SIR BENNET

a novel
NICOLETTE BEEBE

Sir Bennet
By Nicolette Beebe
Copyright © 2021 by Nicolette Beebe

Cover design: Alexander Kopainski, www.kopainski.com
Images used under license from shutterstock.com

Developmental Editor: Hayley Christiansen, Brian Beebe
Copy Editor: Hayley Christiansen, Brian Beebe

Dedicated to my continuing readers

Prelude

▲▲▲

The hell Dexter had endured tonight made the six years with Atraeus feel like child's play. Each awful hour felt like a small piece of time threaded across the span of an eternity. The barrel of the pit grew larger and wider. With every frantic beat of Dexter's heart, it swallowed him in pulses of severe obscurity. The reality of returning to Mount Verta pummeled him in endless waves that beat him senseless. And there was nothing he could do.

Nothing but fall.

Fall and allow the abyss to shred his sanity into discarded scraps of useless fibers throughout existence. His soul was strewn across all the secret places in the universe. It was among the stars, the craggy recesses in the mountain's surface, and the cool night air that spiraled around him as he fell farther and faster toward the bottom.

Broken gasps of someone suffering caught his attention.

Sara.

Her raspy voice was raw as she struggled to breathe. She had fallen long before him. But, the impact hadn't killed her.

Dexter's heart crumpled with the sound of her in excruciating pain as she lay amongst the other deceased sacrifices. As he helplessly reached for her, he let loose a guttural scream. If he could figure out how to defy physics, he might be able to save her. But, gravity had him on a tight and unforgiving leash.

Then, the impact.

There he was.

Then, there he wasn't.

Chapter 1

▲▲▲

Soft tones lulled Dexter into a state of peace. The twins wiggled beneath the covers of their individual beds while Sara sang a lullaby. Not just any lullaby. One Dexter had written in high school. That was how she had been keeping the idea of him alive for their kids. Six years and she had made herself think of him every night, unsure if he would ever return. Touched, he leaned against the doorframe of the kids' room and smiled.

When she finished, Sara kissed their foreheads and went to turn off the lights. Her fingers froze on the switch when Nellie spoke. "Can Daddy kiss me, too, now?"

The request brought a tear to his eye, and his chest burst with pride. He had a son who was asking for his love and affection. "Of course." Dexter walked to Nellie's bedside, laid a kiss atop his head, and placed one more on his cheek while tucking the navy blue comforter under his shoulder. "Sleep tight, Nellie." A part of him wished his daughter would ask as well. But, she didn't. She lay in her bed with a stuffed unicorn snuggled between her arms, glaring at him curiously. It was the first day they had met, so he was content giving Kali time to warm up to him.

"Night, kids," Sara whispered in a soothing intonation. She turned off the lights and closed the door.

As soon as it clicked shut, she took Dexter by the hand and led him down the dark hall in a hurry, past the bathroom and linen closet. At the end was Sara's moody, blue room. He stepped in while she closed the door, evaluating the queen-sized bed against the far wall. It rested between two single drawer nightstands with teardrop shaped lamps upon them. To the right, a gray loveseat was pushed under a large window where he imagined Sara having her morning coffee and reading a magazine. To the left was a door that led to a walk-in closet. Most of the shelves were empty and wooden bars hung just a few clothes. Some shoes were stacked in a pile in the corner. Circling back to Sara, he spotted a white vanity table with cosmetics organized on the surface and a full-length mirror beside it.

Dexter rubbed the back of his buzzed head with both his hands and faced her. "Oh my gosh, Sara. I can't believe how much I love them already. They are perfect." He held her chin between his thumb and folded index finger. "And for the record, I was right. You are a phenomenal mother." The moonlight streaming in from the window shimmered in Sara's electric jade eyes as tears welled between her lids. Her mouth melted to a distraught frown. "You're crying," his voice lilted.

Instead of responding, she glared at him as her energy shifted from loving mother to dark chaos. Mind reeling loudly. Fuck, he missed that.

He took her head between his hands, wiping away the tears just as they spilled over with his thumbs. Something in Dexter broke when she closed her eyes and leaned into his touch, like she was going to crumble into thousands of tender pieces. He rested his forehead against hers, drawing her close by the small of her back. "Don't cry," he whispered. "Not now. Not ever." He shut his eyes to be better lost in her. To pretend she was smiling. "It's been so long. I want to see you happy."

Her head tilted upward until her mouth crashed against his in a frantic rush. With each desperate kiss, her inner turmoil poured into Dexter's soul and smudged the clarity in his brain. The feeling of her soft lips ignited an irresistible desire to tangle himself up in her. He clasped her small frame in his arms and did his best to show her how much he missed her. How much she owned him. Every part. To prove that he was tightly wound around every precious finger of hers.

Her delicate hands grasped the front of his shirt and hauled him toward the bed. One step was all he took before he lifted her. Thin, toned legs wrapped around his hips as she moaned into his mouth. One hand supported her bottom, the other cupped her cheek to bring her closer. When he sucked on her lower lip, salty tears awoke his taste buds. He pulled away and his eyes met her red, teary ones. "What's wrong?"

She blinked and pressed her forehead against his. Her hands hung onto his neck as she whispered, "Love me."

A request he thought she never had to make. He would love her. Always. And, in every possible way. Without her ever needing to say it, he would love her. He set her on the mattress, the cream-colored comforter puffing around her.

Dexter followed her down, lips tangling with hers and groaning at how bad he needed her in that moment. Six years of hell and, damn, did it feel good to hold his lovely reward.

Sara crossed her arms over her torso, grasped the bottom of her knitted sweater, and pulled it over her head in one fluid motion.

Below him, Sara Mar King, half-naked with a white laced bra sparsely covering her pink nipples. The girl who he was madly in love with since before he could remember. The girl who did ballet and sobbed in his arms when her mother abandoned her. The little blonde-haired beauty who he used to help pick up worms with to save them from being stepped on. When she shifted, moving her head to better take him in and expose more of her neck, he saw the protective woman whose blood he could still taste. The woman who used to control the screechers, fought with the wrath of a lioness, and was selfless enough to sacrifice her own precious life to save humanity.

Even now, he still didn't feel good enough for her. But, he no longer cared. She deserved whatever she asked for on a clean silver platter. And if she wanted Dexter, he was thrilled to oblige.

Sara's eager fingers latched onto his shirt and stripped it off. Her scarred palms laid flat over his inked chest, running her warm touch across his skin. Deep within him a hurricane raged and followed the trail of her hands. Dexter couldn't stand the thought of letting a second go by without kissing his blonde pixie soldier whom he had loved for a lifetime. Lust pulled at the corners of his mouth as he reconnected his lips with hers.

11

A soft knock came at the door. Sara pulled away to look, panting with storm clouds gathering in her eyes. The devastating look nearly sent Dexter into the crumbling headspace he was in while Atraeus, the Father of Fear, had tortured him at the bottom of the pit in Mount Verta. He leaned closer to Sara, grounding himself in the moment by tracing his nose up and down her neck in hopes to absorb some of her goodness.

"Mommy?" Kali's angelic voice called.

Sara covered her eyes with a hand and took a hard swallow like her life was ending. "Yes, baby Kay?"

"Can I sleep with you?"

Dexter smiled and stood, gazing at his sexy and beautiful love lying on the bed, emerald eyes beckoning for him to return. Dexter sighed and tossed Sara her sweater. Before putting it on, she dried the tears with the back of her hand, silently observing him. "I'm sorry."

He shook his head, putting his own shirt on. "Never be sorry for this."

Sara looked to the door as she dressed in her sweater. "I'm coming." She ruffled her golden bangs and muttered to herself, "Every night."

"Every night, huh?"

Sara went to the door. "Don't get me wrong, I love it... it's just..." She looked down and rested her hand on the silver knob. "Never mind." She twisted it open, and Kali stood with large cerulean eyes, happy to see her mother. Bright blonde hair cascaded to her belly button and twisted into loose curls at the bottom. Ruby red lips, shiny and parted in a sleepy uncertainty. One of her tiny hands grasped the fabric of her floral-patterned night gown, the other the leg of her stuffy.

Nothing was more beautiful in the world than his stunning daughter. Not once did he think anything could surpass Sara's beauty, but there Kali was, standing like a pretty porcelain doll and proving him wrong. It took mere seconds for her to stake claim in Dexter's heart. Wildly in love with his daughter, he wished he could be the one who could hold her until she felt better.

Sara knelt to lift their daughter in her arms and kissed her rosy cheek. She stroked away a few blonde strands while walking to the bed.

Kali leaned to Sara's ear and whispered, "I don't want Daddy here."

Sara's expression darkened with torture as her apologetic eyes roved over Dexter.

He smiled and said, "No problem. I'll be on the couch downstairs if you need me."

"I'm sorry." Sara laid their daughter in the center of the bed before looking to Dexter. "Please don't leave the house."

"I won't."

Sara's eyes widened as if she was terrified he was lying.

He put his hand up to stop her loud thoughts. "I'm not leaving. I'll be downstairs if you need me." Dexter made his way out, closing the door part way to leave a gap for him to look after his family. He watched as Sara snuggled close to Kali.

"Mommy? Can you sing Daddy's song again?" she whispered in the adorable slur of a tired child.

"You know, Daddy can sing it better."

"No, I want you to sing it."

She sighed. "Okay, baby."

Sara sung, and it filled Dexter with unmistakable love. His daughter requested his song. Dexter stayed until the end before he turned away from the door, already missing both of them.

He plodded down the hallway, running a hand along the white banister that overlooked the first story. After one last peek at Nellie curled up in bed, he closed the door and headed to the top of the stairs. They led straight into a small living room, complete with a TV mounted on the wall, a white sofa, and two other seats surrounding it. A maroon rug lay beneath a wooden coffee table that complemented the cozy room. At the bottom of the steps, he turned into the kitchen to his right. On the far wall was a large window that matched two more on his left and right in size. Covering the walls of the kitchen was pastel yellow paint that, for some reason, he just knew Nellie had chosen. Counters lined two of the walls with dark blue cabinets above. A tiled kitchen island in the center stood beside a rectangular wooden dining table. Everything had its own place and the house was immaculate. Dexter smiled, glad to see she was still the same religiously tidy person.

He made his way around the house to check that all the windows and doors were locked before he plopped on the couch and covered himself with a thin, crocheted blanket. He rested his head on a square throw pillow and closed his eyes, ecstatic that he had found his way back to his family.

Morning sun streamed over Dexter's eyes, waking him from a deep slumber. As he stretched, the covers restricted his movement. Something heavy was lying on his blanket. He slit open his lids and saw Sara curled in a ball at his feet, fast asleep. Black, mascaraed lashes fell over her cheeks and her chest rose with every shallow breath. One elbow leaned on the armrest while her hand propped up her head. Dexter couldn't resist a sleepy grin. He moseyed off the couch and covered Sara with the blanket.

So small, but so damn brave.

In the kitchen, he rummaged through the cabinets and spotted what he wanted. Coffee. He placed a few scoops in a filter then placed it in the coffee maker. He refilled the water reservoir and pressed on. Soon, hot coffee seeped into a white mug with the picture of a fox printed over it.

He placed it on the wooden table near the kitchen before raiding the fridge. He found a bag of bread and took out a slice, toasting it before setting it on a paper towel. As he sat at the table, Sara stepped into the kitchen barefoot and grinning. Dexter eyed his high school band T-shirt that he loved on her so much. The black fabric fell to her mid thighs with the graphic of a skull and the words "The Iron Vikings" surrounding it. Pastel pink and white striped shorts with a small frill at the ends complemented her figure in a way that made him want to tear them off her.

"Hey."

Dexter pushed the mug toward her. "Coffee?"

She nodded shyly and took a seat in front of him. "Thanks."

"I hope you don't mind I stole some toast."

Sara smiled and shook her head. "Eat."

"No strings attached?" he joked as it was what she had said six years ago when he offered food to her in his tower.

She shrugged. "Some strings would be nice."

Dexter winked and took another bite of toast, watching Sara sip her coffee. "How'd you sleep?"

"I thought I was going to wake up today, and you'd be gone." She paused like she wanted to add something but decided against it. Instead, she avoided eye contact as her shoulders slackened.

Dexter's brows creased down the center. "Why would you think that?"

She raked her pixie cut back with her fingers, tucking the longer tresses of her bangs behind her ear. "Nothing. Sorry. I don't want to get into it right now."

Dexter reached an open palm across the table for her to hold. "No. Tell me. Please." Sara took his hand. "I've been so worried about you. Please. How have you been?"

She sighed like she was trying to decipher where to start. In the end, she decided not to even begin. "I am so glad you're here." When her voice cracked, he knew she had been crying last night, and his stomach clenched. "I don't know where you've been or what you've been doing or why you're back. But, please, please say you're staying." Her small hand squeezed his with a desperation so grave that he thought she was going to keel over. "Say you want to be here with us. Please." Her face twisted into a vicious sorrow where tears leaked onto the wooden surface of the table. "You're staying with us, right?"

"Oh, Sara." Dexter rounded the table and kneeled at her feet, looking into her broken eyes.

"Please. I swear, I'll do anything. Just please stay with us—"

"Hey," Dexter hushed in a whisper.

"Dexter, I can't do this without you anymore. Stay. Please."

"I'm staying. I'm staying. Okay? I'm home." He reached up and cupped her drenched cheek in his palm, wiping away her sadness. "I don't want to be anywhere else. As long as you want me, I'm here forever. I'm yours forever."

A glisten in her eyes shined darkly at his words as if she didn't believe him.

"I worked so hard to get here. And, now I'm here and I am never leaving you. Ever. Okay?"

A small grin spread over her reddened face. "Good, because I'm so tired of grieving you."

He took her hands in his, kissing her knuckles. "I'm so sorry. I tried to get back as soon as I could. I promise."

Her glassy eyes held his captive, wanting him to say more.

"You did such a great job raising them alone. I am so impressed with you. You are so brave, Marking."

She sniffed back her tears. "Call me Marking again."

He smiled. "You are my brave Marking."

A small laugh cracked through her chest. She spread her legs, wrapping them around Dexter's torso as she flung her arms around his neck. Dexter came in close, face cuddled into her shoulder. "Why? Why were you gone for so long? Six years, Dexter. I thought you were dead."

"I know. It was either six years or nothing at all."

"Why? Why couldn't you have talked to me, tell me you were coming back. I got nothing from you."

"I would have if I could." Dexter pulled away from her collarbone, a spot he adored. It was where he could hear her heart beating. Beating for only him to love. "You know I would have, Sara. Please, you have to know that. I did my absolute best."

Sara nodded. "Sorry. I didn't mean it like that."

"I'm here now. I want to help. With everything. Starting with you. Tell me how you've been."

She released his waist, put an elbow on the table, and leaned on her closed fist. "I've been terrible, Dex. I don't even feel like myself anymore."

His brows turned up. "Terrible?"

She nodded, averting her eyes while saying, "I've barely been able to eat. I haven't slept. And when I do, I have horrible night terrors."

Dexter brushed away her bangs so he could better see the pain that had been harboring in her eyes. "What about?"

"Like, me giving up the children and you hating me. Or you telling me I am a terrible mother. I get stuck watching you with other women... which made me wonder if you were with other women."

Dexter's heart broke, but he remained silent and listened.

"I kept reliving," she cleared her throat, "Marty Brown... you know, drugging me and everything... but then you'd be there. And you'd have to watch."

Dexter's heart constricted and his lungs depleted of oxygen hearing her words ring true. One of the ways Atraeus had tortured him in the pit was forcing him to watch Marty Brown rape Sara when they were in high school.

"And then, I have one where you'd come out of the pit and you'd push me away 'cause I wasn't real or something. You'd push me so hard that you'd fall back in."

A hard lump formed at the base of Dexter's throat that he couldn't gulp down. "That's all going to change now. Okay? I will be here for every morning you wake up, for every night terror, for everything. For anything you need."

"Where have you been all these years?"

Just then, footsteps pattered down the stairs. Nellie rounded the corner, green eyes wide with happiness. "Daddy!"

Hearing his son so excited to see him melted Dexter to a puddle of love. Nothing else mattered when his son wanted to talk to him. Dexter turned on his knee. "Hey, bud!" He opened his arms to Nellie, lifting him into the air. Repositioning himself in the chair across from Sara, he helped Nellie settle on his lap. "Did you sleep well?"

Nellie nodded and started tugging at different sections of Dexter's beard. "I dreamed I was on the pirate ship fighting bad guys with you."

"Oh, yeah?" Dexter covered one of his eyes. "Give me your best pirate impression."

Nellie smiled and crinkled his freckled nose just as Sara did when she smiled too wide. "Arrr!"

"Wow. You'd make a perfect pirate." Dexter looked at Sara who was grinning. One hand rested over her mug while the other was in her mouth biting her nails. "Look, Marking. We're bonding."

Sara giggled, rolled her eyes, and took a sip of coffee.

Dexter turned his attention to his son. "What would you like for breakfast?"

"Spaghetti!"

Dexter laughed. "Spaghetti? That's a dinner food, silly goose." He took Nellie's small button nose between his thumb and index finger and squeezed lightly.

"Nellie," Sara chimed, "how about some cereal or toast like your dad?"

"No! Spaghetti," Nellie whined.

"Do you have potatoes?" Dexter asked Sara.

She gave a tired nod.

He looked to his son who was studying all of Dexter's facial features, rubbing his palm over his dad's cheeks. "How about some breakfast spaghetti?"

Nellie's green eyes widened in delight. "Yeah!" He hopped off Dexter's lap and raced around the kitchen in his puppy patterned pajama set.

Sara groaned. "Nellie, stop running." When he didn't, she buried her face in her hands like he had exhausted everything in her.

Dexter rounded the table and put a comforting hand on Sara's shoulder. "Nellie, come help me make breakfast spaghetti."

"Okay." His son was by his side in an instant, saluting him. "How can I help you, sir?"

"Can you go to the pantry and bring me the potatoes?" Dexter went to the stove, opened a few cabinets, then looked over his shoulder at Sara. "Marking, do you have pans?"

Sara stood with an amused grin. She reached into a bottom cabinet to the right of the stove. "Um, it's pretty old, but it's good enough." She pulled it out and handed it to him. "Breakfast spaghetti, huh?"

"Hash browns," he whispered while kissing her cheek.

Her hands wrapped around Dexter's upper arm as if still trying to convince herself that he was real. "You can make hash browns?"

Dexter shrugged. "We'll find out. Want some?"

Sara scrunched her lips to the side, deliberating. "Maybe for lunch."

"You think Kali wants some?"

"Yeah. She should be getting up in a couple hours. Closer to nine."

For a brief moment, Dexter saw the dark chaos return to her eyes before she blinked it away. "Are you okay?"

Sara sucked her lips between her teeth like she refused to let whatever was rattling in her brain out. "Yeah."

"Why don't you go relax, and I'll take care of breakfast, keep this ball of energy busy," he explained while nodding his head toward Nellie sifting through the shelves.

She shook her head while hopping onto the counter beside Dexter and crossing her ankles. "I want to make sure you don't leave." Sara rested her forehead on his shoulder and gave a sad laugh. "Now that I can't freeze you."

When Dexter chuckled, Sara lifted her head, eyes brightening at him. "Don't worry. I'm not leaving. Go take time for yourself. I'm sure you're missing the good old, lonely traveling days. Go take a nap or something."

She blinked like she didn't get his humor. "I would love a shower."

He nodded toward the stairs as he turned on the stove. "Go. I got it covered—"

"Shh!" She pressed a scarred palm against his chest. "You're frozen. You can't talk or move… except to make breakfast." After a quick peck on his cheek, she hopped off the counter and left the kitchen on her tiptoes like the white laminate was too cold beneath her bare feet.

Nellie yanked on Dexter's black sweats. "Your potatoes, captain."

He tousled Nellie's caramel hair and smiled with a sinking feeling that something was off with Sara. "You rock, bud."

The shower had been running for over an hour. Dexter kept peeking at the bathroom door, worried. Nellie was by his side on the couch in the living room, devouring his second helping of hash browns. Nellie wanted to eat at the kitchen table, but Dexter coaxed him into eating in the living room so he could selfishly catch a glance at Sara coming out of the shower in a towel. Vintage cartoons blared from the TV, and he couldn't get enough of Nellie's adorable giggle every time something amused him.

With sudden urgency, Nellie placed the plate on the oval coffee table with a loud clang, licked his lips, then put both palms facing the TV screen. One by one, each finger curled into his hand like he was counting down.

"What are you doing?" Dexter questioned.

"Mommy's dreaming again."

Dexter furrowed his brows and glanced at the bathroom door on the second story, curious about what that meant. He looked back to his son who was folding down his last pinky. As soon as Nellie made a fist, Sara's blood curdling scream barreled from the bathroom.

Chapter 2

▲▲▲

Dexter flinched at the torture in Sara's voice as he leapt to his feet, sprinting up the stairs two steps at a time toward the bathroom. He pushed open the door and a tidal wave of steam engulfed him. Earsplitting shrieks reverberated off the bare walls, rattling his core as he slid the frosted glass door out of the way and peered into the shower. Sara's lithe body was coiled in the corner, knees pulled to her chest and arms wrapped around them. Her jaw hung open, screaming under the spray of the water, kaleidoscope eyes open but not really seeing with focus or intention. In hopes to not alarm the kids, Dexter closed the bathroom door behind him and stepped into the shower with her, hot water seeping into his clothes.

"Hey, Sara," he hushed, lifting her tiny frame into his lap and wrapping his arms around her balled form. Her screams vibrated through his chest as she trembled in his arms. He turned his back to keep Sara out of the pressurized water while trying to break whatever spell she was under.

In an abrupt twist of movement, she jerked awake and the screaming ceased. Frantic to escape whatever was going on in her head, she clawed at Dexter's arms.

"Hey, hey, it's just me."

Her head whipped around, eyes widened in shock.

"You're okay. Just a dream."

She squeezed her eyes shut and groaned, leaning a shoulder into Dexter's chest.

"You're okay," he whispered, resting his cheek on the back of her head.

Bangs sounded on the door. "Mommy!" Kali's voice called, sending Sara up in alert.

"Let me," Dexter requested. He took Sara off his lap, scooted toward the door in his soaked sweats, leaned out the shower, and cracked the bathroom door open a few inches while on his knees. Kali's azure eyes that matched Dexter's in pigment were wide with worry. Clasped between both hands was her unicorn. "Hey, pretty girl."

"What's wrong with Mommy? Is she okay?"

"She's fine. Don't worry."

"No, she isn't! She was screaming again!" Tears sparkled in her eyes then spilled down her cheeks.

Dexter reached out with a wet hand and did his best to dry the tears with his thumb. "Mommy's okay. She was just dreaming."

"I'm fine, baby Kay," Sara hollered.

Kali visibly relaxed when she heard Sara's voice. "Why don't you go downstairs and watch some cartoons with your brother? He can tell you all about breakfast spaghetti."

25

Kali nodded, drying the rest of her tears on the fluff of her stuffy before she made her way down the stairs. When she plopped on the couch beside Nellie, Dexter closed the door and got back in the shower. Sara had turned off the water and was eyeing him from the corner.

He put a hand on her bare knee. "Are you all right?"

Sara nodded.

"Did you really fall asleep in the shower?"

She gave him a meek grin. "I'm really tired."

Dexter chuckled, and it caused Sara to as well. "What'd you dream about?"

"I can't remember."

Sara's eyes never left Dexter as he got on his haunches and helped her to her feet. He stroked away a dripping errant lock of her bangs so he could better see her heart-shaped face. Not to mention it also better distracted himself from her sexy, wet nakedness. "Look at me being a gentleman."

Expecting Sara to laugh, he was disappointed when her eyes remained glossy and pained. In a blink, her warm touch met his waist as she lifted the bottom of his wet shirt and tugged it off frantically, whispering, "Don't be."

With her careful enunciation, the two words stiffened him beneath his boxer briefs. His shirt dropped to the wet floor. Then, her hands moved to his sweats, warm fingers curling into the waistband. Dexter's hands rushed to Sara's face, holding it tightly and pulling her in for a hungry kiss, one where he eagerly slipped his tongue between her teeth, anxious to taste her sweetness again.

26

She moaned against him as his pants and everything beneath them fell to the damp floor. He kicked them away and played her scarred ribs with his fingers. "God, I missed you," he whispered in a husky timber as he fulfilled Sara's request and gazed down at her perfection. Raised scars, flat belly, thin but toned legs, and small, teardrop-shaped breasts. Like a magnet, his hand fled to one and massaged while his mouth seized hers, tongue plunging deep into her mouth and refamiliarizing himself with every centimeter of it.

Sara was in his arms, and he melted into her, hoping that he could somehow ease the pain he felt from watching her suffer.

Dexter lifted her, and she secured her legs around his waist. With a hand supporting her bottom, he pushed her back against the wet wall. Suddenly, she was pulling away, shaking her head, "No, no, no! Not against the wall."

"Got it." He got down on one knee then rotated until he was on the floor, his own back against the moist wall with Sara on his lap, straddling him. Before he knew it, she was sliding onto him and everything vibrated with pleasure. In slow gyrations, Sara moved her body while craning her head back. His body went in one direction and his mind traveled in another. "Wait! Sara."

She stopped, dropping her gaze to meet Dexter's, wide with concern.

"We don't have protection."

Her eyes bored into him like he was an idiot. "Shut up and kiss me."

She started again, but Dexter put a hand on her shoulder to keep her from moving. "As much as you're tempting me right now, we can't unless you're okay having another kid or another set of twins."

"I said shut up! I need you," she growled and swerved her hips in a small circular motion, causing Dexter's heart to pulse fiercely and forcing him to keep his mind from roaming to the sudden surge of bliss.

He clamped down on her hips to keep her from moving, leaned forward to press a soft kiss on her shoulder. "Are you saying you want another child with me?" He pulled away with raised brows.

Her eyes met his with a glare so dark and all-consuming he thought he was in the pit again. She averted eye contact, her voice cracking as she said, "Yes."

He took her head between his hands and tilted her face to meet his, but her eyes remained glued to the ground, trying to hide fresh tears. "Why are you lying to me?"

"I already told you."

"Then tell me again," he whispered.

"I'll do anything to keep you here."

The weight of the comment sent Dexter into a painful alert. He pulled her off him and gently set her bottom aside, keeping her legs draped over his. "Sex is not what's going to keep me here, Sara. Rushing into having another kid if you don't want one in hopes it might is *not* why anyone should have a child. I am staying because I love you. I'd want another child because you love me too."

She shook her head and turned her mouth into a deep frown. "That's not enough."

Dexter wanted to find her rose-colored glasses and tape them to her face. "Of course it is."

"You say you love me. You say you'll stay, but then you never do." Scarlet veins spidered toward her emerald irises as she took a slow, shaky breath. "You said you wouldn't let me go when my mom left, then you didn't talk to me for over ten years. And you said you'd never leave me, but then you did for six years. If the kids aren't what you hoped for or-or-or Kali doesn't warm up to you, you're going to leave me again. If I can give you a baby to love from the beginning, maybe you'll really stay."

"Sara—"

"Please, Dex. Give me another child so I'll have more of you to keep with me when you leave—"

"Hey, look at me." When she did, it was like the pixie soldier had left and in her place was the terrified Sara Mar King who had hung over the abyss at the top of Mount Verta, awaiting death—waiting to be the last sacrifice to save the world of its horrid plague. "I'm not leaving you this time. Okay? Trust me. I love you and the kids. Unconditionally." Dexter banded his arms around her body and nuzzled his face against her collarbone. "I need you too much to ever leave." He pulled away and kissed the corner of one of her crying eyes. He tucked her farther into his side, happy to see that she still fit him perfectly. "This is my family. They are mine. You are mine. Forever."

She nodded her head. "You are mine."

"Exactly," he whispered softly.

"But our time is ticking, Dex. I can practically hear it in my head."

He kissed her temple. "It's not, Marking. I'm not going anywhere without you again." Dexter rubbed her bare arm with an open palm when he noticed something inconsistent on her skin. Something dark. Black. He flipped her forearm over to better see. Ink. Three mountains, tattooed just below her elbow crease, in very thin line work. "What's this?"

She sniffed and gave a sad smile as if she was grateful for the change in subject. "Oh gosh, I forgot about that. I'm so sorry. I did it without you."

Dexter beamed. "Mountains, huh?"

She nodded.

"Tell me about them."

"Um. I wanted to match your first tattoo. Also because of what happened at Mount Verta. Just seemed fitting."

"Why three?"

With her delicate index finger, she traced each peak. "You, Nellie, and Kali."

"It's perfect," he leaned in, kissed her on the cheek, and felt everything in his body calm. "What do you say we go dry off, get dressed, and snuggle with our kids. We'll save this sexual adventure for a better time?"

She blinked slowly like she was already falling back asleep. "Yeah, okay. I still have your old clothes in my closet."

He guided her to her feet before towing her thin, naked body against him. Her arms wrapped around his waist. "I love you."

"I love you too, Dexter," she said in crisp articulations that made the hairs on his neck stand on end.

He guided her out of the shower and wrapped a mint colored towel around her. She snuggled into it like a nesting bird.

"Take that towel." She nodded her head toward the towel on the hand rail bolted into the ivory wall.

Sara exited the bathroom while Dexter picked up his clothes and wrung out the excess water. After wrapping himself in the towel, he made his way down the hall to Sara's room.

His old, dark washed jeans and plain black T-shirt were neatly folded at the end of the bed for him. She dressed herself in leggings and his band shirt. "Heads up, I wear this as often as I can."

Dexter dropped the towel and began to dress. "I can tell by the holes at the seams."

She gave him a meek grin. "Yeah. Well, it's been thoroughly loved."

He winked at her and finished putting on his shirt.

"Ready?" she said, walking to the door.

Gently, he took her hand in his. "No, wait. I have to tell you something."

She turned to him with knitted brows, eyes large with concern.

"Nellie did something... strange."

"What do you mean?"

"While you were showering, he put his hands up," Dexter opened his palms like he was giving Sara a high ten, "then started counting down. I asked him what he was doing. He said, 'Mommy's dreaming again.' When he got to zero, you screamed."

Sara's brows creased and her lips parted.

"Have you noticed anything else like that from him?"

Something in her eyes raced through a storm of panic. "No. I haven't." She gulped. "But, I don't know now."

Dexter smiled, hushing her thoughts. "Okay. We'll keep an eye on that."

"No, no, we have to talk to him. Now."

Dexter sighed out the stress building in his chest.

"Actually, you talk to him. You're the one who saw."

He kissed her head. "I'll talk to him tomorrow."

"No. Now."

"Sara, it's my first full day with my son. I don't want to spend it interrogating him after he trusted me enough to show me." He wrapped her in a hug. "Please. Tomorrow?"

"What if it's something bad—"

"Then, I'll find out tomorrow."

Chapter 3

▲▲▲

Dexter threw a piece of popcorn at Sara from the other end of the couch, but Nellie reached up and intercepted it. Kali laughed and threw a piece at her father. "Hey! I can't watch the movie with you throwing popcorn at me," Dexter jabbed.

"You started it!" Kali laughed. Then Sara did too.

A hard knock came from the front door, and Sara looked around with a puzzled expression. Dexter put up a hand and told her to stay snuggled with the kids.

Dexter hopped off the couch and opened the front door. A tall man equipped with a chiseled jawline and deep-set blue eyes stood before him with an endearing smile. His chocolate hair was coiffed nicely to one side. His thick brows raised in surprise as his gaze landed on Dexter. The man had sweats on and a blue T-shirt that stretched over his muscular pecs and biceps. "Can I help you?"

The man let his vision flit behind Dexter and into the house. "Um, yeah, is Sara home?"

A violent shiver rattled his core, watching the man's eyes search for his Sara Mar King.

From behind him, Sara came to the door, flattening a hand on Dexter's back. "Oh, Guy, I completely forgot about my lesson today." As she rounded him, he saw Guy's eyes drift up and down her body with interest, and it took everything in him not to stick out a hand and throw her back into the house.

"Lesson?" Dexter questioned.

"I teach martial arts every Monday morning to whoever wants to join at the wall on the East side." Sara gestured toward her right with a pointed finger.

"She's a really good teacher," Guy added with a wink in her direction.

Dexter widened his stance and folded his arms over his chest, hoping to build a wall at the door entrance to suggest he wasn't welcome.

With a slight whine in his voice, Guy continued, "Though, I think she charges too much."

She rolled her eyes and popped out a hip with an exasperated sigh as if they have had this conversation before. "I have two children to feed, Guy."

"Yeah. That's why I still think you should move in with me." The man's eyes shifted to Dexter and narrowed for a brief moment like he was assessing who'd be the victor if they were to get into a fight. Then, the look of determination was quickly replaced by a fresh smile that indented two dimples over his pitiful five o'clock shadow. Dexter's full grown beard put it to shame. "I make more than enough patrolling the wall to support us all." He folded his arms across his chest and stood shoulder width apart, mimicking Dexter's pose. "I keep telling her that, but she won't listen. The stubbornness of this girl's ass is unbelievable."

Dexter noticed Sara's head tilt down in defeat as opposed to lifting in the fierce determination he had come to expect.

"I'm just teasing." Guy let out a soft laugh. "Her stubbornness is *absolutely* believable once you get to know her. It gets worse with time."

Dexter's temper flared with Guy's unappealing attempt at humor at Sara's expense. His anger quieted as soon as her fingers slid into his palms. Dexter wanted to lean down and whisper that he thought she was perfect just to counteract this man's asinine opinion of the incredible woman he waded through torture just to be with.

Guy's eyes locked on to their intertwining hands then awkwardly fiddled with his wrist watch as if suddenly uncomfortable with Dexter's level of confidence. "Looks like you have company. Want me to tell Lloyd you're not up for a lesson today? I can still take the kids."

"Guy, this is Dexter," Sara introduced with careful articulations.

Guy's brows lifted in surprise. "Oh! *The* Dexter? Seriously?"

Sara nodded.

"Wow. Nice to meet you, man."

The twins ran past Dexter and aimed straight for Guy. In the process, they screamed his name in excitement. Nellie clambered up his back and wrapped his arms around Guy's neck for a piggyback ride. Kali hugged one of his thighs, looking up to him adoringly.

Seeing Kali give affection to another man depleted his lungs of oxygen. Dexter clenched his teeth, hoping at some point they would crack to compensate for his rising aggression. That was his little girl, no one else's. It was a dagger to the heart watching them with this man.

Guy reached down, took Kali's hand, and give her a twirl. And in the process, Dexter noticed Guy's gaze rivet on her tiny palm, checking for something. Why the fuck was he examining his baby girl? That quick action from Guy sent Dexter spiraling to the dark side of his temper. He took a step forward, unsure if he was going to coldcock him or rip his kids off and drag them back inside.

Kali released Guy's hand and wheeled around to face Dexter while Sara maneuvered her body in front of his as if both sensing his desire to assault Guy. When he tried to sidestep Sara, she followed, blocking him. It was too bad she was just as agile as ever.

"Do you, um," Guy started, "want me to take the kids for the day, so you two can catch up?"

Before Dexter could register what Guy said, Sara responded. "That would be great. Tell Lloyd I won't be there please."

"No," Dexter corrected in a low baritone. "We're good. I'd like to see you in action anyway." He leaned to Sara's ear and whispered, "Call our kids back. Now."

Guy's vision shifted from Sara to Dexter a few times before muttering sounds of uncertainty. "So, no?"

Sara looked over her shoulder and said, "Dex, he's babysat hundreds of times. It'll be fine. I need a day with you."

Dexter put his hands on Sara's shoulders. "If you want a babysitter, then get Emily."

Sara shifted her attention back to Guy. "Please. That would be so great. We have to go get Dex a phone and some new clothes."

"Are you trying to give me a heart attack?" Dexter asked in a gruff tone while giving her shoulders a squeeze.

"It's no problem." Guy looked down at the twins. "You kids want to go to the park?"

"Yeah!" they answered in unison.

"Then maybe a movie?"

"Yeah!"

"All right. You ready?"

Nellie jumped off Guy's back and rushed into the house. When he returned, Kali's white unicorn plushy was in his hand. He held it out to his sister, and she wrapped her arms around it, rubbing her precious cheek on its softness. Nellie turned back to Guy and said, "Now we're ready!"

Before he knew it, the three of them were down the block and out of sight. His kids. Gone with a stranger.

Sara turned to Dexter and touched his cheek. "It'll be okay. I promise."

"Who the fuck is that guy?"

Sara rolled her eyes and stormed into the house. Dexter followed and slammed the door behind him, making Sara flinch. Her chest puffed and her spine straightened like she was getting ready for battle. "Geez. Calm down."

"Sara, who is he?"

"He's Guy."

37

Dexter shook his head in disbelief by her ridiculous vagueness. "I need a better answer than that. Who is the man with our kids right now?"

"That man is babysitting. That is all he's doing."

"That explanation doesn't make this bad feeling in my gut go away. Try again."

"Stop!" she screamed, freckled face reddening. "Just stop. Don't do this. Don't be jealous. I've made other friends in the last six years."

"What kind of friend is he? And be very specific, Sara." The thought of his grimy hands on her made his throat burn with envy.

"I said stop! I didn't know if you were ever coming back. I needed help. He and Emily were there for me. I needed support."

Dexter did his best to let her words sink into his wildly raging brain, but all he could think about was his kids under another man's care. His Marking under Guy's care. That smug, slimy guy was definitely not good enough. No one was.

"He's a good person. He'd never hurt the kids."

The image of Guy checking Kali's palm flashed through his head. The moment Guy realized who Dexter was, his eyes narrowed. Small tells were what told Dexter that something was off. "You're wrong. I need you to listen to me."

"And I need you to trust me!"

"I trust you but not your intuition. It's shit."

Her brows lifted. "Oh, wow."

"You know it too, Sara!"

38

She stomped into the living room and folded the still-warm blanket his family was just snuggling under, shaking her head disapprovingly. "I can't even with you right now."

"For heaven's sake, your gut told you it was a good idea to name our son after a man I hated. After another man who kissed you. Even after he knew you were taken." Fuck, fuck, fuck. As soon as he finished the sentence he heard it echo in the space around him. Dexter already knew Sara's good nature. He already knew it was her way of honoring a dead friend who sacrificed his life to save humanity. He searched the air, looking to eat his words before they entered her ears. But, it was too late.

She turned slowly to him. Gone was every trace of his soft, sweet Sara. In her place stood the fearless, hardcore soldier, eyes blazing in hatred, jaw clenched, arms hanging by her side, and hands balled into fists ready to lift for combat. If she still had her powers, her palms would be glowing and seconds away from freezing him. When she took a step forward, he thought she was going to slap him clean across the face. Instead, she gave a low growl and pivoted toward the stairs, tramping up them.

Dexter was on her tail, reaching out for her. "No, Sara. I'm sorry. I didn't—"

As soon as he made contact with her hand, she shrieked and twisted away. "Don't touch me!"

"Sara, stop. I'm sorry."

She went up two steps at a time, ran down the hall to her room, and slammed it shut. Dexter ran to her door, knocking while twisting the knob, but it was locked. "I know you loved

Nell. I was just so upset that he kissed you and could take better care of you. It's not like I could have grown you food when you were hungry or magically grow peli plants for your injuries when you needed it. He was altogether better for you than me."

He waited a moment, pressing his ear against the door and listening. No movement. Just silence.

"But, I was so happy that he grew flowers by your pedestal. They were beautiful."

Still no response.

Fuck, he messed up. He took a beat and scrubbed his face with his hands to take a deep breath. "Sara... Please. I'm sorry. I don't want to spend this time alone with you like this." He knocked again. "Let me in."

"No. Go away, Dexter."

Her request sounded as empty as his heart at the moment. Her voice was soft and hollow, such a stark difference from her typical angsty grit. He knew she didn't really want him to leave. Not with her voice coming directly from the other side of the door. Even after six years apart, he knew Sara. She needed a minute to realize what she really wanted was for him to fix his hurtful and insensitive words. So, he slid down the white hallway wall and sat with his forearms on his knees, waiting.

A few minutes later, quiet weeping sounds ignited his ears. He did this to her. He made her cry. His head buzzed with guilt and his chest caved with anxiety that he couldn't hold her and tell her he was sorry.

More sniffs came before she asked, "Are you still there?"

"I'm right here." The door unlocked and cracked open. Dexter scrambled to his feet and rushed in. Sara was in his arms the second he could get her there. "I'm so sorry. Don't cry."

She huddled to his chest, head resting against his shoulder. "I really like the name Nellie."

"It's not that," she cried, wetting his shirt with her tears.

"Then, what is it?"

"I-I-I didn't want to name him that either, especially because I knew if you ever came back, you'd feel like I betrayed you. It's been haunting me for years."

Dexter pulled away, brushed strands of bangs out of her eyes, and said, "What are you talking about?"

"*I* didn't name him. Emily did. I told her she could name the boy since she was there for me from the very first day I got back to the tower. She helped me through the pregnancy a-and all my grieving and even helped me give birth. I-I didn't know the love of her life was Nell! And I couldn't tell her that he had fucking kissed me and that's why I can't name my son that. It would have destroyed her."

Dexter looked at her, struck by the kind heart she still had beating in her chest. He was so touched by her selflessness that the name Nellie morphed into something beautiful. "How are you this perfect?"

Her wet eyes flitted to meet his. "What?"

"Letting Emily name him might have been the kindest thing you've ever done. You sacrificed your son's name to make someone else stop aching. You are a ray of light in such a dark world. How do you do that?"

The light in her eyes reemerged. "Are you seriously saying these words? How could you forgive me for doing that?"

"Every time I say his name, I'll think of how selfless you truly are."

She collapsed into him, arms reaching around his waist and squeezing tighter than ever before. He supported most of her weight as she sunk to the floor like releasing the exhaustion from holding the burden. "Thank you, Dexter."

"Come here." He lifted her into his arms and laid her on the bed. Dexter remained seated at the edge, arm slung over her legs, not wanting to let her go just yet. "You feel better?"

She grinned and nodded.

"Good. Is there anything else you want to get off your chest? I'm here to listen."

A grave look settled in her eyes as if suddenly being trampled by a memory. She sighed with a sulk overtaking her face. "It's about Guy."

Fuck, they had had sex. Someone else had touched his Marking. He didn't think he could handle listening to it. Not after being subjected to seeing Marty Brown raping her over and over again. He just prayed Guy was a gentleman with the utmost care and patience. Dexter took a deep breath.

Her arm reached out and placed a scarred palm over his hand. "Stop. You think loudly, too, sometimes."

"Just tell me. I'm here even if I hate what you're going to say." He flipped his hand over to hold hers.

"Okay. Well." She cleared her throat and sat up, repositioning herself beside Dexter at the edge of the bed. "A few months ago, him and Emily came over for a movie night.

Emily ended up leaving early because she didn't feel well. Guy stayed. And, um, as the movie was finishing, he leaned over and kissed me."

Dexter narrowed his eyes, staying in check.

"At first, I didn't—uh—stop it. It had been so long since anyone had kissed me, and I tried, for a split second, pretending it was you. But, then his hand touched my face, and it reminded me it wasn't. It felt unnatural and wrong. I pulled away and told him to stop. When he tried again, I pushed him off and slapped him."

"How hard?" he blurted.

Sara smiled and shrugged. "I think you would have been proud. Anyway, what I'm getting at is that I know a lot of guys have kissed me before, but I'm only okay with you touching me. I'll only ever trust you when it comes to that. I know this because I realized Guy had touched the last place you ever did, and I sunk into a deep depression."

A part of Dexter softened. Only he could touch her. She only trusted him to touch her in that way. That felt good to hear. Still, if only he had gotten out of the pit a few months earlier. Dexter knew he couldn't fault her for kissing Guy after his absence for six years, but he still wanted to wring the man's neck—especially after hearing she had protested and he hadn't stopped.

"Anyway, he got mad, asked if I was going to wait for you forever. All I could do was say yes," she explained with an exasperated chuckle. "He called me a lovesick idiot. I told him to leave, and then we didn't speak for weeks. One day, he came with flowers and apologized, said how much he missed the kids. I wanted them to have a father figure, so I kind of just let everything go back to the way it was."

Dexter pressed his lips together, studying hers. Perfect, thin, and raspberry rouge. Another man had kissed them. Jealous fury spiraled into his core and sent a chill down his spine. A wave of thirst for her surfaced, needing to reclaim her mouth for himself, to silently ask her never to kiss another man except for him. If just the kiss made him this wild, he tried not to imagine how out of control he'd feel if they had had sex.

Still, the truth was that even if Sara admitted to falling in love with Guy, he would do anything to get her back. And he would be damn sure to make love to her so thoroughly and so repetitively that the only name she could remember was his.

"Say something."

His line of vision flitted to her and was met by her pleading gaze. "Well, I don't like the idea of anyone touching you because I promised to protect you forever, but thank you for telling me."

"Are you—are we going to be okay?"

Reading her eyes, he saw her focus shift to the darker corners of her mind, and he refused to release anymore of his toxic thoughts on her. "We're okay."

She sighed in relief and a sad grin pulled at her lips.

"Anything else—anyone else?"

Sara shook her head. "Just that. And I'm so sorry for letting it happen. Trust me when I say even if you had never came back, the last man I would have wanted to be with was you."

Dexter took a deep breath and brought her close. Feeling her body snuggle to him set fire to his heart. "I love you."

Her head popped off his shoulder and her eyes turned serious. "Your turn. Anyone you want to tell me about?"

Dexter shook his head. "Only you forever, Marking."

"What happened after you fell in the pit? I saw you with your head cracked open for God's sake, and now you're here. I need to know what happened."

Dexter spent the next few minutes explaining what Atraeus had in store for him. The new six year deal he had made so he could come back to her with an intact body. The camp leader he had been forced to kill in order to be relieved of his duty to be the last sacrifice—the leader who Sara had danced for. "After that, I was frozen in the pit the whole time, going through peli plant-like visions. The first few years were full of physical torture. Then, it shifted to me thinking the six years were done and I could get out. I ran to you, only to find out that," a lump clogged his throat, but he forced himself to speak through it, "you were a drunk and aborted the baby because you hated me. Then, I had to watch myself abuse you. After that, I had to watch you with another man and you had your own little family." It wasn't until Sara's hand met his cheek did he realize he was crying. He turned her hand and kissed her scarred palm. "It was always something new and horrible. I tried everything to get back to you, but every new scenario I'd forget and think I was out again."

"For six years?"

Dexter nodded. "Then, it got so much worse. I was forced to watch..." he pulled her hand to his heart, his other hand

45

crawled up her arm and held the back of her neck, "what Marty did to you. He-he drugged you and you called for me to save you. And I didn't, Sara. I didn't hear you screaming for me. I saw him drag you to his basement thousands of times. I saw him bind your perfect wrists." He kissed her wrists. "I had to watch him rip open your clothes. I saw everything he did to you." He pulled her close so her forehead rested against his, just so he had more of her to hold on to while he spoke. "I heard everything he said to you. And, I died every time. I stayed with you after he left, trying to hold you, but you couldn't feel me. You could never feel me." Dexter sniffed back tears and looked to the ceiling. "Fuck, Sara, Atraeus got so much fear out of me from that."

"Dex." Though her voice came out in a barely audible tone, it was calming for him to hear her in his ear.

"And then I had to see what your dad did to you. God, Sara, I don't know how you went through all that and still ended up a sweet angel. You're still so kind and brave, and you still had room in your heart to let me in six years ago."

Sara turned ghost white, eyes bugging from her sockets in deep mortification.

"How did you possibly trust me in the spring that day?" he said while kissing up her arm.

"Y-you saw?"

Dexter nodded.

"S-so my night terrors were right?"

He nodded again. "I don't know how, but the one of Marty, yes."

She gulped, leaning back. "You heard the things they said to me?"

"Yes." A fresh tear ran down his cheek and into his beard as the voice of Marty telling her that he treated her better than Dexter filled his ears.

"Y-you saw them hurt me?"

A flash of Marty splaying her legs apart and his head crashing violently against her. "Yes. I'm sorry, Sara. I'm so sorry I wasn't there for you."

Sara leaped from the bed and fell to her knees in front of Dexter. "No! *I'm* sorry! Dexter!" she bawled as she clawed at his thighs. "You shouldn't have ever had to see that. I can't imagine how fucking difficult that was for you."

She should not be the one kneeling, so Dexter slid to the ground and tugged her against him until she was in a ball, crying on his lap. "I am so sorry I didn't kill your dad for you. You shouldn't have needed to do that yourself. I would have done it for you. Just like I did Marty. I know it's hard to believe, but even back then, I would have done anything for you."

That made her cry harder.

"I promise, Sara Mar King, I will never let anyone hurt you ever again. Do you hear me? I will protect you with all that I am. And, if anything separates us again, I swear, I will rip this world apart to find you every time."

Tangled together in a mess, they continued to cry. Neither of them able to say anything more. They were broken. Since the moment Dexter made the decision to cut her out of his life in middle school, they had been broken. It finally felt as if they were ready to mend. Ready to bury the past and start an actual life together with the amazing children they would devote themselves to fill with love and joy.

Sara's cell phone on her nightstand repeatedly vibrated, bringing them out of their isolated, cocooned embrace and back to the larger world. She took a deep breath before reaching for it and put it to her ear with a quiet sniff. "Hello?"

Her eyes went wide as they bore into Dexter with infinite concern. "Okay. We're coming."

She hung up the phone and stood, grabbing a black hoodie that was draped over the white swivel chair of her vanity. "That was Guy. We have to go. Something's wrong with Kali."

Chapter 4

▲▲▲

Running with Sara was easier than it should have been. Before, she could have outrun Dexter by miles, but now her breath grew heavier with every step. By the time they reached the tall, green-painted wall that separated the town from the outside world, Sara had her hands on her knees, panting. Dexter rested a hand on her shoulder as she unfurled herself and looked to Guy who leaned against the wall with ankles and arms crossed. Flakes of green paint fell when he moved his shoulder. His navy eyes rolling before they landed on Sara. He marched across the few yards of dirt, out of the sun, and onto the grass that was shaded by a few oak trees.

"What's going on?" Sara huffed, eyeing their daughter.

Kali stood perfectly still, hands tangled together in front of her stiff body. Her ocean eyes were rimmed with puffy redness, and her button nose was a deep shade of rouge. Everything about her sadness put stress on Dexter's heart. A half hour with Guy, and his daughter was a mess. He knelt and opened his arms to her for a hug, but it was Nellie who came running into them. A half-smile caught his lips as his son clung to him.

"The kids are what's going on," Guy answered Sara with exasperation twisting through his speech as he tucked Kali's unicorn under his arm.

Relaxed that his children were back under his supervision, he let go of his son and stood to survey the area. Metal stairs led to a platform where two guards stood on the top of the wall that had a metal railings along either side, monitoring the outside with shotguns. A few yards away from the wall was a crowd of men surrounding a wooden cart on wheels, resembling a kiosk with assorted weapons. Guns hung on every surface while knives were laid out nicely on shelves along with arrowheads, bows, knives, and other weapons. Only one woman was amongst them, twirling a small knife between her fingers like she was testing it out. There was a man in a red hat and black apron handling money and inventory.

Approximately a quarter mile away, he spotted his tower looming far above the crowns of treetops like a mini skyscraper. It casted an eerie atmosphere onto the city like a haunted lighthouse, a warning beacon for trouble. It had been renovated over the years, something he hadn't taken notice of yesterday in his desperate need to find Sara. Where black mold once stained the cylindrical walls that enclosed its spiral staircase was now a hue of pristine white paint that reflected the sun. In blunt contrast, the top of the tower where his small room rested had been painted a crisp black. Around the outer rim were two rows of massive metal spikes jutting out diagonally, both upward and downward. He wondered if they had been expecting some new beast to tear through the city. At least that seemed to be the only logical purpose for this new addition. Instead of the flat roof he had built, it now had a sleek cone-shaped top, its one point standing sturdy and sharp facing the heavens. When Dexter had lived there, it had looked like a self-inflicted prison, but now it resembled a powerful scepter that could intimidate any passerby.

Dexter wanted to continue dissecting the tower's new appearance, but one of the muscular men atop the fence leaned over the railing and shouted toward the kiosk, "Five more minutes before Clive and his weapons are leaving. Make your purchases. He'll be back next month."

Sara turned her attention to the twins. "Are you okay?"

"Kali's upset," Nellie spoke with worry nailed to his words. "She won't tell us why." He let go of Dexter and stepped back.

A growl so faint that only Dexter could hear came from Sara's chest before she turned to Guy. It was a growl he had grown to love because he knew it ignited the feisty side of her that he adored. Preparing to admire her rip Guy apart, he carefully watched as she closed her eyes, sucked in a shallow breath, and disappointingly muttered, "What happened?"

Dexter stood, furrowed his brows, and crossed his arms over his chest to make up for her lack of authority. Closely, he continued to gauge the interaction between them.

Guy raised his shoulders and lifted his thick brows. "They ran off! Nellie went one way, Kali the other."

Sara slumped her shoulders and turned to the children. If Dexter hadn't already been looking at Sara, he would have missed the split second she moved her eyes to him. In that second, he saw everything. Grave darkness had returned behind her eyes, but this time it was splattered with embarrassment and a desperate hope for Dexter to reserve judgment. "Why'd you run? You have to stick with Guy at all times!"

"Mom! We were playing a game," Nellie whined.

"I don't care!"

Guy chimed in. "They met up here, then Kali burst into tears for no reason. Again. Now she's upset, and she won't tell me why. She won't move."

"Mom!" Kali pleaded, tears tracking down her flushed cheeks.

Dexter moved an inch closer to his daughter, ready to build a fortress around her at any given moment.

"What is it, baby Kay?" Sara whispered while getting on her haunches and pulling away a bright blonde strand of hair away from her cheeks. "Why are you upset?"

Her precious hand came up and pointed toward the kiosk behind Dexter. "That man wants to take me with him."

The words spiraled into Dexter's ears like they were made of daggers. "Which man?" he demanded in a deep baritone.

"The one with the red hat."

Taking his baby? His precious daughter? Fuck no. Dexter pivoted on his heel and trooped straight to the man who was minding his own business and laughing with one of his customers. Dexter grabbed his tunic with both fists, dragged him to the wall, and shoved him against it. Just when the man was about to shout, Dexter pressed his forearm against the guy's throat and enjoyed watching his aged brown eyes go wide with confusion and his scrawny face turn red. "What'd you say to my daughter?" Dexter sneered low and rough.

Every wrinkle on his face deepened with a scrunch of pain. "What the fuck, man."

"What'd you say to her?"

"Nothing!"

"Liar!" Dexter bellowed before he moved so close to the man's face that he could smell his nervous sweat and whispered, "Don't you dare even *think* to touch that little girl, you understand me? I swear, I'll kill you without even batting an eye."

After a few suffocating gasps from the man, a hefty hand fell on Dexter's shoulder and tugged. He did his best to remain steady on the red-hatted man, wanting to drain the life from the bastard. Another heave had him backing off.

"Dude!" Guy's gravel voice dug into his ear. "What the hell is your problem?" His piercing blue eyes continued to madden with every second that passed. "Leave the poor man alone! Clive didn't do anything! I've been here the whole time."

The shop owner doubled over, wheezing. "I didn't do anything, you asshole!"

With two hands, Guy shoved Dexter backward. "You better watch yourself!"

When Guy pushed him again, Dexter's temper rose. "Is that a threat?" he spat back at Guy, putting his hands on Guy's chest and thrusted in a spiteful reciprocation.

Guy stood shoulder width apart as if ready to duel for alpha. "She's a kid! You're just going to believe everything she says?"

Sara came up behind Guy, eyes wide with bewilderment and Kali's hand in hers.

"Of course I am!" Dexter answered through clenched teeth. "She's my daughter."

Guy let out a condescending chuckle. "Then you should know that Kali makes things up all the time."

Dexter flitted his gaze at Sara, waiting for her to straighten her spine, say oh balls, then throw a vicious side kick into Guy's stomach. Instead, she stood there, shoulders slack and brows knitted. "Sara," Dexter implored in hopes to encourage her to tell him the truth.

"I-I-I. Yeah, it happens sometimes," she whispered.

"See?" Guy confirmed. "Kali lies. You would know that if you had been here for her entire life. You just hurt an innocent person. You are unstable! You know that?"

Dexter looked to his daughter. And when her eyes latched onto his like he was her only lifeline, he caved. Lying or not, he would defend her until his last dying breath.

Slowly, Kali's fingers detangled from Sara's, and she stepped back, shaking her head and mouthing the words "I'm not lying" to Dexter while her lids grew wet with a stubborn wildness he admired.

Guy narrowed his eyes and brought a corner of his lips up into a smirk. "Let me teach you about your daughter. She lies. It's just a fact."

Dexter moved closer to Guy's face, his nose only centimeters from Guy's pointed one. "You tell me my daughter's a liar one more time. I dare you."

An older hand, one with veins popping out and sun spots covering its olive skin, flew between them and curved to Dexter's shoulders, pushing him away from Guy. "Hey!" a deep voice bellowed before a man's face came into his view. He was bald and had fifty-year-old wrinkles set into his face, and large muscles that put Dexter's to shame tightened around his robust stature. His blue polo shirt stretched over them as if they were going to break free at any moment. "Don't forget you're new around here. You cause trouble for any of us, I'll kick your ass out."

A new hand came between them—a delicate one with a circular scar on the palm. Forcefully, Sara pushed the older man away from Dexter and spat, "Don't you dare, Lloyd! Don't ever say that again. Dexter stays. Always. He built the refugee camp that the majority of these people lived in for four years. Dexter's camp saved you and your niece when you two were dying in the Screecher Age. Dexter. Stays. Always." Her chin lifted and her spine straightened. Dexter wanted to wrap himself around her and whisper "welcome back" into her ear. "Do you understand?"

With every confident syllable she enunciated, Dexter was whipped back to middle school, watching her throw her body in front of his attacker in order to protect him—the kid who tripped Sara until her head smacked against the pavement. The moment he knew he had to cut her out of his life. He'd never make that mistake again. She was sticking by another bad decision of his, and this time he accepted it.

Lloyd took a measured step back, eyeing Dexter.

Guy stepped forward and coiled his fingers over Sara's shoulder, and all Dexter wanted to do was break them off. Guy bent his knees to be eye level with her. "Calm yourself. Remember what happened last time you got angry?"

With those words, her fiery soldier demeanor dissipated within a single deep breath.

He brought her into a hug, whispering, "I don't want you to make another mistake. You couldn't handle it. It'd break you, you fragile little thing."

He wasn't sure what was going on between Sara and Guy, but he didn't want to cause another scene by ripping him off her. Sara was anything but fragile. Averting his eyes, Dexter flitted his gaze to Kali's. Still, she was gaping at him, head tilted and curious. Dexter knelt to his daughter. "Are you okay?"

She nodded.

"No one's ever going take you. Okay? I'll make sure of it." Another silent nod.

"Did that man say anything to you?"

She shook her head and pressed her lips together, keeping her reasons to herself. But, just like Sara, her thoughts were loud. She was trying to figure Dexter out, like he was a calculation she couldn't compute.

Dexter narrowed his eyes, confused. "Why did you say—"

Sara's hand snaked up his bicep, getting his attention. "Kay, why'd you lie? Again?"

Kali clamped her lips shut, rapidly moving her eyes back and forth between him and Sara.

After a few silent moments, Sara scrubbed her face with her hands. "Kali, you cannot lie anymore. It scares us."

Kali's mouth parted, and her whole face scrunched with ire. Her fists balled, her shoulders went up, and her lungs filled, readying for a scream. "I already told you. I'm not lying!" Deep within her cerulean eyes were distress and conflict, magnifying as they moved back and forth between her parents. Her hands made claws as her nails scratched down her own face. She let out a frustrated grunt as she bent, picked up a rock, and hurled it at the wall, screaming.

"Here she goes again," Guy mumbled.

"Kali!" Sara made a move to go after her, but Dexter put out an extended arm in front of her torso to stop her.

"Let her," Dexter requested in a low, confident timber. He stared at Kali who was now taking her rage out on the wall by pounding her fists against it. He remembered doing the same thing to his bedroom wall until he finally punched through it. They had more in common than he knew. From his peripherals, he could see Sara gawking at him with puzzlement building. "Let her finish, Sara," he whispered again with a pleading tone tied to each word.

"You're not going to stop her, Sara?" Guy questioned with an opened hand outstretched toward Kali banging on the wall to better display his point. "She's going to hurt herself again."

Dexter eyed Sara and waited for her to choose which of them to listen to. Her eyes moved to Kali, keeping her ground.

They watched Kali going back and forth between pounding her fists into the wall, stomping on the ground, and screaming. It took about five minutes before Kali calmed and turned to face them. Dexter took a deep breath and slowly made his way to the ground, one elbow hooked around a bent knee and the other propping himself up. He waved Kali over, and when she made a move to approach him, he turned to Sara and said, "Can I have a minute with her?"

"Sure," Sara whispered. "Come on, Nellie."

As the three of them walked away, everyone in the vicinity returned to minding their own business. Chatter started at the kiosk and the guards turned their attention back to the outside.

His daughter remained standing in front of him while intertwining her fingers in front of herself. "Sorry," she muttered.

"Sorry?" Dexter sent her a sullen smile. "Why are you sorry?"

With the back of her hand, she wiped the tears from her reddened cheeks. "I got mad again."

"It's okay to get mad."

Her eyes lit up, but her face remained set in rueful anger.

"And how do you feel now?"

She shrugged. "Still mad."

"That's because you forgot an important step."

She cocked her head to the side.

"You forgot to take a deep breath before. And not just a breath, a deep *belly* breath."

Kali sat down next to Dexter and leaned forward, ripping blades of grass out and making small mounds by her sides.

"Try it with me. You're going to breathe until you feel your belly get bigger."

Together they took three deep breaths.

"And, if that still doesn't work, there's something else you can do." Dexter eyed his daughter who seemed to be soaking in everything. Then, he shook his head and looked away. "No, never mind. You can't handle it."

Kali scooted closer. "No. I can handle it. Tell me."

"No. Only those who have mastered their emotions can do this advanced technique."

She planted her hands in the grass, getting ready to leap onto him if he didn't spill. "I can do it!"

Dexter smiled and looked at his daughter's determined expression. "Okay. If you say so. Can I see your hand?" Dexter held his out for her, and she cautiously put her small hand in his. "Good. Now, point your finger."

She did.

He guided her index finger to one of her thighs and started tracing figure eights. "One loop you inhale, and the second you exhale. It works every time—"

She took her hand back and laid it in her lap. "My mom taught me that."

"Oh, did she?" Dexter smiled wide and leaned closer to his daughter. "Can I tell you a secret?"

She nodded as she bobbed her head into a ray of sunlight that illuminated her bright blonde tresses.

He gestured for her to come closer until her ear was near his lips. "I taught your mom that."

She broke away with wide eyes, loudly thinking again. "Really?"

Dexter let out a soft chuckle to keep the atmosphere light and playful. "You can ask her. It's true."

"But, she said that it's only for when I'm scared."

"Oh no, Kali. You can use it for anything. You think you can try it before you get mad next time?"

She shrugged with a precious grin emerging on her face. "I can try."

"Remember, it's only for people who are masters of their emotions. Use it wisely."

"Okay. Thanks."

Dexter sat up, crossed his legs, and fully faced his daughter. "Want to tell me why you think that man wanted to take you?"

She blinked. Twice. Her thick black lashes fluttered as she shook her head.

"That's okay. Whenever you're ready, I promise I'll listen and believe you, okay?"

She smiled, got to her feet, and ran to Sara, crashing her body against her legs, her sleeveless white dress swaying with her movements.

"You look like you're feeling better," Sara said with a smile.

Kali nodded. "I'm sorry, Mommy. I didn't mean to get mad."

Sara's jade eyes latched onto Dexter, mouth parted, clearly impressed by his ability to make way with Kali.

"Can I still go to the park?"

"Yes!" Nellie squealed.

Sara guided Dexter up by his elbow, stood on her tip toes, and whispered in his ear, "Are you going to get mad if Guy still takes them?" Her forehead came to his shoulder, nose buried into his arm. "I really need alone time with you. We have a lot to get done."

Dexter eyed Guy while he leaned down to grab Kali's hand.

Chapter 5

▲▲▲

The world appeared different now that Dexter was home. Colors were more saturated. The sky was brighter and the gut-wrenching grief she endured for six years dissipated little by little with every minute Sara spent with him.

Dexter didn't forgive easily. So, when he had for naming their son Nellie and her massive lapse in judgement when Guy kissed her, she fell more in love with him. The layers of guilt were peeled away with every time he called her Marking. With Dexter's hand secured in hers, all was right again. Watching him protect Kali sparked an ember within her. A fire that hadn't be ignited since she was surviving in the Screecher Age.

Seeing him act so brazenly sent chills weaving through her muscles, tempting her to smash Clive's face in. A surge of envy beat in her chest as she watched Dexter do something she wished she remembered how to.

She could tell he sensed her loud thoughts because he kept trying to get her to laugh as they walked toward the small downtown.

They passed the residential area where most of the houses were still empty, waiting for new arrivals to claim them. Unlike the area surrounding the walls, these homes were covered in fresh beige and dark blue paint. Each of the corners were adorned with gray accented quoins. Even the rotting home on the corner had just been renovated for possible new tenants. Rustic black lampposts lined either side of the two-lane streets that added to the quaintness of the small town. Some lawns were green, some full of rocks, and others partially neglected. Though most aspects of the town were functional when the world reverted back to normal, it was hard to believe all this was once covered in soot and menacing trees that filled the air with a pungent mold. Sara waved to a couple neighbors who sat on their porches, enjoying the sunny weather.

After the blocks of homes was a red metal arch that spanned from one side of the street to the other and read "Welcome to Downtown Metstraville". Shops lined both sides of the tarred street in a mixture of tan bricked buildings and smaller ones with green bordered accents around the frames of the windows and doors. Most stores had awnings with white, hand painted signs while others had flags that hung outside with their shop's logo on it. The parking meters were expired and with signs that read, "No longer in use". Along the sidewalk were potted plants and small trees waiting for time to grow big and strong.

Chatter from the groups of people relaxing at scattered restaurant tables filled the air with laughter and cheerfulness. The smell of morning coffee alerted Sara's senses as she leaned her head on Dexter's shoulder. He smiled down at her and squeezed tighter.

Two blocks into the downtown, Sara came to a halt and pushed Dexter into a cell phone shop. As soon as Dexter's eyes met the man behind the register, he let go of her and rushed to him. "Zeek!"

Sara laughed with as much excitement as Dexter radiated.

"Dexter! Emily said you were back, man!"

He brought his burly guard of four years into a hug. "You're still around?"

Zeek nodded and released him. For the man who always wore leather and ripped off sleeves, he sure looked handsome in a fitted black polo. Not Dexter handsome, but the heavy five o'clock shadow that came from his Middle-Eastern background and his sun-kissed skin would make any girl mad. Chiseled cheekbones, dark coiffed hair, and mysteriously dark eyes. "Thought you would have liked me to keep a good eye on your girl while you were gone. Make sure she didn't get into trouble."

"Not like you could have stopped me," Sara tittered, placing a hand on a popped-out hip.

Zeek smiled and stuck out his tongue toward her. She stuck hers out too then laughed.

"Thanks, man," Dexter said, patting Zeek on his back.

"When we all heard about your sacrifice for her—for us, a lot of us stayed. You made a lot of good friendships in that camp. Worked out in your favor."

A beaming smile erupted on Dexter's face as he reached out and dragged Sara in front of him.

Then Zeek smiled, showing off his pearly white teeth. "I won't talk about the enemies you made, because those people took off as soon as the world turned back."

"Mostly the women," Sara clarified.

Dexter narrowed his eyes playfully with a smirk.

"And your kids!" Zeek announced. "Aren't they amazing?"

Dexter folded his arms over Sara's chest and placed his chin atop her head. "They're perfect."

Zeek's unique, raspy voice rose in pitch. "Did you know they can destroy a display case in less than four seconds? Real talent there."

Dexter laughed and muttered an unapologetic sorry. "So, cell phone shop? I'd figured you'd be patrolling the fence or something."

"Nah, man. After the apocalypse, I needed something calm and easy. I think most of us did. Most of the stores in this town are run by people from your camp. The majority banded together to get life going again. And once we heard about what happened up on the mountain, we wanted to make sure Sara and the twins got what they needed while Sara got back on her feet."

"You guys are the best."

Zeek crossed his arms and leaned a hip against the counter. "If you go to the right stores, we will get what you need too."

"Thanks, man."

Zeek went behind the register that sat on a clear display case. "So, need a phone to get in touch with this beautiful firecracker?"

"Please."

"There isn't much selection, but why don't I give you this bad boy right here." He reached under the glass and pulled out a smartphone that looked like the one he used to have.

"Perfect."

"All right, I'm going to get it all set up. Come back in an hour, yeah?"

Dexter nodded and gave Zeek another hug. "Good to see you're doing well."

"You too. You need anything, don't hesitate to ask."

Sara slipped her hand into Dexter's and led him out of the glass door. They hit different shops that Sara thought contained people he might know. It wasn't until that day did Sara see how great he was with people and how charismatic he could be. No wonder he was elected Homecoming King in high school. Everyone loved him. Confidence emitted from the way he held himself and the way he made everyone around him feel comfortable. He was able to charm his way into everyone's hearts within a few seconds of conversation. The way he put people at ease with a friendly smile and hug was admirable. Sara started to find herself slightly aroused while watching him be so gentle and kind to people she had known for years. And he was all hers. Right?

By the time they reached the end of the downtown area, he had several articles of clothing and a few other necessities— including condoms—inside a large shopping bag. They sat outside at a table in front of an ice cream shop that was drowned in golden sunlight.

"Sara, I'm going to be straightforward with you."

"Please," she took his hand in hers gently.

Dexter leaned over the table, closer to Sara to ensure he had her full attention. "Something's going on with the twins. First, Nellie's weird countdown thing, then Kali saying someone wanted to take her? You don't find that strange?"

"I don't know about Nellie, but Kali *does* make up stories all the time."

Dexter shook his head. "I get that. And while that's possible, for this specific situation, I believe her."

Sara's brows turned up as conflict burned in her eyes.

"Guy's wrong to tell you she just lies for no reason. *And,*" Dexter flipped her hand over and traced the circular scar on her palm left over from the supernatural energy force she once possessed. "I saw Guy inspecting our daughter's palms. I think Guy knows something's up with the twins, and he's trying to make sure you don't catch on."

Sara took a shallow breath. "I-I-I don't know."

He rubbed her hand with his thumb. "Maybe that's why he's implanted himself in your life."

Sara sighed. In fast spurts, she raced through all the interactions she had witnessed between Guy and the kids. But, nothing odd came to mind. Then again, she knew she was terrible when it came to noticing nuances of social interactions.

"I mean, how did you meet him?"

She shrugged. "Emily introduced me. He must have been in your camp or something because he was just always here." She took her hand back and rubbed her face. "He lost his own twins during the Screecher Age, so I think he kind of latched on to fill that void."

"That's sad."

"Yeah. I think he's still working through it."

He squeezed her hand. "Can we just keep a closer eye on him? Watch how he interacts with the kids?"

"Okay."

He kissed the back of her hand. "Thanks, Marking."

"Will you help me talk to the kids? I-I-I need to know what's going on with them. Nellie's weird hand thing has been streaming through my thoughts on repeat since you told me. You being dead set on Kali not lying makes me believe you— her."

Dexter grinned. "Of course. We'll talk to them when they get home."

"Can we go home and wait?"

He stood, rounded the table, and kissed her lightly freckled cheek. "Let's go." Dexter held out a hand to help her up, and she took it with grace. Sara didn't let go as they walked back toward the residential area. "Sara? What did Guy mean when he said he didn't want you to make another mistake?"

"Oh... um..." She raked her hair back with her fingers and studied the pavement as she walked.

"Did something bad happen?"

"Well... Yeah, I guess. Just...I did something I'm not proud of." It was happening. The images were bubbling up again. Push them down. All of them. Dammit. She didn't want to relive that night, but it was budding in her brain like a parasite feeding on her memories.

Dexter peered at her feet when they lazily scuffed the pavement with every step. "Can you tell me what it was?"

Echoes of aged gunshots stirred a wave of sadness inside her. "It's terrible, Dex. I did something really terrible." If the sun hadn't been glistening through her jade eyes, she would have gotten away with blinking back the tears welling on her lower lids.

Dexter let go of her hand, only to wrap his arm around her shoulders and bring her close. "That's okay. Talk to me."

She took a step out from the circle of his arms, putting a hand to his chest to keep him at distance. She needed room to breathe. "A couple months after I had the kids, there was a breach in the wall. At night, Splitters infiltrated the town." Her voice caught, on the cusp of exposing her tears again. "I hid the kids in my closet and locked myself in the room." *Three short knocks pounded on the bedroom door, knocking the air from her lungs as she spread her arms to protect the closet that sheltered Dexter's children.* "Somehow Guy got in the house, so I let him into the room. We hid together." *It was Guy's arms wrapping around her that kept her extreme fright at bay. Having one more person willing to protect what was left of Dexter was something she would forever be thankful for.* "It was horrid, Dex. A lot of people lost their lives that night. I can still hear the gunshots, the screaming. I relive the panic all the time. All I could do was focus on surviving. It was a blinding state of mind." Her head dropped to both her hands, fingers clawing at her scalp, wishing she could clean out her mind. "I-I-It wasn't supposed to happen, Dexter!"

Gentle pressure of Dexter's hand guided her to a wooden bench, where she could sit.

"The world turned back. Splitters didn't have to be Splitters anymore, you know? We didn't have to be put through anything like that ever again. I shouldn't have had to *still* be surviving. With two kids! How could people *still* want to hurt each other?" Speaking her thoughts that never ceased to repeat in her mind inched up the veil of sadness that shrouded her, only to be replaced with a bubbling rage. "I got so *angry*. I just—I thought about you then. It was the first time I understood your temper. How it could be so *all-consuming*." *A crash boomed from downstairs. Sara stood, back straight, stepping into a fighting stance, clenching her fists by her chin. Her nails dug into her scarred palms. Palms she prayed would spark to a powerful lime green. God knew she used every ounce of her being to summon any residue of power that may have been hibernating in her veins.* "By the time a Splitter busted down the bedroom door, I lost it," Sara's voice hesitated with a quiet quiver. "She hit me in the ribs with a spiked bat." Sara clenched her teeth, ignoring the vibrating phantom pain in her side. "I-I-I ended up breaking her neck." *Between her hands lived the woman's head forever. It took mere seconds for Sara to feel that neck snapping as she forced the chin up and to the left while rolling the back of the head the opposite direction.* Everything about it was satisfying. Killing the Splitter was something she was proud of... for that moment. What still haunted her was what she did next. "And, after that," she scrubbed her face, attempting to hide the tears, "I kept going. And, I *liked* it." *With the bat that had fallen from the woman's lifeless hands, she pounded it into the Splitter's face until she was atrociously unrecognizable, screaming profanities loud enough for others to mistake her as a Splitter herself.*

Dexter turned to her, gently pulling her hands away from her face. "Sara, how on Earth was that a *mistake*?"

She sniffed and began curling into a ball. "I killed someone, Dexter! I did more than kill someone. I lost my fucking mind. I had no semblance of humanity in me! I had no respect for the dead. Poor girl was probably captured by Splitters and had no choice but to participate. I still don't know her story! I should have saved her! That's the Sara Mar King you would have been proud of. Not this! Not me!"

Dexter stuck his hand over her torso, so she wasn't allowed to continue to curl into a protective ball. "Sara! Stop." Dexter lowered his head to ensure she was looking at him. "You protected yourself. You protected our family! You did an excellent job! *I* am *so* proud of you. It's not like you were hurting her after. She was gone by that point. It's *okay*."

"But-but, I—" tears glittered over her electric green eyes.

Dexter's brows knitted into a serious expression that breathed life into her. "No, Sara. You are not allowed to let this haunt you anymore. You did what you had to. It was either you or them."

Her entire body leaned into Dexter's, silently asking him to hold her. "Guy said I went full-blown bat-shit crazy. He said he called my name several times, but I couldn't hear him because I was in a blinding rampage. When he tried to pick me up off her, I broke his nose and swung the bat at him too."

Dexter wrapped his arms around her, slightly rocking her. "You've been through so much. It's okay to have PTSD."

"I do! I know I do!" she sat up and looked at him. "I couldn't have that around the kids!"

Dexter's brows furrowed. "Says who?"

"Guy said I could hurt more people and the kids one day. Especially with my night terrors—"

"Sara! That's manipulative of him, and you know it. It's not true. You'd never hurt those kids. You did that to protect them." Dexter smiled as wide as he could, pulling Sara out of her darkness. "You save worms, Sara!" Dexter laughed, and Sara responded with a half-hearted giggle. She sent him a look that only he could decode. "You still do it, don't you?"

She threw her head back and gave a teary laugh. "Yeah— okay I just did a couple months ago." She covered her mouth as she continued to laugh. "I pictured you helping me and getting all muddy."

"I would have helped you," he said, kissing the corner of a teary eye. "Sara. You're going to be okay."

Because it was Dexter Bennet saying it, she started to believe it. She was going to be okay. Dexter said so.

He stood, and yanked her arm so that she was standing too. "Come on." He laughed and guided her back home.

Dexter set the bag of new necessities he had bought on the dining table and rifled through it. Sara hopped on the kitchen island, crossing her legs and scrunching her lips to the side, studying him. The longer her eyes riveted on Dexter's hands in the bag, the more desperately he searched.

"Whatcha looking for so adamantly?"

Her freckled cheeks seared when Dexter tried to discreetly slip a condom in his back pocket.

"Sly."

He went to her, placed his hands on her knees and gently spread her legs apart to get as close to her as possible. His nose came to her neck and traced her skin while whispering through a smile, "You weren't supposed to see that."

Her legs came around his waist and her lips came to his neck, kissing him softly. "But, I did." She pulled away and leaned back, hands propping herself up behind her as she tilted her head. "Sir Bennet. Were you really going to wait until I came on to you for a third time? I can't believe you'd really make a lady try again."

"Oh, Marking. I wouldn't dare think to disappoint you," he huffed, eyes drifting down her body. One hand snaked around her bottom as he stepped back, sliding her off the kitchen island. She yelped and wrapped her arms around his neck to avoid falling. His cocky, crooked grin met her gaze, like it was his plan to have her this close. "Even though," he whispered as his forehead rested against hers, eyes sinking into lust, "I wildly enjoy you coming on to me."

One hand moved to her cheek and caressed it in the way she loved. Warm but sure. It was okay to lose control with Dexter. With Dexter, she didn't have to think. She didn't have to worry. She could just indulge.

He carried her to her room as tunnel vision surrounded his diamond eyes. As soon as her head hit the pillow, Dexter moved on top of her. His hulky mass created a barrier between her and everything that might still be haunting her. Lips crossed hers and tickles of beard feathered her cheeks. Once his musky scent filled her lungs, worries about the kids and Guy and Dexter's absence were muted. All she had to do was

73

enjoy. That much she could do with a quiet mind. And damn, did she want her mind silenced. The need for him to blank out her thoughts shot through her veins like a ruthless craving.

His hands remained planted on either side of her head, unmoving. Why wasn't he touching her yet? Why wasn't he ripping off her clothes and giving her everything she had been wanting for the last six years? "Dexter, what are you doing? Touch me."

The look in his eyes was filled with uncertainty and fear. They were desperately scanning hers, trying to decipher what she wanted, how fast and for how long. "Sara. I'm sorry I put you against the wall. I *knew* you didn't like that. I *saw* what your dad did to you, and still I lost control."

She growled. Now was not the time. "Dexter! Shut the hell up."

He shook his head with a tortured look building in his eyes. "Listen. If you give me control right now, I'll lose it. You have boundaries and I don't want to cross them. I don't want to hurt you."

Sara pressed her lips together, wishing that him seeing all the horrid things men had done to her in the past hadn't changed this for them. "I'll risk it. I trust you."

He groaned and lowered his head to her neck, kissing softly as if still deciding what to do. "I don't trust myself," he whispered while nibbling on her ear.

"Dexter. I am addicted to the feeling of trusting you."

Another tortured groan ripped from his throat. "Sara."

"If anything happens, I'll let you know."

He parted his lips to say something, but Sara put a finger against them.

"I will let you know." She took his hand and kissed his palm before guiding it down her neck to one of her aching breasts. "Now, touch me."

A carnal hunger filled his eyes and she saw everything. His every desire to claim her, to rip apart all the pain she had ever gone through and replace it with his love. She saw his addiction to her. His hand continued downward until he latched onto her waist, seizing her lips with his. With his other hand, he undid the button and zipper to her black jeans. He earnestly pulled them off her legs. Then, his ocean eyes met hers and held her gaze captive as he ran his hands down the sides of her torso. Every caress had her growing wetter. Every kiss. Every article of clothing that he stripped off of her.

When she was completely exposed, she watched as his eyes wandered over her nakedness with reverence cultivating in his seductive gaze. A tender grin teased the corners of his lips. "You are so beautiful." He kissed down her neck and paused at one of her nipples. Sucking. Teasing. Nibbling. His hand played with the other, kneading and lightly pinching. Sara moaned under Dexter's touch, arching her back toward him. His loving energy swathed her loud mind in so many wonderful ways.

Sara shifted beneath him, writhing in a blinding pleasure. His hand moved down, trailing all her scars until his hand was cupped between her legs. Sara took a deep inhale as he slid his fingers into her heat. A gasp escaped her, but Dexter muted her with his mouth, plunging his tongue between her teeth and groaning against her.

He moved his mouth down her cheek, then to the nape of her neck. When he sucked on the delicate skin on her neck, the feeling of being spellbound by his love spiraled through her with ferocity. With every twitch of his fingers, her pulse throbbed down her body. Her hands came down his back, clawing at his shirt to get it off. And when it did, she admired his inked skin and thickly muscled chest.

His fingers withdrew from her and she watched him hop off the bed. Sara rolled onto her stomach and reached out for him. "No, no. Wait! Why are you leaving?" Her heart leapt from her chest and she reached farther. "Where are you going?"

He towered over her and caught her hand in his, leaning down to kiss the back of it. "Nowhere, Marking."

A relieved exhale exploded from her lungs as she dropped her hand.

He laughed. "Leave you? Like this? I'm not that big of an idiot." He shimmied out of his pants and boxer briefs, and rolled on the condom he had ripped open from the package with his teeth.

"Wait, before you do that." She swung her legs over the edge of the bed. "Did you... um... want me to... you know," she said nodding to his huge length. "I just, um..."

He smiled and shook his head. "We'll take this slow. Let's do what I know you're comfortable with for now."

He was still taking care of her, just like he promised. This was why she trusted him. He knew everything about her and her past. There was never pressure when it came to them, just accepted bliss. "Okay. Maybe next time."

Dexter smiled. "Maybe next time."

He took her ankles and towed her bottom closer to the edge of the bed. He placed himself between her legs. As he bent over, he linked one hand with hers and brought it above her head. "Sara—"

The words he told her in the cabin blossomed in her mind. *This is my hand, Sara. No one else's, okay? If anything else happens, remember that it's me holding you.* "I remember. It's you holding—"

He captured her lips with his as if not wanting to waste another second. Inch by inch, he slid himself deep into her. Sara let out a small cry of pleasure, and she could swear she heard soft music playing in the back of her mind.

When he pulled partially out, he groaned and brought one hand down on her shoulder to get better leverage. As he thrusted into her, he tugged down on her shoulder, which caused her mind to haze into a state of wild euphoria. Nothing was under her control anymore and it felt exhilarating to trust her tattooed warrior. "Fuck." It slipped out as soon as she relinquished all her inhibitions. He stopped, and it pissed Sara off.

Dexter's worried voice sounded in her ears. "You okay?"

"Don't stop," she whined, unsure of what he even said.

He drove into her again and the world around her faded. Damn, she wanted to stay in this perfect state of unclear haze forever. She was so caught up in the need for Dexter after six years that her heart couldn't keep up. It pounded against her chest in thunderous pulses that filled her ears. Or was that Dexter's heartbeat?

He pulled out, panting while flipping her over, taking her hips and pulling them upward to him. "Is this okay?"

She answered by leaning into him, grinding.

"Sorry, Sara. Never mind," he mumbled, while pulling out.

Sara got to her knees and turned to Dexter who was standing at the edge of the bed, face smothered in the same haze.

"I need to see you."

Sara growled, annoyed with the delay. She got off the bed, placed her open palms on his chest and pushed him onto the mattress. As she climbed on top of him, Dexter brought the edge of the comforter over her.

She tittered. "Can you see my face now?"

He took her head between his hands and brought her close. As he kissed her, she eased down on him, sliding forward and backward several times. She pulled away from his lips so she could breathe as she rode him. His hands shifted to her hips, moving in whatever rhythms she desired. She sat up, straightening her spine. The covers bunched at her bottom and her fingers bit into his sides as she gyrated harder. Faster. With every inhale, she let as much of Dexter's intoxicating energy numb her mind and fill her senses.

His perfect blue eyes that protected every part of her. His corded muscles that held her small body, the same ones that carried her when she couldn't walk. His inked skin that she admired and forever inked herself with. His large hands that never hesitated to dry her tears. She let out another cry of pleasure that hardened Dexter that much more.

"Oh, Sara, I'm going to come."

She would have replied, but she, too, was about to finish and wanted to concentrate on staying attached to Dexter in every way possible. Faster. Faster and faster. Everything blurred and her body trembled above his as she exploded around him. His hands pulled down on her hips to keep her in place as he joined her in his own release.

When his hands relaxed, she fell limp to his huffing chest. His arms wrapped around her thin body, holding her tightly against him as he tried to regain his breath.

"I love you so much it hurts," Dexter breathed.

Sara lay atop him, enjoying the feeling of his chest rising and falling beneath her cheek. It told her that he was actually home. He was here to help her and the kids. He was going to protect his family again. By some miracle, Atraeus let him live. Let him come back to her. Let him ease the pain that had been brewing in her mind for so many treacherous years. His arms snaked around her, fingertips lightly tracing the skin on her arms. It wasn't until then did she feel so small compared to him. Always, she had prided herself on standing up to the bulkiest and smartest of men in the camps—even Dexter. But, right then, he was putting her in her favorite place. Small and tucked safely against him where she belonged.

He kissed her head before rolling her to the side and slowly slipping out of her. He moved to the bathroom to dispose of the condom. Sara got between the sheets feeling fulfilled in every way. Soon, Dexter's arms were encompassing her beneath the sheets like he wouldn't dare let her go or he would die.

He kissed her shoulder, sending goosebumps down her arms.

"I don't know how I ever lived without you."

"I missed you so much, Dexter Bennet." Sara shifted so his chest could be her pillow as her arm fell over his stomach.

"I don't know how to ask you this, but... can I have your number?"

Sara giggled.

"Actually, everyone's number from your phone."

"Sure."

"Thanks." He kissed her shoulder again.

A knock at the front door echoed through the house. "That's got to be Guy with the kids."

Sara made a move to get up, but Dexter shoved her shoulder down, and planted a firm kiss over her lips that demanded her to stay put. "I'll get it. You worry about putting your number in my phone."

"No, but we have to talk to the kids."

Dexter shook his head. "Rest. I'd like some more time to bond with them anyway. We'll talk to them really soon. I promise."

She gave a slight grin and relaxed into the pillow while watching Dexter get up. Sara observed as his every muscle tensed when he arched his back to pick up his clothes and get dressed. To stop herself from telling him to forget the kids and get his ass back in bed for another round, she bit her lip and let her mind stay buzzing from the high Dexter's touch had provided.

He tossed her his phone and left the room.

As she was dialing in his number, she heard the kids running into the house and the deep sound of Guy's voice. Her skin tingled, thinking she shouldn't have let Dexter talk to him alone. He wouldn't do anything in front of the kids though, right? She hadn't realized she was holding her breath until the sound of the front door shut and Dexter's happy voice muttered something to the kids.

She turned her focus back to the screen and set her name in his phone as "Sara Mar King".

Then, she deleted it and put "Marking".

Staring at it for a few seconds, she changed her mind, erased it again, and typed in "Sara Mar Bennet", liking the way it looked.

The sound of his footsteps coming up the stairs had her nervously fumbling to clear the name. Dexter opened the door and shut it behind him.

"Hey, what do you want my name to be in your phone?"

His eyes wandered over the outline of her figure under the blankets and said, "Sara Mar King. I want to feel like a kid again when I see your name light up."

Sara beamed and crinkled her freckled nose.

"What was my name on your phone?"

"Sexy Dexy the idiot."

Dexter sent her a heavy-lidded gaze.

"Kidding. Just Dex."

"Then, put that in your phone."

"Okay." Sara's fingers moved to her phone and dialed in Dexter's new number.

"The kids want to bake some cookies. Why don't you hang out up here and rest for a bit?"

"You sure?"

"Yeah."

"Thanks, Dex. I'd love a nap."

He came to her bedside, pulled the covers over her shoulders, kissed her cheek, and grabbed his phone. "Rest, my beautiful Marking."

He left and Sara heard his steps going down the stairs. She closed her eyes and all she could picture was Dexter above her. Her perfect, complete family. Dexter was home. Home for good.

Laughter barreling through the house pulled at the corners of her lips as she snuggled deeper into the pillow. Her body was exhausted, but her mind reeled. Damn, she wanted Dexter back upstairs with her. She wanted her lungs to fill with his scent again.

More laughter. She made a move to get out of bed and join her family, but her head weighed heavy, like she had been drugged by drowsiness. The room spun and the bed swayed beneath her, rocking her to sleep. She had barely slept the night before, afraid Dexter was going to up and leave. Still, Sara didn't want to sleep. She wanted to listen to her family laughing downstairs. It was too precious to miss.

Fighting to stay awake and already craving his attention, she whipped out her phone and texted him.

Sara Mar King: I'm still naked, you know.

Send.

She dropped her phone beside her head, knowing Dexter probably had his hands deep in cookie dough.

To her surprise, the phone buzzed and Sara smiled.

Dex: Whatever you're trying to do... it's working.

She bit on her nails, thinking about what to say next.

Sara Mar King: Round 2?

She watched her screen for a bit, but there was no response. Sara sighed and put down her phone, flipping over. He probably wasn't going to answer, so she could sleep. Luckily that wasn't the case. Just seeing "Dex" flash on her phone brought up the middle schooler in her who was madly in love with him. That same giddy feeling rising up her throat when she got a text from him.

Dex: Nellie and Kali can take care of the cookie making alone, right?

Sara Mar King: Sure! Come back. I'm waiting.

Dex: You're killing me.

Afraid he would really leave the kids to their own devices, Sara didn't respond. She rolled over, closed her eyes, and took a deep breath, praying her night terrors would leave her alone for a cat nap. Soon, her mind blanked, her body molded to the mattress, and she fell fast asleep.

Chapter 6

▲▲▲

Sara Mar King. Texting him. What a wonderfully odd concept. He ran his eyes over her words a hundred times that evening. The sun had set a few hours ago, and he knew it was around the kids' bedtime.

He turned off the TV and the twins whined.

"It's bedtime, kids. Come on. Let's get into PJs, brush your teeth, and I'll sing to you tonight."

"But, Mommy sings to us," Kali complained.

"I know she does, pretty girl, but she's sleeping. Let me try singing to you. If you don't like it, I'll get mommy."

"Okay," she huffed and hopped off the couch and stood at his knees, facing away from him. "Can you braid my hair?"

Dexter's heart pounded with happiness.

"I can do it!" Nellie squealed.

"No," she groaned. "You always mess it up, Nellie."

He brought his daughter onto his lap and pulled her long blonde hair to her back. "Come on, Nellie, teach me."

Nellie stood on the couch, leaned his stomach against Dexter's back, and reached over his shoulders for his sister's hair. "Make three pieces."

Dexter divided her hair in three sections. "Now what?"

"You braid!"

Dexter let out a deep belly laugh and let go of Kali's hair. He reached around and brought Nellie onto a cushion next to him, tickling his belly. "You don't know how to braid, silly goose."

Nellie's nose crinkled as he laughed and rolled off the couch.

"Told you," Kali droned.

Dexter did the best he could to braid her hair, wrapping the bottom with a black hair tie. Yeah, it was lumpy and he missed some pieces, but Kali didn't seem to mind.

As soon as he took her off his lap, everything darkened, and the living room around him melted like paint dripping off the walls. The sudden shift in Dexter's vision had him standing up in a panicked alert. As the TV warped into dribbles of thick liquid, dark slate was revealed. The living room kept dripping until he was surrounded by the craggy recesses that made up the walls of the pit. The decaying smell of the sacrifices filled his lungs with roiling disgust of neglected flesh. Above him was a circular opening that allowed him to peer at the night sky scattered with distant stars... and Sara. Her blonde bangs fell over her forehead as she peered down at him. Tears dripped from her eyes while reaching into the pit for him, crying his name.

Fear pounded in his chest so hard it winded him in a single word. "Holy..."

Before the dread of being back in Atraeus's pit destroyed him, his living room blinked back into focus. He was left with an artificial aftertaste that swirled around him in confusion.

His eyes focused on his beautiful son who was gaping at him, sitting as still as stone with large, guilty eyes. "Oh no," he whispered.

Dexter put a hand on Nellie's shoulder, just to make sure that his son was in front of him. The feel of his cotton short-sleeved shirt under his touch assured Dexter that he and his soul were in fact with his family. Before, when Atraeus tortured him for all those years, he could never feel anything in his visions, and he had used the sense of touch to anchor himself to reality. Dexter even squeezed Nellie's shoulder for good measure. "Nellie?" Dexter questioned.

A horrified expression filled Nellie's eyes. "I-I-I didn't—"

"Nellie, did you just do that?"

Kali tugged on Dexter's wrist. "Do what?"

Nellie pushed Dexter's hand off his shoulder and blurted, "I have to go to bed, Dad. Night." He hopped off the couch and ran up the steps. Halfway up, he tripped and completed the climb on all fours.

"What? What'd he do?" Kali pressed.

He waited until Nellie disappeared behind the bedroom door before turning to Kali. "I think he made me see something."

"Oh no." Her glassy cerulean eyes widened before she turned and sprinted up the steps, yelling, "I have to go to bed too, Dad."

That confirmed there was something suspicious with the twins. But, he clearly didn't have that bond with either one of them yet to pry for more information.

Dexter hadn't earned enough trust from them, so he decided to keep his mouth shut while helping them through the rest of their nighttime routine. He didn't even bring it up when Nellie even whispered a quiet, "I'm so sorry, Daddy," while he crawled into his bed that had a dark wooden frame and navy blue sheets.

"It's okay, Nellie. Talk to me when you're ready."

"You're not mad?"

Dexter grinned, happy to be on the subject. It meant he was making some headway that might help for when he talked to him and his sister with Sara. "Not at all. Okay, bud?"

Nellie's face relaxed with relief as he snuggled deeper into the covers. "Mommy doesn't know. I try to keep it away from everyone."

Dexter knelt by Nellie's bedside and began tucking him in. "Do you need help?"

With an unchanging expression, Nellie shook his head and rolled over, away from him and toward his sister.

Dexter tucked Kali in next and repeated the steps that Sara had done the night before. When they were both under the covers, he knelt between their beds and held each of their small hands as he sang their nightly lullaby. He kissed Nellie on the forehead and went to turn off the light. A part of him silently begged Kali to ask for a goodnight kiss, but she didn't.

"Night, kiddos."

He closed their door and snuck down the hall eager to check on Sara. He stepped into the room and saw her balled form curled in the center of the bed. Head buried in the pillow and covers enveloping her, she slept soundly. Admiring her peaceful slumber filled him with utter peace. He slid between the sheets. As gently as he could, he pulled her against him, knowing he had to have her between his arms if he had any chance of sleeping. As soon as her bare skin touched him, he realized she was still naked. She was happily sleeping, coiled up against him, so he resisted waking her up with his kisses and to start round two.

"Dex..." She sighed while tugging his arm farther over her body. "You're still here."

"Of course I am." He kissed her shoulder.

"The kids okay?"

"Yes. Go back to sleep," he cooed while closing his eyes and breathing in her intoxicating floral scent.

Her body clumsily maneuvered on top of his. "Why'd you make me wait so long?" she said in a tired croak.

"'Cause I'm a stupid, stupid man." He placed his hand on the back of her head and pulled her in for a kiss before setting her head on his chest. Like magnets to her, his arms wrapped around her tiny frame. Her body lay heavy on his and he wondered if she had already fallen asleep.

"Sir Bennet, wake me up," she slurred. "Round two."

Dexter chuckled.

"And since you made me wait, I have some demands. Three rounds." Just then, a soft knock came on the door and a groan ripped from Sara's chest. "No, I don't want you to go," she whined. "You just got here."

"That reminds me. You need to teach me how to braid hair." Dexter sat up with her still on his chest. He made a move to unlatch her from him, but she clung tighter, making him smile.

"I really, *really* don't want you to leave, Dexter. Not tonight. Dexter…"

He rubbed her back, trying to break her drowsiness. "Our daughter needs you."

"Mommy?"

"I'm coming, baby Kay," she hollered without moving an inch. "Dex, I don't want you to go."

"I'll just be downstairs. And now you can text me, okay?"

Sara sighed and fled to the closet while Dexter moved to the door. She put on his band T-shirt and black cheekies. Ones where her pert bottom hung out, teasing him under the shirt.

Once she was dressed, he opened the door and looked down at his precious daughter. Dexter knelt to be eye level with her. "Hey. Can't sleep?"

She shook her head.

"Want to sleep with Mommy tonight?"

She nodded with a grin.

Sara bent down and took her hand. Dexter kissed Sara on the cheek. "Sleep well, Marking." He rustled Kali's hair and imagined giving his daughter a goodnight kiss before he turned toward the hall.

Kali's sweet voice called, "Daddy." Dexter turned to see her little index finger tapping her rosy cheek.

Happiness thundered in his chest and a smile ripped over his face. He leaned down and pressed a soft kiss to his daughter's cheek. "Sleep well, pretty girl."

Dexter made his way to the comforts of the couch, checking the house was locked along the way. He pulled out his phone to text Sara.

Dex: I love you

He fell asleep waiting for a reply from her that never came.

The jingle of keys at the front door woke Dexter. Moonlight seeped through the sheer curtains, casting a silvery glow on everything in the dead of night. He looked to the door and watched carefully as it cracked open. A sudden rush of adrenaline coursed through his veins as he rolled off the couch and got into a crouched position on the ground.

A tall, dark figure slinked in, holding something white. When it entered the kitchen, Dexter made out the shape of a broad-shouldered man. The intruder rested the white object on the kitchen island. When he turned his head, Dexter recognized Guy's features. What the fuck was he doing in their home in the middle of the night? Blood rushed in his ears as his entire being heated into a monstrous rage.

Dexter stood and used light steps to close the gap between them. Guy sighed and placed his elbows on the kitchen island, hands combing through his thick dark hair. In a swift motion, Dexter tugged his shoulder so Guy was forced to face him. Up came his fist and it didn't stop until Dexter sucker punched him in the jaw. Guy yelped and fell to the ground.

"Why the *fuck* did you break into our home?" Dexter whisper-yelled.

Guy's hands went to his jaw, groaning in pain. Dexter grasped his shirt, lifted him, then pushed him against the wall where the back of his head smacked against it.

"Dude, what the hell?" he grumbled.

Unable to ignore the impulse, he clenched his fist and sent a powerful punch into Guy's gut. "I asked you a question!"

Guy doubled over, but Dexter was quick to pin him against the wall again. The small bruise swelling over his jaw wasn't enough. Intense rage overcame him and propelled him into the dark spaces of his mind. A space where Dexter was desperate to show Guy just how dangerous he could really be. That craving to satisfy his anger caused Dexter to grab hold of Guy's collar and send two fast punches into his eye. With the force, he let Guy collapse to the ground.

The man rocked side to side, holding his eye. "Fucking hell! I didn't break in! I used my emergency key that Sara gave me!"

He had a key? That left such a bad taste in Dexter's mouth. Either way, there was no reason for him to be in Sara's home at this time of night while he clearly thought everyone was sleeping. "Why are you here?" Dexter questioned at a much louder volume than he intended. Fuck, he needed to better control his growing ire so as not to wake his family. But damn, that hunger for Guy's blood was barely curbed.

"I-I-I was dropping off Kali's stuffed animal, Jesus."

Dexter got on his haunches, hovering over Guy, who spat out blood onto Sara's nice linoleum. "Now?"

"She has a hard time sleeping without it."

Dexter's vision filtered red. "You think you know everything about my daughter, don't you? About my family?"

Guy's thick brows furrowed into a heated expression. "I've spent more time with them than you." His pointed nose and high cheekbones scrunched as he winced in pain.

Dexter's wrath flared like a thousand suns, and he couldn't resist wrapping his hand around the weasel's throat. Guy pushed at Dexter's hands to free himself, but he was not successful. "What do you think you have planned for my family? Huh?"

Guy tried to speak, but Dexter didn't want to hear it, so he squeezed harder, hoping his stupid excuses would stay trapped in his crushed throat. The more he looked at Guy, the more he enjoyed watching his face turn bluer and the whites in his eyes turn redder. Maybe if he squeezed harder, the bulging vein in the man's head would explode.

Before Dexter even realized, his fist bashed into the side of Guy's head with a satisfying crunch. More speckles of his blood splattered over the ground. "The way you looked at my daughter's hand—told her she was lying. The way you put Sara down. You manipulative bastard."

Guy's eyes closed as his grip on Dexter's hand grew weaker.

A scream burst from the stairs. Dexter looked up to see his innocent daughter standing at the entrance of the kitchen, watching. Her azure eyes wide, mouth agape, and white night dress rocking back and forth with her small shakes.

"Kali—" Dexter released Guy and stood, unsure what to do.

Guy gasped for breath, wheezing in any amount of air to replenish what Dexter had knocked out of him. He, too, turned toward the terrified little girl at the bottom of the stairs. Guy spurt blood from his mouth before saying, "Kali, honey, go upstairs," like he was showing off that she was priority over his own health.

Dexter resisted every urge to stomp on his face for speaking to his daughter with such familiarity.

In the next instant, Sara was behind Kali, blonde pixie cut in shambles and wide-eyed in shock. "Oh my god." She wrapped her arms around Kali. "Kay, go wait for me in your room."

Kali whimpered with an outstretched hand, for which of them, Dexter was unsure. Sara pushed her up the stairs. "Go, Kay. To your room." Kali's footsteps pattered up quickly on the carpeted steps.

Sara rushed to Guy's side, resting a hand on his chest and assessing the damage Dexter had done. "What the hell happened?"

Dexter was happy to explain first, crossing his arms and moving to the bottom of the stairs in time to see Kali closing the bedroom door behind her. "He broke in. I thought he was an intruder."

Sara's confused gaze shot to Dexter then his swelling hand. Her face hardened, but he didn't care what Sara thought. He would have done it again.

Guy's hand came to Sara's shoulder, stealing her attention. "No! I used my key. I-I-I had Kali's stuffy." He wheezed, spurting more blood onto their kitchen floor. "I thought she might need it."

"Shit," Sara huffed, moving her hand into Guy's. Seeing her hold another man's hand sent a wave of acidic nausea boiling up Dexter's throat. "Dex, give me your phone."

Dexter gave it to her with a huff of disapproval, trying to switch off his jealousy. He watched her call 911. Damn, sometimes he hated how sweet Sara was. Just let him suffer for a bit. He shouldn't have come into their home. Didn't she feel violated even a little? Or did she still believe everyone had good reason for everything?

"Hi, I need an ambulance at 811 Malloway Street. Sara Mar King's house as soon as possible. My friend got jumped by a few men on the street. He's in bad shape."

And that reminded him that sometimes her sweetness worked in his favor. The red in his vision petered out as the words streamed into his ears. Damn, he loved Sara. She never thought twice about protecting him back. There she was lying to cover up another one of his violent acts. Just like when she had told Nell her eye shiner was from falling on a rock, not from his peli-induced, hallucinated punch to the face. He wanted to reach out, pick her up, and take her to her room to show her how much he appreciated her steadfast loyalty.

While her lie made Dexter's heart swell with love, it crumpled Guy's face in disgust. "Are you kidding? Why are you covering for him, Sara?"

She rested the phone against her shoulder and pointed a finger at him. "Shut it. You either lie or I hang up and let Dexter finish you off. Which is it going to be?"

"All right. You know I'd do anything for you." He brought a hand to her cheek, and she flinched, slapping it to his side.

Just like that, Dexter was fuming again. He even stepped closer to haul Sara away from him, but he took a deep, centering breath before he acted. "Sara, I'm getting angry," Dexter warned through clenched teeth.

"Shut it, Dex." Sara rolled her eyes and brought the phone to her ear. "Sorry, I didn't hear what you said."

"Yeah, he's breathing and talking… Okay."

She hung up and placed it on the white tiled island.

"Dex, go get me some pants and a jacket."

Trying to block out his feelings and operate like a robot, he went up, grabbed what she needed, including her own phone, and brought it down to her. She dressed herself in front of Guy, which pissed Dexter off that much more. He even watched Guy glance up her creamy legs and lock on her black panties. Disgusted chills spindled up his spine, forcing a ball of acid to take shape in his gut.

"The ambulance is on the way," Sara said while putting on her black bomber jacket and looking at Dexter. "You go check on Kali, and I'm going to the hospital with Guy when they get here."

"Fine."

Once she stuffed her phone in her jeans, she slipped her hand back into Guy's. Because it was Sara, he knew the gesture was just her natural instinct to comfort those who were suffering. But, Dexter wasn't sure if Guy understood that.

Dexter didn't want to wait around to see Guy get any sort of help, so he stalked to the kids' room in search for Kali. When

95

he opened it, he saw Nellie sleeping soundly, like a log, but Kali's bed was empty, blue blanket spilled over the edge of the bed. The window was open and a ladder was hooked on the sill. Dexter's heart sank before he sprinted downstairs. "Sara!"

She turned around with an irked expression on her face. "What?"

"Kali's gone."

She squeezed her eyes shut. "Fuck, she did it again."

"What do you mean 'again'?"

"The ladders," Guy mumbled.

Dexter clenched his teeth and balled his fists. "If you don't shut him up, Sara, I will."

"Relax," Sara ordered while opening her eyes. "Since I got the fire ladders for them, she's been using it to leave the house."

He squeezed one hand on the banister. "Then why the hell do you still have them? She's so young. She could fall and hurt herself."

"Shut up, Dexter! Now is not the time to judge my parenting."

"I'm not judging—"

"Just go get her. She's in your tower. I told her she could go there whenever she's scared."

Dexter snatched Kali's unicorn from the kitchen island and went to the front door to put on his new sneakers. "Can you stay with Nellie? When I bring Kali back, you can go meet him at the hospital."

She huffed. "Yeah. Go."

Just as Dexter exited the house, the flashing lights of the ambulance appeared. Town houses lit up in a parade of racing blue and red. The brisk summer breeze whipped around Dexter's face as he picked up the pace toward his daughter. As he approached the tower only a half mile away, the ambulance faded to the background of his thoughts.

It took only a few seconds from the threshold of the camp, across the grass, and up the repaired spiral stairs to reach the top where his old, circular room from the past resided. Panting, he opened the door and was met by emptiness. He clutched the stuffy tighter when he heard quiet sniffles coming from the smaller room farther back. His old private room where he spent close to four years sleeping in. He drew the dark blue curtain to the side and saw his little girl coiled in a ball on the king-sized mattress, crying.

A flash of Sara six years prior zipped into focus. The image of her curled in the same spot as his daughter hit him and tugged achingly on his heartstrings—as if the memory had occurred just yesterday. Now, it was his daughter who he needed to comfort.

Dexter sat at the edge of the mattress, watching her, letting her cry it out. Then, her wet eyes fastened on him. "Don't hurt me."

His heart shattered into fragile pieces. "No, never, Kali. I would *never* hurt you." He reached out and placed her stuffy in the center of the bed as a peace offering. When he released it, Kali snatched the unicorn and cuddled it to her stomach.

"You hurt Guy."

"I know. But, I didn't know it was Guy. I thought it was a bad person coming to hurt us. I only ever want to keep you safe."

She sat up, wiping her marble eyes with her fingers. "What bad guys?"

"Sometimes bad people may want to hurt us, and it's my job to make sure that never happens. I'm really sorry I thought Guy was a bad person."

She moved into a cross-legged position with the unicorn in her lap and her arms tangled around it, resting her chin on its head. "Did you say you're sorry?"

Dexter smiled. Damn, she was just like Sara. Kindhearted and willing to see past anyone's flaws to fix all the hurt. "Not yet, pretty girl."

"You should say you're sorry."

"I will. But, I had to come find you first. You are more important to me than anyone else."

A sullen grin flashed on her face. "More than Mommy?"

"More than Mommy."

Her ocean eyes widened, and it felt as if he was looking at himself in a mirror as a little boy. All the hope he used to harbor before his endless cycle of bad decisions resided in his daughter. She was all good. That was the difference. Every part of her. And she would make the right choices, because she possessed part of Sara's beautiful soul. "You love Mommy?"

Dexter smiled. "I love Mommy very much. And, I love you."

She scooted over until she was at the edge of the bed with Dexter. "You love me?"

"Always. And I will always protect you. I'm sorry I've been gone for so long. But, I thought about you every single day."

Slowly, Kali leaned over and rested her cheek on Dexter's arm. And in that moment, pure contentment washed through him. "I thought about you too."

He moved his arm around her shoulders so that she was positioned against his side. "Good, Kali. That makes me very happy."

"I'm glad you came home."

"Me too."

"I like you much more than Guy."

He did his best to feel indifferent about the comment, not wanting to read into it or assess his own thoughts about it. He leaned over and kissed his daughter atop her head. "Let's go home. Mommy's worried about you."

She wiped her tears on Dexter's sleeves. "You'll say you're sorry?"

"I will."

He brought Kali into his arms and carried her down the stairs, just like he had done with Sara once before. When his sneakers hit the grass, he whipped out his phone.

Dex: Got her. Coming home.

Sara Mar King: Thank goodness. Hurry.

Chapter 7

▲▲▲

The stench of the hospital seeped into Sara's nose and caused her stomach to churn. Hospitals. Sickness everywhere. White walls covered in sickly viral promises. It was enough to make her want to puke.

Guy was in a bed waiting for his X-ray results. Strong pain meds swirled through his system as the swelling in his face inflated. The ringed bruise around his neck darkened with every second.

Sara sat in a chair beside him, inspecting all the damage Dexter had done. He got Guy good. One eye was a deep shade of purple, as well as his jaw, and a large split down his lower lip still oozed wet with cerise blood. She knew the hurt of one of Dexter's punches firsthand from when he was high off the peli plant and thought she was Marty Brown. An invisible scar was forever etched along her left eye bones. She couldn't imagine what more than one would feel like.

She sighed and leaned back in her chair, replaying everything.

A part of Sara was glad to see Dexter protecting her family like he promised. Dexter thought Guy was an intruder, and he did what she would have wanted him to do, regardless if it was her friend or not. The real issue that banged against her skull wasn't about Dexter. It was about Guy. Why would he ever think it was okay to enter her home in the middle of the night? How many times had he done that? A disturbing feeling shivered through her system, leaving a residue of mistrust.

Perhaps Dexter did have some sort of almighty intuition when it came to judging people's character. Seeing through the crappy overlay of fakeness was something he had always been good at. Damn, and if Dexter was right about Guy, she was sitting with the wrong man. If Dexter was right, why did she still feel this undeniable need to help and comfort Guy? She wanted so badly to find the willpower to leave this suffering person. And, what if Dexter was wrong and jealousy was blinding him? She was so confused.

"Sara?" Guy mumbled.

She sighed and scrubbed her face with her hands before ruffling her bangs to the side. "Yeah?"

"You're beautiful."

She rolled her eyes. "Stop."

Still with his eyes shut and facing the ceiling, he muttered, "I love you."

The words hit her and all she wanted to do was claw them out of her ears. "Oh balls." The only people she wanted to hear that from were Dexter and her kids. A shot of violent aggravation burned at her core as if her powers were still intact and ready to protect her on demand. "If you ever say that again, I'm going to slap that sentence back into your mouth so hard you'll forget you ever said it."

"How could you be attracted to Dexter? He-he's a monster." He rolled his head toward her, blue eyes leeching off her attention. "Do you see my face? Do you see what he did? You want that around the kids?"

She curled a lip and officially felt like punching him too. Guy couldn't have been more wrong. Flashes of Dexter being anything but a monster emerged with extreme clarity. Dexter in his tower giving up his meager food to feed her. Him risking his life outside the safety of his camp to join her on her dangerous journey. Or the time he sealed her wounds and carried her from one camp to the next after she was punished by Atraeus. The gentleness in his touch and the patience of his mind when she asked him to make love to her in the spring. The unbelievable bravery that he exuded when he offered to take her place as a sacrifice to protect her and their unborn babies. She wouldn't let anyone call him a monster. "Shut up and worry about getting better, Guy."

"Think about your precious kids, Sara. He's too dangerous to be around them. You know I'd never hurt them. I wouldn't hurt anyone. He has a very disturbing and out of control temper. And he's rubbing off on you already. Soon, you're going to be just as dangerous as him." He rubbed his face to conceal his exasperated emotion. "Is that want you want? Do you want that future for your kids?"

She didn't want to hear it. Dexter was hers, and she was Dexter's in every universe imaginable. It was in the stars. It was mixed in her blood that he sipped on to keep himself alive.

It was in their troubled spirits tangling between the past, present, and future. It was too late for anyone else.

To hear he was dangerous was probably true, but he wasn't dangerous to her or the twins. He was only dangerous to those who tried to cross his family. He would battle any threat to protect the ones he loved. And, that made her fall harder for Dexter. She was addicted to how utterly safe he made her feel. She was still helplessly addicted to her tattooed warrior.

Dammit, she was with the wrong man. She had made a mistake. "I'm going to go home."

Guy propped himself up on his elbow in a frantic motion. "No. Not back to him. You're safer here. Stay."

Sara stood, adjusting Dexter's band shirt, imagining it was him rather than fabric wrapped around her. "I'll get Emily to come."

"Sara, please," he reached his hand out and touched her cheek.

Flinching away from his touch, she stood and pointed a finger at him. "Stop. You know I don't like being touched." She pivoted to exit, but his warm hand wrapped tightly around her wrist, and it was as if spiders were crawling up her arm.

"He can touch you, but I can't? Are you serious?"

Like muscle memory, she moved her hand in a small circle, twisting his hand enough to make him release her. She took a measured step back and watched him lean off the bed to try grab her again. But, she was quick to move her feet closer to the exit.

"Are you serious? After he basically bludgeoned me in front of Kali for no reason? Hurt the innocent man at the wall the other day? You're going back to *him*? After I've been with you for *six* years? After I've supported you and the kids?"

"Yes." She straightened her spine in a way she thought Dexter would be proud of.

A visible shock spread over his bruised face. He fell silent before swallowing a hard gulp. "I'll worry about you if you leave."

"Then worry."

He said something else, but Sara ignored him and raced to the door. As she twisted the knob, dread seeping down her neck. The new world should be perfect now that Dexter was back. He was home with the kids. Home with her family. She had made a mistake. He was right. She had shit intuition. Six years and she hadn't learned a thing. She just wanted to curl up to him and cry.

She couldn't imagine what was going through Dexter's head while he watched her hold Guy's hand instead of staying with him. Letting Guy close enough to touch her cheek after he had come into their home unannounced. Sitting at another man's bedside. Fuck. She even got dressed in front of him. She could practically hear Dexter's irate thoughts toward her already. What must he think about her now?

She marched out the door and ran straight into a solid body. She gasped and recoiled, looking up into her favorite pair of crystal-clear eyes. "Dexter," she whispered in a relieved breath. She wanted him to wrap her up in his embrace, but judging by the stone-cold expression on his face, she knew that wasn't going to happen.

"How's he doing?" he asked in his typical husky timber underlined with cold coolness.

Guy was none of her concern at the moment, and he shouldn't have been Dexter's either. "Who's with the kids?"

"I called Emily."

Sara took in a deep breath, wrapping her arms around herself and hoping they would be Dexter's soon. "Take me home?"

A sharp look in his eye shifted to something she couldn't decipher. "Let me apologize first."

He made a move to round Sara and reach for the knob, but she stepped into his path. She bowed her head to hide the tears scorching her eyes. "No. Now."

His warm hand tilted her head up. At first, she resisted, but then she wanted Dexter to see the guilt she carried for leaving him and going to Guy's hospital bedside.

Dexter wasn't moving. He didn't say anything.

Suddenly, the dirty walls were closing in. A cough and moan in the distance left her shaking. A clamminess ran through her as her heart rate rose and her hands began to sweat. It felt as if the infectious webs that drifted with the mists during the Screecher Age were covering her mouth and nose again. But this time she had no way of clawing them off her face to breathe. Damn, she needed to get out of there as fast as possible before she broke down and coiled herself into a protective ball. With more conviction, she tried again. "Take me home, Dexter."

He nodded and whispered, "Let's go."

The halls were bustling with sick patients and nurses. Some bumped into her on their way out of the building. Imagining the bacteria suffocating her face, she held her breath until she hit the cool night air. A quick intake of oxygen filled her lungs. She let it out slowly and tried to keep her gag reflex at bay.

"Don't like hospitals?"

She doubled over, hands on her thighs, panting.

"You're okay. You're out now."

She straightened and took another deep breath. By now, Dexter normally would have wrapped his arms around her, but he kept his hands to himself. Was he thinking she had some sort of feelings for Guy? Was that why he wasn't touching her?

They started toward their house in silence at first. But, she always trusted Dexter to break the quiet.

"You okay?"

She just wanted him to call her his Marking again. That was always his tell that they were on good terms. "Yeah."

"What'd he say to you?"

"Nothing."

"Sara, he called me a monster and told you he'd do anything for you. I'm so worried right now. And, I can see you're worried too. A-am I going to lose you? Did I just fuck up everything we have because I hurt your friend?"

Her eyes whipped to his, relieved, but saddened that he was this upset. She wanted to be very clear about where her mind was. "I told you this once before. It's either you or no one."

Dexter gave a crooked smile like he was only half accepting of that answer. "Okay. So, no one?"

She stopped mid-stride and turned her body to face his. "No, Dexter! *I'm* the one afraid of losing *you*! I'm the one who fucked up." Her mind raced, a tired fog shrouded her brain, making her spew everything like she was drunk without a filter. "I should have stood by you, not him. I was an idiot. I shouldn't have taken his hand when I knew it would upset you. I definitely shouldn't have let him watch me get dressed." Tears filled her eyes. "I'm so sorry. I can feel you hating me right now."

His arms came around her so fast, it was as if they had never left. "No, no, no," he hushed.

"I can't believe I let him touch me! In front of you. I-I-I should have trusted you and asked why the hell he was in our home at three AM! I'm so sorry!"

"Sara, stop." He squeezed her harder into his solid chest so that her mouth was smashed against him to shush her. "You're shaking."

"Dexter," she cried.

"Hey, you'll never lose me," he whispered and kissed her head. "Okay? Ever. You've known him for a long time. He's your friend. I get it."

Her arms latched onto his waist, wishing her river of apology could flow into him if she squeezed hard enough. "I'm sorry."

"Don't be. I am well aware of your extraordinary need to help people who are hurting. And in that situation, Guy was the one hurting."

"That's all it was. I promise." The tears turned into a lump in her throat, clogging more words from coming up. He placed his chin on her head and rocked her from side to side.

"It's funny that we're both thinking the same thing. From now on, how about you and I never worry about losing each other again? It's pretty clear we'd follow each other until the world ends... literally." He chuckled. "Okay? Let's never worry about it again. I'm yours."

Sara nodded as his words enveloped her like a blanket. "I'm yours too." Never having to worry about Dexter leaving. What a freeing concept. "Thanks for understanding," she mumbled. "Please don't ever make me go that long without your touch again. When you touch me, it tells me that we're okay."

"Got it, Marking." He chuckled and it filled her with security. "I will keep my hands on you at all times."

He moved them all over her back and pressed his bearded cheek against her head. Sara melted into him, feeling like he was her bed and she could fall asleep in the circle of his arms. Then, his hands shifted to her face, scrunching her cheeks forward so her lips were pursed. She laughed and slapped them away while making a move to shove him, but he took off running down the block. Sara chased him, yelling, "I'm faster than you, you know." Just as she was about to catch up to him, he turned and crouched, sending Sara over his shoulder with her momentum.

He stood and put both hands over her ass. "See? Still touching you."

"Dexter!" Sara let out a deep belly laugh while slapping his bottom. "Let me down!"

"Oh boy, I've awoken the beast." Dexter knelt and set her down.

Sara adjusted her outfit with a smile. "Good choice."

He slid his hand into hers and continued to walk. It was quiet for a few steps, but there was one question that pestered her. Not that it made much of a difference in the end, but she was curious. "Did you know it was him?"

Dexter gave a huff. "At first, no. Then I saw him and, yeah, I may have let my temper get to me a little. Either way, he shouldn't have been in our house while we were sleeping."

Sara sighed. "He told me he loves me."

She swore she heard Dexter chuckling. When she shifted her vision to him, he was. "Of course he does. Who wouldn't? You have a heart of gold, and you're sinfully beautiful."

She gave him a crooked smile. "It scares me."

"Why?" he said, stroking her bangs back.

"Because what if you're right and there's something off about him? What if he wasn't just dropping off the stuffed animal? What if he wants something with the kids? Plus, dhow many times has he come into the house when we were sleeping before you came back? And now that he said he loves me, it makes me think things are going to get worse."

"I'll be here though."

"Yeah, I know. Another part of me thinks he's manipulating me. Like Marty did. Is he manipulating me?" She slumped her shoulders and let out a grunt of frustration. "That would be so embarrassing."

109

"Ah, so what you're saying is you don't trust him anymore?" Dexter smiled. "Look at you thinking more like me."

Sara grinned and nudged Dexter's arm with her nose. "I think we hang out way too much."

Dexter let out a sigh with a smile. "Well, Sara, the kids are safely tucked into their beds. You are safe by my side where you belong. As of right now, everything is okay. We're okay. The kids are okay. And Guy's... probably okay. So moving forward, we just keep a closer eye on everything. You don't have to figure everything out right now."

Sara could still feel Guy's slimy hand twisting around her wrist. "No. Dexter. I don't want him in my life anymore. I mean, it's not jealousy. Zeek looked me up and down and called me beautiful, and you didn't get all panicky. So did half the store owners and still zilch reaction from you. If you have this strong of a reaction to Guy, then I trust you. To be honest, he's starting to give me the creeps."

Dexter kissed her cheek. "Thanks, Marking. I like when you follow my lead every once in a while."

She clung to him again. "I like it when you're here and can take care of us."

"Let's get to bed so we can be rested enough to talk to Nellie about the counting thing in the morning."

However, there was something in his eyes that told Sara he had other plans.

Chapter 8

▲▲▲

Watching Guy's frightened eyes train on him as the meds wore off pleased Dexter. He needed Guy to remember everything. The bruises staining his skin weren't dark enough for Dexter's liking. The creeps. Sara put it perfectly. He wasn't sure if it was his thick brows that seemed to always be set in a serious expression, or the unnaturally severe edge of his jaw, or that arrogant look in his eyes that belittled anyone who doubted him, but Dexter wanted this man to detach from his family immediately.

When the recognition registered, that self-righteous attitude became very apparent. "What are you doing here?"

Dexter rolled his eyes and huffed, "My daughter kind of— sort of told me I had to apologize. So… sorry."

He scoffed, closed his eyes, and faced the ceiling. "You are a danger to your own family."

Dexter clenched his jaw. "I know that."

"You have a violent temper. You do not deserve sweet Sara."

Yeah, that stung. Like doubt poisoning his blood. He was well aware of the awful person he was. Sara had already seen every rigid side of his. But that was the man she fell in love with. "She knows that too."

Guy padded a finger over his lip and looked to see if it was still bleeding. It wasn't. "That girl is an angel. You're around for one day, and she's acting like she used to. Like an angry and selfish monster without care for anyone else's feelings. *I* was here to see how mentally fucked up she was from the Screecher Age. Not you. Me. I took care of her and Nellie and Kali."

Dexter remained silent, antsy about the man's rambling.

"The way you behave is atrocious. You're an animal."

"Good one. Now, my turn." He scooted the chair closer to Guy's bedside, letting the metal legs screech against the floor to keep his attention. Guy rolled his head to Dexter. "Let's talk about some things you can do to not get yourself killed." Dexter paused to let the warning sink into his sobering brain. "Don't *ever* enter our home again. Even if you're invited. You cannot, under any circumstance, examine my children. Lastly, you are never allowed to tell Sara you love her again. You understand?"

Guy linked his fingers and rested them gently on his chest, seemingly unaffected by the harshness in Dexter's voice. "I've been with her for six years—"

"And I've known her since she was born. *She will choose me every time.*" That statement hit Guy like it had physically impaled him. He relaxed into the bed, took a deep breath, and glared at the ceiling. "Trust me, I've tried to change her mind."

One of Guy's hands trembled as he laid it flat over his own heart. "I love those kids."

"That's great. But, they aren't yours."

"Just because you're back, doesn't change anything. Sara loves me too."

"I'm sure she does. But, there's something you've got to understand. Sara loves everyone. It's who she is. She can't help but give love to the world. But, because I *am* back, your life with her and my kids no longer exists."

Guy blinked and a tear rolled down his face, not saying anything.

Dexter put out an open hand. "Give me our key. If there's an emergency, I'll be the one to take care of it."

Guy rolled on his side and reached for the pile of his clothes on the side table. Fumbling for a few moments in the pocket of his jeans, a silver ring with five keys came into view. Guy inspected each, unscrewed one, and handed it over.

Dexter stuffed the key into his pocket, stood, then leaned over Guy's ear. "Just so you know, if Kali hadn't come down, I probably would have killed you."

"You don't deserve your family."

Dexter stood, wanting to clamp his hand over the idiot's neck again, but resisted. Instead, he grumbled, "I know," and walked out.

When Dexter arrived home, Guy's blood was still smeared on the kitchen floor. He grabbed an all-purpose spray from under the sink and cleaned. After washing his hands thoroughly, he headed straight to Sara's room. There, he found both his kids cuddled close to their mother, sleeping. The perfect family he had always dreamed about was finally a reality. He took out his phone and snapped a photo to remember this moment forever. Dexter changed into sweats and a white undershirt before sliding between the sheets, Nellie between him and Sara. He closed his eyes and enjoyed the serene current of peacefulness seep into his body as sleep dragged him down.

Something rapidly poked Dexter's cheek and woke him from his deep slumber. Nellie's green eyes bore into Dexter as soon as he opened them.

"Hey, bud. What are you doing?" he croaked.

"Mommy's dreaming again." Up came his two open palms, counting down the seconds to her scream.

Dexter sprang into action, rounded the bed and shook Sara's shoulder. "Sara. Wake up."

Nellie was down to seven seconds... six.

He shook harder. "Sara."

Five... four.

Dexter scooped her into his arms from between the twins and rushed her into the kids' room. As soon as he set her down on the bed nearest the door, her mouth opened for a gut-wrenching scream. Dexter covered her mouth with his hand, letting the vibrations of volume quiver through his core.

Her electric eyes snapped open, bugging out as she tried to thrash away from him.

"Shh, Sara. It's okay. Just a dream."

She sunk into the bed, closed her eyes, and relaxed her tense body. Dexter released her. "Oh my god," she huffed.

"You okay?" he got on his haunches, hand in hers.

"Yeah. Marty Brown again."

Dexter's brows furrowed as he brought her hand to his lips and kissed it. "I don't want you to dream about that anymore."

She studied her surroundings. "Why am I in the kids' room?"

"Nellie woke me up and told me you were dreaming again. Wanted to make sure Kali stayed asleep."

Sweat dripped down her temples. "N-Nellie did it again?"

Dexter nodded, stroking her damp locks away from her face.

She sat up, reaching out for Dexter with tears in her eyes. "You were there again."

He wrapped her up in a loving embrace and rubbed her back.

"It makes me sad when you watch."

"I know. We'll figure this out."

"I want Marty to leave me alone."

"He will one day. I'll make sure of it." He kissed her forehead. "Come on. Let's go back to the kids. It'll take your mind off it."

Sara's hand flattened on his chest, stopping him. "Where'd you go? I woke up and you were gone. I thought you left us."

He placed his hand over hers. "No, no, no. I was just downstairs. I wanted to clean up the blood before the kids saw it in the morning."

She nodded and slumped off the bed. "Oh, okay. Thanks."

"Remember, you never have to worry."

Reentering the room, Dexter noticed Nellie had fallen back asleep. They snuggled close to their kids between them. Above the twins' heads, Dexter linked fingers with Sara. He took out his phone from the nightstand and quietly texted her.

Dex: Look, Marking! Kali's letting me sleep here.

Sara Mar King: She's knocked out...

Dex: Still

Sara let out a soft giggle. Nellie rolled over and snuggled close to his dad, mouth open and drooling over Dexter's arm.

Dexter awoke to an empty bed. He groaned and wished he had woken up at the same time as everyone else. The house was quiet except for the tones of a muffled voice in the distance. He opened the door and heard Sara talking in the kitchen to someone on the phone. From over the bannister, he peered down on Kali lying on the maroon rug of the living room, bleach blonde tresses falling over a coloring book. He peeked into the kids' room and saw Nellie buried in a cocoon of blankets.

He quietly stepped down a few steps and paused to listen.

The famous Mar King growl rolled out in a pitch so low he almost missed it. "Can't you walk alone?... Okay. I'll get Emily... Then, I'll get Dexter..." He peeked around the wall and into the kitchen, watching Sara pace around the island with her jade eyes glued to the floor. She groaned then huffed. Another growl. "Fine. See you soon."

She put the phone down and placed her forehead on the island's cool tiled surface, groaning. Then, she lifted her head and combed her blonde bangs to the side with her fingers.

"You off somewhere?"

Her head whipped to Dexter and sighed again. "The doctor requested for someone to pick Guy up and walk him home. He wants me to do it." Sara sighed. "I don't want to go, but I figured I could tell him that this would be it." She paused and blinked like she wasn't sure what else to say. "Will you watch the kids?"

Dexter nodded with an anxious feeling bubbling in his throat. Sara alone with Guy, after the conversation he had with him last night. Fuck, he didn't want her to go. But, Sara could handle herself. He had to trust that. Beyond the delicate grace that she embodied, he could never forget her excellent combat skills.

"Sorry, Dex."

As soon as she stepped toward the door, he wanted to reach out, drag her against him, and beg her to stay. Instead, he said, "It's okay. Be safe."

"I'll be back really soon, I promise."

Sara stuffed the phone into the back pocket of her tight-fitted blue jeans, draped her red jacket around her shoulders, and zipped it over Dexter's band T-shirt. She stopped short when she saw Kali blocking the door. Her blue summer dress hung on her like an exquisite porcelain doll. "No, Mommy."

In an instant, everything in Dexter shuddered with sudden fear.

His daughter.

Wide eyes glowing neon green.

Hand open toward Sara's face.

An orb manifesting in her palm.

Just like Sara's old power, it glittered with the same lime green hue and spun as it charged.

"Daddy says to stay." In a flash of lightning, the energy orb shot into Sara's head, freezing her solid.

Chapter 9

▲▲▲

Cold terror paralyzed Dexter as he gaped at his precious daughter who revealed she possessed Atraeus's dark energy. "Holy sh—"

Kali released a scream of bloody murder while shaking her hand to extinguish the light. Tears burst from her eyes as she sprinted to the corner of the living room.

His world emptied. Stilled. A sonic ringing was all that remained, and it drilled through his brain in vicious pulses with each heartbeat. Every movement as he turned to look at Sara resisted him like an anchor dragging on the ocean's floor.

His daughter's terrified cries snapped his attention into sudden overdrive. In a swift sprint, he was kneeling in front of her coiled form in the corner near the window. "Kali, I need you to high five me as hard as you can." He brought his hand up.

"It burns!" she shrieked, looking at her illuminated palm with puffy eyes.

"Let's go. It'll go away if you high five me."

Kali's small hand reached up and barely brushed against his before she cuddled it to her chest.

"Harder," he encouraged. "Give me a real high five."

She tried again, this time smacking Dexter's hand. Still, the energy seared away at his daughter's palm. "Again," he encouraged with as steady of a voice as he could muster. Up came her tiny hand, slapping against his dozens of more times before the energy orb vanished.

Her palm turned bright red as a scar singed its way into his daughter's palm. "Good job, Kali." Dexter's hand went to her cheek, drying her hot tears that burned trails down his palm. Beneath his touch, her skin flared like boiling water. He resisted the impulse to retract his hand, knowing Kali needed the comfort. "Are you okay?"

Her face fell to a haunting ghost white as her line of vision flitted to Sara. "Mommy's dead!"

"No, she isn't."

Kali's focus on Sara never wavered as she ran to her mother and latched onto her hip.

Dexter bent and hauled Kali into his arms, resting her on the crook of his elbow. "Mommy is okay."

"Sh-she's not moving!"

"It's all right." He bent to one knee and pointed to the same scar on Sara's palm. "Look. She has the same mark on her palm." Dexter waited until he saw Kali's eyes widen as she made the connection. "See? You're just like Mama. She used to be able to freeze people too." Dexter chuckled, hoping to not only calm Kali, but to alleviate his own stress.

"She did?"

120

"Yeah. You're okay."

Kali turned away from Sara and wrapped her tiny arms back around Dexter's neck, face buried in his shoulder and crying hot tears. "How do I make her move?"

"Easy. We take a walk."

She lifted her head until her marble eyes fastened on his. "Take a walk?"

"That's it." He put a thumb over his daughter's palm, hoping to rub away the pain. "Do you want to run your hand under cold water?"

His daughter nodded and slung her arms around Dexter's neck again. He brought her to the sink, turned on the faucet, and let Kali cool off her hand.

"Better?"

Kali nodded.

"Okay, pretty girl. I need you to go upstairs and wake up your brother. Tell him to get up, 'cause we are going to take a nice walk'."

"Okay," she sulked, sniffing back tears.

He set his daughter down and watched her sluggishly climb the stairs on all fours. He went straight for Sara, placed a hand over her cheek as soon as Kali wasn't within ear shot. "Holy shit, Sara." He gulped. "I'm going to free you as soon as I can." He lifted her stiff body and brought her upstairs, setting her down in the walk-in closet of her room. "Sorry. I can't risk anyone seeing you like this. I'm going to take the kids to the ice cream shop we went to yesterday. I think that's about a mile. Fuck, I'm hoping it's still a mile. Come as soon as you're free. I'll wait there for about thirty minutes. If you don't come, we're going to move farther in that direction." He kissed her on the cheek like she had done every time she had frozen him and raced out of the room.

Dexter sat at the black metal table outside the ice cream shop. It hadn't opened yet, but Kali and Nellie were enjoying the morning sun while trying to catch small butterflies on the nearby bushes. Dexter stared down the street, waiting for Sara's figure to approach. His leg bounced anxiously on the concrete as he ran a hand over his face then down his beard. Still no sight of her. Not willing to wait any longer, he called for his kids. "Hey, kiddos. Can I ask you a few questions?"

Nellie, still dressed in his dark blue, rocket pajama set, climbed onto Dexter's lap while Kali settled into the chair across from him.

"Yeah," they responded in unison.

"Okay. Has Guy ever said anything that made you think... hmm... that was weird?"

Nellie squirmed on his lap as he played with sections of Dexter's beard. "Like when he said I got my eyes from Mommy?" he turned to his sister, beaming with lifted hands and shrugged for confirmation. "Right?"

Kali laughed. "Yeah. Weird."

Dexter smiled to keep the conversation going with as little pressure as possible. "Anything else?"

Kali blinked her baby blues at Dexter. Just like Sara, he heard a low growl.

"What is it?"

She looked down at her palms, blonde tendrils falling onto them. "He likes my hands." Her gaze riveted on the scar. "I don't want him to see."

Dexter's hand came softly over hers. "Then, we won't let him."

She grinned and nodded. "'Cause you keep me safe."

"Exactly. And to do that, I need to know everything. Like, how did you know I didn't want Mommy to leave?"

She smiled so wide that it affected her eyes, just like her mother. "I see you, Daddy."

Dexter furrowed his brow, trying to understand. "What do you mean?"

Nellie stopped playing with his beard and looked to his sister. "Kay, are you really going to say it?"

She shrugged at her brother before making eye contact with Dexter. "I just see you."

Shallow breaths were all he could manage as he processed what exactly Kali meant. "What did you see?"

"You went to mommy," she wrapped her arms around herself, "and hugged her. Then you said," in a deep mocking tone to sound like Dexter she tilting her head from shoulder to shoulder, "'stay, Mar King'. That's Mommy's name."

How the hell did she know that that was what he really wanted to do? Did she see him act it out? Maybe a ghost version of himself? "Any other time that happened?"

"The man with the red hat. He walked up to me and said I was so cute that he wanted to put me in his pocket and take him home."

That sentence hit him like a freight train. Kali was telling the truth. I bet she had always been telling the truth, but Guy squandered her shy courage.

She looked to the sky, pondering. "When you kiss Nellie, you want to kiss me too."

Dexter's brows lifted. "All right. Well. Kali. That's true. I do always want to kiss you goodnight."

She smiled and sang, "I'm right! And you wanted to hug me in the tower. You didn't want to hurt me."

"Right again. I would never hurt you. So, Kay, you see two of me?"

She sucked her shiny, strawberry-colored lips between her teeth. "Yeah, but only sometimes. I can see through the other you. That's how I tell the difference."

His daughter's eyes twinkled with love for him as she sent Dexter a toothy smile with a crinkled nose. That was why she was beginning to warm up to him. Because she could see, hear, and sense all the love he wanted to give. "Thank you for telling me."

Compartmentalize. That's what he needed to do. It was difficult, but he was desperate for more information. His attention turned to his son wiggling on his lap like a noodle. "Well, Nellie. Kali was brave enough to tell me what's going on with her. Do you think you can tell me how you know when Mommy is dreaming?"

He pointed to his eyes, then Kali's, and back to his. "I see it. It's an accident. Different. I know what makes people scared. And Mommy's scared of the man when it gets dark outside. But, I don't mean to! It just happens. When I'm not trying."

The man. Marty Brown. Dexter's heart shuddered with terror. "Y-you see a man?"

Nellie nodded as he stood on Dexter's thighs, bent over the table, and lay flat on his belly, fingers threading through the metal holes. "He has blond hair." He pointed his finger at Dexter. "Longer than yours. And mean. Mommy calls for someone named Dexter."

Dexter gave a small chuckle. "I'm Dexter, bud. That's my name."

Nellie laughed. "Then, she calls for you. Then, the man opens the door."

The door. Dexter knew exactly which one. The door to the basement where Marty Brown dragged Sara down before he tied her up to rape her. "Do you see anything after the door opens?"

Nellie shook his head and flipped over. "Mommy screams, and it wakes me up. But, I always see you too. Mommy said you had a beard, and so I figured you were my dad."

Dexter's brows knitted together. "You've seen me before?"

"Yup. And you always try to help her. I try to stop the dream, to change it, but it never works."

Dexter ruffled his caramel hair. "You're a smart boy."

He sat up with a pout, feet planted on Dexter's thighs. "If I was smart, I'd be able to change it."

"We can try together."

"And you are really scared of that dark place." He put his opened hands up and gestured around him. "There's rock all around you." Then he pointed upward. "And Mommy's at the

125

top. You're more scared of that dark place than Mommy is of the man. Do you know where the rocks are?"

Fuck, where was Sara? He needed her. She was so much better at knowing exactly what to say.

Just as he wished it, he spotted Sara jogging toward them. Dexter's chest caved with the need for her to be wrapped around him. She didn't know yet, but what the kids were capable of petrified him. "Look, kiddos. It's Mommy!"

Kali turned in her seat and screamed in delight, "Mommy!" In two scooches, she hopped off the chair and ran. Sara lifted her in an embrace, pressing a kiss onto her precious cheek. Then, she came to Dexter, kissed him and Nellie before she sat across the table with Kali secured on her lap.

Sara's electric eyes met Dexter's, widening in shock and mouthing the words, "Oh my god."

"Kali," Sara started, "has this ever happened before?"

Kali shook her head.

"If that ever happens again, you need to run one mile away from the person you froze. Okay? If on accident you freeze both of us at home, come to this spot."

Kali looked at her palm again and nodded.

"So, Marking," Dexter announced, grabbing everyone's attention, "I am pleased to announce that our kids have some pretty awesome abilities."

Nellie gave a wide smile and scrunched his freckled nose. It wasn't until Kali saw Nellie's reaction did she copy it. "Let me introduce you to Nellie Bennet." Dexter put his hand on Nellie's shoulder. "He can create hallucinations. Especially when you're sleeping." Sara's eyes brightened with

126

understanding before she took a deep breath. If Nellie could control his powers, Sara didn't have to suffer with Marty Brown any longer. "As of right now, that's the only power he seems to have discovered."

Nellie jumped off Dexter's lap and put his fists up, punching and kicking the air. "I am awesome!"

"And on your lap is the ever beautiful, intelligent, and unique Kali Bennet. She is able to freeze, *and* she can see a ghost version of people who act out what they really want to do."

"Woah," Sara looked toward her daughter, "how cool is that? My kids are so special."

Kali turned and hugged Sara, ear pressed to her chest.

"Daddy," Nellie asked, yanking on Dexter's blue T-shirt, "can I go play over there?" He pointed to a patch of grass across the empty street where birds were gathered in a group, pecking out worms from the soil.

"Let's all go over there," Sara suggested.

They made their way across, hand in hand with their children. When they let go, the kids ran to the birds, sending them into flight while they snickered. Sara and Dexter settled on a bench facing the twins who knelt in the small patch of grass near a playground picking worms.

"Dexter, what does this mean? Is a part of whatever the hell Atraeus is still here? I-Is it in our kids?"

"I don't know." Dexter took a dry gulp and admitted, "I'm so scared for them."

She threaded an arm under his and linked their fingers together before resting her temple on his shoulder. "Me too."

Dexter watched Kali stand, move to a new spot on the grass, and sit down, blue dress puffing up around her like a delicate, innocent princess. Then, he saw Nellie pick up a worm and put it to his mouth.

"Nellie! Don't eat the worms," Sara shouted, sitting up and readying to leap at him. "Put it down. Now!"

He grunted in frustration, threw the worm to the ground, and moved to sit with his sister.

"Gosh. I'm trying to save the worms, and my son is trying to eat them."

Dexter chuckled then turned to Sara. "Has this happened before?"

"What? Him eating the worms?" She shrugged. "On occasion."

Dexter kissed her head. "No, I meant supernaturally."

Sara giggled. "Nothing I've ever noticed."

"So, as soon as I get back, this happens? Isn't that a little odd?"

Sara sighed. "Maybe? Now that Atraeus is done with you, it moved on to them?"

"No. It told me it's not allowed to kill a single person after the four sacrifices die. The only reason he was still around was because of the deal we made before they died. And now, our deal is done. It should be gone."

"And you believe that?"

He sighed and squeezed her hand. "Well, I guess now I don't know what to believe."

The silence stretched as they both gazed at their kids playing under the golden sunlight. Then Sara said, "What if it's because I got pregnant while I still had its powers. I mean, they grew some with that blood still in me."

Dexter scrubbed his hands over his face. "If that's true then would that mean they feed off fear too?"

"I don't know." He trained his gaze on his children again. Dirt covered their hands and was gathering under their fingernails. Each of them held up different sized worms to show each other. How could they even be remotely connected to Atraeus's evil? They were sweet, innocent, and filled with so much love.

"What do we do?"

Dexter sighed and felt like running to his kids and hugging them to ease his own anxieties. They were handling this better than their parents were. As if this was nothing new. "Well, for now we have to help them figure out how to focus this so that we don't get frozen. Then, we have to decide if we're going to let them keep their powers or start finding a way to get rid of them."

He wrapped his arm around her shoulders and brought her in closer. "Don't worry, we'll figure this out. As of right now, they have something to defend themselves with if anything happens."

Sara gave a sullen smile. "Look at you being all optimistic like me."

"You're right, we hang out way too much."

Chapter 10

▲▲▲

A rhythmic knock sounded on the front door and Sara rushed to open it. Emily was on the other side, plump lips smiling, dark owl eyes shining, and thin legs covered in stretchy leather leggings. What caught Dexter's eye the most was the men's blue zip-up jacket that looked awfully familiar. Zeek had been wearing that exact jacket when they visited him earlier. Dexter couldn't resist a smile as he leaned against the kitchen island and folded his arms over his chest.

In unison, both women got into fighting stance. Emily threw a roundhouse kick across the threshold of the doorway and Sara dodged by stepping backward with a bark of laughter. Emily entered the house, throwing punches while Sara blocked each one like a well-choreographed routine.

"Do you always greet each other like this?" Dexter asked.

"Only when we haven't seen each other in a day," Emily gritted through her teeth as she threw another punch. "Your girl has been teaching me a thing or two."

At one point, Sara jumped onto the kitchen island and hid behind Dexter's shoulders. Emily dropped her hands and tossed her head back to laugh. Sara got off the counter and hugged her friend.

Dexter beamed as the girls' bubbly energy tickled him.

"Hey, Dexter," Emily greeted, going in for a hug.

He met her halfway.

She cocked an eyebrow. "Oh dang, Sara. This hunka-hunka has the best hugs. You lucky girl."

Dexter chuckled then released her. "It's good to see you."

She looked between the two of them, amused. "So," she started, holding out the word while folding her arms, "had to pick Guy up this morning. He looks," she smiled, shifting her gaze back and forth between them. "fantastic. Who did it? You or Sara?"

"Guilty," Dexter said, raising his hand.

Emily playfully punched him in the arm. "You dog, you." She shrugged. "I think he looks better."

"I take it you don't like him," Dexter puzzled.

"Not since I found out he kissed Sara after she told him to knock it off. Coward."

Dexter laughed, but Sara didn't. "I like her," he pointed to Emily while looking directly at Sara.

Emily looked between the two of them. "So are you two together for eternity now? Finally? I've been dying to know what's been going on."

"We have a lot to catch you up on," Sara explained, dragging her friend to the living room and plopping on the couch.

Dexter and Sara took the next twenty minutes telling her about the supernatural phenomena the kids had been experiencing and Dexter's apprehension when it came to Guy. "So that's pretty much what's been happening since Dexter came back. We decided you should know since we might lean on you a bit."

"Whatever you need me for, I'm here for you two," she offered.

"Thanks," Dexter acknowledged.

Emily's eyes wandered the room and sighed. "Supernatural powers. Epic love. Damn, you guys have the coolest family! My family was all crack heads. Meth addicts and big fat abandoners."

"Um hello? My mom abandoned me," Sara reminded Emily while pointing to herself.

"And to leave this gorgeous one," Dexter nodded toward Sara, "she had to have been on crack."

Emily laughed while fidgeting with the two white strings on the hood of Zeek's jacket. One of the strings entered her mouth, nibbling at the frayed ends.

"So, you and Zeek, huh?" Dexter alleged.

As soon as he said Zeek's name, Emily spit the string from her mouth with wide eyes.

Sara's head whipped to him, hand latching onto his arm. "What?"

Emily rolled her eyes then her neck. "How the hell did you know? Did he tell you? That bastard said he wasn't going to tell anyone."

"What?" Sara squealed. "You and Zeek! Why didn't you tell me?"

"Because it's not serious. We just, you know, fuck around. That's it. Then it's, 'bye'." As she spoke, something shifted in Emily's eyes and the exuberance disappeared. In its place was partial confusion.

"Is that why you're wearing his jacket? Because it's not serious?" Dexter questioned.

Emily fiddled with the strings again, raveling her fingers around it inch by inch. "No. I have his jacket 'cause mine kind of got ruined. Since it was his fault, I told him I was keeping this until he gets me a new one."

"Oh," Sara cooed. "How'd he ruin it? Just ripping it right off you?"

Emily smiled and sang, "Yup!" like she was proud of it.

Dexter chimed, "Emily. If all you want is sex, then that's great. But be careful, because that man catches feelings fast. And, he is *very* good at hiding them. Wouldn't want to see either of you hurt."

A telling grin teased at the corners of her bee-stung lips.

The twins' room cracked open and they ran down the stairs, screaming Emily's name.

"Ah, yes! I love it when they attack me." Emily leaped over the back of the couch, ran to the bottom of the stairs, and knelt with her arms open. The twins crashed into either side of her as she lifted them in the air and spun. "My absolute favorite people in the world!"

Dexter leaned to Sara. "You want to break the news to Zeek or should I?"

Sara drew the curtains so no one could see into their home. She positioned herself behind Kali, braiding her luscious blonde locks into one tail that fell to her mid back and matched her pale-yellow dress. Dexter stood behind Nellie with his hands on his son's blue long-sleeved shirt. While Sara, Dexter, and the children stood with their backs facing the drawn curtains, Emily stood on the opposite side of the living room. Beside her was a large, rectangular mirror that hung on a pastel blue wall. Above it was a long white table decorated with green potted succulents and spider plants that spilled over the edge to give it that vintage style that Sara seemed to always be drawn to.

"Sara, did you want to do this in the backyard instead?" Emily offered.

Dexter looked to Sara. "You have a backyard?"

Sara pointed to a door hidden beneath the stairs that Dexter hadn't noticed. "Yeah, it's right over there. It's pretty small. But, I'd rather keep this indoors for now."

"Let's get started then." Emily stretched, touching her toes and making several shoulder rotations. Zeek's jacket was unzipped now, revealing a white crop top with matching high-waisted jeans. "Okay, Kali, tell me what I want to do?"

Kali's small voice giggled as her fingers covered her mouth and said, "Dance on the table."

"Good job!" Emily ran to the coffee table and did just that. "What about now?"

Kali's arms opened wide in Emily's direction. "Hug!"

Emily hopped off the table and picked her up. "Good job!" She looked to Sara. "You have a brilliant child. Can I have her?"

"How about me?" Nellie whined while raising his hand.

Dexter laughed and tousled his son's honey blond hair.

Emily smiled at Nellie and said, "I want you both."

Sara stuck her tongue out at Emily and then laughed when Kali did too.

"Kali," Dexter chimed in, "how long have you been seeing what people want to do?"

She shrugged, swiping a lock of her long bangs backward and clutched the rainbow horn of her unicorn. "I don't remember."

"Before or after I came home?"

"Before," she affirmed, mumbling into the white fluff.

Dexter sent Sara a hard look, trying to communicate that him joining the family hadn't triggered their powers. He cleared his throat and kneeled to be eye level with Nellie. "Okay, I want you to watch what your sister can do with her hands. Then, I want you to try and copy it."

Emily put Kali down.

"Kali, try doing the freezing thing you did to Mommy. But aim at the TV."

Kali faced her scarred palm toward the wooden table, then the lamp in the corner, then herself, but nothing came out. She screwed her eyes shut with concentration. Still, the green orbs still didn't manifest. "It's not working."

"How'd you do it last time?"

She shrugged.

Sara knelt to place her hands on Kali's hips. "Do you feel something hot in your tummy?"

Kali nodded.

"Okay. I want you to imagine that heat moving to your hands."

She shut her eyes and tried again. Nothing. Sara looked to Dexter with turned up brows. "Baby Kay, do you think maybe you're just scared it's going to hurt again?"

Kali nodded.

"Well, it might sting. But, if you want it to stop, you just clap your hands really hard. Can you try it for Mama? We have to practice."

Kali reluctantly opened both her palms toward the wall where the TV hung, allowing the ball of energy growing in her palms to cast a green glow near her.

"There you go," Sara whispered in encouragement. "Now, I want you to use more of that hot ball in your tummy to shoot it out like you're trying to go through the wall."

Kali brought her elbows back then thrusted her hands forward, sending two beams into the television and illuminating the entire living room in neon. The TV shook violently on its mounted hooks and crashed to the ground with a thud. The look on Kali's angelic face darkened into sharp angles for a fleeting moment as she fixated on the broken television. She batted her lids then let out a wild scream from the pain, Dexter grabbed her and rushed her to the kitchen faucet to cool off her hands. "Good job, Kali."

The two rejoined the group and Sara was already beside Nellie. "You think you can try to do what your sister did?"

He tried, but it didn't come as naturally as it did Kali. The skin beneath his palms lit, but it never broke the skin. With every failed attempt, the conviction in his eyes never ceased. Frustrated, he dropped his hands and stomped a foot on the ground. "I want my powers!" he shrieked as he thrusted his palms forward for the hundredth time. A powerful beam escaped and careened to the left, sending a framed photo of a rowboat on a calm river to the ground in shattered pieces of glass.

Nellie shouted in pain and Dexter ran him to the sink. "Great job, Nellie!"

"I love my powers!" He cuddled his hands into his chest like he was hugging the ability with hearts gleaming in his eyes.

Dexter leaned to Sara, whispering, "You really think it can be that easy?"

"It didn't take long when I got the powers. Remember how fast I figured out how to control the screechers? All of two minutes?"

"True."

Nellie turned to face Dexter with a heavy pout overtaking his expression. "What about my other power? I don't want Mommy to dream that dream again!"

Dexter gave a crooked grin at his son's eagerness to protect his mother. "We'll work on that next. First, I need to tell you some rules that go along with your powers."

Sara sat on the couch, towing Kali onto her lap. Nellie and Emily followed suit.

Dexter crouched at the twins' feet. "Kali, Nellie. Now that we know you have these abilities, there are some rules you must to follow. You are *never* allowed to use this on any of us here in this room. Okay?"

As soon as Dexter finished the last syllable, Kali let a defiant smile cross her face, opened her hand, and shot an energy beam into her brother, laughing.

"Kali!" Dexter barked, making her flinch.

Nellie screamed, but was still able to move since he, too, possessed Atraeus's power. Suddenly, his son craned his neck forward, glaring at his sister with resentment. His rounded features converted to harsh edges as he squinted his eyes and clenched his teeth.

Everything about Kali sank into Sara's lap, her cheeks turning a unadulterated white while her brows constricted in anguish. Her arms went up above her head, yelling, "Daddy!"

Dexter lifted his daughter into his arms, confused. Kali's tears poured in waves as she uncontrollably shook with violent hysteria. Wherever he moved Kali, Nellie's vision followed. "Nellie, what are you doing to your sister?"

Instead of answering, he kept intense focus on his suffering sister with a smile tugging on the corners of his lips. Dexter recognized that cruel look. He had seen it time and again over the last six years he had been in the pit. That look belonged to Atraeus. "Knock it off, Nellie!"

With a delicate hand, Sara gently turned Nellie's head to her. As soon as Nellie's line of vision shifted to his mother, Sara screamed and Kali was released. His daughter clasped her small arms around Dexter's neck, panting and crying.

He moved toward Sara, his body stiff like a plank, fingers fisted, and gaze razor sharp. Emily's hands came to Nellie's shoulders, squeezing him to break him of the strange trance.

"Dexter!" she screamed, eyes screwed shut.

"Nellie, stop!" Dexter ordered, rocking Kali in his arms to calm her.

The next words from Sara's mouth told him exactly what was happening. "Dad! Stop! I was just trying to defend myself! I-I-I didn't mean it. Dad!"

Dexter handed Kali to Emily and knelt beside Nellie, brainstorming how to free Sara. "Hey, Nellie." His irises glowed brighter with the energy taking over his mind.

"C-c-can you call him to come get me?" She was dropped into another recurring hallucination of Marty Brown. The conversation continued the same way every time. "I-I-I don't think I can walk home... Call Dexter. Please. Please call him. He's... he's waiting for me... I don't want to go down there! I want to leave!"

"Woah," Emily blurted while putting a hand on Sara's head, Kali clinging to her like she was going to fall off a cliff if she didn't grasp her tight enough.

Dexter took Nellie's head between his hands, trying to snap him out of whatever was keeping him in this spell. "Nellie, do you hear me? Stop." Still, nothing changed. "Hey," Dexter wrapped his arms around Nellie, rocking him back and forth. "When is your birthday?"

No answer.

"I bet your sister's older than you."

His son blinked and his expression altered from hard to heated as he looked at Dexter. "No!" Nellie wailed, moving away from him and pointing a thumb to his chest. "I'm older!"

A gasp from Sara sounded behind him and Dexter released his anxiety in a huff of relief. "You're older than your sister?"

"Yes."

"I didn't know that." Dexter rubbed Nellie's arm.

Nellie shook his head as if breaking free of the cobwebs that had held him hostage over the last few minutes. "Oh no," he whispered.

"Are you feeling okay?"

Nellie nodded and flitted his gaze to Sara on the floor. "Did I hurt Sissie and Mommy?"

"Nellie, I'm fine. See?" Sara put on a fake smile for Nellie's sake.

"Do you remember how you did that?"

Nellie nodded. "But I didn't mean to. I never mean to! I just got so angry at Kali for throwing that hot ball at me. It's only happened a few other times. I promise! It was with strangers."

"That's okay. It just means we have to practice. You can always practice on me. But, never Mommy or Kali. Even if they make you mad. Okay?"

He nodded again. "I'll try." He hopped off the couch and went to Kali who was still clinging to Emily. He wrapped his arms around his sister. "I'm so sorry!"

When Kali didn't turn to forgive her brother, Emily said, "It's okay, Nellie. Go see if your mom is okay."

As he leaped over to a newly-sitting Sara, he crashed his body against hers, knocking them both to the ground. Sara let out an exhausted giggled, assuring him that it would be all right.

"You ready to practice? So you don't do anything on accident again?"

"Yes!" Nellie's head whipped to Dexter, eyes already narrowed as his brain reached for energy inside him that allowed him to give people terrifying hallucinations.

For the thousandth time, the hammer barely grazed Dexter's nose on the way to the cabinet.

Bang!

It swung, sticking into the wooden panel of the kitchen cabinet. Shards of wood splintered as chunks fell to the granite countertop. Sara's parents' kitchen came into a sharpened view. The dark blue walls, the tiled island, dimmed recessed lights scattered over the ceiling, and the stainless-steel appliances.

Little Sara Mar King from high school stood frightened in the doorway that led into the living room. Her long blonde hair was pulled back in a ponytail and fell in a waterfall of liquid gold. It swayed as Sara did. Her arms crossed over her chest, delicate hands clutching the sleeves of her dark gray T-shirt. "Dad, don't." Tears glittered in her eyes as her face fell into a fixed state of sorrow.

"Dammit, Sara!"

Dexter's vision shifted to her father. Angry brown eyes, sweat beading on his temples and speech slurring from all his drinking. The stench of alcohol emanating from his pores, filling every space of the kitchen.

"Go wait for me in your room," her father garbled.

As her father yanked the hammer free from the cabinet, Dexter lurched at it to protect Sara. But his hands went through it as if he was nothing more than a hologram. His eyes widened, poisoned by her distress and her father's perverted abuse.

Sara kept her hands glued to her sides. "No! Dad! Leave me alone!"

"Sara!" her father roared. "Room. Now!"

"No!"

"Where are you going to go? Huh? Dexter's house? He doesn't give a shit about you. No one does."

"Yes, I do!" Dexter's head whipped around to see his precious Sara's face fall to a terrified realization that her father may be right. "Don't listen to him. I'm right here! Sara! Look at me."

"The school didn't even bother to call to say you were absent yesterday—"

Her face scrunched in anger. "Enough!"

The desperate shrill lacing the word triggered something in the depths of Dexter's mind. Something he couldn't hang onto long enough to place. It didn't matter anyway. He had to help Sara in any way he could. "Good, Sara," Dexter encouraged. "Stand up for yourself."

Her father swung the hammer. As if in slow motion, Dexter helplessly watched as it sailed toward Sara's head. "No!" he screamed as he blocked the attack with his forearm, but the attempt was futile. His forearm traveled through her father's.

Sara ducked like an agile tigress, and it surprised Dexter. She was fast. Very fast. Did he know that already? That small spark of something mysterious to return for a brief moment. For a second time, he couldn't latch onto it long enough to uncover what it was.

"Stop! Don't do this anymore!" Sara shouted, straightening her spine.

"Keep going, Marking."

Her father closed in on Sara as he dropped the weapon. While Sara distractedly watched the white tile on the kitchen floor crack with the heaviness of the hammer, her father's hand curled into her hair as his mouth crashed down on hers. Sara recoiled, jamming her open palms on her father's chest to push him away. Dexter watched in terror as two rivers of tears streamed down her cheeks. With overpowering force, he pushed her head down until she sunk to one knee. The sound of her bones smacking against the tile sent a wave of revulsion to clatter in Dexter's chest.

"Fine. Then we'll do it here." Her father unzipped his jeans. "Let's go, Sara. Just like your mother. Fuck, you look so much like her. I can't stand it. I hate you. Just as much as I hated her."

Dexter knelt beside her, praying she could see him. Or sense him. "Pick up the hammer, Sara!"

As if she heard him, she reached down and wrapped her trembling fingers around the hammer's handle.

"Good job. Hit him hard, Sara," Dexter encouraged.

A cry of pain ripped from Sara's throat as her father twisted her hair. Mid-scream, her voice morphed into one of a hardcore soldier. Loud. Confident. And fierce. It sparked again. The memory of something more solid than what he was looking at. He glared at Sara more intently in attempts to hang on longer, knowing it was important. But, like a fleeting thought, it escaped.

She swung the hammer into her father's leg and he dragged her down as they both toppled into the living room. "Fuck! You little bitch!"

With blonde tendrils still wrapped around her father's fingers, she swung again. This time it landed on his temple. Her father's hand fell limp, and she was able to untangle herself. His heavy body thudded half in the kitchen and half in the living room. Sara was able to untangle herself. She stepped frantically back only to train her glossy eyes on the growing pool of blood, quivering hands covering her mouth.

Dexter reached out to turn her away. But, it didn't work. "Don't look."

"I was just trying to defend myself! I-I-I didn't mean it! Dad!"

"It's over, Sara. You did it. It's over." That fluid memory returned with clarity. It *was* over. Fuck, this was over. A long time ago. The spark in his mind ignited into a raging fire built on reality. He had kids with this young woman. Kali. Nellie. He stared at Sara who moved closer to her father's body. "Nellie! Change this for me." Nothing happened. Dexter gazed at Sara violently sobbing as she fell to all fours before her father, convulsing with dry heaves. "Nellie, please." This had already happened. And, Dexter was probably only a few yards away in his own house most likely self-absorbed with playing guitar. Playing guitar! While Sara suffered. Fuck, he was probably in his room writing a stupid love song for her too.

Why did he ever think writing a song for her was going to bring her back to him when this was what she was facing. "Change this, Nellie. Help."

These hallucinations never got easier. And now he was sure that Nellie could see exactly what his mother went through in high school.

Then, Sara's blonde hair swayed as she lifted her gaze and latched onto Dexter's. In a slow cautious motion, she got to her shaky feet, blood dripping from her fingertips.

"Sara? Y-you can see me?"

She gave a sullen nod. "Dexter! Help me! Please!"

Relief swathed him as he kept his mind steady on talking to his son. "Keep going, Nellie. Take us somewhere else. Somewhere happy."

In a brush stroke of paint, Dexter's surroundings morphed. The scent of clean air mixed with a particular perfume relaxed his tensed muscles. Something soft brushed by his hands in waves, like hundreds of petals. His smudgy surroundings glowed blue and orange as they continued to transform and polish around him. On all sides of him, everything refined. It was just him and a teenage Sara in an enormous field of orange poppies. The shining sun blanketed the field with warm, golden rays. Black birds with white stripped wings sung as they flew in a v-shaped pattern overhead. No signs of her house or the blood remained. He made a move to close the distance between him and the love of his life to give the comfort she so needed, but his feet were glued to the ground.

"Yes! Nellie, you're getting it. Can you make Mommy walk to me?"

With tortured eyes, young Sara Mar King took a hesitant step toward him. "D-D-Dexter," her raw voice cracked.

He nodded, egging her to come closer to his open arms.

She sniffed and wiped her tears with the back of her wrist. "I need you."

"I'm right here," he coaxed.

Just how he had always wanted, she stepped into his embrace as she broke down crying. He wrapped his arms around the beautiful eighteen-year-old who needed his attention, his love, and his protection. Her quakes vibrated through him as he silently promised to never let her go. He closed his eyes and kissed the top of her head.

When he opened them, her pixie cut came into focus. His arms were encircling the Marking he had grown to love. The living room surrounded him with Nellie standing on the couch smiling wide enough to reach his green eyes.

He let Sara go to hug his son. "Great job, bud. You think you can do that again tomorrow? We'll keep practicing."

"I *love* my powers." He gave a toothy smile while he clapped his hands and brought his elbows into his chest as if hugging them.

Sara's phone pinged and the kids ran into the kitchen, playing some tag game and speaking in pirate jargon. He was prepared to follow them, but when Sara checked her phone, a visible quiver shook her. Concerned jade eyes remained transfixed on her screen and tension dominated beneath her muscles.

With a sinking feeling, Dexter questioned, "You okay?"

Emily leaped after the kids and played their seemingly made up game of Pirates and Sharks. With her hands shaped into a fin above her head, Emily tramped toward the twins, making gurgling shark sounds.

There was a strong tug on that invisible thread Dexter felt every so often between him and Sara. She shook her head to let her blonde bangs fall over her forehead, hiding her expression from Dexter's questioning gaze. But, he did see her bite her bottom lip harder the more she honed in on the phone that dinged a second time. A third. A fourth.

"Sara?"

Her electric green eyes shot to him. "Yeah?"

"Who's texting you?"

She cleared her throat, turned off the screen of her phone, and stuck it in the back pocket of her denim jeans. "No one."

"You look spooked." With his words, the thread between them vibrated with Sara's quick shiver.

The phone chimed again and her face hardened. She sighed to consciously relax her facial expression and whispered, "It's no one important." After a curt grin, she brought her phone out and set it to silent. As she was turning her phone to place it back in her pocket, Dexter eyed the dozens of texts being sent to her.

"That's a lot of messages." He nodded at the phone while massaging his own hands for comfort.

"Leave it alone, Dexter," she requested with exasperation as she pivoted to make her way around the couch and enter the kitchen.

Dexter caught her by the upper arm and tugged her to the front of him. "Who is it?"

Chapter 11

▲▲▲

Dammit. Over the course of the last day, she had received hundreds of texts from Guy. Each more desperate than the last. She hadn't responded to any of them. She also hadn't given him any reasoning as to why she was ignoring him. But, truthfully, the idea of talking to him made her nauseatingly sick. If only she could go back in time and never invite Guy into her life to start with. Then, the thought of the last six years without his help also turned her stomach. That was the only reason she felt the need to give him closure. Could she be that cold? Could she, for once, ignore someone else's feelings? Especially a friend who had gotten her through so much?

She looked at the tall, hulky man in front of her, cerulean eyes hunting for the truth in her own and wanting to fix whatever she needed mending. When she looked at Dexter, there was no Guy. Hell, there wasn't even an Emily. All she could see was the tunnel vision of him and the trust that he threaded through her weakened soul after living without him for so long.

Sara kept her lips pressed in a straight line.

"It looks like someone's harassing you." He loosened his grip. "Is it Guy? What's he saying?"

A lot. Guy was saying more than she ever wanted him to. Every word she read sent suffocating waves of guilt that constricted around her throat, burning hotter than the ball of Atraeus's energy that used to wring her neck whenever he spoke to her.

The texts started out with him wanting to talk to her. Then, they moved to him saying he was waiting for her in a certain place at a certain time to speak in person.

After was a slew of increasingly angrier texts about how she had the audacity to stand him up.

They became more frequent as the hours passed. More frequent and more vulgar.

More degrading.

"Can I see your phone?" Dexter let her go and held out an open palm.

Sara looked at Dexter's hand, his eyes, then back to his hand. That was the last thing she wanted. For Dexter to see the texts, then hunt him down and beat him to a bloody pulp. She quickly turned her head to the kitchen and called, "Emily, come here."

Dexter brought his hand to his beard and stroked it while narrowing his eyes at Sara.

"I'll tell her," she grumbled under her breath.

He sighed and turned toward the kitchen. "Okay then. I'll make lunch."

As soon as Dexter crossed paths with Emily, guilt settled in her arid throat. Anytime he was upset with her, disappointment drowned her.

Sara invited Emily to sit on the couch in the living room.

"Woah. What happened to Dexter? He's in a mood."

Sara scrubbed her face with her hands as she pulled her legs into a crisscrossed position. She handed her phone to Emily. Her dark eyes lit up as Guy's texting continued to plague her phone.

"Ew! What the hell's the matter with him?" She gasped as more came through. "You are *not* a failure as a mother."

"I can't bring myself to tell Dexter."

Emily began punching in a text.

Sara swore before reaching out to snatch the phone. "No!"

Emily swatted Sara's hand away from the phone and continued typing. "Stop, Sara." Once she was finished, Emily handed her phone back to her. "There. I blocked him and deleted his texts. You're welcome."

Sara looked at the blank screen that used to be filled with Guy's harassment. Could it really be that easy? Would he leave her alone then? Something stirred in her that told her that wouldn't be the end of it. "I don't need to feel guilty, right? He did help a *lot* with the kids for the last *six* years."

She gave a heavy-lidded glare. "Did you read those texts? He can go fuck himself."

Sara sighed, ruffled her bangs, then grinned at Emily. She was right. Hopefully it was over. All she wanted now was to get more alone time with Dexter—to make it up to him for not sharing her phone, for stressing him out. "Can I ask for a big favor?" Sara questioned.

"Sure."

"Any chance you could sleep in the kids' room tonight? I need a night with Dexter without Kali coming in."

Emily narrowed her eyes with a knowing smile. "That little cock block."

Sara giggled.

"Yeah, you need to take your mind off Guy's texts anyway," Emily answered while pulling out her phone.

Sara put a hand over the screen. "You were planning on seeing Zeek tonight, weren't you?"

Emily shook her head and brought her phone back to her face. "Yeah, but it's fine. I'll just let him know."

In a swift motion, Sara stole the phone out of Emily's hands. "No, no. It's fine. Maybe another night."

Emily's eyes bugged and shot to Sara as she stole the phone back. "If you ever touch my phone again, I'm going to have to pound on you a little."

Sara laughed then jokingly frowned.

"You haven't had a night alone with Dexter in six years. I kind of want you two to work out. How is that ever going to happen if you can't sleep together."

Sara shrugged. "We seem to find ways. But, I'd like a whole night, you know?"

"Oh, I know." Emily said while lifting her brows several times suggestively. "Besides, I'm curious to see Zeek's reaction if I don't show up for once."

Sara elbowed her in the arm. "You like *like* him, don't you?"

"No! *You* like him," she spat defensively before rolling her head back, straight black tresses scattering in raven waterfalls over the armrest of the couch. "Okay, yeah, I like him. But, he was the one who made it very clear that it was only a sexual thing. Not me." She picked up her phone and texted. "Watch."

Sara leaned over Emily's shoulder.

Emily: Can't come tonight.

A few seconds later.

Zeek: k

Emily rolled her eyes. "See? Romantic tension at its finest."

Sara shrugged. "I don't know. Dexter said he's good at hiding his feelings."

"Hiding them? They're nonexistent. He doesn't even glance at me when we do it. I think he's pretending I'm someone that died years ago."

"You'll never know unless you ask."

Emily shook her head. "And ruin perfectly great sex? I don't think so."

"Well, if anything, absence makes the heart grow fonder. I mean, I wouldn't suggest six years, but maybe a night apart will make him miss you."

Emily lifted crossed fingers with hope.

The kids reentered the room, Kali with stickers on her forehead and Nellie acting like a robot. For the next half hour, Emily and Sara played with the twins.

Dexter came into the room with two plates full of fettuccine pasta with alfredo sauce, garlic, and some parsley. "For my lovely ladies."

"Oh yum!" Emily exclaimed and snatched one of the plates. "And he cooks too. What can't you do, Dexter?"

He thought about it while handing the other plate to Sara. "Get Kali to sleep in her own bed."

Emily laughed. "Say no more. Emily Merrit is here!"

The center of Dexter's brows creased in confusion.

"I'm staying with them so you two," she said while pointing to them with her fork, "can have some alone time tonight."

Dexter's eyes brightened and a crooked smile raced across his face. "Is that right? Zeek will be so disappointed."

"Why?" Emily snapped, reaching a hand out and grabbing Dexter's wrist. "Did he say something to you?"

Dexter's brows shot up. "No, I was joking. But, good to know it's not serious."

Emily's cheeks seared as she dug into her meal.

Sara laughed and spun her fork to wrap the pasta around it.

"Wait." Dexter put a hand out to stop her from eating. "Are you still vegan? I can make you something else."

Sara smiled and shook her head. "Not anymore."

"Enjoy!" Dexter said, kissing Sara on the cheek.

They smiled at each other before he took the kids to eat in the kitchen.

Sara took several bites, letting the creamy pasta fill her empty stomach while Emily hopelessly chatted about Zeek with a mouthful of food.

The next thing Sara knew, Dexter stood in front of her holding a large piece of cardboard on his knees. Kali was smiling and holding her own on the right side of him and Nellie on the other. All three of them had smiles wider than she had ever seen before. Nellie was hopping in place while Kali was rocking her hips side to side, letting her dress sway.

"Okay, ready, set, go," Dexter whispered.

Kali lifted up the cardboard above her head. On it, in Kali's handwriting, read: "Will you"

Next, Dexter flipped his up and it read: "go out"

"Okay, Nellie, your turn," Dexter cued.

Nellie flipped it over and sprawled across the cardboard in Nellie's shaky penmanship was, "with Daddy?"

With a vision of writing signs to each other and taping them to the windows as kids, Sara was whipped back to feeling like the little girl who was in love with the boy in the house next door. She shoved her plate into Emily's hand, jumped off the couch, and wrapped her arms around Dexter's neck, giving him a delighted kiss that ended with her saying, "I'd love to."

"She said yes, kids! What do we do?"

The three of them did an adorable dance where they spun in a circle and raised their arms, chanting, "Yay!"

Sara giggled as her heart filled with overwhelming joy.

"Good god," Emily chimed, "stop, I'm going to gag on your cuteness."

Dexter kissed Sara's cheek, grabbed her plate out of Emily's hand, and said, "I'll pick you up at eight tonight."

Sara took her plate and plopped on the couch. "We live together," she retorted as she took another bite of food.

"Tonight. We don't."

"Shopping time!" Emily exclaimed with a mouthful of chewed pasta. "Let's get you all dolled up."

Within the hour, Sara and Emily were out the door and perusing different clothing shops downtown. Dress after dress, Sara tried each on but felt either too ugly in them, too much like someone else, or way too sexy. She wanted to find a happy medium that would make him think she was beautiful. All he really saw her wearing were dirt stained clothes from the traveling days or his band T-shirt. And although she had relied on the comfort the old clothes brought her to make it through the long days and sleepless nights, she finally felt ready to dip her toes in her new reality.

She drew back the sky-blue curtain of her tiny dressing room and made her way to the full length mirror, not sure what Emily would think of the lavender dress she had put on. It went from a halter of frills around her neck to an elastic band cinching her waist, then a flowing skirt that fanned when she spun.

Emily put down her phone and leaned forward on the red velvet stool in the corner. "Dear lord, Sara. How do you look so good in absolutely everything?"

Sara gave Emily a meek grin. "Still not good enough though."

"No. Of course not. 'Cause you're picking all the wrong things. You keep looking at clothes you think Dexter will like. But, what do you like?"

She thought about it with a hand on her popped out hip. "I don't know. Maybe something sophisticated. A high-waisted black skirt and maybe a crop top."

Emily's owl eyes lit up as a smile sprawled over her plump raspberry lips. She jumped from the stool in excitement. "Oh! I know exactly where we can find that."

Sara rolled her eyes and curled her upper lip. "You're going to say the cell phone shop, aren't you?"

"No," she said with a heavy-lidded stare. Then, her face shifted to a hopeful, wide-eyed expression. "But, maybe when we're done here." She took Sara by the arm and guided her back to the dressing room. "Come on, get dressed!"

Emily hurried her across the street and down several blocks to a vintage clothing store where she and Sara sifted through hundreds of more clothes. "I saw it somewhere here. I wanted it myself, but I couldn't afford it." She leaned to Sara's ear and whispered, "Maybe they'll give it to you for a discount, and then I can wear it for Zeek." Emily pulled out skirt after skirt from the racks, but nothing was appealing.

A sudden squeal erupted from Emily and echoed through the shop. "Found it!"

Sara eyed the two romantic garments clutched in Emily's hands and smiled so wide that her freckled nose crinkled. Sara grabbed them with urgency and fled to the fitting room at the back of the rose gold themed store. As soon as the outfit was snug on her body, Sara knew it was exactly what she had been looking for. The outfit was a perfect blend of comfort and sexiness that left her feeling desirable. She opened the door to reveal the skirt and matching crop top to Emily who was sifting through some accessories in a brass bowl hung on the wall. She dropped a small trinket into Sara's hands and clapped with a beaming smile.

The high-waisted black maxi skirt was covered with hand painted roses on the overlay of tulle that flowed overtop the silk fabric. It swayed gently with every movement, her leg peeking out of the thigh-high slit. The matching crop top fit to perfection as if it were tailor-made just for Sara. Translucent tulle covered her from atop her breasts to over her shoulders that flared into cap sleeves. The rest of the top was opaque. A small strip of her midriff poked through with her subtle movements, making Sara feel self-assured and alluring for Dexter. Damn, she wanted to impress him so badly.

"Dead gorgeous. Screw Dexter, *I'll* take you out."

Sara tossed her head back and gave a belly laugh. "Yeah. I really love this."

Emily meandered to the other side of the store while Sara did spins in front of the mirror, checking that she appeared well assembled on all sides and at every angle. When Emily returned, she had two black strappy heels that sparkled under the store's fluorescent lights.

"Oh dear, I haven't worn high heels," she paused to think, "ever. I'll just wear my sneakers."

Emily's jaw dropped while she said, "Excuse me?" with a wounded overtone in her voice.

"What? The skirt goes to the floor. No one will see them."

"I'm going to pretend I didn't hear you say that before I drop kick you." She held out the shoes. "Put these on. Now."

Sara gave a reluctant groan as she took the heels and slid them over her bare feet. She did another twirl, sending the bottom of the skirt off the ground in a flare of fabric and revealing the sparkly straps that clearly completed the chic look she was hoping for.

"Perfect, Sara. That'll definitely get you laid."

Sara paid for the outfit at a discount thanks to the store owner being an old friend of Dexter's. She and Emily walked back to the house, giggling as they passed Zeek's shop.

By the time they got home, the sun was making its descent into late evening and the kids were doing some drawing project with Dexter in the living room. The coffee table was pushed aside, and the three of them lay in a messy pile of crayons and construction paper. When his blue eyes hit hers, Dexter eagerly stood to kiss her on the cheek. "All done?"

"Yup."

"Do you mind if I take off until our date?"

"Nope," Emily answered for her. "She needs to get ready."

Dexter kissed Sara again. "Good, because I do too. I'll pick you up at eight."

Sara peered at the silver framed clock hanging in the kitchen. Three hours. "Okay."

She carefully watched Dexter's muscular shoulders and tattooed arms exit the house. The second the door shut, anticipation crept into her psyche and anxiety found a home in her stomach. Her vision zoomed to the laminate beneath her feet while her palms clammed up and butterflies flapped in her chest. A date. The only date she had ever been on was with Marty Brown.

"You okay?" Emily said. "You're looking like you saw a ghost."

Sara moved her gaze to Emily as her breathing went rigid and her heart rate sped. "No. Not okay."

"What's wrong?"

"I'm going on a date."

"So?"

"I've been on one date. With Marty."

"And this one is with Dexter."

Sara shook her head, green eyes widening into saucers. "I-I-I'm not ready."

"Yes, you are."

"No. I'm not. My whole life I've wanted to go out with Dexter. And now it's happening. And the only practice I've ever gotten was with Marty Brown."

"Sara, it's not like this date is going to change anything." Emily put a comforting hand on Sara's trembling shoulder. "That man is a fool for you, you don't need to worry about impressing him. You've already banged. Hell, you already have kids together. You have nothing to worry about."

"Yes, I do! It's Dexter fucking Bennet, Emily!" More wings tickled the inside of her stomach at the feeling of his name rolling off her tongue. Now, Sara was panting, trying to get a grip over the irrational response to a date with the love of her life.

Emily took her by the arm and dragged her into the kitchen. "You are losing it, Sara. If you're going to swear, do it away from the kids."

"I can't do this. What if I'm horrible on the date, and it changes everything?"

Emily's owl eyes rolled. "I'm pretty sure you could sit there and insult him for an hour, and he'd still want to bang you when you got back."

Sara shook her head violently as she began circling around the island, nails between her teeth. "No, no, no. No date. We've gotten this far without a date."

Emily's voice chimed in the distance. "Yeah, I think the pressure of this date broke your girl." A second later, Emily's body blocked Sara from making another round. In her hand was her phone that she was shoving into Sara's face. "Talk to him."

Sara shook her head violently before Emily pressed the cool surface of the phone against Sara's ear and Dexter's voice rang out. "Sara?"

A sharp intake of breath was all she could manage when his familiar husky timber registered in her mind.

"Hey, Marking. It's going to be all right."

"Come home. I can't do this."

She heard him chuckle on the other end and it quelled a small part of her building apprehension. "Yes, you can. You can do the impossible. I promise you, it'll be fine."

"It's too much for me."

"There's never any pressure with us, remember? But, I do want to take you on an official date. Don't cancel this."

She grabbed the phone from Emily's hand, staying silent.

"It'll be okay. Please trust me."

She groaned and clutched her belly. "I feel like throwing up."

Another laugh. "You can take on Splitters and Atraeus but not a simple date with me?"

When he put it like that, it did sound ridiculous. Still she couldn't keep the panic from flipping her brain into overdrive, racing through any valid excuse to justify canceling. "What if something happens with the kids? What if they freeze Emily? What if Guy tries to break in again and we aren't here?"

"You're worrying too much. None of that will happen. We won't be out long. I only need an hour."

Sara groaned into the receiver.

"I want you to go take a shower. Then, get dressed in whatever you're comfortable in. It doesn't need to be what you got today. When you're done, go lay in bed and relax until I get there."

She nodded her head as if Dexter could see her. One of her palms fled to her eye, rubbing it as she rasped out, "Okay."

"All right. I'll see you soon."

"Okay, I love you."

"Love you, Marking."

Emily took the phone and hung up, crouching in front of her and resting a hand on Sara's shoulder. "You good?"

"He wants me to take a shower."

Emily smiled. "That's easy. Go do that."

The next couple hours went by in a blur. The strength of her old self crept to the surface of her mind as the hot water of the shower calmed her nerves. She could do this. She deserved a little fun. A little fun with Dexter. Especially after the day she had, she needed it. She got out of the shower and dressed in her new outfit. When she looked in the mirror, she found some courage to be brave now that she felt put together. She went back to the bathroom. Emily was seated on the counter sifting through the ever-growing makeup collection in Sara's large black case.

Makeup had always calmed Sara. She enjoyed being able to alter the way she looked. If she didn't like what she saw in the mirror, she would change it. But, tonight, she wanted to impress. With care, she applied foundation, concealer, and a dark cat eye with black eyeliner. Soon, it just felt like she was creating art with cosmetics like she used to as a teenager. The idea of going on the date vanished. She applied brown pencil to her brows and a set of fake, luscious lashes. Using her ring finger, she patted on red lip stain in a shade that matched the dark red roses on her outfit. Next, she placed some curls into her pixie bangs and ruffled them so that they came to life.

Emily rounded the corner into the bathroom. "Holy shit, you clean up good."

"I look all right?" she questioned in clear articulations, needing her best friend's reassurance.

"Are you kidding? Dexter is going to drop dead when he sees you." Emily jumped onto the bathroom counter then insinuatingly shrugged. "I guess you don't have to worry about going on the date then."

Sara giggled. "Thanks."

Nellie and Kali wandered in, wanting to join their mom in getting ready. Emily put braids in Nellie's hair while Sara put a light layer of makeup on Kali. With her curling rod, Sara styled soft waves in her daughter's bleach blonde hair, relaxing her knotted stomach.

Right as the clock struck eight, there was a knock at the door.

Dormant butterflies stirred awake, taking flight in various directions while trying to escape.

"You're on, Sara. Go get that hunka hunka," Emily encouraged.

Sara descended the stairs before intently staring at the door. "It's just Dexter. It's just Dexter."

A trembling hand reached for the knob as Emily and the kids watched from the second floor through the white slats in the banister. After a deep breath, she cracked the door open. And, what she saw caused a fresh wave of panic to roll through her.

Dexter.

Dressed in black jeans with a white buttoned up shirt under a denim jacket.

A bouquet of roses in hand held out in her direction.

Along with adoration shining in his eyes, a charming smile was sprawled on his face.

The epitome of Sara's kind of handsome.

To top it all off, he was clean shaven.

It felt as if she was thrust into an alternate dimension where she wasn't going out with her tattooed warrior, but with the Dexter Bennet from high school. It made her stomach twist and turned her into the giddy little girl who used to gawk at him from across the classroom.

"Wow, Marking. You look—"

Sara yelped and slammed the door in his face.

"Well, that was unexpected," Emily huffed as she marched down the stairs.

"Sara?" Dexter called with a light knock on the door.

His voice flung her against the wall as her breathing went harsh.

Emily opened the door and peeked out. "Holy damn." She, too, shut the door on him and turned her attention to Sara. "Dude. Your man is smoking hot."

She shook her head. "Nope. Tell him to go away. I'm not ready to go out with Dexter from high school. I'm not nearly good enough or ready enough." Her voice lowered to a hushed tone. "I should have put something sexy on, not this! I'm not ready! Tell him to put his beard back on."

"Sara," Dexter called, "what's wrong?"

"You're ready. Don't leave him waiting," Emily squealed as she reopened the door to let Dexter in.

Sara smiled sheepishly at him and let out an ugly, nervous laugh before hiding her face in her hands. "Oh my god."

"You broke your girl's brain, remember?" Emily warned, raising a brow.

He put down the bouquet and wrapped his arms around Sara as she trembled into his chest. "What's the matter?" he whispered.

"You look like you did in high school and it's freaking me out."

"I'm sorry. I thought you'd like it."

She nodded, feeling her cheeks burn as she released several nervous giggles. "I do. You look *really* good." Sara turned her head to Emily and said with disbelief. "I'm going out with Dexter Bennet."

Emily laughed and shooed both of them out the door. "Go on. Get."

The next thing Sara knew, she was under the stars outside the house and alone with Dexter. She couldn't help but feel like a lovestruck teenager who had finally caught the attention of hottest guy in school. She stole a peek at him again, eyeing his chiseled cheeks and a jaw line that could cut glass.

"Do a twirl for me," he encouraged while taking her trembling hand and spinning her. He tugged her into him and smiled. "You are a vision, Marking."

For all she knew, she vomited butterflies at that very moment. His face came down to hers for a hungry kiss, but she pulled away, unable to stop herself from tittering like an idiot. Strings of nonsensical syllables spilled from her lips.

"Dang. Your brain is broken, isn't it?"

More words and sounds she, herself, couldn't even comprehend spewed from her mouth.

He leaned to her ear and whispered, "Just wait until I get you in bed."

Quakes zipped through her stomach and down to her knees, threatening to knock her over. The remnants of his husky timber buzzed through her core and between her legs. "I can't even look at you." In her mind, she tried to morph him into the rugged man she had traveled with six years ago. Right now, they seemed so separate. Her warrior was sweet and kind and caring. Dexter Bennet was rude and had ignored her for over a decade. Yet, they were the same person.

"I'll grow the beard back."

"I'm having a difficult time."

"No kidding."

"For so long you looked like a different person that it was easier to leave behind the version of you that was mean to me. Now, you are that person, and it's coming back up. It just took me off guard."

"I get it. I'd be pretty thrown if you came out with long hair."

She offered a grin, but kept her eyes glued to the pavement as they took steps toward wherever he was taking her. "Hey, check it out." Sara pointed at a worm wiggling across the sidewalk. "It's a sign." She knelt down, picked it up, and placed it in the grass to the side. "There you go, buddy." When she got up, sprawled across Dexter's face was befuddlement. "What?"

"Okay. Now, I know why not having a beard freaked you out." He draped an arm around her shoulder and kissed her cheek.

Dexter walked her to the downtown. They passed most of the restaurants and stopped in front of Zeek's store.

"You're taking me cell phone shopping? Sounds like a date for Emily."

Dexter shrugged. "You'll see."

He opened the door and led her into the darkness. The only light source was a small candle in the center of a white clothed table. It wasn't until hundreds of fairy lights flickered on did she see everything that Dexter had been working on for the last few hours. Nothing about the place resembled Zeek's shop. The perimeter of the floor was littered with gorgeous bouquets of assorted flowers. There were even wall hangings of roses and cascading ivy dripping to the floor. The ceiling glowed with tiny, warm lights to create a star-like skyscape. "Wow!" Sara walked in circles, trying to take everything in. All this for her? "This is beautiful." Across the hardwood flooring were thousands of different colored rose petals. The feeling of walking into a fairytale burst through her chest in exuberant awe.

"Take a seat," Dexter encouraged while pulling out a chair for Sara to sit in.

When she looked to Dexter, she saw familiar gentleness smiling back at her. That meant more to her than all the love he poured into the decorations. Seeing that glimpse of the man she fell in love with eased her mind. Taking a calming breath, she sat and absorbed the gorgeous variety of flowers that covered all four walls. "I feel like a princess."

"Then I've done my job." Dexter sat across from her and held out an open hand. She took his with more unstoppable chuckles erupting from her mouth. His ocean eyes were smoldering at her in the dim lighting and a genuine smile emerged across his face.

"Giggles still got you?"

"You're making me so nervous."

"Same."

"Liar," she said, sticking her tongue out.

The door in the back of the shop opened and Zeek stepped out. He was dressed in a white button up shirt, black slacks, and a bow tie. In his hand were two plates. When he approached them, he said, "Your salad, miss," and placed it in front of her.

Sara's eyes shifted to Dexter and laughed. "You're making him wait on us?"

Zeek answered for him with a wink. "He promised Emily would be free every night after this."

Dexter shrugged and picked up his fork when Zeek left. "So this is a Caesar salad brought to you by a restaurant that I have forgotten the name of."

"Yum," Sara said, taking the first bite and crossing her legs under the table, allowing her toned leg be exposed from the slit in her skirt. "My favorite." She swallowed and took another bite. "So, Dexter Bennet, is this what you did with all your women? Sweep them off their feet by decorating a cell phone shop to look like the setting of a fairytale wedding?"

Dexter scoffed. "The romance always came straight from microwave TV dinners." He smiled and shifted his voice into a sexy rasp. "Especially when they'd watch me slowly peel back the plastic."

Sara couldn't contain a laugh. "Panty dropper."

He chortled at her joke, which filled her with certain pride. "Every time."

Zeek cleared their plates when they were finished and replaced it with grilled chicken, roasted vegetables, and rice with a type of sweet teriyaki sauce.

Sara took a bite and moaned when the flavors burst in her mouth with a perfect balance of savory and sweet. "This is so good."

169

"Aw man, I know. Remind me to buy this once a week."

"Screw that. I want to learn how to make it."

Dexter swallowed. "That sounds fun. Let's do it together."

"We both know I'm the cook out of the two of us," she answered with a bratty smile.

He laughed at her humor that he had missed so much.

Movement just outside the doors caught her eye. Two small figures ran past, holding hands. One had long blonde hair and the other honey bangs falling over his forehead. Kali and Nellie. Alone on the street. Sara frantically stood, took off her heels, and ran to the door, black skirt flying behind her. "Dexter! Our kids!"

Chapter 12

▲▲▲

It took a second for Dexter to process what Sara had said. One moment he was lost in her beautiful aura, the next, her seat was empty. The sound of the door opening snapped him to the present. Sara's skirt almost caught in the door as it shut behind her. His kids! Dexter was out of his seat and pushing open the door within a breath, trailing behind Sara. He turned to the left and chased after them. She already had Kali in her arms and was reaching out for Nellie's hand with the other.

Before her hand made contact with their son, Dexter rushed to picked him up under his armpits. "What are you guys doing outside by yourselves at night? Where's Emily?" Dexter questioned in a tone so serious that the twins burst into tears in unison.

"Kay, what's wrong? Where's Emily?"

Between her labored breaths, Kali said, "We-we accidentally froze her."

"Oh geez," Sara murmured under her breath, eyes latching onto Dexter's.

Zeek's large frame sidled Sara. "Froze? What the hell does that mean?"

"Emily will catch you up, just go to her," Dexter promised as he pointed in the direction of their home.

Zeek took off, sprinting down the sidewalk like a lion on the hunt.

"We're sorry!" the twins cried.

Sara hushed Kali while Dexter rocked Nellie, each whispering that everything would be all right.

In step, they hurried down the street toward the ice cream shop, making sure the kids made it the full mile from their house. It took the entire trip there to hush their crying. When Kali reached out for her brother, Sara and Dexter put them down, so they could hold hands back to the cell phone shop.

Dexter wrapped an arm around Sara and rested his temple against her head.

"Dexter, we have children together," she whispered in a gentle hum.

"I know. For a while I kind of forgot we weren't in high school."

Sara giggled. "I'm glad we aren't though. I'm so glad we skipped all this dating stuff and have our family. It means so much more to me."

"I know what you mean. It may have been unconventional, but I love every second of being here with you."

When they reached the cell phone shop, they spotted Zeek and Emily conversing as they stropped along sidewalk.

Nellie and Kali screamed her name and charged at her. Emily knelt down and wrapped them up in a big hug. When she released them, Emily gave Sara a hug. "I'm so sorry, guys. This must have ruined your date."

Sara shook her head. "No worries." She put a hand atop both the kids' heads. "What do you say?"

"Sorry," they recited in unison. Kali finished the apology by saying, "It won't happen again!"

Emily kissed both their cheeks. "Apology accepted."

Sara smiled and suggested, "Let's all go inside."

"No, no," Emily insisted, taking the twins' hands in hers, "I'll take these brats back home."

"No, it's okay. I want them here," Sara admitted while looking to Dexter. "Is that okay?"

"Of course," Dexter chimed. "It'll be more fun to have them with us."

"Okay, then," Emily let go of their hands. "I guess I'll wait for you all back at the house."

When Emily turned her back, Sara punched Zeek in the arm.

He shook his head, but Sara widened her eyes, silently telling him she was going to do it harder if he didn't call Emily back. Dexter wildly enjoyed the way she could exert authority over anyone, especially the seven-foot, rock-of-a-man Zeek.

Zeek sighed and said in a raspy voice, "Stay, Em. I want you here."

Emily whipped around, straight tendrils of dark hair flying over her flushed face in scribble-like patterns. If Emily's eyes weren't wide by nature, they were now.

The group went into the shop, and Zeek put on soft piano music through the speakers and winked at Dexter. Within the first two notes of the gentle tones, Dexter faced Sara and bowed. "May I have this dance?"

Sara playfully curtsied back with a smile that reached her eyes. "How could a girl deny such a request from Sir Bennet?"

He brought her against him by the small of her back and enjoyed the feel of her cheek pressing trustingly against his chest. Her dark lashes fell over her lightly freckled cheeks as she closed her eyes and listened to his heart. The world faded. All that mattered was holding her—lovingly enough to remind her that he was never leaving again. She was strong and well protected.

He spun her and whispered, "I am so in love with you, Sara Mar King."

She smiled, fraying his nerves into euphoria for the thousandth time that day. In a flash, she was on her tiptoes, kissing him.

Soon, Dexter was dancing with Sara, Kali was dancing with Nellie, and Zeek with Emily.

When the song ended, a more upbeat one rang from the speakers and the kids jumped in circles and ran around the shop.

After a good thirty-minute dance party for the sake of the kids, Zeek walked everyone back to the house while Dexter took Sara to a wooden ladder in the back that led to the flat roof of the shop.

Set up was a blanket and a box of Oreos. Dexter wrapped the two of them up to protect them from the cool night breeze as they fed each other the cookies. They sat in happy companionable silence, enjoying the fleeting moments of what felt like stolen time together under the unmarred night sky filled with stars. After scarfing down a sleeve of Oreos, Dexter looked to Sara and asked, "Remember when we were on the roof of the last camp, eating that Oreo."

"Yeah, the stale one that made us feel like vomiting?"

Dexter kissed her cheek. "That's the one. I started talking about the future and you got all tense because you thought there wasn't going to be one?"

Sara nodded.

"Look at us now. We made it."

Sara turned, resting her warm lips on his bare cheek. "I love you. You are perfect for me. And the kids are so lucky to have you as a father. Thank you for working so hard to get back to us."

He squeezed her closer. "I'd do anything for you and the kids."

Sara smiled and munched on another cookie. "Same."

While Sara admired the sparkling stars, he admired her electric eyes. Sara Mar King. In his arms. He was in awe that this stunning, courageous woman let him call her his. And he wasn't going to let her go anywhere. He made a silent promise in that sweet moment that she would never be a sacrifice for anything ever again. This time he would ensure she knew there was always something to live for. He would work each day to be worthy of her love. The love he had always wanted.

Nothing was going to ruin this.

His hand brushed up and down her arm. His nose traced the nape of her neck, inhaling her intoxicating floral scent. He kissed her shoulder and watched the goosebumps ride down her arm. She gave a small gasp as she felt her body melt into his. "You look so good, Sara. I think I died a little when you opened the door."

She giggled.

"I mean I love this outfit, but all I want to do is rip it off you."

Sara brushed her lips against his. "Thanks, but you can't because Emily wants to borrow it." It took all of a second for Dexter to seize her lips, ruining her perfectly reapplied lip stain. He sucked her sweet-tasting bottom lip into his mouth and nibbled.

"You know," he whispered, "that tattoo on your arm," he kissed her again, mind hazing as he drank her in with his eyes, "is damn sexy." She kissed him with lust gathering in her own eyes. "To know you marked your skin forever with the same tattoo as me," he traced his lips down her cheek to her ear, "makes me wildly happy."

With every stroke, his heart's pace quickened to a point of near bursting. For years he had fantasied about touching her like this, caressing her in the way he had craved to. He could barely stand it.

She jumped back and stood. "Let's go."

"Where?" Dexter groaned.

She pointed down the street. "My room."

"But, everyone's there, and the kids are probably asleep by now."

"We'll be quiet."

He kissed her neck.

"Dex..."

"Let's go."

Hand in hand, Dexter rushed Sara to the house with her hanging off his lips. Her warm hands buried beneath his shirt and ran along his heavily inked skin. He hadn't gotten nearly enough of her on their date. The way she was giggling as she fumbled for her keys in the dark, the rosiness in her cheeks that told him she was in love, her body pressing against his, and everything about her had him struggling to resist taking her there and then.

Her nervous laughs kept her feet nailed in the entryway. Dexter had to lift her in his arms and carry her upstairs with her legs wrapped around his waist. Bursting through the bedroom door, he tossed her on the bed and ordered, "Get undressed. Now."

Sara got to her feet and jumped on the bed with a sultry giddiness taking over her expression. "Make me."

Fuck. He wasn't interested in games, no matter how happy they made her. It was just going to take longer to get her in his arms, and it was close to driving him mad. Dexter tackled her legs, sending her falling onto her back, beige comforter enveloping her momentarily as she sunk and bounced back up. He trapped her hips and said, "Tonight, I make the rules for you. Get undressed."

She gave a disobedient smile, and he knew she was calculating how to get out from under him. To get her to stop thinking, he kissed her with immense pressure, hands shifting to her thighs and bunching up her skirt.

When he pulled away, she pouted. "You're no fun."

Dexter smiled and neared the hollow of her collarbone, making a trail of kisses down to her cleavage. "Let me prove you wrong."

Her hands cupped his clean-shaven cheeks, and it drove him to hardness. Feeling her touch on his face was something he wasn't used to. There had always been a barrier of a beard preventing it. But this time, he felt it all. All her trembles when he kissed her. He slid his hand higher up her leg until his fingertips reached her red panties. He rounded his hand to her bottom, lace running along his touch. "Get undressed."

In an angelic plea, she said, "I need help." When she shifted her gaze to meet his eyes, her pupils dilated, causing a perfect storm of love and lust to flourish inside him with burnished desires.

She stood and turned to show him the two gold zippers on the back of her outfit.

A smile caught his lips as he tugged it down, revealing her bare, scarred skin. As he brought the fabric of her sleeve off her shoulder, goosebumps rode down her tattooed arm. A soft giggle sounded, stiffening him.

When she was stripped from her skirt and top, he gazed at the pure sexiness of her red laced pushup bra and matching panties. He carefully watched her cheeks heat in shy embarrassment and was quick to remove his own clothes to even the playing field.

She moaned in sensual amusement and ran her hands across the patterned ink on his chest. "My tattooed warrior," she hummed.

He grinned and brought her close enough to be sucked into the gravity of her beauty. On her tiptoes, she kissed him softly as his hands dipped down to her pert bottom. She smiled against his lips as if she was lost in him as well.

Sara was his everything. She gave him her trust, her precious love, and his perfect kids. And, what had he ever given her? Fuck, he wanted to give her the world. But all he could offer was the broken version of himself. Each time she kissed him back, his love for her filled to the brim, threatening to spill over in an overflowing torrent of devotion.

Her delicate fingers journeyed down his torso until they wrapped around his length. A jolt of energy awakened his nerves as she brought her fist up to the tip, then down to the base. He resisted falling to his knees as he yanked down the cup of her bra and massaged until her nipples hardened. A cloud of lust fogged around his heated body. Smokey wisps of sexual hunger overcame him. An aggressiveness awoke deep within his chest, demanding to take Sara, urging him to show her how fiercely he needed her.

"Sara," he growled, as her hand continued to move at a perfect pace. Like she knew exactly what he liked. In a smooth motion, he unclasped her bra and threw it to the ground. Dexter moved her hand away, worried he was going to come simply from her touch. Reaching down her hips, he slid his hand into her panties and towed them down her thighs until those, too, hit the ground. Dexter bent and lifted her legs around him before laying her on the mattress. He guided her legs over his shoulders, needing control. One slipped off, but he was quick to reposition it over him as he thrusted into her more forcefully than he ever had before. His brain hazed and he knew his mind was entering into dangerous, uncontainable territory.

Dexter tried, but he couldn't get it together. He couldn't find his way out of her sensual energy as he drove himself into her again. Sara's leg slipped off his sweaty shoulder, and he took this movement as she needed some control back, so he let her keep it down, hoping it would resurface his mind. However, his body was in control now. He leaned on her other leg until it couldn't bend back any farther and thrusted again. A quiet whimper flew from her lips, and his mind was quick to decipher it as pleasure. It was pleasure, right? Fuck. He needed to keep his head on straight, keep reading her facial expressions to see if there was any pain. Even if it was painful pleasure. But, he couldn't keep himself from diving into his carnal desires for his Sara Mar King. Being lost in the smell of her sweetness did things to him that he was not prepared for mentally.

Her nails bit into his shoulder, pulling him from his intoxicated haze. Electric green eyes swimming in his. He could always read her eyes. And right then, they were telling him that she was in love. And that was it. All control lost. He fully entered into the darker places of his mind that thrived on desire and selfishness. He needed her in the way that he always wanted her.

And he needed more.

He shoved her leg down and guided both around his waist, happy she was trapping him in place. Pleasure spiraled through him as he indulged in the feeling of his building climax.

Her eyes closed and a shot of clarity struck him for a brief moment. He grabbed her hand and brought it above her head, but that was as much willpower as he could muster. A condom came to mind, but it was a fleeting, foggy thought. Vibrating from the high Sara was giving him seemed to short-circuit his mind.

She gasped when he drove into her harder. He was being too rough. Rougher than any time before. He knew it, but his body didn't care. All he focused on was the desperate need for more of the tantalizing thrill that blazed through his body. He dipped his head down, sucking the skin on her neck into his mouth to mark her for himself. For everyone to see. Her sweet skin between his teeth had him biting, harsher than just a nibble. She gasped again, but this time with a hint of pain behind her moan.

"Tell me to stop," he grunted, knowing he would stop as soon as she said to. But just as the warning dripped from his lips, he drove into her deeper, praying it would keep her from saying anything and let him have her in this way.

But what came through her sweet-tasting lips was, "More, Dex."

With that, he was dragged to the bottom of Sara's ocean and mercilessly drowned in her. Faster and harder. She had him on a silver platter just like she wanted. Her thighs tensed harder around him, and he knew she was close. But, Dexter wasn't sure if he could wait her out. She squeezed his hand until her nails dug into his skin.

In an utter impulse, his other hand twisted through her hair and grabbed a strong hold of her bangs. As if a distant part of him whipped him across the back, screaming to let her go, he clenched his teeth and did the best he could to resist pulling her. To compensate, he dug his own nails into the back of her hand and rammed into her again. When he forced himself to peer into her gaping, gorgeous eyes, Dexter exploded every ounce he had in him. Even when he thought he was emptied, more of his love poured into her. He observed the expression of pure ecstasy on her face that told him she may have been riding out an orgasm.

He waited until she closed her eyes and her body sank into the mattress, panting. Watching her chest rise and fall and her eyes screwed shut like she was in pain had his mind finally resurfacing. Scanning every part of her, his eyes absorbed the sight of the reddened bite mark on her neck that was disguised in a nasty burst of blood vessels.

He had hurt her. Fuck. His lungs hitched, threatening to cut off his breathing altogether. Then, he felt her hand begin to let his hand go and brought hers into view. Dents from his nails were imprinted on the back of her hand surrounded by an aggressive redness. Fuck! Did she tell him to stop? He couldn't remember.

He pulled out of her as gently as he could, dismounted the bed, and swore under his breath. He had fucked up on so many levels.

If he had hurt her physically, she was sure to be hurting mentally. He didn't hold her hand from the beginning, didn't concentrate on what she needed. He hadn't worn protection.

Now that he had gone and fucked it all up, she probably wouldn't want another baby with him. Every muscle fiber in his body tensed, writhing in self-loathing and aggravation.

"Dexter," she called with a quiet sniffle.

Dexter looked at her. Naked, sweaty, and so sexy. To get him out of his own selfish desires, he rubbed his face in his hands to scrub away the nightmarish fog that caused him to lose control. "I am so sorry. I wasn't thinking clearly."

She sat up and tilted her head, rubbing her scalp where he had grasped her hair. "What?"

His head whipped to her, watching her brows turn up and the water line forming on her lids. She was crying. Soft, articulated tones leveled out his emotions. "Did I do something wrong?"

"No," he released in a breath. "I did."

She furrowed her brow. "No, you didn't."

He reached out for her hand and showed her the horrible marks he had made on her skin. "Yeah, Sara. I did." With his fingertips, he gently stroked the bite mark on her neck. "I did everything wrong."

She withdrew her hand. "It's fine. I don't care."

He sighed. "I hate that you learned how to lie to me."

She blinked a few times, sending the tears down her porcelain cheeks. Her cheeks were scar free, but the tears over what he had done tainted them. "I'm not lying," she defended, getting off the bed and standing in front of him with a straightened back and her chin held high. If she weren't crying, Dexter might have believed her. "I didn't notice. It's fine, Dexter."

"That's not even the worst thing I did. I didn't hold your hand."

Her brows knitted together in further confusion. "Yes, you did."

"After. After we had already started."

She gave a comforting grin and took his head between his hands. "It's fine. I'm fine. I'm more than fine."

Running his opened palms up her arms, Dexter felt a lump forming in his throat. "I was too rough, wasn't I? I am so sorry."

She rolled her teary eyes and smiled like she was relieved. "You weren't, I promise. Dex, that was perfect. My pain tolerance should win a fucking award. I didn't feel anything except pleasure. I feel happy. I'm crying because I'm happy!"

Dexter heard her words, but they barely made a dent in his self-loathing anguish. "And I thought about protection in the middle of it and didn't stop myself."

She smiled, and flattened her hand over his chest. "I know we only touched on this before, but I don't mind growing our family. We're committed to each other, and we love each other, and I'd love another little one with you. Okay? That's only if you do too."

He leaned into her, forehead pressing against hers. "I didn't hurt you?"

"No."

"Are you sure?"

"I'm sure," she persisted with a kiss on his cheek before wiping away her tears.

Dexter let out his anxiety in a huff of frigid air. She hadn't slapped him, so that must mean she was telling the truth. He observed each perfect freckle lining the bridge of her nose. "I love you so damn much." He took the back of her hand and brought it to his lips, pressing a soft kiss over the deep marks. "And if you are pregnant, I will be there for you every step of the way this time." He hauled her to the pillows and laid her down.

In a fast motion, she cuddled him under the sheets and Dexter followed suit. Just as her leg wrapped over his, she smiled and her eyes went wide. "I got you something."

"Yeah?" She made a move to leave his arms, but Dexter was quick to tighten them. "Where do you think you're going?"

She giggled. "Well, I have to get it."

Dexter kissed her neck, sucking on it lightly. "No. Don't move."

She did anyway and somehow maneuvered out of his grip within seconds. "I waited six years to give this to you." She hopped out of bed, entered the closet, and came back out with an acoustic guitar. The alder shined in the moonlight streaming in from the window and small white dots were scattered strategically between the frets. It was an identical match to the beaten down, used version of his old guitar.

Dexter's heart pattered with the promise of music at his fingertips. Music. She was bringing music back into his life.

"It's not the exact one you had, but I found the same model." She sighed. "I wanted to learn for the kids. But, I couldn't. I needed a good teacher." She stepped to the bed and held it out for him. "Will you play me something?"

Dexter's fingers wrapped around the neck of the Fender and the steel strings like it was second nature. He brought the instrument to his lap and draped his right arm over the body and stroked the strings. Vibrations buzzed up his arms and rattled his brain with exhilaration. "Oh my god, Sara. This is the best gift I've ever gotten."

Her heart-shaped face was smiling wide enough to reach her sparkling eyes. Her hands came to a prayer position and rested them over her lips, thumbs under her chin. "You like it?"

Dexter would have answered, but he choked up as he stroked the strings downward. If he closed his eyes, it *was* his guitar. And, he had loved his acoustic Fender. It was always there for him during every heartache, every test, every show, every major event. He had his creative outlet back. And it was all thanks to her. If only he had had it during the Screecher Age. It definitely would have come in handy to calm his temper whenever he felt it rise out of control.

A part of him had even forgotten that playing music was how he coped with anger. In an upward stroke, he pressed his fingers down to play a C chord, instantly feeling at peace. The strings let out a semi-unpleasant ring. But, only because it needed tuning.

It didn't matter though. His eyes were already closed, channeling his high school-self who had wished Sara could hear the new song he had written for her. Hearing her laugh spurred him to jump on the bed and strum as he sang *Didn't I*.

One of Sara's hands covered his mouth, giggling with happiness. "You're going to wake the kids, Dex!"

With careful movements, he laid the guitar at the edge of the bed and dismounted. "I got you something too. But, it's not as cool as this."

She rested on her knees, eyes wide with mystery. "You did?"

Dexter went into the closet, grabbed a piece of folded fabric on the top shelf—a place he knew she wouldn't be able to reach. He stepped out and unfolded a gray heather T-shirt. In the center was the logo of his old band, The Iron Vikings, wrapped in a circle. But, instead of a dagger stabbing through the skull, mountains that matched her tattoo were printed in the center. "I figured you could wear this while my band shirt is in the wash. I think all the songs I wrote were about you, so I thought the band logo deserves to match."

Sara's hands fled to her mouth, cheeks searing. In her eyes was something he couldn't decipher.

"I'm sorry. I know. It was stupid. I can think of something better."

In a blur of colors, Sara leaped into Dexter's arms while squealing. He caught her, spinning to slow her momentum. "I love it! Give me!" She reached down to the hand that grasped the shirt, grabbed it, and put it on while still in Dexter's arms.

He smiled and put her down.

She whirled in a circle, modeling for him. "How do I look?"

"Like my biggest fan."

She put a hand on a popped out hip and curled her lip. "Don't flatter yourself."

Dexter grabbed at her, sending her over his shoulder. "Don't do that lip thing." He tossed her onto the bed, loving her deep belly laugh. "You are my biggest fan, and you know it, Marking."

Dexter was on his stomach, passed out in bed, but Sara was finding sleep more difficult. She didn't want to sleep and be stuck in a nightmare again. Being tortured by night terrors wasn't something she was willing to risk after a flawless day. She had spent hours observing the indents on top of her hand, hoping they would last forever. Of all the scars etched into her skin, she would like one she could look at and remember pleasure, not pain.

She moseyed over to the window and sat on the love seat, watching the stars. With hundreds of cities that were either vacated or deserted after the world reverted, seeing the Milky Way was almost always promised. Like tonight, millions of stars shone brightly in clumps that formed a strip of pastel purples beneath a few clouds. It was in that moment that Sara felt secure. Everything was going to be all right with Dexter back.

Sure, her kids had powers and that terrified her, but they were okay in that moment. They were sleeping soundly in the next room with her best friend.

She sucked in a fresh breath of contentment before her eyes flitted to a dark figure pacing in front of the house. She leaned closer to the cool glass, fogging it with her breath, only to make out Guy's face in the moonlight.

Chapter 13

▲▲▲

"Oh balls," she whispered. She would have told Dexter, but anxiety prickled at her feet, urging her to confront Guy alone. Dexter was sleeping, and she didn't want to interrupt his rest in any way. Tonight they had their marvelous date and that's how she wanted it to remain for Dexter. She wanted him to wake up more in love with her, not rudely awakened by some jackass that had been harassing her. Besides, she had years of practice standing up to men. She could handle Guy on her own. It was time to tell him to take a hike.

She slipped into a pair of black leggings and buttoned up Dexter's denim jacket from off the floor. Then, she tiptoed out of the room and down the stairs.

When she opened the door, Guy's hooded navy eyes met hers. He took his hands out of the pockets of his maroon zip-up jacket then nervously placed them in the pockets of his black sweats. "You blocked me?" he grumbled in a breath that seemed to heat the air between them. He hurried up the cemented path until he was only a few feet away from her. "Are you serious?"

Sara rolled her eyes as she shut the door behind her. "Good. You got the message." She tilted her head and directed a bratty grin at him while she crossed her arms. "Are we done now?"

"After six years, Sara. This is how you want our friendship to end?"

"Yes. Is that all you're here for?"

"No." His eyes flitted to the top room where Dexter lay sleeping. "I'm making sure Dexter didn't murder you in your sleep."

She curled a lip and placed a hand on her hip. "For your information, I could kick Dexter's ass if I wanted to. Go home."

Guy sighed as his eyes softened and refocused on hers. He made a move to touch her cheek, but Sara was quicker this time and swatted it away while stepping aside. She pointed a finger at him and clenched her teeth. "Don't ever touch me again." She pointed down the street toward his house. "Go home."

He gave her a hard look. "So that's just it with us. Dexter comes back and what we had is gone."

"Us? There was never an 'us'. You kissed me once, and I told you to get the hell out, and you called me a lovesick idiot. I'm going to make this very clear for you. It was always Dexter. It will always be Dexter."

"You're wrong, Sara. I have a horrible feeling about him. Something is wrong with that man. You don't just stay under Atraeus's control for six years and end up completely fine."

She dropped her arms to her sides, readying to ball her hands into fists. "How do you know that?"

He blinked. "This small town talks, Sara. And with Emily's loose lips, everyone knows. And everyone is scared. For you."

"You're pissing me off."

"Please, Sara. Listen to me. He might be hiding it for the time being, but he's a sick freak."

She pressed her lips together, trying to defuse her rising aggression. The need to protect Dexter and his image emboldened her as she clenched her hands and snarled, "You have no right to talk about him."

"Use your little head."

She crossed her arms over her chest and stood shoulder width apart, elongating her spine. "I am. And it's telling me that it's best if you no longer come around me or my family. You entered my house without permission and at an inappropriate time. I just don't trust you anymore."

His thick brows turned up. "You're only saying that because it's what Dexter wants. He's manipulating you."

Her fingers tingled, needing something to punch, and his bruised face looked good. She let loose a growl, readying to release some of the rage building in her body. "Go home."

"Dexter is—"

She couldn't handle one more word. All she wanted to see was his ass walking home. If he wasn't going to follow directions, then she was going to make him. As her fists tightened and her foot stepped toward Guy, the front door swung open behind her and something caught her wrist before she could make contact.

Dexter marched out of the house and tugged Sara behind him. "That's the third time she's asked you to go home. Be smart and listen to her."

Guy stood his ground, taking his hands out of his pockets and pointing a finger at him. "Stop messing with her head. I don't know what you've done to her, but she can't see through your bullshit."

As if an explosion went off in her brain, Sara saw red and she twisted her hand free. Dexter's arm flailed outward to stop her, but she crouched past him and lunged for Guy. Just before her fist slammed into his eye, Dexter caught the back of her collar and yanked her against him. His arms banded around her front, securing her to his chest. "Leave before she fucks you up," Dexter huffed out.

Guy's eyes shifted to Sara. "Dexter's going to kill you one day."

A vicious snarl barreled out of her throat as she stomped on Dexter's foot, then head-butted him in the face. When he didn't release her, she grabbed his palm and twisted until the pressure had him sinking to one knee.

Free, she sent a fast side-kick into Guy's chest. "Say one more fucking word about Dexter. I dare you!" As Guy doubled over, she kneed him in the nose. His head flung back as he cried out.

Dexter's arms wrapped around her torso, dragging her away from Guy and spinning her toward the house. "Enough, Sara."

"Shut up, Dexter!" she screamed, feeling the rage boil in her brain. Without the element of surprise, it was more

192

difficult to get out of Dexter's grip, but she continued to try even as he rested his chin on her shoulder so her mobility was limited. "Let me go!"

"Calm yourself, Marking," he said in the natural, soothing intonation that made her want to do whatever she could to impress him.

Then, she heard Guy grumble something about Dexter in a vicious tone which caused her anger to surge. Another low growl tore out of her throat. "Hypocrite!" she yelled to Dexter while attempting to break away as his strong arms clamped more tightly.

"He's not worth it. Don't get worked up over this."

Her face tensed, and she felt the blood rushing to it as her whole being stiffened with rage. "He's pissing me off. He's not allowed to talk about you like that."

"He can say whatever the hell he wants about me."

"No, he can't!" She thrashed under his embrace until she tired herself out. "I want to rip him apart."

"I know. And while that is cute as all hell, and I know you could kick his ass," his lips came to her shoulder, sending goosebumps down her arms in rising waves, "I would like you to leave that stuff to me."

"No, Dexter."

"Listen, I don't want you stressed or getting in a fight if you're pregnant."

"Pregnant?" Guy groused loudly in disbelief. "Are you serious, Sara? Are you that dumb?"

Sara flayed again, letting out a long-lost warrior cry. "What'd he just call me?"

Dexter's arms released her while turning to Guy. "Dude! What the hell is your problem?"

Sara spun and admired her handiwork as she took in Guy's swollen eye and nose dripping with crimson blood that reflected the silver light of the moon. But it wasn't enough.

"I hope to god you're not," he muttered, wiping his nose with his forearm.

Sara pitched forward, saying, "I can't believe I ever let you around Kali and Nellie!"

Dexter stuck out a hand, twisting the fabric of the denim jacket to keep her from advancing. "Get the fuck off our lawn," he ordered Guy.

Guy took a deep breath and roved his gaze all over Sara. "Come to me when you've figured it out. I'll be happy to take over and take better care of our kids."

That sentence took Sara a minute to process as it sped through a head full of roiling repugnance and hatred.

In a slow, steady stream of words, Dexter cocked his head and said, "What did you just say?"

Guy's eyes went wide, hearing what he had said.

"Did you say Nellie and Kali were y,*ours*?" Sara questioned in the clearest enunciations she had ever articulated.

His brows set back to their typical determinate fashion. "I've been with them for six years. For all intents and purposes, I've been their father. They are my kids! And I *will* fight for them."

Sara reached over her shoulder, doing her best to claw at the hand wrapped around her jacket. "Dexter. Let me go! I'm going to kill him." She tried to maneuver out of the jacket, but his rigid arm secured her around the belly.

"You and I could be something," he continued. "Something great."

"Now look who's the lovesick idiot," she snorted in derision and spat at his feet just as Dexter hauled her into the house, shutting the door with a hard slam and locking it.

Then, he grabbed Sara and secured her to his chest. "Ignore him."

She wedged her hands between their bodies and tried to push Dexter away. "How come you get to beat on him, but I'm not allowed to? Dexter! He said they were *his* kids! Doesn't that piss you off? Move the fuck away from the door!"

"No." Dexter hushed her before letting her go. "And lower your voice. The kids are sleeping."

Sara placed a determined hand on her hip. "Move your ass, Dexter."

"It doesn't matter what he said, okay? Nothing's going to change the fact that we are together and *we* have two beautiful children. He can go fuck himself." He tucked her safely against his chest again, one hand around her shoulders and the other on the back of her head. "Let's go back to bed."

"I don't feel like sleeping," she muttered as tears streamed down her cheeks. "I'm fucking *angry*."

He rocked her to the beat of unplayed music. "I know, Marking. But we aren't in survival mode anymore. We never have to be again. You can get angry without killing him."

Sara softened against him with every sway. "How are you the calm one between the two of us?"

195

"I'm learning. And, you're a good role model to admire."

She could hear the cheer in his voice, and it caused the anger to simmer down. "How is that possible after I smashed his face in with my knee?"

Dexter chuckled. "Because I'm a bad role model."

Sara grinned as the guilt for the whole situation settled into her chest. "I'm so sorry he said that." She screwed her eyes shut as she felt the detrimental words forming behind her teeth. Words that were unkind after she knew what he had gone through to get back to her and the kids. But, before she could stop herself, they came out. "I wish you hadn't left me. Ever. This never would have happened—Guy would have been a nobody." She knew that was going to hurt him. She could feel it. She was fighting unfairly. "I wish you had stayed! You should have been with me. If you had been here, he wouldn't think he had a right to Nellie and Kali."

"I know," he said still rocking her. He took a deep breath as if he was breathing her in. "But, honestly, I'm just glad you waited for me and that you decided to have our kids. Nothing else—no one else matters. Only my family. And, I promise I will protect all of you." Dexter laid a soft kiss atop her head. "If Guy tries to pull anything, I'm here. You're not alone anymore."

Her love for Dexter expanded larger than she thought was possible. His understanding and calmness in direct contrast to her level of irrationality soothed her anxiety. "Thank you, Dexter."

The night grew darker as he held her in place. When her knees buckled, he carried her to the couch where she remained in his loving embrace until they fell asleep.

Sara awoke to Emily's voice and the morning sun streaming through the sheer white curtains. "Love birds," she sneered with an eye roll as she put her shoes on.

Dexter shifted beneath her, half asleep and holding onto her more tightly.

"Jealous," Sara chided while resting her tired head on Dexter's shoulder.

"I'm out of here. Kids are still asleep."

"Thanks, Emily."

Emily blew her a kiss and left.

When the door closed behind her, Dexter murmured, "Did Emily just leave?"

"Yeah."

"My nose still hurts from your headbutt last night."

Sara turned her head to kiss the tip of his nose. "I'm sorry. Want me to get you ice?"

"No," he nuzzled his face into her neck, "that means you'd have to get up."

Sara laughed as she rolled in his arms to face him. "Thank you for the best date ever. I'm sorry Guy ruined the night."

Dexter smiled. "Are you kidding me? I love watching my blonde pixie soldier at her finest." He sleepily kissed her forehead. "I'm so attracted to you. Every side of you." He moved to her lips and sucked on the bottom one until she let out a moan. He gave a satisfied smile before saying, "So, what do you want to do today?"

She shifted her body until she was mounted on top of his. "I know what I want to do," she whispered in his ear.

His hands wondered over her sides, down her waist, and rested on her hips. "What's that?"

She leaned down and nibbled on his ear. "You."

"Here? Now? With the kids sleeping upstairs?" He cocked a devious smile. "Dangerous."

The kids' door flung opened, and Dexter practically tossed Sara to the other side of the couch. Nellie stepped out in a pair of his wizard patterned pajamas and rubbed his sleepy eyes. "Mommy? Can we go to the park today?"

Sara and Dexter gaped at each other, trying their best to contain their laughter. "Yeah. We can go after breakfast. And as long as you don't eat the worms this time," Sara agreed with giggles threading through the sentence.

Dexter and Sara watched the kids run around their town's playground equipped with a metal slide, monkey bars, and a sand pit. The area was slightly out of the way from the downtown, surrounded by trees and a field of grass that was half brown. Sara curled herself into Dexter's side as they sat on a wooden bench that creaked with the weight of their bodies.

"Zeek and I redid this park," Sara whispered.

Dexter's brows rose in surprise. "Yeah?"

She nodded. "Everything was rusted and the slide was falling to pieces. The sandpit was a larva trap. He helped me bring it back to life."

"At that point, why didn't you just build a new one in the backyard?"

She laid her arm straight on Dexter's thigh and yawned as if she was beginning to fall sleep. "The backyard is really small and at least this gives us a place to go."

"An outing is always good. Plus, if any kids come to town..."

Sara let out a snort. "There's not many women around here if you hadn't noticed. Nonetheless any who are willing to reproduce."

"Maybe one day."

"Nellie!" Kali whined, taking a handful of sand and chucking it at her brother's face. All at once, Kali's face fell into a deep, wistful frown as her arms reached out to her brother who was falling to his knees, holding his eyes in pain. "Sorry! I didn't mean to!"

Dexter jumped to his feet, letting Sara fall to the bench.

"I hate you!" Nellie screamed as he shot out a green beam from his palm into Kali's arm.

The famous Mar King growl rolled out of Kali's little chest as she shot a beam back at her brother just before Dexter could pick him up. "I said I didn't mean to, Nellie!"

Sara sprang into action just as the surrounding pine trees lit up in a green glow. Her hand came down on Kali's forearm, pulling her to her side.

"You two *cannot* do that outside the house, do you understand me?" Dexter barked as if he were a drill sergeant ready to make them drop and do push-ups.

"But, Daddy—" Nellie complained.

"No! Our rules were very clear. We are going home." His kids' eyes turned into wet marbles, looking at each other as if in a silent conversation. In that instant, Dexter prayed Nellie would keep his peli plant hallucinations to himself.

He looked to Sara, signaling it was time to go home. But, a crease formed down the middle of his brows when he saw her gaze was elsewhere. Her body went stiff as she cried, "Dexter!" A tremor of hesitancy rolled through his name. She didn't use that gravely tone for any reason other than desperation and disbelief.

Dexter turned in dire need to know what had spooked her to such an extreme degree. A tall, built man wearing all black stood by the nearest tree like an ominous shadow glaring at Kali. As the figure stepped forward, Dexter made out Guy's beaten face. Stings of panic raced down Dexter's arms as Guy blinked and ignited his eyes in a neon green light show.

Chapter 14

▲▲▲

It took a moment for Dexter to understand if he was really witnessing Guy with glowing eyes. "Nellie? Are you doing this?"

Kali screeched, "He's going to hurt Mommy!"

"Kids, stay behind us!" Dexter snapped out of impulse. Nellie hid behind Dexter's legs and Kali behind her mother's. Sara came shoulder to shoulder with Dexter to make a stronger wall for the twins to hide behind.

A sinister smile tugged at the corners of Guy's thin lips and vibrant orbs manifested in his hands as a nasty cackle barreled out of his throat. Nellie's grasp on Dexter's jeans tightened. In an instant, the dark bruises on Guy's olive skin melted away, leaving behind untouched smoothness.

"Atraeus?" Dexter growled.

Guy's head tilted down, looking at him from beneath his brows. "The one and only," he cheered while the orbs grew to the size of snow globes. Flakes tore off the spheres, floating away for a brief moment before getting sucked back by their pulsating gravitational pull.

He noticed Sara bend her knees into a loose fighting position as if preparing for battle.

"Why are you still here? Our deal is finished!"

Guy cocked a brow. "Is it?" His hands rose in a swift movement and sent the two orbs into Dexter and Sara's chest, trapping them in their own bodies. Frozen.

Shit! Dexter thrashed within his skin, trying everything to break free, but it was futile. The kids screamed as Guy approached.

Bang! The swing of Sara's father's hammer flew past his nose. The playground blurred, the trees muddied, and Guy's face smudged in a moving paintbrush stroke until his surroundings resembled Sara's parents' kitchen. Her teenaged scream barreled through her core, shrieking for her father to stop.

"Daddy!" a different, smaller voice squealed. A voice he would recognize anywhere. His son's. He followed the sound, which led him to the corner of the room where he spotted Nellie huddled into a ball.

"Nellie! You and your sister, run in different directions!"

Dexter's environment snapped back to the playground surrounded by pine trees with Guy's gruff face standing directly in front of him.

"Kali, run that way!" Nellie shrieked as his grasp on Dexter's leg released.

From Dexter's peripherals, he saw Nellie sprinting.

A smug smile broke over Guy's face. "Nice try." His hands shot out to the sides and a spindle of energy flashed like a lightning bolt while weaving through air like a horrific spell.

The two paths of electricity assaulted the kids, dragging them to his side like a lasso. Nellie's limbs flailed, trying to escape the energy engulfing him and his sister inside a growing sphere.

Kali came into Dexter's view. An expression he hadn't yet discovered was forming over her face. Her features fell still, more fearless than Sara's soldier façade.

She was concentrating.

Watching.

Learning.

Seeing what Atraeus wanted to do.

What she could do.

He positioned the kids on either side of his hips. Into view came the flash of a silver bladed pocket knife gleaming green from the spheres that encompassed his kids. Guy disappeared from Dexter's line of vision as he side-stepped to Sara. "What a disappointment you turned out to be. I gave your pretty face too many chances to be obedient. You and I could have been something. You had such potential to be the perfect mother. What a shame."

Suddenly, Kali's face morphed into a desperate cry. "Mommy!" Her nose scrunched, her jaw fell open, and tears fell to the bottom of her sphere. "No!" She lifted her hand and Nellie copied, sending beams from their palms into Guy, but all it did was make him laugh as he approached Sara, blade in hand.

Don't! Don't fucking touch her! Dexter couldn't see, but he heard the quiet sound of her flesh ripping open.

The twins squirmed and jerked at the energy entangling them. "Mommy!" Kali screamed, like her high-pitched yell would break Guy's attention. She bashed her hands against the sphere, but all it did was redden her precious fists.

Guy came back into view, lifting the knife covered in Sara's blood. "Remember this?" The blade plunged deep into Dexter's forearm then was wielded down to his wrist.

"Daddy!" Nellie screamed.

Guy dropped the knife and tilted his head to the side, green eyes sparking like wasted electricity. "You like my new trick? Your fear let me perfect every millimeter of this world. Every touch of your hand felt something, didn't it? Every detail in the thread counts of your sheets. Every memory I didn't haze. You were just so willing to turn a blind eye to be with your precious Sara. You were just going to live on forever, pretending this was your reality, weren't you? Didn't even catch a whiff of the artificial."

What the fuck? Dexter's mind reeled into pitch darkness.

Guy's lips twitched to a grin. "I'm getting better. You're making me stronger." In a spiral of his hands, the twins dissipated into thin air, like Guy erased them off the chalkboard of the pretend world he had built to deceive Dexter.

No, no, no, no.

Guy morphed into his true form in a quick swirl of colors. A green orb that pulsed like a swimming jellyfish, stars weaving in and out of its body and circling in the air around it. "Did you forget I'm the Father of Fear? Are you enjoying my playground?"

A prickle of fear spiked painfully down Dexter's limbs. *No!*

"I'm going to let this one ride out a bit, because your fear right now is fantastic. You've got two more years, big guy. I can't wait for you to see what I have planned." In a flash, the sphere shrunk into a vacuum in space and blinked out of view.

Chapter 15

▲▲▲

The words settled in his ears and proliferated through his body in a vicious virus threatening to shut down his organs. All that was left was the fake sound of his heart pounding in his ears. Beating closer to detonation.

Nellie? Kali? Dexter's heart fragmented into tiny glass pieces that he couldn't ever put back together again. Not even Sara could fix it. *My children. My Marking. It was all fake.*

His body freed and he crumpled to the ground in desperate sobs that battled through his closing throat. Everything was blackness. All around him. He wanted to reach into his chest and rip out his heart. Gut-wrenching depression seeped into his veins, hardening his blood.

None of it was real.

Lost.

He was lost without his perfect little family, all a show to squeeze out as much fear as possible. And it worked.

He leaned his back against the corner of the sandbox, head buried in his arms, sobbing for his fake family that expired his heart. "No, no, no." Ruthless fear fled through him without hesitation. Atraeus earned it. It successfully broke him. His everlasting love for Sara. The unwavering desire to have a family with her. He fucking earned it.

Dexter screwed his eyes shut, trying to use any sort of energy to rewind time back to the first day. Back to kissing his nonexistent twins goodnight. Back to making love to Sara. Back to laughing with her and braiding his fake daughter's hair.

Then, Sara's warm touch came to his cheek, trying to force him to meet her gaze. But he didn't look up. He couldn't bear looking at how perfectly Atraeus conjured her. She was only there to drive him closer to insanity—to suck every last ounce out of him.

Dexter snatched her into his arms and brought her on his lap, hugging her close, already missing her tremendously. Wisps of her floral scent overwhelmed him until it drew him close enough to bury his face into her shoulder. "Please don't disappear yet," he cried. He clawed at Sara's scarred skin just to have something to hold on to. To take his rage out on. "Don't. Don't leave me. I can't keep going."

Her muffled voice was distant, and that was the way he preferred it. He had no intention of listening. Whatever she was saying was what Atraeus wanted her to say. His hands migrated to under her shirt and flattened on her back. The scars beneath his fingertips were rough, but so real. Fuck! She couldn't feel anything. She couldn't feel him. She was miles away. He dug his fingernails into her back, praying it would mean she would stay for just a little while longer. Before he figured out how to take his own life.

"I'm so sorry. I give up. Atraeus broke me." He squeezed her until he couldn't breathe. "I can't keep thinking I have you then finding out it's all fake. Especially when this life was so perfect. Fuck, I would have loved this life with you."

He brought his eyes to her electric jades, and they were glossed over with wetness. One glance. That was all he allowed himself. He buried his nose against her collarbone, watching his tears drip onto her scarred chest. "Sara. If you can hear me, go to Mount Verta and drop a boulder in there. Please. End this for me. Please." His heart twisted into a shattered mess, wishing somehow Sara would answer his prayer. "Please."

Her hand came to his cheek again, pulling it up to meet hers, like Atraeus was doing everything he could to wring every last drop of hurt from his soul.

Fine.

He looked at her.

He watched her pretty, dark lashes bat over her gorgeous eyes.

He observed every fucking perfected detail of her. Even the small hazel starburst surrounding her pupil that he only noticed when he was this close to her. He hugged her tighter, feeling for the last time that her body perfectly fit his. He wouldn't survive another second—nonetheless the two more years he had left. "End this for me," he whispered in profound desperation. This is what he thought dying felt like. Losing absolutely everyone he loved.

Her lips were moving, but no words registered.

And all at once, like Atraeus turned up the volume, Sara's voice came screaming into his ear. "Dexter! Listen to me!"

He groaned, tears dampening the sleeve of the T-shirt he had made her. "No. I'm done listening. I'm done feeling. Let me die, right here. Right with you. When you leave, I'll leave."

Her chest rumbled with a growl. "Shut the fuck up! Don't say that to me! You're not in the fucking pit! He's messing with your head, Dexter!"

Fuck, did he wish that to be true. But, he had seen it. He had seen his children turn into orbs. Humans didn't do that. "I'm sorry, I wasn't strong enough to make it back to you. I tried, Sara. I promise I tried my best."

"Dammit, look at me!"

Dexter did. He would do anything she asked of him right now. Atraeus or not. He would pretend. His gaze drifted over her face. Blood dripped down her cheek from a large gash that split her flesh from her temple to the corner of her lip in a harsh zigzag line.

Dexter's chest clenched as he wiped the warm blood away, only to see that his nails were already covered in blood. He looked at them, unsure where it had come from. That was what told him that his mind was getting dragged back to the pit. Things were expected not to make sense.

"Dexter! It's me. You are not in the pit," she cried. "Please! He took your son. Your daughter! Get it together!"

Dexter stopped his tears as soon as hers commenced. "Don't cry, Marking. I want to see you happy before a new vision starts."

"For heaven's sake!" She made a move to get up from his lap, but Dexter wrapped his arms around her like steel bars and forced her to remain in his embrace. "Dexter. How do I prove this is real to you?"

He shook his head. "Everything is fake. It always is. You're never real."

The sound of her voice cracking was done flawlessly. "Dexter. Every second you don't figure this out, the more time Atraeus has to hurt our children."

"I don't have two children with you, do I? Fuck, I wish I did though. I'd love them so much. I'd take care of you all so well. My perfect pixie soldier."

Gritty angst poured from her mouth. "I'm giving you one more minute to figure out this is your real life before I slap the shit out of you. Now, you listen here, Dexter fucking Bennet. You were in the pit at the top of Mount Verta, but it *has* been six years. You have a daughter. Kali. You have a son. Nellie. And they *need* you! We have a war to fight."

Sara's eyes widened and closed throughout her speech, but all he could think about was how perfect she was.

"Dammit. When you figure it out, come find me. We've wasted enough time." She let out a roar of frustration.

Chapter 16

▲▲▲

Atraeus was good. She had never seen Dexter so lost before. His cerulean eyes turned dark with rage and pain and something else morose. Dexter believed he was still in the pit. His body seemed to be collapsing in on itself. And, when he asked her to kill him, a part of her broke. She would never know the true torture he had endured unless she lived it. But, she did know the amount of torture someone had to live through to want to end their life. This was the outcome of what Atraeus had done to him. It had its hooks in him deep. Blinding him so deeply to the point where reality was no longer a realm of existence.

Seeing Dexter suffer and having zero idea on how to free him was crushing. Tears burned her eyes like draining acid, but she didn't have time to let it take over. When he figured it out, he would be glad she had gotten a move on. She maneuvered from his grip and marched into the street for some clue to where their children were. Where Atraeus was. She growled and turned her back on Dexter. Warm blood poured down her back from the burning trails where Dexter had dug his nails into her. Her shirt clung to her skin in so many places. Down her elbow, drops of blood dripped to the floor. Dexter's crimson blood from his wounded forearm drenched her left shoulder.

She felt wrecked. Haggard. Alone. The blade Guy had carved into her cheek was enough to turn her mind to a helpless heap of sharp pieces. But, for the sake of her kids and Dexter, she swallowed the agony as best she could.

"Sara?" Dexter called, and she whirled around, her body a magnet controlled by his husky timber.

Dexter got to his feet, one hand covering his forearm, and rushed to her in a few long strides. His arms came snaking around her. Yes. Please. In his eyes, it seemed as though something had distorted, bent in the right direction. Sara was waiting to hear him say that this was reality and not the trick that had been played on him.

Wild ocean eyes traveled along her shoulder, like he was in a bobbing lifeboat helplessly screaming for an uncertain rescue. "You're hurt. Who did this to you?"

Sara's pain transformed into a deep rage. "You did! You idiot!" she wailed. "You scratched me really fucking hard."

Her words seemed to have punctured a hole into his boat. Down his mental stability went, dragged down by the storming seas of his vast mind. "I did?"

"Yes! Now make it up to me and help me find our kids."

He brushed away a few tendrils of her bangs, and it almost sent Sara to her knees, begging for him to say he believed her.

Instead, what he said was, "Sara, I'm so sorry. Let's get a peli plant on it."

She rolled her eyes and dropped her jaw, bending her legs while balling her fists and shoving him in the chest. "For the love of god. There *are* no peli plants anymore!" Her hand raced through the air, slapping Dexter's cheek with striking pain. "Snap out of it! I can't get Nellie and Kali back without you."

Slowly, he looked back with a hand covering his bare cheek.

"I just lost our kids. I can't lose you too."

His blue eyes shifted as if the sun rose on his storm and the rescue boat threw a life preserver ring. But he remained silent with the whiplash of confusion.

She let out a grunt of frustration and began moving. Any step in any direction would be a step closer to her children.

Dexter's fingers curled around her upper arm and tugged her back to him. With brows pulled down in determination and a strict rigidity in his jaw, he mumbled, "This is real?"

With eyes widened into saucers, Sara screamed, "Yes! He's messing with your head and it's working."

"This is real," he said more as a statement rather than a question.

"Yes, Dexter!"

"It's really you."

In came a deep breath, readying to enunciate clearly and push him off the cusp of illusion. "Yes. We have kids together. We have Kali and Nellie. They are *real*."

She blinked, unsure where his mind was taking him.

"Say you believe me!"

His expression relaxed and said in a torrent of words, "I believe you, Sara." Even though a minute part of her wondered if he had just said that to appease her, it was good enough for now.

Bang! The hammer. One of the many weapons Sara's father used to control her flung past her head. She shrieked and ducked out of the way, long blonde tresses swaying down her back. "Sara! Room. Now!"

She held her own arms to keep from shaking. "Leave me alone!"

A warm hand touched hers, and the memory of her peli plant experience came to the forefront of her mind. The reassuring touch of Dexter's hand reminded her he was there and that what she was seeing was her mind playing tricks.

"Mommy!" Nellie's voice screamed.

She turned and saw her son bawling in the corner. She ran to him just as the entire scene thawed to a field of orange poppies. She brought him in her arms and snuggled him tight. "Nellie? Are you okay?"

He shook his precious freckled face.

She pressed him harder into her. "Where are you? Daddy and I are coming."

"We don't know." The poppies dripped like liquifying paint to reveal a place she knew all too well. Beneath her feet were thousands of English daisies scattered over luscious blades of sparkling grass. Only one man could have created something this extraordinary. She recognized his creations in a split second. Nell Maddows. And, this splendid scene was his creation at the top of Mount Verta. Her eyes dashed to her surroundings to reaffirm herself. Before she could take it all in, the image snapped away, and she was between Dexter's arms.

Sara gasped and locked eyes with him. "They're on the mountain."

"Verta?" Dexter asked in faltering words full of cautious belief. It didn't matter if he couldn't truly accept his life as reality. Sara knew he would see it in time and at least right now he was cooperating.

"Yes."

"That's really far from here."

Sara's eyes teared. "I know."

Dexter's scanned the park, contemplating. "Zeek has a car. We used it to bring the flowers for our date."

Sara dialed Zeek's number. As the seconds ticked by with each ring, it became tougher to breathe. "Pick up, pick up."

Voicemail.

She called Emily.

Voicemail.

She placed her phone back in her pocket, gazing hopelessly lost at Dexter.

"Come on." He tapped her arm and took off running toward Zeek's shop.

With feet of boulders, she painfully trudged forward. Her heart throbbed closer to bursting. Her lungs weighed with a treacherous ache that inflicted a searing heat to well in her eyes.

Shapes blurred.

Colors blended.

Her world was claimed by thick darkness.

The only thing keeping her anchored was Dexter's hand in hers, dragging in a direction toward help.

They banged on the locked glass door and attempted to open it several times. It took a dreadful minute, but Zeek huffed to the door to let them in. A second later, Emily's ebony hair bobbed behind him with an embarrassed smile and burnished cheeks. Sara didn't have the mental capacity to even entertain anything other than the dire situation at hand.

"What the hell happened to your face, Sara?" Emily screeched as she covered her own mouth with her hand.

In that moment, she lost it. Everything. The pain came screaming back to her face. Her mind spun out of her head and a gigantic hole ate at her heart. "He took my babies!" Sara shrieked in an agonizing cry as she fell to her knees, sobbing with her hands buried in her hands. "Atraeus took my babies!"

"What?" Zeek uttered in a breath of disbelief.

Dexter got on his haunches beside her, a hand on her back as she rocked back and forth. "Get it together, Marking. I need your courageous mind cleared and focused."

Dexter was right. She needed to uncloud the fog of desolation fast and get back into her hardened soldier brain. But, she had to face the sad truth. Dexter softened her bulletproof exterior. Her kids smoothed out all her jagged edges. That fearless soldier Dexter met six years ago died when she thought he had. That part of her went extinct a long time ago. It had been a lifetime since she had done her damn hardest to block out every trace of who she was from the Screecher Age.

She no longer thought of herself as brave. She had been a grieving, single mother for six years. Every day, it disassembled her to tiny pieces. It wore her confidence down to a nub. Every time she pictured Dexter's head cracked open at the bottom of the pit. She had failed him. There was nothing left in her that she could conjure to transform her back into the well-trained sacrifice Atraeus had wanted her to be. The same Atraeus who called himself Guy and had hacked away at her self-confidence for six successful years.

"Wake up that soldier that I know is sleeping in you. Our kids need her."

"She's gone," Sara cried. "I don't have powers. I don't have energy and I am *not* brave." With her scarred palms, she wiped at tears and focused on Dexter's eyes, but she wasn't able to discern what they were trying to tell her. "How are we going to fight it, Dexter? How! That one thing took over our entire planet. Killed *so* many people. How are we going to stop him? Dexter! It's a losing battle." A desperate cry of agony blew through her chest as she fell into Dexter's side. "He took them," she sobbed. "He took our children!"

Warm hands covered her back.

Dexter.

Emily.

Zeek.

All wishing to send her their energy to get the kids back.

"You're right," Emily said, kneeling beside her. "You're not a soldier. You're a goddamn mother."

"And Atraeus just messed with the wrong one," Zeek huffed out in complete confidence.

Dexter's folded index finger lifted her chin until she was looking into his determined eyes. "Get your brave ass up, Marking. I need our kids to prove this is our real life. I need to see them. I need to hold them. I need to kiss them. That's the only way I'll know this life that I've been praying for isn't an illusion. Fight for them. Fight for me. Fight for my humanity this time." He swallowed hard. "Sara, I need you."

Yes. Dexter had a way about his words that always seeped into her soul and awoke some withdrawn part of her. And it unleashed in a zealous frenzy that fed off fearlessness and bravery. And, damn, she wanted to impress him. She always did. She wanted him to continue to think she could do the impossible. With Dexter's love, maybe she could. With her friends behind her, maybe she could kickstart the solider lying dormant in her and find enough strength to take on Atraeus and save their children. Dexter needed her. Her children needed her. That was enough to rip the world apart.

Dexter guided her up by her elbow as she dried her eyes with the back of her hand. "You're right. All of you are."

"Atta girl," Dexter praised. "Let's fuck him up."

Zeek put a hand on Dexter's shoulder. "How can we help?"

"They're at Mount Verta. We need your car."

Zeek reached into his pocket and pulled out a ring of keys. He spun off the black clicker and handed it to Dexter. "It's in the back parking lot."

"Thanks, man."

Emily left and came back with an entire roll of toilet paper. She shoved the roll into Dexter's hand. "Wrap your arm. Then give it to Sara for her face."

Dexter gave her a flash of a sullen grin, took the roll, and gave a wad to Sara.

"What else can we do?" Emily queried.

"Stay by your phone," Dexter urged as he grasped Sara's hand and took off around the corner into the nearly empty gravel parking lot.

They got into Zeek's black SUV, Dexter in the driver's side. While Sara settled into her seat, he wrapped his arm, throwing the rest of the roll in the back seat.

"Want me to drive?" Sara nodded at Dexter's injured arms, clicking the seatbelt secure in the passenger seat.

He stuck the key in the ignition and put on his own seatbelt. "Nellie tried talking to you earlier." Dexter backed out of the spot and got on the main road that led through the downtown toward the wall on the outskirts of the city. "Let's not have you hallucinate while driving."

"Good thinking," Sara said, sinking in the seat. "You think Atraeus already killed them?"

"No, I don't. But, you are my optimistic compass. We both need that right now. We don't know anything yet. Stay positive."

Sara put her elbow on the sill near the window and rested her head in her hand with a soft groan. When Dexter didn't say anything to distract her, the jagged wound on her cheek blazed, fraying her nerves. "My face, Dexter."

He took a hand off the wheel and placed it on Sara's shoulder. "I'm so sorry. Look in the glove compartment. See if he has a first aid kit. Maybe there's painkillers in there."

Sara leaned forward and unlatched the compartment. With a quick rummage through, she found some napkins under the car manual. "It hurts," she whispered as she shut the drawer with a mild slam.

His eyes flitted off the road and onto her for a second. She could see his gaze in her peripherals, and it numbed some of the pain. "I know. Fuck, Sara. I wish I could have stopped him. I wish I hadn't been so easily tricked. And I'm so sorry I scratched you that hard."

"My face hurts more right now."

Dexter fell quiet, focused on increasing his speed down the street toward Mount Verta. Minutes passed and the tension in the air amid them built. Dexter's mind was loud.

Guilt.

All of it.

Guilt for not seeing through Atraeus's deception quicker.

Guilt for hurting her.

Guilt for not protecting his family.

Sure, her face was pulsing fire with every beat of her heart, but the loss of her children was agonizing in its own surreal reality. She wanted to help him, but the pain was extraordinary. Everything she wanted to say was just going to weigh more heavily on Dexter's shoulders. She bit her tongue.

"We're going to get them back, right?"

She faked a grin, pressing the paper harder against her face. "Right." She leaned her temple on the cool glass, sending a silent prayer into the universe for her children's safety.

Buildings passed and all she could think about was that they weren't going fast enough. It felt like they had been driving for an eternity already, and yet they were still in the same town. They hadn't even reached the wall. Few people walked on the sidewalks even though it was a sunny afternoon. Dexter could go faster, but Sara kept that comment to herself, for fear of upsetting him more.

As they approached the edge of the downtown and ventured toward the massive wall that lead toward the mountain, the engine revved into high speed and roared in her ears. Sara jolted up from her slouched position despite the force sending her against the seat. Their speed increased from thirty to fifty-five in a matter of seconds. Her head snapped to Dexter, whose eyes were anything but focused on the road. They were blinking fast, his hands slipping off the wheel.

"Dexter!"

No response. He lazily fixated on the road like he was under a blinding trance.

Sara leapt for the wheel, make-shift bandage falling from her cheek. Her fingers wrapped around the wheel, doing her best to keep it straight with the restriction of her seatbelt locking.

"Pick up the hammer, Sara," Dexter muttered.

A terrified jolt zapped her core. He was reaching fifty miles per hour, the wall approaching fast. "Dexter!"

"Good job. Hit him hard, Sara," he groused.

She peered at his foot heavy on the gas pedal. With a closed fist, she hit his thigh for any hope to signal him to lift it, but it wasn't working. Sara looked back at the road, eyeing the five patrol men at the top of the wall turning with their guns drawn toward their car out of habit. Sara's fist slammed on the horn, letting the sound vibrate her bones and resonate in all the corners of her mind. The men lowered their weapons and began shouting incoherent warnings for them to stop. Even if they had begun opening the doors, it would never have been fast enough.

The top of the wall disappeared from view and all she saw out the windshield was a sea of green painted metal flaking apart by rust.

Knowing these were her last moments, her mind processed in slow motion. With every centimeter their car barreled closer to the wall, she thought of Dexter. She thought of her children. Between the two of them, Dexter was far more capable of rescuing the kids. Of raising them. So she made the only decision that she had ever been confident in.

With a grunt, Sara tugged the wheel toward the left so her corner of the vehicle crunched against sturdy wall first.

Her vision resembled a glitching screen. Flashes of different scenes passed by her eyes as her sense of sound muted everything except for the drumming of her heartbeat. And it drummed until all that was left was her dissipating being.

There she was.

Then, there she wasn't.

Chapter 17

▲▲▲

It was the outrageous pain that Dexter noticed first. It came in radiating pulses and expanded to every cell in his throbbing muscles.

Had it started again? A new vision?

All was dark. Just like the pit.

That sinking feeling of being Atraeus's enslaved fear producing possession fucked with his human mind in ways he couldn't comprehend. Expecting the scent of the four other sacrifices' decaying bodies to hit him, burning metal surprised him instead.

Slitted lids.

A mix of red and blue hues strobes exploded around him like fleeting stars. Dexter attempted to lift his head, but the world spun around him like a whirlpool amassing all the colors from his sight. Too stiff to move his neck, he rested his forehead against something rough, a type of fabric he couldn't decipher. He tried again and saw a screen of white with splotches of crimson liquid splattered across it in an arching pattern. His blood? Just above the white material, he saw the resemblance of a steering wheel.

He groaned, not ready for this new vision to begin. Whatever it was, he already felt he was far under prepared. As a nasty headache drilled through his skull, he rolled his forehead on the wheel and riveted his eyes on a horrifying scene. Sara's tiny frame was slumped forward, limp in the passenger seat with her seatbelt preventing her from falling forward.

Eyes closed.

Lips parted.

Slender arms limp by her sides.

Blood streamed over her lids in two paths from the top of her head and branched out in different directions, dripping to the floor.

Smeared across an airbag was more of her blood in a gory stroke of a hand.

His vision narrowed, black at the edges and terrifyingly cold. The longer he examined Sara's unmoving body, the faster he fell into a cavernous hole—the pit Atraeus had chained him in for far too long.

The world felt hollow. Like a spoon had scraped out every corner of his being and tossed it to the wolves.

Violent quakes of panic crashed into his chest, breaking through the gray cobwebs that obscured his dazed mind. Adrenaline spiked in a painful wave throughout his body, giving him enough strength to lean back in his chair. "Sara?" he muttered, unsure if he had said anything at all.

Blaring sirens came screaming into his ears.

He put a trembling hand on Sara's shoulder. "Sara..." It came out as a faint whisper even though his intention was a loud, clear scream.

A man yanked on Sara's door several times before it opened. He put his hand onto Sara's head to keep her neck from bending.

Muffled voices emerged from his left, but they were a mix of disjointed, muddled sounds.

Hands on his arms had him twisting his sore neck to his now opened door. Paramedics were talking to him, but he couldn't answer, only grunt. A few more moments and a single voice sharpened.

"Are you okay? Can you hear me?"

"Help her."

"We are helping both of you."

Dexter made a move to exit the vehicle and the paramedics stepped aside, keeping a hand on his shoulder for support. Cool air hit his face as he stood beneath the darkening sky. The residual blurs in his vision refined as he fixated on the fragments of glittering glass scattered throughout the grass. Horrified, he looked to the front of the vehicle. The front corner of Sara's side was crushed against the wall in dozens of metal wrinkles. He wheeled to Sara, ducking his head under the hood of the car to ensure she was awake, but she wasn't moving. In a panic, he pushed away the insistent hands of the medics, rushed around the car, and threw the two other men hovering over Sara backward by their collars. Vision or not, he would ensure her safety in every world Atraeus created.

"Sir!" one said.

He grabbed Sara's face between his hands. "Sara? Sara!"

No response. Not even a flutter of her eyelids.

Each time he said her name, his heart sank. "Sara! Dammit, Sara. Wake up."

"Sir! We need to help her!"

He checked her pulse, relieved to find a very shallow one. That was enough reassurance for now, so he stepped away and the two men rushed to her side. He watched, terrified that she was still limp and unresponsive.

Was this what Atraeus wanted him to see? Sara dead?

They carefully took her out of the car and put her on a gurney and wheeled her toward the back of an ambulance. Time stilled in that moment as he trailed his fingers along her scarred skin.

The memory of her voice tangled around him from all sides. *Snap out of it! I can't get Nellie and Kali back without you.* A surface level sting of a Mar King slap tingled on his cheek. Dexter had to touch it just to confirm this memory was his, not Atraeus's.

Dexter screwed his eyes shut and rested his fists against his sockets. "Fuck," he whispered under his breath. Nellie and Kali. What was real? Were they real? Was this real? "Fuck!" he shrieked, but no one took notice with the sirens wailing and the calamity of medical professionals chattering. He blinked again, remembering his precious children. Remembering Sara saying they were on Mount Verta helplessly waiting for him. His real children. This was real. He couldn't risk believing in the alternative.

As Sara was loaded into the back of the ambulance, the unthinkable reality trampled him. Sara needed to go to the hospital. Their mission to get their kids was over. He had to go with her.

But their kids.

How could he leave Sara's side? Like this? How? His feet remained stapled to the ground unsure whether to take off toward Mount Verta or go to the hospital. He needed her to get his kids back. She knew how to do everything. She knew how to talk him off any ledge. How to keep him optimistic. How to fight. And, fuck, she was so clever. Clever enough to get out of any sticky situation they might find themselves in. He wouldn't be successful without her, especially with the constant worry over her. He couldn't decide this on his own.

Dexter whipped out his phone and dialed Zeek.

In a quick, deep rasp, he said, "What do you need?"

"We got in a crash at the wall. I think Nellie was showing me something, and I couldn't see the road. A-a-and now Sara's not moving!"

"Shit, man."

Dexter turned toward the path that led toward the mountain. "They're taking her to the hospital. W-what do I do? I can't leave her."

"She'd want you to go get your kids, and you know that."

He did know that. And that was what he would have ended up choosing, but hearing Zeek say it took some of the weight off his shoulders.

"Emily will meet her at the hospital, and I will drive you to where you need to go in case Nellie talks to you again."

"No. I need you with Sara. She's a sitting duck if Atraeus shows up."

"I'll get some of your other old guards to keep surveillance over Sara. It'll be okay. Sara will be fine. Stay where you are. I'm coming."

Dexter hung up and jumped into the back of the ambulance beside his sweet and delicate Sara. She already had needles sticking in her and her shirt was cut down the middle, exposing her bra and a scarred stomach covered with wires. "Is she going to be okay?" Dexter asked the medic beside him while taking her unmoving hand into both of his.

"Too early to tell," she answered without looking. "We need to get her to the ER stat."

"Dammit! Tell me she's going to be okay! Lie to me if you have to!" Dexter roared.

"Sir, with all due respect, every second you don't let us help her, the more danger she's in. Do you understand?"

That was when he realized how small her hand was in his. How tiny and fragile she was. But, she was a fighter. He had to remember that. Remind himself that she was a soldier. "What's going to happen to her?"

"She'll probably get a pan-scan to check for internal bleeding. We won't know anything until we get her to the ER."

Dexter turned and kissed her precious knuckles. "Get better, Sara. Whatever you have to do to come back to me, do it."

Exiting out the ambulance, he told himself it wasn't too late. He could turn and hold Sara's hand on the way to the hospital. Make sure she made it safely.

"You need to get checked out too," the woman advised.

"I can't."

"Sir, you are risking your life."

"And, I have two others to save. You do whatever you have to do to keep her alive." He turned and walked away.

The doors to the truck closed with an urgent slam, and Dexter watched the ambulance drive in the opposite direction of Mount Verta, back into town with sirens blazing and lights flashing.

His heart slowly—brutally tore in two.

Lost. He was lost. And he had lost everyone. Sara, Nellie, and Kali. His family. Gone. None of them within reach. Fuck, he wished he *was* still in the pit. Anything was better than this. Better than losing his entire family.

Dexter stood near the totaled vehicle as the two large doors to the wall lumbered open inward, pushing the car to the side with a disturbing screech. Though the path toward the mountain was laid out before him, he kept his eyes fixated on watching the ambulance blip out of sight. Fixated on watching Sara leave. Maybe forever.

Chapter 18

▲▲▲

Moving with aching muscles felt unnatural. Nausea gathered in a hard ball at the pit of his stomach. Dexter kept his eyes fixed on the totaled car and the empty passenger seat with Sara's blood sinking into the fabric. He doubled over and let vomit ride up his throat in several waves. At the tail end of the last heave, he fell to his hands and knees, staying there until the nauseous feeling subsided. His stomach burned and his eyes watered, but the determination in his blood still simmered hot.

A red SUV slowed near Dexter. The window rolled down, revealing Zeek's wide eyes that were riveted on the ghastly crash. Dexter staggered to the passenger seat and buckled himself in after a few tries.

"I saw the ambulance pass on the way here."

Dexter lay his head on the headrest as the wooziness abated. "Zeek. I can't lose her."

"You won't. You won't lose anyone."

Slowly, as not to jostle his brain, Dexter lazily observed the crash as they crossed the threshold of the wall. The moaning of it closing behind him sent such a profound dread, it nailed him to the seat.

There may not have been screechers circling above him, but he sure felt them in his heart. If he couldn't save his family, the winged monsters were going to saw their way out of his chest with their serrated beaks and eat his carcass.

The image of Sara's unresponsive face between his hands haunted him. The memory constricted around his throat until he physically coughed to break free of the suffocation.

Several minutes into driving, Dexter's phone dinged with a text message.

Emily Merrit: I'm with her at the hospital.

Dex: Keep me updated.

"She's at the hospital," he whispered to Zeek while rubbing his buzzed head. "If anyone could get our kids back, it was her. She's a fucking beast. Did you see that girl six years ago?"

"No. I didn't." Zeek wrinkled his brows as he recalled a memory. "Because she was so damn fast. And somehow snuck out of our secured camp."

Dexter scrubbed his hands down his face, smearing a stream of warm blood across his cheek. "I have no idea how I'm going to do this."

"Sure, she could do this. But, so can you. And you got me. I'm not letting those kids get hurt." With a dark glint in his eyes, Zeek glanced at Dexter. "So tell me where the hell we're going."

Dexter straightened in his chair. "It's a straight course to the mountain if you stay on this road. I don't know how long it'll take. I mean, it took us a little under two weeks to walk there from the tower. Between seven to ten miles a day? So, I don't know. Couple hours maybe."

Soon the sun dipped below the horizon, setting the sky ablaze in layers of cobalts, magentas, and heated golds. Silhouetted against a line of dark clouds were a flock of birds flying in a "V" formation. Dexter was brought back to witnessing a similar sunset six years prior with Sara by his side in the depths of the rotting forest. He tried to harness the memory of her spunky, fearless spirit, but as soon as his eyes scanned the ghost town they were entering, his confidence leaked away like molten lava. Roofs were demolished from the onslaught of winged screechers years ago. Glass on the storefronts were shattered and fabric awnings were ripped, waving in the breeze as tattered strips. Plants were decomposing and small rodents scurried away from their car's headlights.

Zeek rotated toward Dexter to rest a hand on his shoulder. "You feeling all right from that crash? It looked bad."

"No. I feel sick." Dexter exhaled in a breath he hadn't realized he had been holding. "And, I want to punch something."

"Let's keep your hands working for now. You have a gash on your brow, man. Looks gnarly." He released Dexter and placed his hand back on the wheel.

Dexter raised his fingers to the injury, but decided against touching it. Also against looking in the mirror. It didn't matter. He just buried his face in his shirt to wipe away some of the blood.

"Fuck, man. What if we get there and the kids are gone? What do we do then?"

"Let's cross that bridge if we get there."

Dexter gave Zeek's sharp profile a hard look, angered by his pessimism. "You're supposed to say they'll be there."

Zeek cleared his throat while turning the wheel to follow the slight bend in the road. "Okay. They'll be there," he rephrased curtly.

Unsatisfied, Dexter focused his attention on the dilapidated town. Just beyond the crumbling buildings lived a flourishing forest.

More driving.

More contemplating.

More worrying.

It's either you or no one.

Sara's sweet voice called to him.

Breakfast spaghetti, huh?

Dexter held his temples with flat hands, trying to keep her from leaving his skull. "Fuck. I'm hearing her in my head."

"Because you miss her, not because she's dead." Zeek sighed while checking his mirrors. "Emily would have called to tell you."

Will you play me something?

How could she be there one minute and gone the next. He could still feel her in his arms, rocking her.

Dexter sighed while continuing to listen to the detrimental thoughts ebbing through his brain in the unrelenting surges of a vicious hurricane. "Fuck. I don't even know if this is real, man. Are you real or am I still in the pit?"

"You are very much out of the pit. It *has* been six years. You *do* have twins with Sara."

"Then why the *fuck* is Atraeus still here? What does he want with my kids?"

Zeek sighed and changed his grip on the steering wheel to a more relaxed one. "Emily and I were talking about it. You said that Atraeus had to leave after the deal, yeah? The only reason that we could think of that is strong enough to make him stay here is if—maybe—Kali and Nellie are his kids too."

Dexter's head whipped to Zeek's so fast that his neck kinked, sending hot chills from his neck to the base of his skull. "What did you just say?"

"Think about it. Sara got pregnant while Atraeus's energy was still in her. It would make sense that the kids she had would be partly his too. Why else would he keep your kids alive right now? Why else would they have those powers? And now they're magically on the same mountain where Atraeus is supposed to depart from?"

I'll be happy to take over and take care of our *kids,* Guy's voice rang out with obnoxious clarity.

Dexter kicked, foot striking somewhere under the glove compartment. "Fuck! I hope you're wrong."

"Calm down. Clear your head," Zeek encouraged with a veil of flat emotion.

I'd love another little one with you, twinkled Sara's melodic voice.

"Shit!" How had he forgotten?

The phone rang as he was dialing. He picked it up and Emily's raspy voice rang out. "They finished her tests, and we're just waiting for results."

"Is she awake?"

"No, she's banged up real good. But, I'm with her. And, so are four of your other guards."

Dexter let a frustrated grunt tear through his chest and into the phone.

"They're doing everything they can for her," Emily comforted.

"Emily, she might be pregnant. It'll be too early to tell, but just let the doctors know, okay? Maybe they can do an ultrasound or something."

"I will."

"Call me for everything."

"She'll be okay, Dexter. Focus on Kali and Nellie."

Dexter hung up and stuffed the device into his jean's pocket. He couldn't help but think that maybe Sara would wake to his touch. To him calling for her. If anyone was going to coax her awake, it was him.

Bang! The swing of the hammer. This time he didn't bother even a glance at young Sara. Dexter had no time to find his way out of the hallucination. Little Nellie was curled in the corner, trying to shield his eyes from the scene. "Daddy!"

Dexter ran to him, holding every shaking part tightly. "Nellie! Are you okay? Is your sister okay?"

There was no answer, but his jade eyes were large and pleading for his dad.

"I need you to talk to me, bud. Are you still on the mountain?"

Nellie nodded.

"Is your sister okay?"

"Yeah," he cried, wrapping his small arms around Dexter's neck and burying his face into his shirt.

Dexter laid a flat hand on his back and lifted him into his arms. "Where's Guy?"

"Not here."

"Are you hurt?"

"No."

He did his best to pour every ounce of his love through his fingertips, wishing his son could feel it and gain comfort from his touch. This little body in his arms refocused Dexter's mind. He couldn't live without Sara, but his soul would be decimated without his kids. He finally believed that this was real. "Okay, Nellie. Don't worry. I'm on my way right now—"

The vision cut off, and he was back in the car with Zeek. Dexter took a large inhale of air and felt a bit more revived. "Nellie just talked to me."

"What'd he say?"

"Both of them are still okay on top of the mountain. Atraeus isn't with them."

"Good, but you need to rest. You're looking pale." Zeek cleared his throat and ruffled his dark hair off his forehead with a large hand. "Don't need you keeling over on me right now."

The next empty town passing by his window resembled the first, if not worse. Black and white graffiti marked the sides of buildings and some had been torched. Dark soot streamed down windows and walls were collapsed to rubble.

Zeek slowed the car, swearing under his breath. The car gave a gentle swerve around something large blocking the road.

When Dexter realized what it was, he sat up and shouted, "Stop, stop, stop!"

Zeek's thick brows rose in alertness as he slammed on the brakes and put the vehicle into park.

Dexter hopped out and gazed at it. Standing before him was the second of the three log cabins that signaled the ending of Sara's journey to the mountain. This was where he had stayed his last night with Sara before being torn apart for six years.

Nell's creations still surrounded it. Avocados, cherries, oranges, and lemons thrived. Dozens of rose bushes fared well. Like they were all frozen in time. Even though it seemed impossible that anyone would travel all this way to care for a garden, it had survived to an impeccable degree.

Nell's creations were miraculous. Flourishing with fortitude in an eternal bloom. A spark of an idea flickered awake. Before Dexter dismissed it, it rose, spun, and ignited into an inferno of a complete belief. Dexter wheeled around to Zeek who was stepping out of the car.

"Zeek, I know how to save Sara."

Chapter 19

▲▲▲

Zeek's sharper features scrunched as he scratched his head. "You do?"

Dexter gazed down the long stretch of road they had just driven, visualizing all the pieces of what needed to be done. "Yes." He sighed and rubbed the back of his head. "But, it's a detour."

Immediate rejection came from Zeek's shaking head. "No, man," he said in a deep, commanding voice. "We aren't going backward. Whatever it is, squash it. Your children are in danger. There's no time for detours."

Dexter narrowed his eyes at Zeek. "Sara's in danger too!" In a hot breath, he released the rest of his anger and took a measured step toward Zeek, flatly saying, "I can do it." Dexter pivoted back to the cabin sheltered by the heavenly luscious variety of plants, gesturing to it with both opened palms. "This is what Nell created. And it's all still here." He dropped his arms and turned to Zeek, visually seeing his answer like the memory happened yesterday. "Six years ago, he created a ring of peli plants around him and Sara. That ring of pelis has to

still be out there. If I can find them, I can save Sara. I just..."
Dexter looked beyond the buildings and to the treetops of the
forest behind them, "I don't remember exactly where they are.
We'd have to backtrack."

Zeek made sharp gestures with his hands as he spoke. "Sara
is at a hospital. She is protected and people are taking care of
her. She is safe, Dexter. Your children are not. They are
vulnerable and need our help. Don't risk their lives for a
maybe."

"You didn't see her!" Dexter roared, tears welling in his
eyes. "She wasn't fucking moving. She's not going to make it. I
can feel it. That crash fucking broke her! The kids need her,
and I need her. I *have* to get those pelis for her."

Zeek's angled jaw clenched, searching Dexter's serious
gaze and finding complete devastation. "We can get them on
the way back."

*But our time is ticking, Dex. I can practically hear it ticking
away in my head.*

Dexter's jaw went rigid, taking what Zeek was saying under
consideration. In the end, he was dead set on saving his whole
family. A father shouldn't have to choose. "Having the kids
with me, fumbling in the dark is more of a liability. We have to
do it now." Dexter looked to the sky, imagining the screechers
circling aloft. Between the time Nell grew the peli circle and
this second cabin, they rode on a screecher. Who knew how far
it was from the exact spot he stood. Dexter strode past Zeek,
but Zeek put a flattened palm on his chest to stop him. They
both looked at each other out of the corner of their eyes for a

brief, silent moment before Dexter mumbled a quiet, "She'd do it for me."

Zeek nodded briefly and released Dexter. They both jumped into the car, Dexter clicking in his seatbelt while Zeek turned it on.

"This is a bad call," Zeek expressed with a hard look of exasperation.

"My family, my call."

Zeek huffed and threw the car in reverse, making a three-point turn back in the other direction. "How far?"

"At least a mile. Then, we'll get out and look."

Zeek remained silent, letting the tension build.

"You're going to take the peli back to Sara when we find it." Still, Zeek didn't say anything, which pleased Dexter. He didn't need more doubt in his head.

After a mile of silent driving, Zeek finally spoke up. "This is a mistake, man."

Dexter's fists clenched impulsively and slammed one against the center console. "Shut up before I strangle you." Instead of flinching, Zeek rolled his eyes. A sudden tidal wave of nausea passed over Dexter.

Zeek sighed. "I can't bring the peli back to Sara, man. You need me to help them down the mountain and you need someone to drive you and the kids back in case Nellie can't keep his hallucinations to himself."

Fuck. He was right. "Maybe there's a way I can make sure Nellie has them under control while I'm with him."

"Or maybe not."

Sara was a much better partner in crime than Zeek. Sara was game for anything, and at least she made him laugh. With Zeek, he was slowly sending Dexter deeper into a dark spiral of uncertainty. "Fine. Keep driving."

As the drive went on, Dexter roiled over his decision, bouncing back and forth from being extremely confident to wondering what the hell told him this was a good idea in the first place. That was all he had the capacity to contemplate. If he ventured out to any of the other dark places of his thoughts, he'd never resurface.

In another mile, Dexter ordered him to stop. Zeek parked the car in the center of the two-lane road, and they both hopped out, making their way straight into the dense forest behind the heavily graffitied buildings that lined the main road.

The two trudged into the forest with a sense of dread looming over them. A fresh woodsy scent was a welcome relief that calmed Dexter's nerves. They did their best to keep their eyes peeled for the small shriveled leaves of the peli plant. Its brown crinkled surface hid the weight of the sack of steaming hot salve beneath. Their feet snapped twigs that carried the sound through the seemingly hollow forest in a loud echo. Trees stood strong, despite the rodents scurrying in all directions, away from their flashlights. Surrounding Nell's gift to Sara was a conspicuous dome of elegant flowers that would attract animals and people alike. For all he knew, the peli's had been used by scavengers already. But, there was no room for doubts. He remembered it had been hidden deep in the forest and everything had seemed abandoned. The odds that

241

there were enough people to comb through the forest to find this little sanctuary seemed unlikely enough that Dexter kept his mouth clamped shut.

"We've wasted an hour," Zeek huffed, still beside Dexter and scanning the area with the flashlight. "I don't even know if we can find our way back to the car, and Nellie hasn't spoken to you in hours. You're being a delusional *idiot*."

Sure, it had been a while and there was only moonlight shining, but he couldn't give up. "Keep looking," he groused.

The dozens of boughs and bent branches danced like fleeting shadows in his terrible night vision. Not to mention the pulsing headache and upset stomach from the crash he attempted to ignore. But even when he dared himself to focus harder, shapes and objects remained blurred and indistinct. Dexter wasn't worried though. He didn't need to see more than the shape of the circle the peli plants were arranged in. Plus, he had Zeek's keen night vision too. Between the two of them, they would find Sara's only lifeline.

"We're wasting time we don't have," Zeek argued for the hundredth time. "We have to go back. Now."

Dexter kept his feet moving deeper into the forest, eyes scanning every inch of soil. Small critters sang all around him as the sun set. Twigs snapped beneath the weight of his body and leaves crunched. Each time, there was a short pause in the insect cacophony of music. "Then you can go. I'm not giving up. The kids need their mother."

Zeek let out a frustrated sneer of contention and remained by Dexter's side. Just as he had always done. "She might not even be a mother right now, Dexter!"

Dexter filled his lungs, prepared to shout back at him and maybe punch his daylights out for that insensitive comment, but in the corner of Dexter's eye, he spotted something large and bright that reached the treetops. In a quick spin of his head, he stared dead straight into the eye of a dome. Purple Wisteria spilled like a rainfall of petals into the center of a clearing with a variety of fruit trees standing strong and tall. Littering every branch were coiled morning glories. Poppies and orchids arched through the wild dome-like fountains. A flash of Sara admiring the beauty entered his head. He distinctly remembered her breathing in the colors, the artistry, and the creation with the utmost admiration.

With the back of his hand, Dexter slapped Zeek in the chest then pointed. "Look!"

Dexter sprinted to the wonderland and fell to his knees, feasting his eyes on a dozen peli plants bending into a large circle. He could have cried at the relief, wishing this was all he had to accomplish, but he didn't have it in himself to celebrate.

"Start plucking!" Dexter shouted while fisting each thin stem and yanking them from the soil. "Careful, the bottoms are scorching hot." He retracted his hands, took off his shirt and tied the sleeves to create a makeshift bag. The two scavenged each one and placed it gently in the shirt. They gave each other a mutual look of understanding before pivoting and sprinting through the darkness that blanketed the forest.

Though their flashlights were helpful, it only illuminated their path at a concentrated diameter. After Dexter almost ran into a tree, they were forced to slow their pace.

The line of buildings came into view, and Dexter was about to announce it to Zeek, when a mix of voices filled the air. The two broke their strides and hid behind separate trees. Yard by yard, they snuck closer to the buildings, darting from one tree to another. They crouched and joined behind one dilapidated structure. Around the corner was a surreal sight. One he never thought he'd have to ever see again.

Four men surrounded their car. All were massively built with tribal tattoos running down half their skulls and their milky arms. Two wielded a butcher knife while another had a bat with nails sticking out at the end. Each had black leather pants and tunics paired with combat boots. There was a fifth member. A thin woman. She stood on the hood, feet shoulder width apart and chomping on half an apple before tossing it to the side.

"Fuck." Dexter whisper-screamed. He hid behind the building to look at Zeek. "Splitters?"

"Bastards," he spat while disgust alighted his expression.

"We need the car."

"No, we don't. Not worth it. Let's go on foot. You walked to Mount Verta once before. You can do it again."

"We need the car to make up for time." Dexter peeked back at the Splitters, analyzing their positions for the best attack approach.

Zeek's strong hold on Dexter's shoulder surprised him as he was shoved against the wall, dark eyes boring into him and jaw clenching like he was going to kill him long before the Splitters would have a chance to. "Listen, Dexter. You have wasted enough time. Nellie and Kali are scared and need you. Splitters will fuck you up. Get your ass up that mountain before I impale you with that butcher knife."

Dexter shoved him off with the sinking realization that he needed to listen to Zeek.

"If you don't return with your kids, Sara is going to kill you herself," he reminded.

Dexter grunted and took a step toward the mountain on foot with Zeek trailing close behind, so close that Zeek kept a hand on Dexter's upper back.

Ring.

The initial beep of his phone echoed louder than the crash. It shot him straight into disbelief. For a miniscule second, he consciously ignored it, praying it was a figment of his dark imagination siphoning energy from his pooling temper.

Ring. Ring. Ring.

Fuck! In a frantic rush, Dexter fumbled with his phone to shut it off, but its flashlight momentarily blinded him. In a few short seconds, everything about the device shut down. He looked to Zeek, wide eyed and panicked.

The two glared at each other as they heard the Splitters' questioning voices.

Run or hide was the silent question that passed between them.

"Run," Dexter urged.

The two took off toward the mountain, makeshift bag of peli plants bouncing on Dexter's hip. It hindered his speed, but he held on to the bag for dear life, knuckles whitening around the cloth. Dexter's eyes did as good of a job as they could in the dark, but his night vision was anything but keen. He stumbled over a protruding root but was lucky enough to catch himself before falling, the bracing impact in his aching knee joints. A few pelis slipped out of the bag and tumbled to the ground, rolling behind him. Sara's ticket to life! They didn't come all that way to lose what little they had. Dexter stopped in his tracks.

"Leave them," Zeek barked, not hindering his strides and grabbing Dexter's arm to drag him forward with his momentum.

Dexter eyed the three pelis hitting the ground and tumbling on the unleveled forest floor. Two split open, spilling its steaming contents in a wasteful ooze. Dexter grunted in frustration and continued with Zeek.

Splitters' voices echoed through the forest. "There!" a male shouted several yards behind.

"Don't let them get away," the woman shrieked like a bobcat, warning against failure.

Adrenaline released in an agitated frenzy, sending Dexter's feet propelling forward faster than he thought his sore limbs would allow. Shadows passed in front of his vision, but he kept his eyes glued to Zeek's back, following in his steps to keep on the best path. Something swung from the trees, striking Zeek in the head and knocking him to the ground. His massive body crashed onto his side, causing Dexter to screech to a halt.

Pain spread through Dexter's temple, chasing him into a blackness darker than the pit.

Chapter 20

▲▲▲

Vibrations buzzed through Dexter's brain in horrifying waves. Even the gums in his mouth felt like his teeth were shifting to new positions. A high-pitched ring pulsed in his ears. The smell of blood filled his nostrils with the stench of rusting iron. Something sharp penetrated his temple, like it was digging a hole into his skull.

Sir Bennet. Were you really going to wait until I came on to you for a third time?

Marking?

Where was she?

Pressure wrapping around his body drove him closer to awareness. His wrists had little mobility. Each finger swelled with pooling blood, impeding his sense of touch. Both arms were wrapped behind something solid and bound together. Dexter brought his aching neck up from a hanging position and opened his eyes to see a mantle of darkness. Focusing his gaze by narrowing them, he made out the silhouettes of hundreds of trees in front of the moonlight but not much else.

A groan sounded to his right. "Sara?" Dexter turned his head and saw Zeek's hulky figure bound by chains to a tree trunk. Wrists behind his back, neck and ankles secured.

Zeek?

A male dressed in a black tunic and pants with chains dangling off the belt loops stood in front of him. He was just as tall as Dexter but with skinny muscles. Hooped rings ran along the cartilage of his ear and a silver bar pierced through his one missing eyebrow. The angles of his face were hard to make out as Dexter tried to gain his bearings, but his darker clothes and a butcher knife taped to the end of a stick were dead giveaways. "What's the hold up? I feel like chopping," he grumbled.

"Because I know this mother fucker." The woman stepped into a beam of moonlight that sliced through the darkness, revealing herself. Sunken onyx eyes with thin lips and a pointed nose. Her eyes emitted years of pain and sought merciless revenge. She had a mousey appearance, but her ears were small. The corners of her mouth turned up as she cocked a thin eyebrow. Her brows crinkled in the center as she dipped her chin down so her cutthroat fierceness was exposed.

Dexter grumbled and focused on the woman's blurred, lithe shape. A shadow veiled her features, but he could decipher the outline of her diamond-shaped face and bald head. "Have we met?" he huffed in a baritone. He studied her hairless scalp reflecting the sapphire tint of the moon and the tattoos running down her cheek.

"Have we met!" She let out a snort of derision. "Really?"

Behind her, silhouettes of more Splitters stepped forward, weapons in hand and tattoos darker than the night. Dexter closed his eyes, half from drifting awareness and half hoping he would wake up beside Sara in bed. That wasn't the case. The woman took another step forward, coming up to Dexter's chin. She raised her brows and crossed her arms, awaiting a response. Was he supposed to have one? Her crew had him beat. What more did they want?

"So you know the guy," the male Splitter announced, looking to the rest of his team. "Who cares? I say, let's get to slicing already!"

The crowd behind them gave a cheer of agreement.

"Shut up!" she screamed, tone dipping lower with authority while she shoved the male with the cartilage earrings back. "This one is mine!" Her small nose crinkled as her head bobbed with the impact of her fist into Dexter's jaw. The blow amused Dexter. It barely tingled compared to Sara's vicious slaps. The woman's nose wrinkled again, readying for a scream. "You killed my father, you asshole!"

The male leader smiled at her confession as he stepped back. "This one's hers, boys." His figure faded into the shadows with the rest of the members.

The volume of her voice didn't affect Dexter's fatigued apathy. He cleared his throat. "Sounds like me," he croaked. A specific shrill of a scream reverberated in the depths of his mind. A scream that had haunted him over countless days. Pure piercing shrieks of desperation. *You killed my father.* The image of a deteriorating infected man, swaying in his tower surfaced. *No! Dad! No!* The woman's torturous cries blared like a siren, loud enough to evacuate cities. "Jane," he grumbled.

"There you go." A satisfied smile spread over her face as she took a step out of the moonbeam, blending in with the backdrop of darkness. "Almost didn't recognize you without the beard. But, I could never forget those monstrous eyes and those tats."

"I'm sorry," he said, because it was true. Since the first day the screechers arrived, he was sorry. "I made the mistake of letting an infected in the camp once. That decision cost an eight-year-old boy his *life*." That statement brought her back into the light, arms swaying loosely at her sides and palms facing her thighs. Her thin lips were parted like she was ready to shout something, but Dexter beat her to it. "There was no way anyone could have helped your father. Believe me! I tried! I'm sorry!"

The words shifted the intensity in her eyes, but the harshness of her expression remained unwavering. She blinked as if warding away the logic of his explanation. As if she knew he was right but didn't want to admit it. Something passed between them. An understanding? A shallow sense of respect? Maybe sadness? Letting go of harbored anger was something she didn't seem capable of. It must have been brewing in the root of who she was for the last six years. That one statement he made was not going to undo all he had put her through. But, something had resonated that triggered her to lower her guard. Whatever it was, Dexter was thankful for it. Quickly blinking back new thoughts, she changed the subject. Into view came his makeshift sack. "What are these?"

His numbed mind teetered on the brink of awareness as it expanded and contracted in waves of panic. The bag. Pelis. Fuck! Sara was in the hospital! The memory of her lifeless body winded him, crushing his ribs toward his spine. Then, images of Nellie and Kali emerged. Nellie's eyes the color of his mother's and Kali's the pigment of his own. Both scared. Both in need of rescue. The two he was devoted to protect at all costs. His brain was wrecked, as if he had already failed—as if they had already died.

"What are these?" she yelled, shaking the bag in front of his nose.

It was his only chance to secure Sara's life. He had already dropped some, and he couldn't afford to lose a single more. "Plants," he griped.

"Yes, plants," Jane repeated in a hard laugh. "Plants from the Screecher Age. Why do you have them?"

"My girl's a botanist," Zeek baritone chimed. "I've been collecting strange plants for her to learn about."

"Is that so?" She spilled the contents of the bag on the ground, lifted a foot, and stomped on one. Jelly salve splattered everywhere, and Dexter thrashed against his restraints. Before he could even voice his rage, she brought her foot up again and smashed another.

"No!" Dexter roared. Immediate tears sprung to his eyes as he imagined Sara fighting for her life in the hospital. "Stop! Please! Stop!"

Over Jane's lips was the most satisfied smile. "Now we're getting somewhere. Why are you hoarding these?"

"Because they heal injuries," Zeek admitted.

"Zeek!" Dexter barked, struggling against his chains again, wrists seeking any point of weakness for escape. Something rumbled deep in his chest, wishing he had some underlying, supernatural ability like his children did.

Jane's slender frame moseyed to Zeek. "Liar!"

"Put it on Dexter's cuts and you'll see."

"Zeek! What the hell are you doing?" That was all he needed. To be tripping on pelis while Sara and the kids were in danger. "Jane, Jane, Jane—"

"But, you'd be wasting it on him instead of your own people," Zeek warned.

"Zeek!" Dexter warned through gritted teeth. "Jane! Listen to me! Those are going to—"

Jane looked behind the trees into the distance. "Bring me the hostage."

"No! Jane! You can't use them on anyone." His hope of spending the rest of his life with Sara Mar King, the one reason he had agreed to waste six years of his life in complete misery, was slipping from his grasp with every treacherous second that ticked by.

A gaunt male who looked like he hadn't eaten in years was hauled in front of Dexter and forced on his knees. His skeleton protruded through his translucent skin, and his cheeks were hollowed out from lack of nutrition. No hair, but also no tattoos.

Bang!

Wind from the swing of the hammer grazed across Dexter's nose. The florescent lights of Sara's old house poured through his eyes in cool, dim hues, immediately signaling it as artificial.

"Daddy!" Nellie's voice begged from the corner.

Nellie. Fuck, Dexter couldn't say anything. If he did, the Splitters would hear.

Small arms coiled around his thighs. "Come, Daddy!"

Dexter laid a hand on Nellie's back for comfort as he twisted his torso to open a kitchen drawer. He took out a paper and a pencil and wrote, "Dad in trouble."

His jeweled eyes studied the sign then frowned in distress. "Sara! Room. Now!"

Nellie's attention shifted to the scene unfolding, but Dexter was quick to kneel and hold this son's attention at eye level. His gestured to both his son's eyes then to his own, hoping to convey not to let his eyes wander. Nellie kept his eyes glued to his father's. "Dad...in...t-t-tr-tr. I don't know the last word!"

The dark forest came back into view. Jane was cursing while shaking her hand wildly to extinguish the burn of the boiling salve.

"Emily," Zeek mumbled. "We can't."

Dexter whipped his head to his friend, seeing an unsteadiness in his eyes that he recognized.

"You think you love me. But you don't," he huffed with an ache in his voice Dexter hadn't heard since his infected friend had died.

Either Nellie is trying to talk to Zeek or Jane slathered peli over his skin. Through his hazy mind, he remembered the plant hadn't ever worked that fast.

"This is as far as we will ever go. If you can't handle that, then I don't want to see you anymore." Zeek shook his head and the focus in his eyes returned.

"The fuck?" Jane spattered, eyeing Zeek.

"Gotta get out," a male mumbled from behind Dexter. "Gotta leave. Fuck, we have to go! Now, Rodney!"

The chains around Dexter's arms clanged as they loosened from his sore body.

Jane's shadowy eyes fastened on the man behind Dexter as she cradled her injured hand to her chest. Her other hand now aggressively pointed at the man behind the tree Dexter was tied to. "George!" Jane shouted, reaching into one brown boot and retrieving a small knife while keeping her eye on Dexter. "Don't you fucking dare!"

"Gotta get out," George muttered more quietly as the chains clattered.

It clicked. Dexter knew what was happening. Nellie was sending hallucinations to everyone around him. Perhaps it was his way of trying to help.

As Jane marched toward George, Dexter's chains fell to the ground. In a blink, he rammed his shoulder into Jane's chest, knocking her to the ground. The blade fell from her fingers, and Dexter's longer arms allowed him to grasp it before her. He hoisted Jane upward, blade pressed against her throat.

"Let my friend go or she goes," Dexter roared at the other Splitters. A sudden burst of laughter filled his ears. They were laughing.

"We don't care about her. Hell, we don't care about anyone but ourselves. It's how we operate," a man wielding a bat informed.

Jane's body stilled as she shrieked, "Dad! No! Dad!" Her knees buckled as she bawled. "What did you do! He just needed some help! He would have been fine!"

Holy hell. Dexter's heart sank. Jane was talking to him in her hallucination. That was one of the scariest moments in her life. When Dexter brutally murdered her infected father. Dexter let her go with trembling hands as she fell to the ground, hovering over an invisible father with his neck sliced open. He had caused her enough pain. What he was doing now wasn't right.

Voices sailed into the air. Everyone's talking overlapped each other's in garbled and fragmented sentences. The Splitters dropped their weapons as they mumbled through their own hallucinations.

Fuck. Nellie was so bright. So intelligent. So Sara's son. Nellie gave him a window of opportunity, and he wasn't going to lose it.

"Hurry!" Zeek growled.

Dexter rounded the tree his friend was chained to, spotted keys in the lock, and snatched them. Every second that passed as he tinkered with Zeek's lock felt like an eternity. First key. Didn't work. The second key didn't work. Dexter was free to get his kids and for a fleeting second, a part of him wanted to drop the keys and make a run for them. Third key. If the hallucinations ceased, Dexter was running the risk of getting recaptured. Running the risk of losing his family—a risk he had already taken too many times.

On the fourth try, the chains dropped, and he watched as Zeek knelt to pick up a blade and jab it into the skull of a male Splitter to his right. Then, he moved like a swift ninja in the night to the next Splitter and repeated the attack.

Dexter pushed Zeek's chest back to get his attention. "Zeek! We have to go!"

"And risk running into them on the way back?" he answered as he side-stepped Dexter and continued his assaults. Then, Zeek lunged for Jane who was a crying heap on the ground, sobbing over the vision of her dead father. A gasp escaped Dexter's lips, feeling an overwhelming desire to protect her from any more pain. To save Sara's friend. She was Sara's friend! Fuck! How could he have just remembered that? Sara was the one who had taught her how to defend herself— to save herself from more pain. All Sara did was try to save Jane, and Dexter would to be damned if he didn't follow in her footsteps. He stepped in Zeek's path and shoved him back. "No, Zeek!"

Zeek spun the knife backward so the blade was adjacent to his forearm, the black hilt grasped tightly in his fist, knuckles whitening. He stepped forward, shoving Dexter aside.

"He attacked me," Jane whispered in a blind, agonizing sob.

Dexter rammed his shoulder into Zeek's side just as he leapt for Jane again. "Leave her alone!"

Zeek's massive body bulldozed Dexter as he let out an annoyed grunt.

"She was Sara's friend! Maybe Emily's too. Don't touch her!"

Dexter's words must have registered, because Zeek stiffened with a clenched jaw and a look of indecision raging in his eyes.

The two eyed Jane who was rising from a hunched crouch on the forest floor, curious eyes absorbed with the vision of Dexter. Her hands relaxed and her shoulders went slack as the glossy, wet tracks over her face reflected the silver of the moon. She didn't bother wiping them away as her entire demeanor shifted. Jane resembled a lost little girl as her arms hugged herself, eyes now scanning her dead mates sprawled everywhere. The longer she drunk them in, the more relief overtook her expression. Zeek visibly straightened and disengaged as she brought her line of vision back to Dexter.

"Th-they're dead." The shock in her eyes was both pure and frightening at the same time. Almost like Zeek had released invisible chains that had been suffocating her. Her eyes roved over Dexter's. "I'm not. Why? Why didn't you kill me too?"

"I didn't want to kill anyone," Dexter sneered. "Including your father. We've all been hurt too much. Right now, I have to get those peli plants to Sara and rescue our two children from Atraeus," he blurted, not caring if it made sense or not to Jane. He needed the audible reminder to keep himself focused. "I really don't care about anything else."

"Children?" Jane whispered.

"Yes. They are being held captive by the one thing that caused more than half the world to die out. The Father of Fear." Dexter knelt, gently moving the fabric covering the remaining peli plants to count the remaining few. Slinging the makeshift pack over his shoulder, he adjusted it and looked back at Jane, whose entire demeanor had altered.

"Sara?"

A sharp exhale cleansed his soul as he readied to continue to Mount Verta. "Listen, I don't have time to explain. I am deeply sorry about your father. I was a different person back then. I hope you accept my apology." Not bothering to stick around for her response, Dexter grasped Zeek's sleeve and hauled him toward the car, passing Jane on the way. "Let's go."

"Wait!" Jane announced while jumping in front of them, palms out to their bodies. "Sara? Mar King? Like, from your camp, Sara? Blonde hair, pixie cut? The one who taught me to fight?"

Dexter nodded.

She pointed to Dexter. "You two are... together?" she asked, thin brows furrowing.

Dexter huffed, unsure where the conversation was leading, but he clenched his jaw and said, "She changed you. And she changed me. It's what she does."

Her brows lifted, eyes widening to black marbles. "Y-you have children with her?"

"Yes. And right now she's in the hospital not fucking moving, and my children are about to die at the hands of Atraeus. So you got your fucking wish. If I lose them, I lose everything. Just like you lost your dad."

She blinked her wet onyx eyes. "She's in the hospital? What happened?"

"Car crash," Zeek muttered.

Desperate for something, her eyes shifted between the two of them, lips parting and body stepping closer. "I want to help," Jane blurted, dropping her arms and holding her open palms by her sides to show trust.

"I may have saved you from this idiot," Dexter said, pointing to Zeek, "but I sure as hell don't trust you with Sara's life." He made a move to continue to Mount Verta, but Jane stepped in his path.

"But, she helped me. I-I-I want to return the favor. What she taught me saved me three separate times from getting attacked. Please. I have to help her."

Dexter's stare cut into her soul, deciding.

Chapter 21

▲▲▲

Moments of silence passed. Jane stayed unmoving, giving Dexter as much time as he needed.

Zeek huffed behind Dexter impatiently before snatching the makeshift bag of the remaining peli plants from Dexter's shoulder. "You want to help Sara? Take these to the hospital," he said while holding the bag out to her.

Dexter shoved Zeek's arm down and away from Jane. "No! She's a Splitter, Zeek. She's going to use them herself. This is all we have." He shook his head. "I'm sorry, I can't chance it. She hates me!"

Jane's expression changed to pleading, brows up, lips parted, and ready to defend herself, but Zeek shoved Dexter and straightened his back to be a bit taller to assert his dominance. "Every minute you waste is a second she could die. I'm *so* sick of you wasting time. Those kids need their mother and this is an opportunity to make sure she lives."

"I promise," Jane chimed. "I'll help."

Dexter never let go of Zeek's stare. "She just tried to kill us!"

"Yeah, I know." She sighed and let her shoulders go slack. "I'm sorry. Seeing you there after so many years of hating you seemed like too good of an opportunity to pass up. Plus, the guys wouldn't have let you get away anyway. If I didn't ask them to save you for me, you'd be dead right now." She scratched her temple and eyed the men bleeding out on the floor, including the hostage, a misstep Dexter was furious about. "Listen, Sara helped me in a time when my life was over. Let me repay my debt."

"No," Dexter growled.

In a gruff response, Zeek shoved his shoulder and said, "Yes, Dexter. It's what Sara would do."

"I said no! It would take too long for her to walk there anyway."

Her brows furrowed in determination. "It wouldn't take long at all. I have a motorcycle. You really think I walk everywhere?"

Dexter gave her a hard look. *It's what Sara would do.* Trust. She'd fucking trust. She trusted everyone. It was no time to think as himself. He needed to harness the loving powers of Sara Mar King. He needed to think for Sara—like Sara. Dexter turned to Jane, eyeing her carefully, studying the look in her eyes. Was she telling the truth? Could she be trusted?

"Fine." He took the bag from Zeek's hand, took out one peli plant and tossed the rest to Jane. She caught it between her fingertips. "She's at the hospital in the nearest town, within the wall. Follow the road and rub this on her head and her arms and her back. Hell, just bathe her in it. Her friend, Emily will be there to help you."

"You can count on me," she assured as she slung the bag over her shoulder.

Seeing her physically holding Sara's lifeline sent him into more eddying conflict. Just a second ago she was wielding a blade meant for him. Zeek better be right about this.

He wanted to threaten Jane. Wanted to tell her that if she didn't follow through, he was going to hunt her down and take her life as he had her father's. But, his lips remained pressed shut, not willing to risk pissing her off.

"Oh, here." Out of the back pockets of her black jeans, she took out two flat objects and tossed it to Zeek and Dexter. "Your phones."

As soon as the phone was in his hands, he unlocked it and called Emily on speaker, unsure if he could keep it to his ear with trembling hands.

"Dexter! I've been calling you!"

"I know. We got, uh, held up. How is she? Is she awake?"

"No, she's not. But, her tests came back. Dexter," she paused, "it's not good. The doctors said to prepare for the worst."

Fear turned his blood cold. Dexter couldn't speak. He was hollowed. A miserable lump hardened at the base of his throat that threatened to cut off his will to live. Sara wasn't going to make it. His eyes trained on the phone, unsure if it was possible to answer. Maybe if he didn't, the news wouldn't be real. *Prepare for the worst.*

Zeek took it out of his hand and said, "Thanks, Emily. We have someone bringing peli plants. Her name's Jane, and she looks like a Splitter. So, don't freak out."

"Jane? Everkin? I know Jane. She's alive?"

"Hey, Emily," Jane called into the phone.

"Jane! You're okay—"

Zeek huffed. "Not the time, Em. Call us if anything changes or if she doesn't show up."

"I'll show up," Jane announced into the phone.

"Okay. Hurry. Sara needs those plants, like, yesterday."

Zeek hung up and handed the phone back to Dexter. "Let's go."

The three of them ran back to the car. On the way Dexter had to endure Jane apologizing for the delay. She kept saying something about having to play a part. Between that and her incessant pledge to get to Sara, Dexter wanted to clothesline her.

When they reached the vehicle, Jane gave one more promise to reach Sara as fast as she could and revved her black motorcycle hidden behind an overgrown bramble. In a split second, she peeled down the street in the direction of the hospital. Zeek and Dexter settled into the front seats. Dexter opened the glove compartment and placed a single peli plant he had pocketed for safekeeping. In case Jane decided to betray them, like he felt she would in the pit of his stomach, he would be ready. His intuition was hardly ever wrong.

"Zeek, what if Nellie talks to you again?"

He cleared his throat. "Then we crash." The engine roared and Zeek slammed his foot on the gas, barreling toward the mountain.

Dexter whipped his head to Zeek's half-assed grin. "Not funny," he groused before resting his head and taking in a deep inhale that stretched his abdomen and cracked a few of his ribs, leaving an unbelievable ache in its wake. "Distract me from my children's imminent deaths, would you?"

Zeek shifted his hands on the wheel. One remained on the top, the other ruffled his thick dark locks. "Oh, sure. What would you like to talk about?"

Dexter rolled his eyes. That wasn't what he meant. Slouching in his seat, Dexter mulled over what he could talk about. "So, you and Emily? What's going on? I heard your hallucination."

Zeek sighed as he turned the wheel with the bend of the road. "Never mind. I'd rather you worry about your children's imminent deaths."

Dexter slouched in the chair and leaned it back to accommodate for a blaring headache that pressed behind his eyes. "Come on, man. She told you she loves you and you rejected her. What's that about?"

He struggled and kept a steely eye on the road. "And I'd do it again."

Dexter shook his head. "No, Zeek. I see the way you look at her. You are drowning in her every move. Why not? What's the problem?"

He shot Dexter a hard look, a dark vortex gathering in his eyes. "Because I don't want to be her second choice. I want to be someone's first choice. That terrifies me."

Dexter furrowed his brows. "What do you mean?"

"She always says Nell's name in her sleep, man." Zeek swallowed hard and rubbed his eyes with one hand.

In an impulse, Dexter opened the glove compartment to reassure himself that at least one peli was, in fact, in his possession. "So?"

"She'd be with him, not me."

"You don't know that."

"I do."

Dexter sighed. "We've all been traumatized."

"Dexter. She named your child after him!" His grip on the steering wheel tightened. "I can't just ignore that. My mom was not my dad's first pick, and it messed them up. I don't want to repeat that."

Dexter rubbed the back of his neck. "First, you are not your parents. You can't put that on Emily. It's not fair. Plus, she never got to say goodbye to him. I'd cut her some slack."

Zeek gave an impressed frown. "You think if I take her to the mountain to say bye, she might get some closure?"

"Yeah, maybe." Dexter folded his arms, eyeing the millions of stars and the moon shining brightly. "You know, I don't think Nell really cared about her as much as you think. Their love wasn't some whirlwind romance. He kissed Sara a few days before the mountain. He tried to convince me Sara liked him more. Though he had some other—less offensive— qualities, I don't think you need to be worried about Nell."

Zeek's heavy brows shot up. "Really? Can I tell Emily that? Maybe she'll start to hate him."

Dexter gave a crooked grin. "Go back to wanting to take her to Mount Verta for some closure. That's probably more productive for your relationship."

After that, Zeek's thoughts rang loudly. Dexter let him have his space and time to think about how much he actually liked Emily.

The craggy mountain hadn't changed. Nell's unyielding creations held strong. It was a sight Sara would have taken a moment to admire if she were with him. Running along the rocky surface lived an assortment of horizontal trees with both thick and thin trunks jutting out into the air that formed a ladder leading to the summit in a serpentine design. The mountain was adorned with luscious oaks, pines, cherry blossoms, and birches. Coiled around the branches were waterfalls of green vines waving in the slight breeze, covered in a mixture of spade-shaped leaves and vivacious flowers. The colors meshed in a cohesive pattern, like a vibrant lure to commence the climb and celebrate at the peak. But Dexter knew better. Dexter knew at the top lay death, torture, and inescapable nightmares. And that reminder felt like the cold legs of spiders swarming down his back.

His skin buzzed with the sharp memory of his flesh splitting open and melting off. Pain in his knuckles stiffened with the recall of each of his fingers being dislocated and torn off. An overwhelming instinct to flee for his life jolted through his legs when that sense of dread closed over his mouth and nose. He resisted. His feet remained stone, anchoring him in front of the place he feared the most. Amongst the images of the torture clobbering him were Sara's jade eyes pleading to get Marty Brown to stop hurting her...hurting him. Being back here hurt, and the terror of the residual memories froze his blood.

"You okay?" Zeek's voice was smooth with tender understanding.

Dexter clenched his jaw and sucked in air between his teeth. "No," he croaked out of a sore throat. The recollection of Atraeus's sweltering energy noose tightening around his neck sent another shudder through his body, building up in a hard lump he couldn't swallow.

Dexter unbuckled himself as Zeek parked a few yards away from the base of the mountain. Another breath had his eyes lowering to his forearm where his first tattoo was. Mountains heavily inked by shadowing as the sun set behind them. It wasn't the mountain hacking away at his sanity. It was the cavernous abyss at the top. It was the pit that stole years away from his family. The hellish cage that was Atraeus's den of terror, and he had no desire to ever return.

Dexter exited the vehicle and began the gradual slope up to the base of the mountain. He placed a hand on its surface, assessing how deep his fear ran. The cool stone pricked at his nerves like it was alive and nipping at him. He dropped his hand and placed it on the first of Nell's trees. It was a thin birch, one that fit his grip perfectly. In contrast to the craggy mountain, the strength of Nell's tree seemed to sing a lullaby of security, protecting him from the trauma he associated with it. As long as he kept true to the path Nell had laid out, he could tolerate the climb. Still, that sense of dread lingered on his skin and clung to his soul like tacky, old dough. This must have been how Sara felt the day they scaled Mount Verta together.

Dexter lifted a leg, set it on the trunk, and hauled upward to start his ascent. He leaned forward to clasp the next tree, and up he went. Conscientious to keep his attention on the ladder and not the vertical tunnel inside the mountain running parallel to him, he kept going. Even when he worried Nellie might talk to him while he continued with his momentum, it didn't hinder his speed. He was close to seeing his son and daughter. That was what mattered. Not the real fear of being trapped in the pit or reliving the trauma that settled in his muscles with a lurid throb and sucked him beneath the raging undercurrent of distress.

On the cusp of moving his limbs automatically, a floating black dot entered his peripherals. He blinked, thinking it was a side effect of his crash and his eyes were playing tricks on him. But it dwelled. That small, black tear in the universe beside him grew. If he were to lose focus and look away from the endless trees, he would dive head first into the pool of anguish that persisted at the edge of his mind that was already brimming on the edge of insanity. The dot continued to widen until he could no longer ignore it. In a slow shift of his gaze, he stared down the mouth of the abyss. The pit wasn't going to wait for him to reach the summit before swallowing him whole. When he sucked in a ragged breath, something worse caught his attention. Something worse than the vision of the dead sacrifices tangled together at the bottom. It was Sara Mar King's slender shape limp amongst them all. Arms contorted the wrong way, skull cracked, and *blinking*. She was blinking!

Reverberating through the stony walls was Sara's small gasps of breath mixed with her attempts to call his name but only getting as far as the first letter. She was *alive* and suffering at the bottom of the pit.

The zap of terror had him miscalculating where the next branch was and he missed with a clumsy reach. As his torso fell amid the two trees he was positioned between, he gave one final grasp to catch himself, but it was too late. The momentum he had gained from his mistake dragged him into a fast free fall. As he tumbled to the trees below, the dark chasm filled with the sacrifices swung above his face like a three dimensional hologram. It followed him down so he was forced to watch Sara suffer at the bottom while he tumbled to his own death. It hovered so close that he could smell the death seep into his nostrils like essence of a cruel monster.

"Dexter!" Zeek called from below.

His back slammed against something solid that knocked the wind from his lungs. When the leaves clattered together beneath him from the impact, the holographic disc vanished like the poof of a magic trick. Stars glittered in the sky and Zeek's shadowed figure was making his way back down the mountain. Everything around him silenced. Unable to move while he replaced the air in his empty lungs, his body helplessly slid off the trunk. Desperate, he forced his arms out to grasp something—anything, but he missed again and tumbled between the opening of two more trees.

And down the mountain he fell.

Chapter 22

▲▲▲

The night was dark, but the bottom of the pit was even darker. Dozens of black holes encircled him, exponentially growing in size. Encompassed in fear, the rotting smell of the dead sacrifices barely registered. One by one, the floating chasms engulfed him, hauling his body straight into the belly of the mountainous beast. Doom swathed him as the agonizing reality cinched around his throat. Returning to the one place that haunted him pierced his wall of hope, plunged into his ribcage, and punctured his chest in an endless series of holes.

The wind roaring in his ears stopped as all the organs in his body shifted from the impending impact. His speed slowed with a loud creaking. The pressure of something flexible burrowed into his back and stretched as his speed decreased. Each snapping sound came from a different vine that threatened to cut him into useless pieces. The stress of gravity and his body mass sent an initial pop from weaker vines echoing into the vastness that surrounded the mountain. As if the dozens of black holes had a mind of their own, each snap closer to his doom had the circles responding in a happy frenzy. They danced from his left to right in quick spurts until they engulfed all of his vision and swelled into an expansive wall of nothingness. Another groaning of a vine on the verge of cracking rumbled. If he didn't find a way to safety, he'd continue his descent down the mountain and to his inevitable death. He grunted and shot his arms out for something to grab. As he moved, another vine ruptured and resounded with a crack. Rough bark treaded beneath his fingertips. With a quick roll to his right and an arm extension, his hand brushed against something rough. More tree bark. He clutched the tree with one hand as the last three vines broke apart. His body dropped and swung into a vertical position. Dexter screwed his eyes shut and braced himself for falling if he couldn't hold himself up with one hand. The weight of his body put immense strain on his shoulder and his grip slipped a centimeter.

"Dexter!" Zeek called from above.

He grunted with determination and reached up with his other arm to readjust his grip. To better survey his dire situation, he opened his eyes. Still, an immersive layer of darkness blocked his view to all potential paths to safety. "I can't see anything!"

"Hang on! I'm on the way!"

Using the little strength his shaking biceps allowed, he pulled himself up and was able to swing a leg over the trunk. From there, he hugged it, panting from a dangerous mix of adrenaline, relief, and intoxicating terror. "No, no, no," he repeated to self-soothe, still feeling like he was being dragged to the bottom of the pit. His mind ventured into the dark spaces of his memories to rationalize the poignant torment. It must be just Nellie, sending him his nightmares. It had to be. With the fourth time he whispered "no" to himself, it dawned on him how real the fear of the pit was. His voice caught and came out as a croak of desperation. "No!"

"Dexter!" Zeek's raspy voice approached as Dexter did his best to keep his mind present. Zeek was not in the pit. Dexter was not in the pit. What he experienced was a terrible hallucination.

"No, no, no!" He wasn't ready for this. Not ready to face returning to the place that had torn his family apart. To the place where he had been brutally tortured. To the place he had learned just how much hurt Sara was in.

"You good?" Zeek muttered in his ear, his hot breath landing on his cheek with the comfort that someone could watch out for him while he took a second to refocus.

When Dexter reopened his eyes, the night had returned to its norm. "Pits. Everywhere. They were everywhere."

"You think Nellie did something?"

"I don't know, but I can't do this. I can't go back up there," he admitted, fully disgusted with himself as he said it.

Zeek's arm squeezed Dexter's shoulder. "You can and you will."

"You don't know!" Dexter shouted, shrugging off Zeek's hand.

"I don't!" he barked back with a certain type of bite that Dexter felt himself respond to. "But I know your kids. So, let's go."

Dexter squeezed his eyes shut, reliving the drop into the artificial chasms. The shudder that traveled through his body felt like his bones were breaking. "I'm sorry. Zeek, I didn't realize the PTSD was going to be this bad. I can't breathe. I-I-I can't move." Dexter clamped his arms tighter around the limb of the tree. "You have to go up and get them. Please get them."

"You are almost there. Maybe a quarter mile left. You can do this."

Shameful tears welled between his lids. "I can't."

"Fuck. Dex. You can't be serious right now. I'm not leaving you clinging to a fucking tree miles above the ground."

Dexter let loose an exasperated growl. "I'm terrified, Zeek."

"So are Nellie and Kali and Sara! Now, let's go, man."

He watched the blur of Zeek's hulky figure leap to the next tree through his tears. After a long, slow breath of fresh air, he blinked them away and loosened his grip around the tree. *So are Nellie and Kali and Sara!*

Dexter gulped loudly as he positioned himself to leap to the next tree. In the midst of his jump, a primal, distant roar from beyond the tree line let loose. The deep, inhumane yell of utter aggravation grew increasingly closer with every second. A faint glow of neon green brightened Zeek's left side before the screaming hit his ear in increasing volume. Dexter gazed at the bright sun racing over the horizon toward them and braced himself for impact. As the object barreled through the sky, he could make out the millions of green particles crawling in a bug invasion frenzy and bent to the features of Guy's head. His mouth was open, tongue pulled back, brows dipped into a twisted and sadistic anger.

Zeek and Dexter watched in horror as the particles crashed against some invisible barrier not more than a few feet from their noses. Molecules recoiled in on themselves, reformed into Guy's screaming face, then lurched forward again. As Guy's likeness ricocheted off the barrier, it shifted into a sphere that pulsed like a jellyfish, glowing orbs escaping the center, only to be sucked back into its gravity. Atraeus's true form.

"No!" Atraeus's baritone boomed.

Dexter and Zeek didn't dare take their eyes off the extraterrestrial creature, ensuring whatever miracle kept him at arm's length remained intact.

"Let me in!" It thrashed against the barrier again, trying to reach them—trying to reach the mountain. A frustrated growl rumbled through the air. "Don't do this, Verta!"

Dexter willed himself to look at Zeek. Neither of them said a word. Dexter just pointed to the top to signal they needed to continue the climb.

"Dexter!" Sara's velvet voice swirled around him with comfort and grace. "Please."

"That's not—" Zeek warned.

"I know," Dexter growled back.

"You can't keep them from me," Atraeus garbled. "I saw they have my powers. They are mine! And I'm not leaving without them. I will find a way to them before you do!"

Zeek's dark eyes clung to Dexter's, silently agreeing they needed to pick up the pace and get to Nellie and Kali before Atraeus could.

275

The two climbed with utter ferocity and speed, but this time, Dexter kept close enough to Zeek to cling to him whenever the hallucinations of the pit reemerged, which they did. Constantly. Each time he was barraged with another illusion of the pit at the top, it grinded him to dust. With the incessant assault of Atraeus's screams mixed with the dozens of black pockets swallowing him, he hit rock bottom and slowed way down. Each grasp on a new limb was cumbersome and laborious. His head throbbed, nausea swirled his vision, and bruises from the crash were contracting his ribs.

"Keep going, Dex!" Zeek barked. "You can do this!"

That was it. That was all life could throw at him. Everything he feared in one poisonous mixture of mental insanity.

"I swear, Dexter Bennet," Atraeus's voice turned demonic and reverberated against the mountain, "if I was able to kill one more person without it costing my life, I'd pick you. I'd fucking dismantle you alive, muscle by muscle. But, this time it would be real."

His bottle of fear was capped off. If he was going to be the man his family needed, he had to liberate one of his fears to proceed. Overcoming the power held over him by Atraeus's demonic voice seemed easiest. When Dexter turned his focus to the disks containing the pit, Atraeus turned into a pesky fly buzzing in his ear. One that bothered the shit out of him, but he was better able to tolerate the berating. "Shut the fuck up," he whispered under his breath as he leaped onto a new tree.

"Let me in, Verta!" Atraeus roared and it rumbled through his chest, awakening Dexter's focus. The sound waves hit the trees and they vibrated beneath his hands. "Fine. If you won't let me in. I will find a different mountain worthy of sending me back home with *my* offspring." He sneered and his green glow zipped through the air toward distant mountains.

Mount Verta nestled back into the darkness of the night and the faint illumination of the moon.

"We're almost there, Dex. Keep going."

They rounded the peak in the dead of night, and Dexter felt like he had already been dismembered. He bent over, hands on his knees, and let out a stream of vomit until nothing was left. He wiped his mouth and blinked a few times before straightening. The world spun in a dizzy blur of gray and lime. With Zeek keeping him steady, his vision soon sharpened on the two orbs that were shrouded by a buzzing electricity that arched in zig-zagging patterns from one place to another. The energy wisped upward and outward before sparking. Between the spheres was a solid rod of light that kept them separated by a foot of distance, like a barbell. The rod hovered above the old slab of aged concrete Sara had called her pedestal. The one he had stood on as a sacrifice before Atraeus sucked him into the pit and tormented him for six years. Amongst the dark floating circles that had stalked him, the pit rested just behind the orbs. It was wider, darker, and far more intimidating than the fabricated ones that had taunted him up the mountain.

Dexter crumbled to all fours and gave another exhausted dry heave. Grabbing a quick breath, the green spheres recaptured his attention. In them were his children. Nellie sat in a crisscrossed position, eyes closed and facing Kali. Kali's eyes were wandering in every direction, whispering, "Dad?" She went silent again before uttering, "Zeek?"

"Nellie! Kali!" Dexter called, getting to his feet.

The moment Nellie's jade eyes landed on Dexter, the hallucinations ceased. He twisted his small body toward his father and laid two open palms on his glowing cage while screaming, "Daddy!"

Kali's eyes continued to wander like she was sensing he wanted to be all around them. They finally locked on Dexter as she yelled, "Daddy? Daddy!" Her fists slammed on her sphere with such force that her skin darkened with a purple bruise. "Daddy!"

"I'm here! I'm here!"

Dexter ran to them, reached for the rod to pull them away from the pit, but a zap of electricity ripped through his palm. Dexter jumped back and cursed.

"Daddy! You can't touch us," Kali screamed, still pounding her little fists against the orb. He fell to his knees between them. "You'll get hurt."

His eyes wandered over his amazing daughter who was expressing the need to protect him. "We're going to get you guys out of this, don't worry."

"We can't get out!" Nellie explained, placing his hands against the textured surface.

"Has Atraeus hurt you?"

"No," they said simultaneously. "He can't get to us," Kali finished. She wiped her tears away with the back of her hand. "When we got close to the mountain, it sucked us to the top even though Guy tried to keep us with him."

"Get me out," his son squealed.

"Any ideas, Dex?" Zeek called anxiously from behind him.

Dexter let his eyes rove over his imprisoned children. Ideas rolled in and out. One in particular may have been more effective but would cost him his hands and arms.

Sara. Fuck. Sara would know exactly what to do. Her strategic brain could do the impossible.

It tickles!

Sara's voice. But, what could that have been referring to? He had never tickled her.

It tickles!

Her sweet voice crisply rang in the exact same happy tone. He had to pinpoint it.

It tickles!

Exhaustion dragged his awareness down the rabbit hole of the past.

It tickles!

Yes, he had heard her say that once before. But, it was so long ago. Dexter threaded his fingers between the millions of English Daisies that Nell had grown overtop the luscious grass. Nell. It had to do something with Nell.

It tickles!

But what did Nell matter right now? Why was he even wasting time pinpointing something that tickled Sara? Dexter took in a swift breath before giving in. He let his body relax. Hearing Sara's voice was calming, reenergizing. Let her take over.

It tickles!
It tickles!

It tickles!

The daisies. The neon hue of green distorted the patterns of the glow in the grass like a reflection of running water. Sara laughing amongst it.

The image of Nell and Sara holding hands and lighting up their palms together pummeled him with clarity. That was it. That was what Sara was trying to tell him.

Kali and Nellie may have another power.

Chapter 23

▲▲▲

"Nellie, Kali. I need you two to touch your palm to the bar in the middle and light up your hands. Could you do that for me? I want you to try and freeze each other. Not just one beam. I want you to keep your palms lit for as long as you can."

His kids looked at each other with strict determination rising in their eyes. Their hands lit up against the inner wall of their orbs. The bar between them increased in illumination, casting a glow over the flat top of the mountain.

"That's it. Good job. Keep it up."

"Do you know what you're doing, Dexter?" Zeek questioned behind him.

The twins' hands released a beam toward each other and their bodies shot back to the opposite side of their orbs, heads hitting the solidness with a yelp.

Something changed with the orbs. Rippling waves in the bubbles transformed into different sizes. Expanding and contrasting while Nellie's eyes lit up with a type of fire—rage Dexter recognized as his own.

"Nellie!" Kali screamed as her bottom bounced on hills moving through her orb. "Stop!"

Dexter's eyes shifted to Nellie who was rubbing his hands together before separating them like he was flinging a card. His cage shattered into smoky wisps before it was sucked into Nellie's palms in a ribbon of twinkling fairy lights. As it traveled into his son, Kali's jail burst and retreated into Nellie's palms. Both sat on the grass, staring at each other, rapt.

Dexter immediately opened his arms. He felt Nellie's wrap around his neck first. Dexter kissed his cheek a million times, wishing he could squeeze his son so hard that he would become a part of him. His eyes flitted to his daughter who was standing with her hands linked behind her back and her vision darting all around Dexter. Like a bug was encircling him.

"What's that?" she said hesitantly, taking a tiny finger and pointing it just above Dexter's head.

"Let's go!" Zeek boomed, already halfway to the edge of the mountain.

Dexter ignored his friend and peered aloft, but there was nothing other than the billions of stars that created a canopy of sparkles. "What are you looking at?"

"You have red all around you," her sweet voice shook.

"Red? What do you mean?"

"The outline of you is bright red." Kali's hand drifted toward Dexter's head. As soon as her fingertips neared his ear, his daughter flashed out of existence.

Disappeared.

Gone.

"Where the hell did she go?" Zeek screamed.

"Kali!" Dexter called.

She reappeared with her hands covering her ears. "Ow! That was loud!"

Dexter let out a huff of air and reached out to hold his daughter. As soon as his hand neared hers, she vanished again. But he could feel his daughter's hand in his. Invisible. "Look at your brother. What color is around him?"

"Pretty Gold," said her floating voice.

"And Zeek?"

"Green. But, Daddy, yours is very, *very* bright! Very red!"

Dexter let her go and his stunning daughter came back into view. What were these colors Kali was seeing? Auras? Was she reading a type of aura? "I want you to touch your brother's gold light."

She stepped closer, twiddled her fingers, and reached out to her brother. Their bodies glitched before they both disappeared.

Suddenly, a large hand clamped down on Dexter's arm. "We have to go before Atraeus finds a way to get to us," Zeek demanded.

Dexter stood and faced his friend. "Okay, Kali. Let go of your brother."

Silence.

He scanned the area, doing his best to avoid eye contact with the pit, and waited for his kids to respond. "Kali!" Dexter's eyes roamed the mountain for several more seconds before he realized neither were reappearing. "Nellie!"

"Where'd they go?" Zeek questioned with a frantic catch underlying his voice. "Fuck. If we had just gone when I said to—"

"Kali! Nellie! Where are you?" Dexter whipped his head around the empty mountaintop, fearing they were gone forever.

Chapter 24

▲▲▲

The edges of Sara's vision were smudgy. Wispy even. Each jab of her knuckles against the black vinyl bag bolstered her sense of security. She had to train. Had to break the muscle memory of ballet and build martial arts into her body's knowledge. After punching a hole in the wall of her bedroom, a spark of freedom twinkled in front of her and extinguished. Control. That's what she needed. Within twenty-four hours she had purchased a punching bag to take out all her anger on.

Sometimes the bag would be Marty Brown. Sometimes Tyler Grant. But today, sprawled across the black fabric was her father's face. Punch after punch, kick after kick. Again. Each strike suppressed part of her past for the duration of her workout.

After two hours, her arms shook and her legs burned with muscle failure. Once her breathing turned laborious, she rested her head against the bag and her foot on the base for a short rest. Sweat from her forehead poured onto the fabric as she listened to the boom of the bass blasting from speakers on her dresser. This playlist that she had named "Be A Badass" always amped her up.

That was good enough. She couldn't fathom lifting her wrapped knuckles for one more punch. She moseyed to her computer to shut off the music. And, what filled her ears was madness.

Screaming.

Sirens.

Distant, inhuman screeches.

An ear-piercing shriek sent her to her knees as she slammed her reddened palms over her ears.

The sound of her heartbeat battered in her head as she ran to the window to see what was going on. Blue and red flashes from police cars filled the night and engulfed all the townhouses on her street as dozens of people clambered in different directions. Some held their children, some held their pets, and others, their loved ones.

Gunshots erupted from the ground just as an impossibly large, winged creature swooped down from the sky, plucked a man from the street, and lifted him into the air and out of sight. Then another. Sara let out a horrified scream as adrenaline surged through her coursing blood.

There was no time to process. She grabbed a black backpack from under the bed, went to her drawers, and stuffed clothes into it. Then, she looked down at herself. Short shorts and a nude bralette. "Dammit." She pulled on black jeans and the first top her hand reached for. A white "V" neck shirt. After that came on her black bomber jacket that was slung over her desk chair. She rushed into the hallway, opened the medicine cabinet, and stuffed a handful of meds and bandages into the pack. Down the stairs she went in a frantic hurry, snatching her father's hammer covered in his dried blood and a few water bottles from the fridge. The walls of the house shook with gunfire and evil screeches of the monster.

"Come on. Hurry!" she encouraged herself as the calamity outside amplified. She zipped on gray high top sneakers by the front door while planning an escape route. In her dad's room was a balcony that had a few branches she could jump to. She could hide in the trees and figure out where to go from there. Maybe get out of the city.

As the second shoe came on, the thought of Dexter Bennet smothered her mind. And, she was utterly pissed at herself. Why the *fuck* was she thinking about him? Now of all times? He hadn't thought of her in years. He didn't deserve space in her brain. But, she listened to the thought, listened to her body that urged her to flee to his house and see if he was all right. She let out a low growl. No. Fuck him! He never cared if she was all right. He would probably be gone by now. He would check on perfect, popular Debrah Kassini far before ever checking on her.

But, what if...

What if he had headphones on, or if he was practicing a song and couldn't hear?

Dammit!

She didn't have to listen to the side of her that hoped he would be there with open arms, welcoming her with joy. Because that side of her was sure to be disappointed. Instead, she listened to the logical side. He was a neighbor. That was all. There was a rightful duty in helping a neighbor, friendly or not. "Dammit, Dex! You better fucking be alive."

For all she knew, he went to his friend's house for the weekend. But, she had to check or she wouldn't be able to live with herself.

She opened the door, prepared to brave the several yards to his house, but a large body propelled toward her, crashing into her at full force. With the momentum, she fell to the ground, back aching and chest compressed with the weight. Then, she heard it. His voice. And it filled her with miserable peace.

"Sara!"

The wind was knocked from her lungs, so all that came out were grumbles and gasps.

Dexter's hand rushed to her cheek, guiding her face toward his. "Are you okay?"

The moment his cerulean eyes met hers, she dove in. He was actually looking at her. He was seeing Sara for the first time in years and it choked her. It caused a swirling storm of lust to churn, and she had to resist the impulse to kiss him even if these could be her last few moments alive. What would the scruff on his face feel like against her cheek? What would his arms around her feel like now that he was muscular instead of scrawny? Instead, what she spat out was, "Dude, what the fuck? Get off me!"

His brows knitted together as he rolled off. "Did you just swear?"

She got to her feet, bent over his hulky mass that was sprawled on the floor, and grabbed his hand. "Come on, you idiot! We have to go!" she tugged, letting him pick himself up before sprinting up the stairs. His heavy footsteps behind her mixed with his breathing sucked the air from her lungs and was replaced by his musky scent, an intoxicating aroma that she hadn't smelled in years. A lump formed in her throat that wanted to break free in the form of tears. That he came for her in a time that seemed like an apocalypse was on the rise. That was how their relationship was, right? The underlying love they had shared as children would have lasted this long. She pushed aside the need to sort out her inner turmoil for a better time.

Sara led him to her dad's bedroom and slid back the glass door to the balcony just as a crashing sound exploded from above. Debris rained on them as an ivory beak pushed through the ceiling, aiming for Sara. She yelped, pulling the backpack in front of her chest for protection and fell onto her back. A serrated beak speared the pack, grazing her stomach. Sara let out a wild cry as it ripped open flesh on her abdomen.

"No!" Dexter grasped onto the beak, cutting open his own hands, and pushed it to the side with all his might.

The beak retracted only to come down again, but Dexter grabbed onto Sara's waist and dragged her away just as the beak speared through the floor and into the downstairs. Dexter hauled her to her feet. "Get your ass up, Marking! Hurry!"

She hefted herself up while she spun to the open door and sprinted into the cool night air. In a quick jump from the wooden balcony, she made it onto a branch and moved toward the bough of the pine tree to make room for Dexter.

A cracking rang out behind her as Dexter's voice echoed from below. Sara peered down and saw him lying on the ground next to a snapped tree branch. With a quick climb down, she put a hand on his thick bicep as one of the large creatures flew overhead. Its massive body blocked the moon while letting out a terrifying screech that started from a low growl then morphed into a high-pitched cry. "Get up!"

He got to his feet, took her hand in his, and sprinted down the street, crossing into back alleyways to flee the city as quickly as possible.

They ran side by side for miles before most of the screaming faded. They slowed their pace as they neared the beach. There were a few people walking along the shore, unaware of the catastrophe that ensued a few miles away. Dexter squeezed her hand hard, telling her that even though danger wasn't immediate, to still stay alert. He didn't let go until he tucked her safely inside a shallow cave in a rocky cliffside that lined the beach. Their heavy breathing filled the small cave as they listened to the screaming of citizens slowly approaching. His open palm rubbed her back gently.

"What's happening?" Sara asked between breaths.

"I don't know. But, let's catch our breath here for a moment."

"What the hell are those things?"

Dexter didn't answer. He just pulled her into his chest, mumbling into her hair. "I'm so glad you're okay. I don't know what I would have done if one of those things got you."

She molded to his sturdy form. Words nestling in her ear with love and light. Just for a moment, she let herself pretend the last ten years had never happened. Just for a minute, she let Dexter mend her.

The sound of a cocking gun clicked in her ears, awakening her senses.

"Get out," a deep voice demanded.

Dexter pulled Sara behind him in a swift motion, but as soon as he let her go, she ducked under his outstretched arm and repositioned herself between him and the gun.

"Sara!"

His husky urgency shook her to the core, but she was determined not to let it show. Instead, she grabbed the barrel of the Glock, pushing it to the right while her other hand shoved the man's wrist in the opposite direction. The man was forced to release the gun as she turned it to face the intruder.

"Whoa, Sara," Dexter breathed out behind her.

Fuck yeah. It felt good to impress him. Show him what he had been missing for ten years.

Ten years.

Ten fucking years!

What was she thinking letting Dexter affect her like this? Was that all it took? A few seconds of being in his arms to forget how much she *hated* him. For her heart to lurch for him? She grasped the gun tighter to compensate for the war igniting in her brain.

She had no time to think through her confusing feelings, so she quickly buried them and turned her attention on the hooded teenager standing just outside the entrance of the cave. "You going to leave or should I just shoot you now?" Sara huffed with authority.

The teen raced off and Dexter's hands snaked around Sara's shoulders, but now she had no desire to be touched by him. Not until the war between the love and hate she felt toward Dexter had been won, one way or another. She twisted out of his embrace and aimed the gun at his forehead. "You," she growled out in disgust.

His apologetic eyes were wider than saucers. But, they were also familiar and filled with an aching love she had never been in the presence of before. "Sara. What are you doing?"

"Why?"

"Why what?" he said, bringing his bloodied hands up in surrender.

"Why'd you come for me?" she gritted out from between her teeth. "Why now? Why fucking bother after this many years?"

Dexter dropped his hands, repositioning them over his heart. "Hey," he whispered, "let me explain. Just please, put the gun down. I'm not your enemy."

As much as she was swooning over his attempt to rescue her, she was just as disgusted by his face. She grasped harder onto the cool metal of the gun, feeling the rage of his absence suck her into a tunnel of darkness. "Fuck. You. Dexter. Bennet."

"Sara." His brows turned up, and he flinched at her words. He gripped the grey T-shirt over his chest like he was trying to rip out his heart to hand it to her. "Please. You're scaring me."

"It took flying beasts for you to talk to me again? Are you fucking serious? This is what needed to happen?" she screamed. "For people to die?"

She could see it on his face as each word of her sentence registered. His shoulders went slack. His vision roved over something else. Her belly. "You're hurt," he whispered.

He prepared to take a step closer to her like he wanted a closer look at her wound, but Sara shook the gun to hold him at her mercy, ignoring the feeling of her blood leaking into her jeans. "Like you give a shit."

His jaw went rigid as his lower lids layered with tears. She was hurting him. The deep-rooted sadness set in his eyes told her which side of the war won. Love. Nearly ten years and she still couldn't stand seeing him upset, or sad, or anything in between. She loved him. Dammit, she still fucking loved him. But, that didn't mean the hurt in her chest just disappeared.

His eyes raised to hers in appalled horror. "I've always cared about you, Sara. Always. Put the gun down and let me explain."

A close lick of the monster's screech echoing through the universe had her loosening her grip on the gun. "Why? Why now? Why not when Marty Brown *raped* me?"

"Sara—"

"Why not when Tyler Grant punched me and knocked me out? Why not when," her voice turned into a visceral shriek, "*my dad violated me!* Dexter! Where the *fuck* were you then?"

His eyes turned to wet sapphires, and all she wanted to do was live in the light they radiated. In that moment, under the pain, she recognized his love for her. That was all she had ever wanted. But, this one enlightened moment wasn't enough for her to get over her own pain. This was not enough. Life had taught her nothing good ever came out of anything. She would

293

be delusional to expect a reconnection with Dexter after all this time. If this was how agonizing it felt to see Dexter's love, it wasn't going to get any better. Better to go out now knowing he cared about her than to continue to live and become disappointed and hurt all over again. She stepped backward.

"What are you doing, Sara?"

Another step.

"Don't," he said, stepping toward her. "You stay in this cave, Sara."

She shook her head and the gun. "I'm done," she explained, letting the tears stream down her face. Letting the pain in her stomach numb—letting Dexter's eyes heal her. "I've been done for a long time." One more step and she was fully out of the cave. She lowered her gaze to the ground and watched her own tears drip to the white grains of sand beneath her feet. The gun juddered as she trembled. "This is enough, Dexter. Of all the fucking people, *you* hurt me the most. I loved you, and you punished me for it. I don't want you if this had to happen for you to want me."

"Sara," he whispered, stepping forward again. She noticed the way her name came off his lips. Like it had always been on his tongue, waiting for the chance to say it. "Please. Stop."

His gentle touch cupped her cheek, tenderly wiping away the tears with a thumb before his other hand wrapped around her hand that held the gun. She loosened her grip and let Dexter take it. His loud exhale of relief filled her ears as he dragged her to the back of the cave where they were concealed by shadows.

He turned on the safety before tucking it into his waistband and brought her into his arms where she mourned for all the things she wished he had been there for. Her legs buckled with the feeling of Dexter holding her. He guided her to the ground where she curled into his lap and cried. "I've always cared about you, Sara." He rubbed her arm up and down and kissed the top of her head. "I've always been with you for everything horrible that happened. I *never* stopped caring about you. I swear on everything that I am."

"Liar," she whimpered, not caring to listen to another squawk of the creatures. This was more important.

"It was me, okay? It was because of me that Marty died." He squeezed her harder. "I killed him after I found out what he did to you. I *never* stopped caring for you."

Her head popped off his chest. "What?"

"And I fought Tyler after he hurt you. That's how I broke my arm." He wrapped a hand around her head, and brought it back to his broad chest, rocking her back and forth. "And if I had known about your dad, I'd have killed him too. No one is more important to me than you. No one. And, I'm so sorry for hurting you."

Then, she bawled her eyes out, chest convulsing with sobs.

"Shh," he hushed, holding onto her more tightly. "I love you, Sara Mar King. So much."

She didn't answer. The hate she felt for him still swam through her blood and wouldn't go away with a simple admission. But... she loved him too. Always.

The world smudged at the ends as it morphed. She didn't want to leave the cave. She didn't want anything to change.

She wanted to stay curled on his lap and let everything sink in. "Dexter..."

"I'm right here," he whispered. "You're okay. We have to get through this. We'll survive together. Okay? Say you'll stay with me."

Just as she was about to respond, everything about him went slack. The arms around her fell to the ground in a thump. She looked up only to see a white beak speared through his skull, slowly extracting.

She clutched the beak, ripping open her hands. "No! Dexter!" As it let him go, she turned to him, clawing at his chest, screaming his name until her voice went hoarse and her throat turned raw. His face blurred as tears filled her eyes. She *just* got him back! This couldn't be happening! It couldn't be real! If she screamed his name louder, he would hear her. She could wake him up. He would wake up for her, right? "Dexter!" She took his heavy head between her hands and watched a stream of blood drain over his closed lids. Her voice cut off when the winged creature screeched in her ear.

She spun to face its sharpened beak, flattening her back against Dexter's chest. It hovered inches away from her forehead, and wherever she moved, it followed. Green filtered through her vision and a burning appeared around her neck. She arched her back with a cry for help, clawing at her throat to extinguish the heat.

You have the rare opportunity to save humanity. I will give you a powerful gift that will make you immune to what is happening to your world. To live without worry. In exchange, you must sacrifice your life at the top of Mount Verta in four years. Do you accept this deal with the Devil?

The deep, invasive voice rang in her head. While she endured the burning, she did her best to relax against Dexter, grab his arms, and wrap them around her, pretending he was still there. Four more years without Dexter. Four years to mourn him, just to die in the end. When she could die right there in his arms? Where she felt she had always belonged.

She yelled out a harsh, "No!" before she watched the beak approach as fast as lightning.

There was a distant screaming. The soreness in her throat told her it was her own. Sara jerked to clear her mind of dying with Dexter in a cave the day the screechers arrived, but something restricted her arms and legs as she flailed to escape the vision.

"Sara!" a female voice calmed.

She thrashed again, needing to get as far away from the horror as possible. When her eyes slit open, white fluorescent light poured in, hurting all her nerves.

"Dexter!" she cried in sobs. "No! Not Dexter!"

"Sara. Calm down. Dexter's okay," the woman comforted.

She squeezed her eyes shut. "No, he's not. It got him."

"Sara, whatever it was, it was just a dream. Dexter's okay."

When she opened her eyes, expecting to see a beak, she saw a woman with a round face and large, brown eyes come into view. Sara gasped at the confusion. "Who are you?"

The woman's brows furrowed. "I-I'm Emily Merrit."

Her eyes shifted to another woman behind her who had a bald head, onyx eyes, small features, and zig-zag shaped tattoos down her skull. "Who are you?"

"Jane. I know why you wouldn't remember me, but you don't remember her?" She pointed to Emily.

Sara shifted her vision between the two women, eyes pleading for help. "Where's Dexter?"

"He's coming," Emily said through a smile.

For a moment, that was all she wanted to hear. She relaxed into the bed. Dexter was alive. "How'd I get out of the cave?"

"It was a dream, Sara." Her voice fuzzed, but Sara did her best to stay concentrated.

It was a dream? But, it was real. Right? No. A dream. Her eyes scanned her surroundings to see she was lying in a hospital bed with a thin cotton blanket over her lap. She gripped the blue fabric once her eyes riveted on the needles sticking into her skin and the silver machines surrounding her. The moans of other patients in different rooms filled her ears and sent her stomach into a turbine of nausea.

But, she was not in the cave. "Where's Dexter? Did they take him?"

"No, no. Sara, Dexter is alive and well. He's coming."

Alive and well. It had been a dream. So where the hell did she stand with Dexter? Did he know her? Had they spoken in the last ten years? The desperate need to understand reality swirled through her fogged brain. "Is he still talking to me?"

Emily smiled. "Yes. Of course he is."

Sara's brows turned up as tears filled her eyes. "He is?"

"Yes. Relax. You had a lot of peli."

298

"Peli?"

"I need you to relax."

In her peripherals, bodies appeared out of thin air. Two small children. Sara shrieked, and shrunk away from them. "What the fuck!" She looked down at her arms that were in foam restraints. "Help!" she yelled, thrashing beneath the bands. "Let me out of here!"

"It's okay, Sara." Emily let go of her hand and rounded the bed to the children. "Kali! Nellie!" She reached down and lugged the two into her arms.

As she did, the little blonde girl frowned and burst into tears. "What? Mommy doesn't remember me!"

Emily's head whipped up. "What? Why do you say that?"

Mommy?

The child sprinted to Sara, arms outstretched as she climbed up the bed and snuggled into her side. "Mommy! No!"

"Me?"

Emily's eyes went wide. "She's your daughter, Kali. And this is your son, Nellie," she explained while pointing at him. "You had twins with Dexter. Do you remember?"

All Sara could do was take in the information and try to breathe deeply. When the little girl curled to her side, head under her pit and crying, she couldn't believe what she was hearing. *This* was the dream. Right? Having kids with Dexter? How? That meant she had to have had sex with Dexter Bennet? What the fuck was going on? Why couldn't she remember! Sara screwed her eyes shut and prayed for something to clear up.

"Mommy!" the little boy screamed as he, too, clambered into the bed and snuggled on her other side.

She looked down at the two, faces reddening, tears drenching their cheeks, and arms clinging around her belly. "This isn't happening. I'm dreaming, right?"

"You're not. I promise. This is your real life."

She looked to Emily, who was unwrapping Sara from the bounds. "Where's Dexter? I need him right now! Get me Dexter. Please!"

Emily whipped out her phone and pressed buttons. "Let me call him and see how far away he is." She bit her bottom lip, glaring at Jane with worry before saying into the phone, "Dexter! Sara's awake. And the twins are here." She was going to continue talking, but stopped to listen to what he had to say. "Yeah, I don't know how they got here either." She paused. "Okay, she doesn't remember me or them... Yeah, she remembers you, but it's weird... Okay. She's scared. How far away are you?" She listened again before holding out the phone to Sara. "He wants to talk to you."

Sara snatched the phone and brought it to her ear. "D-Dexter?"

"Hey, Marking. How are you feeling?"

It was him. She could never forget his husky timber she loved so much. "What's going on? Where are you? And..." she took a hard gulp, "are you really talking to me again?"

There was a stretch of silence on the phone. "Yes. We've been talking for a long time. Don't worry, I'm coming to see you right now. I promise I'll explain everything."

"W-What happened after the cave?"

Another pause. "You and I were never in a cave."

Tears streamed down her face. "Yes, we were! The big monsters were coming and we ran to the beach. You brought me to a cave and then—and then you died! Dexter, you died! I saw it!"

In the most calming tone she'd ever heard him use, he said, "Just a dream, Marking. I'm alive. Everything is okay. Trust me, please. It was just a dream, and I'm just so glad you're okay."

"No, Dexter. It did happen!" She could practically feel the cool metal of the Glock still in her hand. "And I pointed a gun at you. I'm so sorry!" Tears poured through her vision. "Don't leave me again."

He sighed. "Please, try to relax. I know the world seems scary right now. But, I promise, it'll be okay. I'm talking to you, which means it wasn't real."

"Where are you?" she said, putting a hand on the little girl's back who was still crying by her side. "I need to see you."

"I'll be with you in a few hours. I'll get to you as fast as I can."

"Are you just saying that?"

"No. I'm not. I'll be there for you. Emily is a good friend. She'll help you with whatever you need until I get there."

"Okay," she agreed as she sniffed back tears.

"Is Jane still there?"

Sara nodded, forgetting she was on the phone.

"Sara?"

"Yeah. Jane is here." Sara looked at Jane, whose eyes were locked on the phone.

"Then you can trust her too."

Sara cleared her throat and looked back to the kids. "Are these really our kids?"

"Yes. And you're a phenomenal mother, Sara." She could hear his smile through his words, calming her frayed nerves from hearing the children cry. "Please know everything will clear up soon, okay? Just enjoy being with the twins."

"I-I don't know them."

"And that's okay. I'll be there soon. I have to get off the phone, so that I can get to you."

"Okay," she muttered, wishing he could stay on the phone with her until he walked through the door.

"Okay, Marking. I love you. See you soon."

The sound of him calling her Marking. Saying he loves her. It itched a part of her brain that was still asleep. She was missing something. A hole in her mind. "I'm forgetting things, aren't I?"

"Yes. You were given a drug that made you confused. I'm hoping everything will clear up soon."

She looked down at the kids huddled on either side of her. "Hurry. I need you."

"I'm coming. I love you."

She squeezed the phone tighter. "Do-do I say it back to you?"

"Well," his laugh rang through the phone, "you usually say it first."

"Okay. Then, I love you too."

"Deep breaths. Figure eights if you need to. Okay?"

"Okay."

"Bye, Marking."

The phone disconnected and she was left with two children she didn't recognize crying at her side and two women staring at her.

To escape their gaze, she looked to her lap and rubbed the backs of the two children. "Why am I in a hospital?"

"You were in a car crash," Emily informed, sitting in the chair beside her and crossing her legs. Jane followed suit. "We gave you a lot of a powerful drug to make sure you're okay. The doctors weren't sure if you were going to make it. You scared all of us."

A thunderous sound erupted through the halls of the hospital, sending Sara up in alert and a cry from her lips. Then, she heard it. The screech of the winged monsters. Its low rumble licked to a high, piercing pitch. Sara scooted herself against the wall behind her. "They're back!"

Emily and Jane were quick to scoop the children up and bring them onto their own laps. "What's back?" Jane asked.

"The monsters! They're coming. They're coming for us! We have to get out of here!" Sara jumped out of the bed, dragging the machines she was attached to. She clawed at the wires to free herself in petrified terror.

"Doctor!" Emily yelled down the hallway.

"Mommy!" the little girl screamed, arms reaching out for her mother.

The boy stuck out his palms toward her. "It's not working! Emily! I can't change it."

"Keep trying if you can, Nellie."

A crowd of people in white coats rushed in, cornering Sara against the wall. The saw-like beak crashed through the ceiling, spraying debris in every direction. Sara let out a bloodcurdling scream, thrashing against the people's hands who were trying to restrain her. "You don't understand! We have to leave! Now!" Sara urged as two nurses latched onto her arms.

Her breathing staggered as the panic restricted her lungs. All she could think about were the walls closing in on her. The viruses and bacteria lurking on the skin of the people who were touching her and the inability to escape the creatures.

Then, the screech of the monster rang out as its ivory beak impaled the little girl on Emily's lap through her tiny belly. Her blonde tendrils bounced as her head flung backward. "No!" Horrified, Sara pitched forward, trying to make a mad dash for the girl before the creature hoisted her into the sky as the hands clamped down on her harder to keep her in place. She twisted, swung, and thrashed, but her attempts were futile. There were too many people to fight against. Sara was forced to watch the horrifying scene unravel. "Let me go! It's got her! It's got the girl! Emily! Do something!" A prick in her arm let a cool liquid into her system. "Let go!" The edges of her vision darkened with fatigue. Everything blurred and her head grew heavy. She fought the urge to stay awake for the girl's sake. "Let... me..."

She could feel herself falling forward just before her world detonated to a blackness that would put midnight to shame.

Chapter 25

▲▲▲

Dexter stormed through the hospital like a force of nature waiting to be reckoned with. Emily led the way with Zeek trailing behind. Dexter ignored the two guards standing outside Sara's door as he entered her room. His whole body heated with startling shock upon seeing his Marking bound to a bed by foam restraints. It was something he could not have prepared for. There was barely a trace of blood running through her pale cheeks. Sunken in a pool of gray were her closed eyes.

"Daddy!" Nellie screamed. He looked down at his son who sprinted to him from Jane's lap.

"Hey, bud." Dexter leaned down and lifted his son into his arms, kissing his cheek several times. He put Nellie down and opened his arms for Kali. "Hi, pretty girl. Come here."

She cautiously dismounted Emily's lap then plodded over with tears in her swollen red eyes, lips pursed in a pout. "Mommy doesn't remember us," she cried. "She was really scared." She stumbled into Dexter's arms like it was taking extra energy to maneuver her legs. As soon as she was in his arms, she disappeared. But, he could still feel her pressed against his body. He lifted her, kissing what he thought was her cheek, but was really her ear.

"I can't see myself," she simpered.

"I know, pretty girl. When you touch me, you turn invisible, remember?"

"Whoa," Jane muttered from the chair beside Emily's.

Dexter shifted his attention to Jane's sunken eyes. "Thank you. I don't know how to repay you. For saving her," he said, gesturing to Sara. "You saved my family while I destroyed yours. I didn't deserve it, but thank you. Whatever you need, I'm here for you."

It looked like she was going to say something but decided to give a sullen grin instead.

He looked to Emily as he approached Sara with an invisible Kali still in his arms. "How is she? Is she okay?"

"She's okay. We used all of the peli. Hallucinations started again after you called. They had to give her a sedative to sleep it off."

Nellie was at the foot of the bed with his hands on Sara's feet. "Nellie, next time Mommy's scared, do you think you could change what she's seeing?"

He frowned, rubbing his hands over his heart-shaped face. "I tried! But, it didn't work."

Touched that his son had tried to protect Sara, he leaned over, ruffled his caramel hair, and said, "That's all right. Thanks for trying, bud."

Dexter pulled up a chair on the opposite side of the two women and positioned Kali on his lap the best he could before unwrapping Sara from the restraints. He held Sara's hand as Kali wrapped her arms around his neck. Dexter put his other hand on his daughter's back. "She doesn't remember me," she whimpered.

"She will, Kali."

"What happened? Is she sick?"

"Well, she got hurt. So we gave her medicine to feel better, but that medicine made her a little confused. She'll get better. Don't worry."

"What about me?" Nellie asked.

Dexter smiled. "She'll remember you too, Nellie." He closed his eyes and took the first deep breath of that day. He had Sara's hand in his, Kali around his neck, and Nellie clinging to his mother. He had his family.

He did it.

They were all alive.

He had saved them all.

And he couldn't have done it without his friends. "I love you guys." Dexter took a moment to make eye contact with each person in the room. "All of you." He noticed Jane shift in her seat, straightening her back. "I owe you all my life." Tears welled on his lids, so he lowered his head and squeezed hard to keep them from spilling over his cheek. "They are the reason I keep going."

"We're here for you, man," Zeek rasped, taking Nellie into his arms.

Kali clamped tighter around Dexter's neck. He sighed to escape the weight of the situation. "Hey, Kali?" he said in her general direction, sniffing back tears. "What happened when you touched Nellie?"

"I don't know. I wanted to be with Mommy. And then we were here."

"Teleportation?" Zeek chimed in as he moved to Emily and put a hand on her shoulder.

Emily covered his hand with hers. "Want to fill us in?"

"They have new powers. Nellie can suck the green energy into his palms. And, Kali sees different colors around people. So far something new happens when she touches different people."

Emily looked to Kali. "Cool! What color am I?"

She shifted on Dexter's lap. "Purple."

Emily leaned forward. "What happened when you touched me?"

"I heard what you think."

She made eye contact with Zeek. "That's good to know."

Suddenly, Zeek, Emily, and Jane all flinched in unison. Their eyes grew wide with both fear and shock while gawking at something behind Dexter.

"Hello again," a deep voice rang. The same voice that crawled under his skin from the entity that wanted to rip his family away from him.

Guy.

Atraeus.

Chapter 26

▲▲▲

Dexter growled as he turned to face his enemy, placing Kali on Sara's bed in the process. He spread his arms to protect his family. Zeek, Emily, and Jane rounded to Dexter's side, creating a wall of protection.

Guy's cobalt eyes darkened to an endless obsidian. His thick brows lowered in anger while a crooked grin formed over his lips, face covered in thick scruff. He appeared bigger than he used to. Taller and more muscular. A black shirt stretched over his muscles and snug jeans fit over his hips.

"You cannot have my family," Dexter roared.

"Well, I can. And I will. My kids are inside your annoying brats. I need yours back to get mine out." He bowed his head and glared at them from below his brows. "Don't worry, you can have your kids back when I'm done with them. Whatever's left of them."

Dexter stepped forward. "I fulfilled your stupid deal for six years. Our contract is done. We are done. You shouldn't even be here right now. You need to leave us humans alone. You've tortured us long enough."

Guy cocked his head to the side as a sinister smirk spread over his thin lips. "I'm not leaving without my children. Thanks for getting them off that mountain. I found a better one."

"Kali, take your brother somewhere else—" Dexter ordered.

Just as he finished his sentence, a scream burst through the air. So loud, it had Dexter wheeling around to see who it was coming from. Nellie was standing on Sara's bed, straighter and more confident than Dexter had ever seen anyone before.

Eyes glowing.

Palms facing Guy.

Neon orbs claiming his palms.

Screaming, "Leave us alone!"

"Nellie! What are you doing?" Dexter shouted, reaching out for him.

But, when Guy let loose a torturous cry, he turned back to see Guy's body begin to bubble, swirl, and warp. Flesh peeled off his face and arms, revealing the swarming green energy beneath. The clumps of skin dissolved to the green substance before it flew into Nellie's hand like a vacuum. Layers of Guy kept disintegrating until he was in his true form. A green orb with small glowing particles circling it. And that, too, didn't stand a chance against Nellie's newfound power.

"Nellie!"

Once every ounce of the green sphere filled Nellie, his hands dropped. His eyes rolled to the back of his head as he toppled backward.

Jane was fast to reach over the bed and grab the front of his shirt to keep him from smacking his head on the ground. She let him go when Zeek's arms were beneath Nellie's back, scooping him up to hand him to his father. Dexter cradled him in his arms, calling for him over and over again.

Nellie's eyes flew open in all their radiating glory. His hand shot out to Dexter's throat, but it barely made an impact.

"Are you trying to choke me?" Dexter said in a confused laugh.

Nellie dropped his hand and what came out of his mouth was the voice of Atraeus. "You're lucky my child is in here. If not, I'd be shredding this kid's organs." His eyes went back to vibrant emerald and brows turned up, tears dripping over his lightly freckled cheeks. "Daddy! Guy is yelling at me in my ears. He's really mad."

"Hey, bud. It'll be okay. Listen, I want you to show Guy space. Okay? Stars, galaxies, planets. Anything you can think of to calm him down," Dexter urged, forcing a composed expression on his face.

"I'm scared," he mumbled.

"I know. But, you did good. Show him some stars. Go to sleep."

"I'll try." Nellie shut his eyes and in a moment everything about him relaxed.

Dexter kissed Nellie's forehead, loving him that much more for being as reckless and brave as his mother. He sighed and looked to Emily. "Could you take Kali home? It's been a long day for her. She needs her rest and her stuffy."

"Of course."

Kali hugged Dexter's legs, turning invisible in the process. He bent to her level and kissed her cheek. "You did good too."

"I don't want to go. I want to stay with Nellie and Mommy. I want to stay near your red light!"

"I know you do. But they'll be okay. Emily will be with you at home and I'll be there soon too, okay? With Nellie and Mommy."

As soon as he let her go, Kali reappeared. Her head hung heavy on Emily's shoulder, eyes closed. Emily looked to Jane. "Want to come? I can catch you up on everything that's been going on."

"Go," Dexter offered. "Feel free to eat, shower. Whatever you want."

Jane graciously nodded and headed out with Emily.

Zeek put a hand on Dexter's shoulder. "I'm going to drive them, but either Emily or I will be back."

Dexter grinned with a nod.

Then it was just Nellie and Sara. Both unconscious. Dexter placed one hand on Nellie's arm and the other on Sara's. "Sara, wake up. I miss you so much. We need you back." She had new scars over her face that the peli had healed. A thread-like zig zag from her temple to the corner of her lips and a few others over her hairline from the crash.

She didn't move. But, she was breathing.

"I want to see that you're okay." Dexter took in a deep breath, pulled up a chair, and leaned over to rest his head against the edge of the mattress. Once he closed his eyes, exhaustion dragged him into a deep sleep.

Pressure on his hand had him up in alert. Sara. Her beautiful green eyes were open with curiosity and her strawberry lips were pressed in a straight line.

"Sara." Dexter smiled, squeezing her hand with one of his and rubbing the sleep from his eyes with the other. "You're awake."

Her eyes looked as muddled as the time she had first seen him with a beard. Confused and unrecognizable. Her eyes flitted around the room before returning to his. "Are you my doctor?"

The question blew a canon-sized hole through his chest. She didn't recognize him. Dexter's brows creased, retracted his hand from hers, and placed it over the ache in his heart. "No. I'm Dexter. You're boyfriend. You don't remember me?"

Her cheeks flushed as a smile ripped over her face. "No." She giggled. "That can't be right." More laughing. With both hands, she pushed herself into a seated position. "But, holy damn, I wish that were true. You're one handsome hunk."

Dexter laughed, unsure what to make of her silly, playful mood. No matter what she was saying, he was beyond ecstatic to be talking to her. "You're not so bad yourself," he expressed.

She covered her mouth with her hands and looked away in a sheepish gesture while bringing her knees to her chest. "I don't know who you are."

A slow breath with his eyes closed was all he needed to make her words sting less. "I know. But we know each other very well. And we have two children. Nellie and Kali."

Sara snickered like she was on laughing gas, and it filled Dexter's soul with uter peace. "No, we don't. Stop lying! What's happening?"

Dexter sighed. "Well, at least you're laughing," he mumbled to himself. "What's the last thing you remember?"

She scrunched her lips to the side, thinking. "I-I... I. I can't remember."

"It's all right. Everything will come back soon, okay?"

With a quick tilt of her head, she narrowed her eyes, and asked, "You're my boyfriend?"

"For now," Dexter answered. "I intend on proposing to you soon."

She let out a deep belly laugh that calmed his frayed nerves. "Stop lying! Where am I? Freaking Land of the Perfect Men?"

Dexter couldn't resist a smile, admiring that she probably felt like shit but still decided to put on her rose-colored glasses. He swooned hearing her call him attractive despite all they had gone through. "Sara, I need you to try and remember."

She eyed him, relaxing her laughs. "Okay. How do I do that?"

Dexter shifted his eyes to his son who was still sleeping at the foot of the bed. "Do you remember your son? Nellie?"

Her eyes turned serious as she looked to analyze him. "I-I-I'm really a mom?"

"Yes. And you have a daughter named Kali. But, she's at home sleeping."

"Who's their dad?"

Dexter furrowed his brows. "I am."

There went her darling, deep cackle of hers again. "What! No. We've never had," she hushed her tone to say it, "sex. I've never even seen you before!"

Dexter smiled. "I hate to break it to you, but we *have* had sex before. Many times."

"Liar!" she said through the tail end of her laugh.

"And you liked it too," he said with a wink.

Her cheeks flushed with embarrassment. "I would have remembered having," she softened her volume again, "sex with a hottie petottie."

Dexter grinned. Fuck, he wanted to enjoy her like this, but he just wanted her back. He needed her back. Needed her help to fix what was happening to Nellie. "Try."

She scrunched her face in a show of remembering then threw up her hands. "Nope, nothing."

"Try again. You're a mom. Kali and Nellie are your kids. And they love you so much."

Her laugh faded and in its place emerged a frown. "Kali and Nellie?" she whispered to herself.

"Yes. And, I'm Dexter. Bennet. We've known each other since we were kids. We lived right next to each other. We used to walk to school every morning. I helped you pick up worms off the pavement. Um," he thought about what else to say that could jog her memory, "you used to do ballet and tape notes for me to your bedroom window. I used to have a beard. And—"

Her eyes roved over him. "Bennet." Silence stretched while their eyes remained locked on each other. "Sir Bennet."

"Yes! You call me that." Dexter leaned over and kissed her forehead. "Say you remember me." When she didn't answer, his heart sank.

She shrugged, yawned, and lay back down. "Doesn't ring a bell," Sara hummed as she pulled the covers over her shoulder. "Sorry, Dex-Ben. Wait, what was your name again? Sorry," she paused to rub her eyes, "I feel all loopy."

Dexter sighed and put energy into suppressing the prickly panic bubbling to the surface that there was a very real possibility that she would never remember. "It's okay. Can I get you anything? Food? Water?"

"No thanks." From soft and tired, she shot up out of bed in all of a second, alert and wide eyed, fear growing on her face. Whatever made her switch from silly to gravely serious was something dangerous and wicked. "Did you hear that?" she whispered.

"No?" Dexter questioned looking out in the hallway where nurses were chatting leisurely at their own desks.

"That screeching sound. I've heard it before." Her eyes shot to the ceiling as she yelped in terror, drawing the staff's attention. "Watch out!" In a quick lunge, she jumped from the bed, pushed Dexter and his chair backward by his shoulders with herculean strength then crumbled before him.

"Sara," he called to wake her from whatever peli vision she was living in and caught her waist before she hit the ground. When her body went slack, he gathered her to his lap and waved the doctors away from the door frame. "Sara, it's the peli. You're okay. You're safe."

"D-D-Dex—" She coughed and her eyes closed.

"Nothing's going to hurt you, Marking."

A gurgling sound came from her throat before she fell silent, limp.

"Sara?" Dexter filled his lungs and held it until she curled on his lap like a cat that had found enough comfort to sleep. He let out the breath with relief and held onto her for dear life. "You're okay, Sara. You'll remember us. It'll be okay."

The comforting words never ceased for an hour. They were meant for both Sara and Nellie, possibly even becoming a prayer to the universe. One arm was wrapped around his precious Sara and the other on Nellie's stomach.

Every few minutes, Dexter kissed the top of her head, keeping his nose buried in her floral scent. "You're okay," he whispered.

When she awoke, he laid her on the bed so her drowsy mind could better filter the information around her. Her eyes fluttered to Nellie with a wrinkled brow of confusion then to Dexter. "Hey," she croaked.

His chest contracted, anxious to know if she recognized him. "Hey."

Her eyes went wild, scanning her hospital room then Dexter. "A-are you my doctor?"

The question deflated him. "No, I'm not. I'm Dexter."

Batting her eyes, she wiped some of the confusion off her expression before she sat up and pulled the covers over her bare legs. "Oh. Hi, Dexter." She said his name precisely as if trying it out for the first time.

"Hello." This time, he was far too exhausted to even crack a smile, but he tried to keep his expression welcoming.

She cleared her throat. "I'm sorry, but who are you?"

"I'm a friend. You were in a car crash. I'm here to help you."

Her eyes flitted to Nellie. "Okay?" she held the word out questioningly.

"This is Nellie."

"Nellie?"

"He's—" Dexter stopped himself, suddenly refraining from wanting to give her too much information. Overloading a clouded mind wasn't going to do either of them favors. "He's my son. We came to check on you."

"Oh," she grinned, wrapped her arms around herself, and let her fingers fidget with the sleeves of the thin hospital robe.

"How do you feel?" Dexter asked as he grabbed a paper cup from her bedside table and moved to the sink to fill it.

"I think I'm okay." When he brought the water to her, she snatched it, tilted the brim to her lips, and chugged.

He held his hand out. "Let me get you more."

She shook her head and placed it to the side. "No thanks. I'm good." After a long, deep breath that she let out excruciatingly slow, she stole several glances at Dexter. "I'm sorry, but I'm having a very hard time remembering... anything."

It hit him then. The weight of her erased mind pounded on his shoulders. Anything. She couldn't remember *anything*. In that moment, he realized what a possible gift this could be if it were permanent. She didn't remember Marty Brown, or Tyler

Grant, or her parents. She wouldn't have that grit of angst that derived from the immense pain that cut her soul in thousands of lesions. She wasn't suffering. Time in the Screecher Age, completely wiped squeaky clean. Years of being under Guy's manipulation, gone. She no longer had to suffer from any form of PTSD. She had reverted to the innocent Sara Mar King he first fell in love with, the one who enthralled him and enticed him to be curious about life and taught him what loyalty truly meant. He could be the man she had always wanted. One that knew how good he had it straight out of the gate.

This could be so good for her. So healing for her.

Sara couldn't remember the years of pain…or him. She couldn't remember him. Didn't remember any rendition of how deep their love went, how intimate he was with her and only her. She-she didn't love him. And that thought alone sliced him in half. Which was worse? Which was best? Which should he be hoping for?

She leaned forward like she was going to whisper a secret, so he did too, hoping for some clarification. "I'm so embarrassed to ask this, but I-I don't remember my name. Do you know it?"

"Sara Mar…" "Bennet" was at the tip of his tongue. Just give her the name. She would want it after all, wouldn't she? If her mind was intact, she would have wanted him to say "Bennet", right? Maybe it would lend as a subtle reminder every time she heard it to who he was to her. Or, it could further separate her from the only name she ever knew. The only name that might bring her beautiful mind into the light and back to him.

Her innocent eyes went wide with unyielding trust that he knew he would never earn if he wasn't truthful. If this was her forever, he would want her to want his name. "King." He shifted uncomfortably in his seat before repeating, "Sara Mar King."

A sparkle in her eyes glittered as she giggled, leaned back, and drummed her fingers on her thigh. "Oh, right. I knew that."

Dexter grinned as her laugh filled him with love. "Did you really?"

She nodded. "Yeah. Sara Mar King. Sounds familiar." She cleared her voice. "Are my parents coming?"

How was he supposed to navigate these questions? As a brand new Sara or as the Sara from yesterday? God, he wanted to shake her and tell her to wake the hell up and tell him what to do. He placed one hand on Nellie as a tether to the truth to keep his mind straight. "No. I'm sorry, they aren't coming."

A sadness creeped into her eyes. "Oh. Good." She leaned in again to him. "I don't think I liked them. Right?"

Dexter grinned. "Right. You and I have only ever had each other."

She grinned like that statement pleased her. Well, that was what he'd hoped the happiness dancing on her face meant.

"Dexter," she said while staring at her hands. His name repeated on her lips, holding out the "R" at the end of his name longer and longer. "Dexter B-B-B."

His eyes raced to her face as they narrowed in her direction, desperate for her to get there.

"Dexter...B-B-B." She huffed and scrunched her mouth to the side. "Does your last name start with a B?"

Dexter smiled and nodded. "Keep going, you're doing great."

"Dexter B-Ben-Bet?" she enunciated with a charm about her he had always adored.

"Yes! Great job, Sara."

Her eyes latched on Nellie and pointed. "Nellie Bennet?"

Dexter nodded as an impulse to grab her hand and kiss her cool knuckles overcame him. Even after his lips made contact, he rested them on her hand a few moments longer.

She retracted as her eyes budged. "I thought you said we were just friends."

"Did I?" he nudged with a hooked brow.

Her cheeks seared with heat and he wanted to bathe in it. Her neck craned forward with squinted eyes. "Did you used to have a beard?"

"Mmhmm."

"Yeah, you kind of look familiar."

The words cradled his ear, and he decided it would be best for her to remember him, remember everything. He wanted his Sara back. Marred soul and all. And he vowed to support her and to heal her tortured soul every day if that was what it took. Dexter rested his elbows on his knees.

She adjusted herself and said, "Can you bring my son closer?" The words fell from her lips like a splendid waterfall of pure honey. Sweet and smooth. Her eyes widened at the shock of her own words before they fixated on Dexter. "My son? Is he my son?"

Dexter chuckled. "He is."

"But, he's yours too."

"He is."

The heels of her palms dug into her eyes for a moment before she looked up and out the door. "Oh my god! Kali! Where's Kali!"

Dexter put a hand up to keep her from jumping out of the bed. "She's okay. She's fine. She's at home resting with Emily and Zeek."

Panic possessed her as she moved to her knees to dismount the bed and run. "Dexter!"

He lifted his open palm higher and closer to her. "I promise. She's okay, Marking."

After a few blinks of her deciding whether to trust him or not, her body went slack and she doubled over to rest a hand on Nellie's head. "Marking. Mar King. Marking." Her eyes shifted from the left side of her bed to her right in a rapid repetition. "Marking."

Dexter waited, hoping for the peli blanket covering her memories to lift and bring his Marking back to him.

"I'm so confused! You can't be Dexter Bennet," she uttered.

"No, no. I am," he corrected, desperate for her not to go backward.

She eyed him. "You can't. He hasn't spoken to me in years." The feeling of her gaze on his skin lulled him away from panic. "You have tattoos. Dexter? You got tattoos?" she pointed to one of his sleeved arms.

"Yes. I got a lot."

She smiled, sweeping away a lock of bangs. "My hair." She shoved her fingers into her the tresses and ruffled it. "Where the hell did my hair go?"

"You cut it. A while ago."

"Oh," she giggled out, "I forgot."

In a whisper, Dexter murmured. "Look at me."

Her sparkling green eyes electrified him with a hint of recognition as she dropped her hands to either side of her body.

"Keep looking at me."

She did.

"I'm right here, Marking." He took her hand and wrapped it in both of his. "Keep looking."

She followed his command.

"Say you remember me."

"I do remember you. I remember Kali and Nellie. But everything else is fuzzy. I'm sorry. I just…"

He licked his lips and sucked them between his teeth.

A subtle shift in her eyes had Dexter reeling with hope. She threw her legs over the side of the bed and scooted to the edge. Her slender hand came to his cheek before the other followed. "Dexter Fucking Bennet," she said with a half-smile. "I love you…right?"

Selfishness overcame him. Her touch coaxed him to lean forward and brush his lips across hers as if they had a mind of their own. But it was his natural reaction to having her so close to him. After how many hours went by, wondering if that moment was ever going to happen again. She didn't back away, her sweet breath filling him. He pressed his lips more firmly against hers in a cautious pressure. When she took a swift intake of breath, he sucked on her top lip, to keep her where she was. Immense joy sprung in his heart that she was alive and well while praying the kiss would trigger something more in her. Trigger all of them. She rested her face on his shoulder and her arms fled around his neck in a tight squeeze.

"I love you, Sara."

He heard her sniff as she coiled herself onto his lap and snuggled her face into his neck. "Kali's okay?"

"Yes."

"Where's Atraeus?"

"I have a lot to catch you up on, but just hush for a minute." He stroked her hair and kissed her head. "Be still," he cooed as he held onto her tighter. "I missed you so damn much."

"I'm sorry," she simpered.

"Don't be." With his cheek, he nuzzled her temple. "You scared me."

A few deep breaths went by in peaceful silence. "Are you okay, Dexter?" She unfurled herself, leaned forward to cradle her son in her arms, and kissed him. "What happened? You got them back without me. How?"

While he recounted the events, Sara fell silent.

With each part of the story Dexter retold, she clutched onto Nellie tighter, kissing his temple dozens of times. "What do we do?" Sara asked.

Dexter scrubbed his face with his hands. "I'm still thinking."

Just like that, her thoughts reeled loudly. Back to her old habits. Her eyes shifted from one spot in the room to another like she was reading her own ideas. Then, chaos erupted in her mind, causing her to look at him wide-eyed.

"What? What are you thinking about so loudly?"

"I think I know how to get rid of Atraeus for good."

Dexter grinned. He knew she'd come up with something. She was fucking brilliant.

She scrunched her face in apprehension and was disgust by her own plan. "But, you're not going to like it."

Chapter 27

▲▲▲

In front of her was no longer the sweet Dexter she adored, but the strong, obstinate warrior that looked at her with an annoying and overwhelming need to protect. "No! Absolutely not." He stood from his chair and paced the room with a rigid spine.

She straightened herself in the bed, crossing her legs and resting her hands in her lap. "It'll work," Sara coaxed. "We have to try it."

"I said no," he barked.

Sara rolled her eyes.

"Stop it and get it out of your mind. I'm not risking your life. Especially after a horrible crash where I almost lost you."

With hands flat over her heart, she smiled. "I feel fine."

Dexter folded his arms over his chest. "Because of the peli, not because you actually are. Think of something else."

Sara sighed then gritted her teeth. "It'll work and you know it. We need to save our son and the rest of humanity! What is there to think about?"

His jaw went rigid. "Sara. No."

Chin tilted upward, back straight, and arms crossed, Sara did the best she could to overpower his authority. "Yes, Dexter! Don't you have more peli just in case?"

He shook his head. "There's not enough peli in the world that would ever get me to agree to this!"

Sara rolled her eyes. "Worrywart."

Emily's fluid form rounded the corner with a handful of clothes for Sara, saying, "Whoa. What are you two fighting about?"

"Emily!" Sara squealed.

"Sara? You remember me!" Emily leaped to Sara's side and squeezed her friend. "Oh thank everything good in the world!" As soon as she noticed Dexter fuming, she readjusted her face to a serious one. "What's wrong with him?"

"Emily. Back me up here. I have a foolproof way of getting rid of Atraeus for good. And Dexter doesn't even want to try it."

"Okay, shoot," she expressed, repositioning herself in a chair, crossing one leg over the other, and giving Sara her full attention.

"If Atraeus kills another person on Earth, he's done for. The easiest way for that to happen is—"

"Did you just call this 'easy'?" Dexter might as well have been foaming at the mouth. "There is nothing 'easy' about your plan."

"Will you let me finish?" Sara growled, her tolerance for his skepticism nearing its limit.

Dexter sighed and paced the room.

Taking the lack of pushback as a momentary acquiescence, Sara started again. "If we get Nellie to kill me, boom, bye, Atraeus."

"Sara—" Emily interjected.

Sara put up a hand to stop her. "But, it'd be fine because he can bring me back," she explained with jazz hands.

"What do you mean he can bring you back? How would you die and come back?"

"Well it's not like I'm going to give Nellie a gun to shoot me. So I thought, why not drowning? Dexter can use CPR, and it's all good. People flatline all the time and end up fine."

"No!" Dexter roared, blue eyes searching Emily's for support. "I'm not risking her life. Again. Our kids need their mother. And, I don't have enough peli to bring you back from the dead if this doesn't work!"

Sara's head whipped to her best friend. "Emily! Help me out here."

Emily shrugged and took Sara's hand in hers. "I mean... it sounds logical."

"Get out, Emily," Dexter ordered in his booming baritone while pointing toward the door.

Emily lifted her brows. "Yeesh. I've awoken the monster." She looked to Sara, clearly the only one who would listen. "There are a lot more questions I have, like do you know for sure it would work?"

"Well, no, but he let it slip to Dexter that he couldn't kill anyone else. So I'm guessing it might mean he'd either sky rocket back to where he came from or die. I'm cool with either." She looked to Dexter who was still pacing, stroking his chin like he missed his beard. "You sacrificed your life for kids you didn't even know yet," Sara argued. "You should know damn well what I'm feeling right now."

"You cannot ask our son to drown his mother!"

Sara's eyes went wide. "Our son is in danger! And, we are his parents. We make the choice. And I choose to get that son of a bitch out of him before it kills Nellie. We don't have time to think of another goddamn plan."

Dexter eyed both women. And when he didn't say anything, Sara knew she was gaining ground.

"I think it could work," Emily chimed.

He huffed and said, "Fine. If you want to try this, then I'm the one going underwater. You understand?"

"No," Sara said, shaking her head. "I don't have enough strength to bring you back."

"Zeek will. And you can stay home with Kali."

Sara jumped off the bed to face her match head on in a duel. "No, Dex. I need less peli than either of you. And, I've already had six years with the kids. If anything goes awry, it's your turn. You don't get to just leave again. You promised!"

"I'll do it," Emily offered with a hand up in the air. "That way both of you are safe. They can't lose either of you, especially after all they've been through."

Both of them looked to her, but it was Sara that spat out, "What? And get bludgeoned to death by Zeek for letting you? I think not."

Emily sent her a heavy-lidded stare. "I'm serious. I adore your kids. This way I'll make sure they keep *both* their parents.

Besides, how hot would it be to have big, strong Zeek save my life?" She explained with a dreamy smile.

"Thank you, but no. He's my son. This is my family. I wouldn't ever ask—let anyone else to do this. And if it's me, I *know* Dexter will bring me back."

Dexter rubbed the back of his buzzed head with both his hands as he sighed. "Right now, I still have peli in me. You can do this, Dexter. It'll take all of five—ten minutes."

He stared at her nice and long. "But, what if..."

"I'll come back. Okay? You're going to bring me back."

His face paled and sweat beaded along his hairline as he said in a slow groan, "Sara, I can't live with the what if."

She smiled, recognizing his walls coming down. He knew she was right. This was the safest way to save Nellie and get rid of Atraeus. "It's going to be okay."

"But, what if I can't bring you back?"

"Then, it will still be okay." Sara turned her back to Dexter's broody atmosphere, content with the little wiggle room he gave her so far. She busied herself with getting dressed and tucking Nellie safely in her arms. "Can we finish this conversation at home? I want to get out of the hospital."

Dexter didn't wait. He couldn't. The whole way home he lit Sara's ears with his many concerns while she and Emily did their best to put them out. When they entered the house, Emily went upstairs to the kids' room to tell Jane and Zeek what had been decided.

One of Sara's arms was tucked under Nellie's bottom while the other hand cupped Dexter's cheek. "We need Kali, Dex.

She can tell you when I've stopped wanting to leave the water. That way you can get me out as fast as possible."

Dexter's knees buckled with hopelessness, taking Nellie into his arms and holding him tight. "I can't do this. I'm sorry. I can't lose you. I can't put Kali and Nellie through it. To put you in danger on purpose. I can't. You better think of something else."

Sara laughed. "Do you remember how many times you've put me in danger before this? What's the big deal?" she said with a popped out hip and an eye roll. "This is nothing new."

Nellie was so small. Even his sensitive soul was small. Killing his mom would destroy him. And Kali. How could he make her see this? Nothing he said seemed to penetrate Sara's cool, determined resolve. This could destroy the kid.

Sara leaned to Nellie's ear while stroking errant strands of hair off his forehead. "Mommy and Daddy are going to save you. Don't you worry your pretty little head," she whispered.

Emily was zipping up Zeek's grey jacket as she marched down the stairs.

"We need Kali," Sara called.

"Sara, please." Dexter put a hand on her shoulder, squeezing it.

In that instant, gone was his fun-loving Sara Mar King. In her place was the pixie soldier that had survived in the rotting forests for four years. "Listen closely, Dexter Bennet," she said stepping forward and pointing a finger at him. "That is enough. I am doing this with or without you because it is going to work. I *will* save our son and our planet. If we kill this thing, he cannot come back ever again. Not in four thousand years. Not ever. Do you understand? I can still fulfill my purpose of saving humanity."

"Is that what this is about? You still *want* to sacrifice yourself? After all I've done to make sure that never had to happen again? After you had kids you're still responsible for?"

"We are all more responsible for this world, because without it, there is no us, there is no family. When you agreed to that stupid deal, you screwed over everyone in the future, and our kids are part of that future. This is our chance to undo that and *still* have our family." Her jade eyes turned wild. "We could literally have *everything* we have ever wanted. We don't have to live in fear from anything or anyone ever again. We need to kill this bastard. And, you know it."

Kali's footsteps pattered down the stairs beside Emily. Behind was Zeek, a shadow attached to Emily's heels.

"I'm putting my offer on the table," Zeek huffed. "Just to be clear."

"Well, take it off!" Sara sneered. "He's my son. I would never let any of you do this for my family." She looked to Dexter. "It has to be me."

Fuck! He just wanted to shove her in a closet and lock her in there until he could think of some other way out of this mess.

"Why does Daddy want to lock you in the closet?" Kali spewed in a tired slur directed at her mother.

Sara whipped her head to Dexter. "Don't you dare."

His jaw went rigid, anger outweighing panic.

Sara moved to Kali. "Kali. I need to ask you something. It might be scary."

"No, Sara!" Dexter interjected, grasping onto her upper arm and hauling her away from their daughter.

Sara's green eyes narrowed with anger and a low growl rumbled through her throat.

Kali held out a hand for Emily to take.

Emily looked down and jerked her hand away. "Sorry, Kali. You can't read my thoughts right now. You'll have to listen to your parents to see what's going on."

"It's fine," Sara said as Dexter bulldozed over her words with a "Don't."

Kali let out a similar growl in protest before she took an aggressive step closer to Emily and grabbed her forearm. Then, his daughter's eyes became two cyan saucers.

Dexter rushed to his daughter's side and held her now invisible body into his side. "Kali, don't worry. That's not going to happen."

"My neighbor has a pool," Emily offered, hesitantly peering at Dexter.

"Jesus! Everybody out! I need a minute with Sara." Dexter ordered, not taking his eyes off her for a second. Zeek took Nellie while Emily took Kali.

"We'll meet you at my house," Emily said.

Dexter looked up the stairs that led to the closed door of the twins' room. "Where'd Jane go?"

"She's in the kids' room... crying. She said we could do this without her."

He grumbled at the fact that they wouldn't be totally alone but snarled and continued. "Fine! Just go." Then, they were gone. All that was left was Sara's pleading eyes. "Use that perfect brain of yours and find some other way."

"It'll be okay. Trust me."

"It's not going to happen. I swear, I will lock you in my tower if you don't bend."

Sara let out a childish cackle and playfully punched him in the arm. "I'd like to see you try."

Dexter's fists clenched and his nostrils flared, trying to suppress the rising temper Sara was instilling in him. "Sara Mar King. I'm telling you it's not going to happen. Either think of something else or let someone else do this. Our kids need their *mother*. And *I* need *you*."

The hardened fog in her eyes cleared and she morphed back to his lovely, genuine angel. She took a measured step closer and held his head between her hands. He closed his eyes while her floral scent filled his lungs, praying for her to let this idea go. "It's exactly why you won't give up on me. Our children are my life. I might as well kill myself now if we can't protect them."

That was not what he was expecting his sweet Sara Mar King to say. In a quick movement, he pushed her hands away from his face and stepped back. "Sara. I'm fucking *begging* you right now."

Half expecting the hard-edged soldier to remerge, he relaxed when her devoted tenderness remained set in her green jeweled eyes. "I hear you, Dex. And just like you said to me a billion times six years go, I'm okay with whatever happens." Then a smile touched her lips, and he knew she had won. "But... also, bring me back. Okay?" She cocked her head playfully. "You know CPR right?"

His shoulders slouched as he nodded.

"Great." She kissed his cheek.

He knew once Sara was hellbent on doing something, nothing was going to change her mind, especially when it involved the greater good. Fuck, how did he agree to this? He would do anything to save his son, right? Even lose Sara? His heart pumped out ice-cold blood that chilled his veins and made him cherish each beat of time they had together as he tugged her into his arms and rested a kiss atop her head. "I'll bring you back, Sara. I promise."

Chapter 28

▲▲▲

Every step along the pavement felt like he was leading her to her own memorial service. As if she were a ghost already, he could have sworn she was floating beside him. While he took slow laborious steps, she tugged on his arm to keep him moving forward. She was alive and leading the way, clinging to his arm. Every so often she would kiss his skin, sending goosebumps down his spine. Would this be the last of her kisses?

Flashes of watching her twirl in her high school bedroom filled his mind, blonde tendrils spinning in a fan of sunshine. In his hands, he could feel the slimy wetness of the hundreds of worms he helped her pick up as a child and the unique giggle she let out whenever she'd set them down in the grass. The neon glow of her eyes was all he could see. Then, he felt the patter against his chest from the cherries she threw at him while at the cabin, surrounded by Nell's garden of flowers. He drowned in the tears of joy that filled her eyes when she found out she was pregnant, which urged his own to well.

"Don't cry, Dex. I need your mind clear for this."

He wiped the tears on his shoulder and sniffed back the rest. What if... What if this was the end?

In a swift impulse, he spun in front of her, and got down on one knee. He looked up into her emerald eyes unsure if he was ready to beg her or marry her.

Her eyes grew large with confusion. "Dexter? What are you doing?"

Reaching out for her, he held onto both hands for dear life. "Marry me."

Her brows turned up as she shouted, "Dexter!" She tried to take her hands back, but he held onto them tighter.

Her reaction to pull away from him closed his throat. "Say you'll marry me."

She said nothing and blinked.

"Dammit, Sara!"

She flinched at his volume.

He softened his tone. "Sara. Mar. King. Be my wife."

She wasn't smiling, or frowning, but water glistened between her lids, amplifying her electric green irises and pummeling him with a need to save them. Inundated with sheer protectiveness for this tenacious woman, he watched her slowly get on both her knees and rested her forehead against his.

"No matter what happens now or in the future, I will choose you every time. I love you and only you."

Still she remained quiet.

"Please," he whispered, one hand wrapping around the nape of her neck. "I don't know how many different ways I can ask you, but I swear I will ask as many times as you need me to for you to say yes. Will you marry me, Marking?" He looked up to kiss her forehead and saw a smile rip across her face. "Say yes." Then, she started laughing and it clicked. "Don't you dare say, 'oh balls'."

Her deep belly laugh exploded from her chest. "Dexter! Yes! Of course, I'll marry you. I honestly thought you'd never ask me. I'm sorry, I just needed a second to process. But, yes, Dexter Bennet, I'll marry you a hundred times over."

Dexter smiled so wide he thought his face was going to shatter from happiness. Everything in him burst with overwhelming love for her. He pressed his lips against hers fervently and prayed the moment would last until they both died from old age. "I-I don't have a ring."

Sara kissed his cheek. "I don't need one."

"Want me to tie a worm around your finger?"

Another belly laugh gushed as she stood. "Ew!"

Dexter stood and dragged her into him. "I love you so damn much."

She grinned against his chest. "I bet I love you more."

"Not possible."

She giggled and his soul filled with love, strength, and everything in between. He wasn't going to lose her. He couldn't. He was going to marry her. It was set in stone. "All right, Sara. Let's save Nellie."

The two fell into step as they approached Emily's two-story townhouse that was painted a bright yellow. But, in the dark of the night it appeared more foreboding and ominous than cheery.

Sara knocked on the door, but there was no answer. After a second knock, Dexter pounded his fist against it. "Emily? Zeek?"

Sara scrunched her lips to the side, thinking loudly. Her eyes wandered to the two neighbors' houses. "Didn't they say meet at her house?"

Dexter furrowed his brows. "No, I think they said their neighbor's house? Right? Because they have a pool."

Sara shrugged and looked to the house to the right of them. "I think I remember this neighbor having a pool. The kids played in it once after they moved."

The two moved to the neighboring home, walking the paved path on the side of the house hand in hand. At the end, Sara peered through the slats in the wooden gate and froze with fear. "No!" Sara unlatched the lock on the other side with a loud clunk and swung open forward.

Dexter trailed behind Sara into the backyard, only to feast his eyes on Nellie and Zeek submerging their hands into an oval pool to hold Emily beneath the surface of the water. Locks of her black hair spread out like the legs of a dead spider. Over Zeek's wrist was her wet hand, white knuckles gripping it tightly. But, whether it was to signal that she was okay or to cue him as a plea to let go, Dexter did not know.

Overwhelmed with guilt-ridden relief that they hadn't gotten there in time to stop them, he watched Kali's blonde hair bounce behind her back as she charged toward Sara, palms open and energy orbs manifesting. The beams shot out into Sara's chest and she helplessly stilled. Plastered over Sara's face was a look of absolute horror, like someone had eviscerated her from the inside out, piece by grueling piece. Then, Kali's eyes shifted to him and she dropped her hands. She could see Dexter wasn't going to stop what was going on.

Dexter went to Sara's side and kissed her cheek just before a dreadful scream echoed through the night, disturbing the silence in the seemingly deserted neighborhood. He shifted his gaze to Nellie who had fallen limp by Zeek's side then violently convulsed. His eyes squeezed shut with a contortion of agony.

Zeek's right hand kept a firm grip on Nellie's arm to keep him in contact with Emily, knowing it was the only way to rid Atraeus from stowing away inside of him. With his other hand, Zeek tried to keep him from falling into the pool with his spastic movements.

Dexter ran to his son, placing a hand on either side of his body as a protective cage. "Nellie!"

A deep roar cried from Nellie's mouth. Atraeus. "Stop!" it shrieked. "No!" Nellie's glowing green eyes flew open and his brows turned up. More spasms overtook his small body as drool spilled from the corners of his mouth.

"Kali!" Zeek roared.

"Not yet!" she cried, clinging to her mother's leg.

"Hang in there, Nellie. You can do this," Dexter whispered while wrapping one arm under his son's head to keep his upper body elevated. As he wiped the sweat pouring down his temples, Dexter felt Nellie's skin heat to a scorching burn that stifled the air around them. A green light swam just beneath his chest, glowing under his indigo T-shirt and casting a shadow on his organs and rib cage.

Emily's hand slowly released Zeek's and it drifted away, up and out flaccidly. Each finger was slightly curled and paled.

Nellie's eyes opened wide and his mouth dropped to release a terrified scream. The light erupted through his abdomen in a spindle of buzzing, sparkling energy. In Atraeus's natural form, he swirled in the air around Nellie, spiraling in and out of his chest as it fought to reenter his son. The toxic energy branched into dozens of diverging pieces, like fraught cobwebs, a few feet above Nellie. The splitting of each tendril snapped and crackled like a firework as more reached out toward Dexter, the sky, the pool, the ground, the universe. More and more of Atraeus's infection poured out of his chest in neon specks which zipped back and forth in a glitching, dying frenzy.

The more the Father of Fear spiraled out of Nellie, the hotter his body became. Hot enough for Dexter to feel his fingertips burn. But, he didn't care. Dexter fought through the pain to keep hold of his son while Nellie fought to keep his own body intact the best he could.

"Almost done, Nellie! Stay with me!"

"Stop!" Atraeus's voice was arcane, terrified, and layered in panic. In a sudden explosion, Atraeus's atrocious being erupted in a rain of glowing particles that blanketed the entire backyard. One by one, each green speck burned out like fiery embers extinguished in the breeze. The pavement sparkled in a wonderland of unearthly glitter. Pieces sunk to the bottom of the pool, silhouetting Emily's unmoving body as those, too, burned out and brought them back into the dark night.

Nellie's body sagged in Dexter's arms as the last light burned out.

"Nellie!" Dexter bellowed.

"Now!" Kali screamed.

Zeek released Nellie's hand and reached into the water for Emily. Her head hung forward as he hauled her from her watery grave. Thick droplets dripped from her wilted body, darkening the pavement in puddles.

Jet black hair streamed over her ghostly pale face in straight inky lines. Zeek laid her on her back beside the edge of the pool, tilted her head up to better open her airway, then began chest compressions. His face was full of extreme focus. Thick brows tugged downward, eyes wide with concentration, and lips pressed together, punctuated with a rigid jaw.

Dexter tore his eyes away from Emily and put his fingers to Nellie's carotid artery in search of a pulse. A shallow beat fluttered beneath his son's skin, and everything about Dexter relaxed with relief. "Nellie's okay, Sara!" he announced without looking at her.

Grunts from Zeek stole Dexter's attention.

"Come on, Emily. Come back to me," Zeek called in short grunts with every compression.

Her eyes remained closed and her jaw hung open.

The minutes that passed without any sign of Emily's return had Dexter clinging to his son tighter.

Tears spilled from Zeek's eyes onto Emily's torso as his efforts dwindled to slower, more laborious pumps. "Emily!"

Chapter 29

▲▲▲

Kali rushed to Emily's side, put a hand over her forehead, and closed her eyes. "Keep going!" she encouraged Zeek.

He gaped at Kali for a millisecond before he pressed onto Emily's chest harder and breathed into her mouth again.

"Keep going!" Dexter commanded.

The two words seemed to give Zeek enough strength to keep the rhythms.

Kali let go of Emily and ran to Dexter. He brought her into his side and kissed her rosy cheek as she wrapped her arms around his neck and disappeared.

Water spewed from Emily's mouth and poured down her chin, followed by a visceral cough.

"Emily!" Zeek cried and snuggled her close.

Dexter reached out for Zeek's arm. "Let her go. She needs room to breathe."

Zeek shrugged Dexter's arm away and continued holding her.

The mix of coughing and deep gasps of breath erupted from Emily as her arms clung to his arm that was wound tightly around her torso. "Did it work?"

"Yes, Emily. Good job."

Kali moved to Nellie and rested a hand on his head. "I see him getting up and crying. He doesn't feel good." Her arms wrapped around her brother and stayed there in a long embrace. They both disappeared and reappeared just behind Dexter.

"Whoops," Kali uttered. "Mommy's really mad."

She was dying within her skin. As if her soul clobbered against the cage of her body. Emily. Nellie. Both in danger and she was frozen, forced to watch everything.

By the time Emily came to and Dexter announced Nellie was alive, Sara had exhausted herself. She had ridden out the relentless panic invading her mind.

Dexter held Nellie in his arms, and Kali followed close behind. He walked to Sara and kissed her cheek. "We'll be back."

"No, I want to take Nellie," Kali urged, peeling off Dexter's fingers off her brother.

"Kali, I have to go with you, sorry."

"No! I want to go with Nellie alone." She scrunched her nose, squinted her eyes, and pouted with an awakening temper he recognized all too well.

Dexter knelt but twisted his body so Nellie was out of reach. When she tried again, he jerked her brother farther away.

She stomped a foot and whined. A low growl rumbled out of her tiny chest. "He's my brother!"

"I know, Kali. And I'm going to let you, if you can follow my rules."

What? Sara's own body vibrated with a growl that would go unheard. *Dexter! You better fucking go with them. They are six years old and Kali doesn't have the best control over her powers yet.* She thrashed again as Dexter continued.

"You are only allowed to think about two things. Zeek's shop and this spot right here. Take a good look around at where you are."

Kali sucked her bottom lip between her teeth and did a slow spin to imprint her surroundings.

"You think you got it?"

She nodded with a thumbs up. "Got it."

"If you can't come back, you stay in Zeek's shop and you do not leave. And you don't talk to anyone. Do you understand me?"

Another nod. "Yup. I can freeze them if I have to."

Dexter twisted her brother back to her. "Make me proud, pretty girl."

Her fingers inched toward Nellie, a face of solidified determination before they both blipped out of sight.

Sara remained watching Zeek and Emily together.

When Zeek held Emily in his arms, it was like he was enveloping her with his entire body. Every inch of her was covered—cradled against him. He whispered things in her ear that made her smile through the laborious act of breathing. He didn't dare let her go even when she tried to get some space.

He kissed her forehead and smiled against her cheek. She wiggled out of his secure grip, muttering, "You're acting like you were scared." She weakly stood, staggered back toward the pool, and was caught in Zeek's arms.

"I *was* scared," he huffed out. With him standing so close to her, Sara realized what a stark difference in height they were. Zeek towered at seven feet while little Emily came to his mid-chest. Where she lacked in height, she made up for in spunk, enough for Zeek to be entertained for decades.

No matter how much they embraced—no matter how much they had succeeded, they had done this without Sara. And that infuriated every fraying fiber in her body.

Released in a fall of motion, Sara balanced herself before stalking straight up to Zeek. Dexter lazily stepped into her path like he could sense she needed to release pent up energy.

"Sara," Dexter warned.

He couldn't stop her when she ducked, spun around him, and advanced toward Zeek. In a fast spurt of movement, Sara lifted her arm and readied it to smack him across the face. Zeek caught her hand and squeezed.

"How dare you!" Sara shrieked in a tone so primal that her vocal cords seized up.

Zeek towered over her, dark eyes boring into Sara. "Emily remembered that you might be pregnant. You couldn't have done this."

The words registered like she had slapped herself. She dropped her arm and her jaw. How had she forgotten? She would have never forgiven herself.

Sara looked to Emily. Her brown eyes sparkling with tears that now matched the ones falling down Sara's cheeks and smiled. Sara wrapped her arms around her best friend and cried into her shoulder. "I love you, but I'm so mad at you for doing that. For putting yourself in danger. Please. Tell me you're okay."

"I'm okay, Sara."

Sara's shirt absorbed the water still dripping off Emily. "Thank you. So much."

"Love you."

"I love you too. Thank you."

"You better be my best friend forever now."

Sara gave a sad chuckle and said, "Always!"

They stayed like that for a long while before she moved to Zeek, hugging his waist tight. When his arms came around her, she felt the warmth and security she was sure Emily experienced whenever they embraced.

Small hands wrapped around her legs. Sara looked down and saw her children. She bent down and wrapped the two up in a bear hug that they couldn't have gotten out of if they tried. She kissed them a hundred times over and cried. "I love you two so much! I'm so proud of both of you!" She looked to Nellie and took his head between her hands. "Are you okay? How are you feeling?" She ran a hand over his forehead to feel his temperature. It was as warm as a mild fever.

Then tears gushed from his eyes in torrents.

"What's wrong?" Sara moved her hands over his arms, rubbing them for comfort.

He wiped his eyes with the back of his hands. "I don't have my powers anymore."

Sara's eyes enlarged. "No?"

"No."

She studied Nellie as he cried. Red nose scrunched, frown opening into a sob, and shoulders slack. His whole world had ended. "Oh honey, it's okay."

"No! I want my powers back. I loved them!"

Sara snuggled him close. "I know you do. It'll be okay though. Mommy and Daddy don't have powers. Zeek and Emily don't have powers either."

Kali moved to her brother and wrapped her arms around him. "It's okay, Nellie." She kissed his head. "I can try to give you mine."

"You're so sweet, Baby Kay," Sara said while stroking her hair back. "Here, I think your brother needs a sister hug." Sara stood and looked to Dexter whose arms were open. She melted into him. As soon as his arms enclosed around her, she felt free. For the first time, she could breathe easily.

A loud yawn from Emily sounded behind her.

"Come on," Dexter announced to everyone, "let's go to our house. We'll put the kids to bed and relax."

"Sure. Let me go shower and change into dry clothes first." Emily looked to Zeek and smiled. "Want to help?"

Zeek tucked her into his side and looked to Dexter with a wink. "We won't be coming, but thanks for the invitation."

"Fair enough. Our house tomorrow for a thank you dinner then."

"Cooking from Dexter? I'm in." Emily smiled while wringing out her hair.

Sara gave her best friend one last hug.

Nellie rode on Dexter's back all the way home while Kali galloped beside Sara.

"Hey, Kali?" Dexter asked as they strolled down the street.

Kali slowed as she looked to her dad, bright, golden hair illuminating in different shades and tints with the incandescent moonlight.

"What color is Mommy?"

She blinked, expression dropping. "Silver."

"What happens when you touch her?"

A frown pulled down on her lips. "I don't want to talk about it."

Though curiosity swathed him, he stroked her hair back and whispered, "It's okay, Kay. When you're ready you can tell me."

She shook her head, turned back to the street, and continued to gallop away.

Sara arched her brow at Dexter, asking him to investigate.

Chapter 30

▲▲▲

The kids were tucked in. After Nellie whined for Jane to stay in the room with them, she begrudgingly agreed even though she preferred the seclusion of the couch downstairs. Her slender body rested on a makeshift bed Sara had made out of comforters and stray blankets, just like she normally did for Emily. Nellie passed out from exhaustion by the end of Dexter's lullaby, but Kali's eyes were wide awake and staring at her mother. The curious look in Kali's eyes struck a chord of confusion Dexter couldn't extinguish.

"Daddy? I want to tell you something." She gestured with her index finger for him to come closer. When he knelt, she cupped his ear with both her hands. "Silver. I can tell you what Mommy wants."

Dexter smiled, admiring his daughter's strength and trust. He turned his head to whisper in her ear. "And what does she want?"

She giggled. "She will tell you soon. But when she does, know that I'm okay with it."

"Okay, pretty girl." He turned his head and gave her a quick kiss on the cheek before she could vanish for too long. She snuggled farther into her covers, wrapped her arms around her stuffed unicorn, and closed her eyes.

"Goodnight, my perfect children," Sara cooed.

"Sweet dreams," Dexter echoed to his kids. "Night, Jane."

"Night," she repeated, glaring at Dexter in a probing way that he was uncertain about.

Sara turned off the lights and closed the door. Her warm hand latched onto Dexter's forearm and dragged him to the bedroom down the hall. She spun in his arms and kicked the door closed. He wasn't sure if she was aroused or ready to break down crying. But, once he took her into the circle of his arms and rocked her side to side, tears pouring from her eyes.

"Dexter," she cried out.

"I'm right here."

She gripped the back of his shirt. "I forgot I could be pregnant."

Dexter sighed then groaned. "I did too, Sara." He squeezed her closer to his chest. "Between the chaos with Nellie and me almost losing you, I-I-I lost my mind." She could hear the heartache lacing his words. "I was so scared. I can't believe I forgot."

Sara rubbed his back with an opened palm. "We have really great friends."

"We do. I love you so much, Sara."

She kissed his bicep that was still tangled around her. "I love you too." She could have said more. It felt like she wanted to say more. But, she trembled quietly against his chest. He guided her to the bed where he lay down and dragged her against him, cocooning around her.

In her ear, he whispered, "Please tell me we're done with all this. I just want to enjoy you, Sara Mar King. And our kids. I want us together forever." He kissed her neck. "I want to love you forever. And, I don't want it to be cut short. I have sixteen years to make up for. Please—*please*, don't risk your life anymore. Tell me it's done."

She kissed his cheek with a smile. "It's done, Dexter."

Chapter 31

▲▲▲

The morning came and Dexter was awoken by a quiet knock on the door. Not wanting to wake Sara, he moved with care and precision to untangle himself from her lazy embrace and dismounted the bed. He pulled on his sweats and went to the door.

Jane's onyx eyes were on him as soon as the door opened, and they were running down his bare, tattooed chest before they refocused on his eyes. Dexter gave a smirk. "Hey."

"Hi. Yeah. Sorry." She twisted her torso to look down the hallway, a slight blush rising on her cheeks. "Just thought I'd let you know that Nellie and Kali are up. They're asking for breakfast spaghetti? I don't know what that is, and I—I don't—I don't mix well with kids."

Dexter smiled as she bit on the side of her nail. "No worries. Ignore them and I'll be down in a sec. Go get yourself some breakfast."

She nodded then pivoted on a heel.

Dexter closed the door quietly before moseying to the closet and throwing on a plain blue T-shirt. He took one last glace at Sara to ensure that she was still sleeping before he snuck out and went down the stairs.

Like magnets, his kids slammed into him as he entered the kitchen.

"I'm hungry!" Nellie complained.

"Can I have cereal?" Kali asked.

"Cereal it is, kids," Dexter announced.

"No! I want breakfast spaghetti!" Nellie whined, twisted his body, and let his arms smack into his dad. "Kali just said she did too!"

Dexter laughed as he saw his daughter put a hand on a popped out hip and fling her luscious locks over her shoulder. "But, now I want cereal."

If their life was officially starting, he needed to parent. He looked to Nellie and said, "Maybe you can try asking nicer at lunch time. So, now you'll have cereal with your sister."

"Aw man!" He slouched in the chair beside his sister, pouting and looking at Jane who was sipping on some coffee and intently looking at the two kids.

Dexter observed her as discretely as possible while he fixed his kids breakfast. There was an insecurity lingering behind her eyes as they switched from his daughter to his son, then back to his daughter again. As she took another sip of coffee, he heard her stomach rumble. She tried to mute the sound by hugging her middle. Dexter grinned before making a third bowl of cereal for Jane.

He set all three down, specifically making eye contact as he scooted a bowl in front of her. "Eat."

She shyly grabbed the bowl, grinned, and whispered, "Thanks."

The kids dug into their breakfast like Dexter had starved them their whole lives, milk and flakes spilling onto the wooden surface of the table. Nellie finished first, climbed onto the table and hurdled himself toward the living room. He didn't make it past the stairs before Dexter called for him. "Hey! You put that bowl in the sink before you watch TV."

Nellie whipped his head toward Dexter as his mouth turned to a frown. "But, Dad!"

Dexter widened his eyes and pressed his lips in a line while pointing at the sink. "Now."

Kali wiped her mouth with the back of her hand, got off the chair, and took her bowl to the sink with a competitive smile directed at her brother.

"Just like your sister or no breakfast spaghetti for lunch."

Nellie crossed his arms, stomped to his bowl, and picked it up. The bowl made it to the sink, but not before he haphazardly tossed it in with a loud clang.

Dexter grinned as Nellie tramped to the living room, sat on the couch, and grabbed the remote from Kali's hands.

"Hey!" Kali's eyes glowed green. "That was mine!"

Nellie stuck out his tongue toward her. "I got up first!"

"But, I put my bowl away first!" She reached forward and snatched it back. "Daddy!"

"Nellie. The remote is Kali's. You should have put your bowl away to start with."

"It's not fair! I lose my powers *and* don't get TV!" Nellie's face reddened as he got up from the couch and ran upstairs to his room, slamming the door behind him.

Kali looked over her shoulder at Dexter, waving the remote. "There's not even a TV!"

Dexter laughed, remembering they had broken it when practicing their powers and he forgot to throw away the remote.

A small giggle spilled from Jane. "That kid's going to be trouble."

He raised his brows. "I'll have to see about that."

"Looks like you have a handle on things."

Silence passed between them for a few moments before Dexter addressed the elephant in the room. "Hey, I'm really sorry about your dad."

She shrugged and took a bite of cereal. "I know you did him a favor that I never could have done." After swallowing, she trained her eyes on Dexter. "I didn't know an infected couldn't be saved."

He sent her a sullen grin of apology. "Why'd you join the Splitters? You could have stayed at my camp forever, you know. Food, shelter, security."

She went to take another bite but decided to play with the food at the last second with an audible sigh. "I used to have a brother."

"Yeah? Didn't make it?"

Jane pulled up the hood to the gray zip-up jacket Sara had lent her. "He was with my dad and me for a while. I was actually surprised at how long because he and my father never

356

got along. That honeymoon period between them didn't last long. They got in a horrible fight, and my brother decided to join the Splitters since they had protection, weapons, and loyalty. I was stuck in the middle. Both wanting me to go with them. I chose my dad since he was older and wouldn't have stood a chance without me." She shrugged. "After my dad..." her dark eyes flitted to his and intentionally chose not to finish the sentence, "I went to find my brother."

"Did you find him?"

A thin film of tears glimmered in her eyes. "No." Then, she gave a sad smile. "But, he could still be out there. I thought the longer I stayed with the Splitters, the more of them I'd get introduced to. I asked, but no one had ever heard of a Tyce Everkin."

"I'm sorry." He suddenly wished Sara was here. She was better at this comforting thing than he was.

Her smile left. "So, how did you and Sara meet?"

"Oh, her and I go way back. I've known her forever. We were neighbors growing up. Never treated her well. Still don't think I do, but somehow, I'm lucky enough for her to stick by me."

She took another bite. "So, you and her are pretty tight then?"

Dexter saw visible tension build in her shoulders before he nodded.

They slumped forward as she picked at her fingers. "That's too bad," she absently muttered to herself.

The comment struck Dexter in an odd way. Was she trying to say she was interested in him? After he killed her father?

Dexter's brows raised, wondering how much the Screecher Age had messed her up.

"What's too bad?" Sara's angelic voice called from the bottom of the stairs as she rounded the corner and ruffled her bangs.

Before Dexter could interject, Jane said, "Nellie can't have breakfast spaghetti until lunch. And only if he asks nicely."

She lied. That had to mean... great. He watched Sara tiptoe on her bare feet to the coffee maker, but Dexter was desperate to get out of the awkward conversation with Jane. He let the chair screech behind him as he stood and raced to the pastel pink mug Sara was reaching for. "I got it."

"Oh." She giggled and let go of the mug. "Thanks, Dex."

He threw away the old coffee and began making a new pot while Sara took his spot at the table.

"Were you comfortable last night?"

Dexter heard the crunches of Jane's cereal as she continued to eat. "Yes. Very. Thank you."

"Great. Later we can go to the downtown and get you some new clothes, some toiletries, a phone—"

"That's okay. I was actually planning on taking off today."

Dexter's head whipped around, glaring at the back of Jane's inked head. Then his eyes flitted to Sara who was staring at him funny and said, "You okay?"

"Yeah," Dexter mumbled out. "I—uh, just never asked how you like your coffee. One scoop or two?"

Sara smiled. "One please."

When he nodded at her, she turned back to Jane. "Are you really planning on leaving?"

"Yeah." Jane sighed.

"No, you should stay." She shifted in her seat. "We love having you."

"Nah. Me and kids don't mix."

"You don't have to hang out with them. Emily and I need more girls for an actual girl's night anyway," she jabbed.

As much as he suddenly didn't want Jane around, he knew there was not much outside this town if she began to travel. Jane was confused and tired, he didn't want her ending up with the Splitters again. Plus, Sara really enjoyed having friends. "Where would you go?" Dexter chimed.

Jane turned her head with a weird look in her eye. "Not sure yet. Why?"

"You should stay," Sara offered. "And you can stay here for as long as you'd like. No rush."

She peered over her shoulder to Dexter once more before looking back at a beaming Sara. "I don't know. I wouldn't want to impose."

"You wouldn't be. And we can go house shopping. There are plenty here that are empty. We can spruce it up. It'll be a nice project."

Jane looked back over her shoulder. "What do you think, Dexter?"

"I think you should do what makes you happiest."

She took a deep breath and turned back to Sara. "Okay. Well, I guess I'll stay then."

"Yay!" Sara squealed, clapping her hands in celebration.

Dexter chuckled, happy to see Sara could still be her exuberant self, even after all the chaos of the last few days.

"But, we go house shopping today. I don't need kids drool waking me up again."

"You got it."

As the coffee streamed into the mug for Sara, Jane stood and took her bowl to the sink, directing a sly wink at Dexter. Then, she looked back to Sara. "I'm going to go clean up the covers from the kids' room then shower if that's okay."

"Go for it," Sara said, taking the mug from Dexter's hand.

When Jane left the room, Dexter took her spot across from Sara and the two glared at each other until they heard Jane close the kids' room.

Sara rolled her eyes. "So she likes you."

Dexter smiled and reached across the table for her hands. "Your intuition is getting better."

She giggled. "It's not. I saw her wink at you."

"Want to send her packing?"

Sara stood and rounded the table to Dexter, sitting on his lap and wrapping her arms around his neck. "You said we don't have to worry about either of us leaving, right?"

"Of course."

Sara shrugged and looked to the stairs. "She'll get over you. Lots of guys to pick from here." She gasped in delight. "Emily and I could set her up on dates! It'll be so fun!"

Dexter kissed her cheek. "Let the girl bonding commence."

Sara kissed him on the lips, hard and fast. "Why does everyone like you? You're not that great."

Dexter lifted her, then roughly placed her on the counter, spreading her legs, and moving in with his hands firmly on her waist. "I'm not that great, huh?" He kissed her fervently, separating her lips and teeth with his tongue.

She moaned against him before her hands moved to his chest and pushed him away with flushed cheeks. "I'm not jealous if that's what you're thinking."

"You? Jealous?" Dexter smiled. "Never."

Chapter 32

▲▲▲

One week later...

Everything was set. Down to the last detail. Dexter had checked, and rechecked, every final touch. The sun warmed every part of the town. Sara was out with Emily, distracting her as best she could.

A knock on the door followed by Sara's angelic giggle sent spirals of butterflies to take flight in him. He rubbed off his sweaty palms before opening the door. Sara stood there, smiling and oblivious as to what he had planned. Doting green eyes on him as if her whole world revolved around Dexter and only Dexter. Her thin frame was dressed in the black "Iron Vikings" T-shirt he had made her with her tattoo imprinted on the logo's skull, paired with ripped white skinny jeans that hugged in all the right places. When she reached out for him, he brought her in close, lifting her up slightly to kiss her.

"You okay?"

He glanced at Emily behind her who was winking at him and giving a silent applause. "Yeah. I'm fine."

Sara took a step back to really look at him. Her brows were furrowed in concern, but she was still wearing a precious smile. "You look frazzled."

"No. I'm good. I just want to show you something."

She looked over her shoulder to Emily for a hint of what it could be, but Emily went back to her normal smile as she shrugged. "Your dude be weird."

Dexter wrapped an arm around Sara's shoulder and guided her through the living room toward the door under the stairs that led to the backyard. He watched her carefully as he opened the door, not daring to miss a single one of her over-the-top reactions.

He melted when her eyes went large with amazed shock. As her green gems glided over everything he had been working on for the last few hours, a giddy warmth filled him. He knew exactly what she was looking at with every small twitch in her expression.

First, her eyes swept across the grass that was littered with thousands of colorful petals. In the middle of it all were two lines of white roses that created a pathway that led to their children. Both were smiling at their mother and holding their own square piece of cardboard. Nellie in a buttoned-up, white collared shirt and tan khakis. Kali in a pink dress that poofed at her waist and a white headband that held a large white flower that glittered in the sunlight.

Then, her vision moved to the dark wooden fence lined with wired lights drooped in a romantic series of waves. When her jaw dropped, he knew she was looking at the lace covered table to the side that held a single tiered white cake and two small figurines pushed into the top.

Then she saw Zeek and Jane smiling off to the side. "What's going on?"

"Come," Dexter said through a smile. He directed her down the path to their two children, stopping two feet away from them. "Stay right here."

Dexter went to Zeek to grab his own cardboard before positioning himself between Nellie and Kali. "Okay, Nellie. Go."

Nellie lifted up the cardboard that had his sloppy handwriting sprawled over it in the word "Daddy?".

"No, wait." Dexter laughed. "Kali and Nellie switch! It's backward."

Nellie let out a loud belly laugh that put Sara's to shame as he sprinted to Kali's spot and shoved her to his.

"Okay. Kali, go." With a wide smile and a scrunched nose, she lifted hers which read "Will you".

Dexter lifted his. "Marry".

Nellie swung the last piece of cardboard over his head and hopped in place. "Daddy?"

Sara smiled so wide that it reached her eyes as they filled with happy tears. "Dexter, you know I already said yes."

"Is it a yes again?"

"It's a yes every time!" Sara laughed.

He watched Jane, Zeek, and Emily walk up behind her and throw white petals in the air. Seeing the confetti rain down over a glowing Sara made him cheer along with the rest of them. Just like he had orchestrated, his kids ran to Zeek and Emily so she was only facing him.

Dexter got down on one knee, holding out an opened black box that held two rings he had spent days in search of. Everyone offered him their most expensive rings that had been imported from other revitalized towns. But, they weren't for Sara. Though she deserved the biggest, most brilliant diamond, he wanted the one that felt most like her. He had chosen two golden bands. One as her engagement ring and one as her wedding band. The engagement ring had three diamonds. There were two small ones on either side of the larger round stone. Just like the peaks of the mountains on her tattoo, each diamond represented him and their two children. For the wedding band, he had chosen a gold band that was encrusted with smaller diamonds and shined as bright as her eyes. The diamonds traveled around her whole finger to show that their love was endless. The simplicity of it reminded him of how easy it was to love her.

"Dexter!" she squealed.

He laughed and took out the engagement ring, slipping it over her trembling finger.

"It's beautiful!"

He stood and kissed her in epic euphoria. "Happy wedding day."

Sara stepped back with wide, panicked eyes. "What'd you just say?"

"I'm giving you this wedding band tonight. I am marrying you right here. You have two hours to get ready."

"Two hours!" Sara shrieked.

Dexter rolled his eyes with a crooked smile. "I wanted to marry you right now, but Emily and Jane got mad at me. And, once Kali got mad, too, I couldn't say no."

Emily reached out a hand to Sara's shoulder and spun her around. "Don't worry! I got your dress and your shoes. They're upstairs."

In squealing delight, Sara asked, "How did you do that?"

"What are Maid of Honors for?"

Sara hugged Emily tight before Zeek chimed in. "Dex and I took the kids shopping for their clothes. They're all set."

"Mommy!" Kali called, pulling on her shirt. "Daddy said you can do my hair!"

"Well, of course I will, Baby Kay!"

"I'm not the biggest makeup person," Jane added, "but I went out and found some you might want for tonight."

Sara moved to Jane and gave her the biggest hug. It was the first time Dexter had seen Jane smile, and it melted his heart. That was because of Sara. She could make absolutely anyone happy.

"Sara," Dexter started, "get your cute butt upstairs, because now you have one hour and fifty-eight minutes."

"Oh, shut up, Dex," Emily jabbed. "This bride is going to take as much time as she'd like!"

Chapter 33

▲▲▲

Upbeat music played from the speakers as fragrant hairspray filled Sara's lungs. She put on a smoky eye and a neutral lip that complimented her complexion. Next, she brushed the sparkly, gold highlighter that Jane had picked out over her cheekbones, cupid's bow, the tip of her nose, and the inside corners of her eyes. When she had completed the look, she put some of the highlighter on Kali. Emily warned Jane that Sara was going to do her makeup one way or another. Jane lost the argument and within twenty minutes, she had a light layer of makeup. Sara did her best to cover the zig zag tattoos over her bald head at Jane's request.

The dress was exactly what she would have picked for herself. Flowy white fabric that fell to the ground and had a slit up her leg. Beneath the slit was beautiful white lace that peeked through the opening. The soft fabric rounded her bare shoulders and left a deep "V" neck that led to the beaded gold belt around her waist. Her shoes were simple, sleek sandals that matched the muted yellow accent. The straps stretched upward in a "V" shape before rounding her ankle.

"There's no heel because I know you're uncomfortable in them, and you're going to want to run around with your kids for the reception."

"Emily. It's perfect."

"Oh!" Emily darted out of the bedroom and was back in a quick minute. Breathing heavily, she handed Sara something shiny. "Here. To complete the look. But, if you don't want to wear it. It's all good."

Sara gently took the thin, gold head piece with white jeweled flowers branching off in different directions. She looked into the full-length mirror near her vanity to carefully place it over her beach-waved blonde hair. After a single twirl, she felt like a bride. Behind her, Jane was in a lavender dress that hung to the ground to compliment her slender figure while Emily was dressed in a fit and flare pink dress that came to her midthighs. Looking at the picture in the mirror, the weight of the situation struck her. "Holy shit. I'm going to *marry* Dexter Bennet."

There was a knock on the door and Zeek's voice boomed. "Dexter's getting impatient. He sent me up here to tell you that it's been two hours and four minutes."

At his words, the three of them began shouting to tell Dexter to suck it up and Zeek to take a hike.

"Dear lord! Okay. I get it. Kali, your dad wants you."

Kali took off down the hall with Zeek after giving Emily a once over.

The three girls laughed and huddled in a hug. "You look beautiful, Sara," Emily said.

"Yeah, really stunning," Jane added.

"Love you girls. Thank you for doing this."

"Let's go get you married!" Emily squealed.

Down the stairs the three went while Sara's stomach tied itself in a million nervous knots. Not only because she was marrying Dexter, but because it was her wedding day, and she didn't want to forget a moment of it. Before she knew it, she was standing in front of the door that led to the backyard. It opened and Emily and Jane walked through first and down the path. She could hear her kids off to the side humming *Here Comes the Bride*.

The sun had set and the lights strung around the backyard illuminated every inch of the makeshift venue in a beautiful, glowing atmosphere of romance.

"Mommy! It's your turn," Kali called.

She laughed and looked down the path where Dexter was standing in a fitted navy tuxedo, smiling wide at her. When she saw his eyes tear up, she could feel exactly how much she meant to him. She walked down the path, feeling like a princess in a fairytale. Every part of her happiness was dedicated to Dexter Bennet. Sara was alive because of Dexter. Her kids were alive because of Dexter. The world was alive because of Dexter.

He held out a hand for her to take as she approached him. "You are breathtaking, Sara Mar King."

Sara giggled. "Look at you all handsome."

She looked around, waiting for it to start. "Who's going to marry us?"

"I am. Apparently, religion is not a thing in this town and no one is ordained. But, I don't care. I'll marry you in every

369

religion or in the absence of it." He pulled out the diamond band from his pocket and took a deep, steadying breath. "I'm going to keep this short because it's already been way too long." Another deep breath. "Sara, if I explained exactly what you mean to me, we'd be here for years. Instead, I'll spend the rest of my life telling you every day how in love with you I am." He slid the ring over her finger. "And I want everyone to know that you are taken and you are mine. I love you more than you'll ever know."

After she tilted her hand several times to admire its clean vibrant glittering, Sara felt a tap on her shoulder. Emily was there holding out a dark gray band. "This is for Dexter."

She took it in her palm to better examine it.

"This one," he flattened her hand to see the ring, "has the gold on the edges too so we are always connected. And in the center is meteorite. I thought it was a nice touch to say we defeated unworldly events together."

Sara was touched by his words, accepting them and their meaning. She placed the ring on his finger with a smile. "You're mine, Sir Bennet."

The crowd behind them started chanting, "Kiss!"

Sara gave her famous deep belly laugh while Dexter took her head between his hands and brought her close. Her arms flew over his shoulders and around his neck as their lips met in demanding, yet loving, kiss that sealed their love.

"Dexter! We're married!" she squealed.

He whispered in her ear, "Fucking finally," before kissing her neck.

Upbeat music thumped from a large speaker that Zeek had hooked up to have a dance party. Nellie brought out a water gun and began attacking everyone. Sara was quick to get the gun without a drop getting on her dress and turned it on Dexter.

Sara smashed the cake into Dexter's face even though he was a gentleman and didn't retaliate. Then, Nellie smashed a piece into Kali's hair. Nellie laughed while his sister cried.

By the time Sara cleaned Kali up in the bathroom and brought her back outside, the stars had appeared in full force and it was way past the twins' bedtime.

Emily offered to put the kids to bed while everyone else relaxed by the new fire pit Zeek had installed. They roasted marshmallows and told funny stories. When the conversation veered toward stories of the newlyweds, Sara's memories were different from Dexter's. They each told their own side for hours.

When midnight neared, their friends let themselves out. Dexter took out a blanket from under his seat and wrapped it around them so they could continue to stargaze alone. Though Sara found herself thinking how much more comfortable she would be curled up in Dexter's lap, his arms wrapped around her in a cradling kind of love had her soothed just as much.

"We did it, Sara." He kissed the top of her head before resting his chin on her. "We found each other again. We cheated death. We have two beautiful children that we get to raise together. That weird alien thing is obliterated. The future of our world is saved. We fucking did it."

"I love you, Dexter." She decided to stop looking at the stars and snuggled her face into Dexter's chest, letting his musky scent assault her senses as she whispered, "I'm not pregnant."

His body went rigid. "You're not?"

"No. I got my period this morning." Dexter sighed, but Sara wasn't sure what that meant. "Are you upset?"

Another audible sigh. "No."

"Dexter, I want another child with you."

"Oh yeah?" he smiled.

She will tell you soon. But when she does, know that I'm okay with it. Kali had given her blessing and it pleased him to no end.

"I would love to have another child with you. One where I can be there for you from the beginning. I didn't get to spoil you." He kissed her temple, warm breath gliding by her cheek. "When did you want to start?"

Sara looked into his eyes and kissed him, so he couldn't finish the sentence. "Maybe tonight?"

Dexter smiled. "Then, what are we waiting for?" He scooped her up, her legs draped over his forearm and an arm supporting her back as she laughed. "Let's get our life started, Sara Mar Bennet."

Connect with Nicolette Beebe

Want more of Sara and Dexter's story?

Follow Nicolette Beebe on Instagram, @33nbeebe, and sign up for her newsletter for updates on book III, *Send Your Ghost*, and new romance series, the Thin Skin Series.

The official hashtag for this series is #markingseries

If you enjoyed this novel, a review on Goodreads and Amazon would be greatly appreciated!

For all of Nicolette Beebe's links, look up Msha.ke/33nbeebe/

Interested in Nicolette Beebe editing your novel? Contact her through Instagram or email, 33nbeebe@gmail.com.

Other works by Nicolette Beebe

Post-apocalyptic romance
Mar King Series

Mar King

Sir Bennet

Send Your Ghost (Releasing soon)

Nell's Story (Releasing soon)

Dark, contemporary romance series
Thin Skin Series

Many Punctured Wings

Few Working Minds (Releasing soon)

Acknowledgements

I cannot thank my readers enough! I appreciate all the love and support. Thank you for continuing to be curious about Sara and Dexter! It means the world to me.

Thank you to my husband, Brian Beebe, for helping me weed out all the plot holes, finalize the edits, and for listening to me babble about these two characters to many hours of the day over many years.

Thank you to my editor, Hayley Christiansen. Without you this book wouldn't have the magic and life I wanted it to have. The time you invest in my novels are extremely appreciated.

Thank you to Melyssa West for saying, "...But I'm not done with them," after reading "Mar King". Without you, there probably wouldn't be a book II.

Thank you to the talented cover designer Alexander Kopainski for this creating this amazing cover! You've outdone yourself!

Thank you all kindly.

Printed in Great Britain
by Amazon

72653369R00225